BY CALLAN WINK

Dog Run Moon

August

AUGUST

AUGUST

A NOVEL

Callan Wink

RANDOM HOUSE

NEW YORK

Published in the United States by Random House, an imprint and division of Penguin Random House LLC, New York.

Random House and the House colophon are registered trademarks of Penguin Random House LLC.

Library of Congress Cataloging-in-Publication Data
Names: Wink, Callan, author.
Title: August : a novel / by Callan Wink.
Description: New York : Random House, [2020]
Identifiers: LCCN 2019016807 | ISBN 9780812993752 (hardcover : acid-free paper) | ISBN 9780812993769 (ebook)
Subjects: LCSH: Domestic fiction. | GSAFD: Bildungsromans.
Classification: LCC PS3623.I6626 A95 2020 | DDC 813/.6—dc23
LC record available at https://lccn.loc.gov/2019016807

Printed in Canada on acid-free paper

randomhousebooks.com

2 4 6 8 9 7 5 3 1

First Edition

Book design by Caroline Cunningham

AUGUST

BONNIE AND DAR WERE sitting at the end of the dock at Bonnie's parents' lake house. Torch Lake stretched out in front of them, so blue it seemed impossible, unnatural, almost as if it had been dyed. They were going to the cherry festival in Traverse City that night, and Bonnie had worn a sundress for the occasion—white, decorated with a pattern of brilliant red cherries. She was slim, but her belly was just starting to round out, and it was more noticeable, sitting the way she was, with the dress tucked up underneath her.

"So," she said. "You wanted a few days to sleep on it. It's been a week. How about it? Augie—it's got a certain ring to it, doesn't it? It could be August, properly, but Augie for short."

Dar had his socks and shoes off; his feet, accustomed to work boots, hung pale and hairless above the water's surface. "I've been considering it," he said.

"And?"

He tried it out. "*August.* My son, August." He disentangled himself from her and leaned back on the dock, his hands laced behind his head. "My father's name was Alexander."

"I know. So?"

"Alexander is a good name."

"You told me you and your father got in a fistfight when you were fifteen years old. A real fistfight."

"It's still a good name. My mother would be happy."

"Your mother." Bonnie snorted. "Well, there's that." She reached over and pinched his leg. "They close the streets off for the festival and they have music. Will you dance with me?"

"Hmm." Dar had his eyes closed. "Maybe."

"I'll find someone else to dance with if you don't."

"You know none of those assholes will dance as good as me."

Bonnie got to her feet suddenly and stood above him. One of her hands was resting on her belly, something he'd noticed she'd gotten in the habit of doing lately. She nudged him with her bare foot and then stepped over him, pausing momentarily to give him the briefest flash under her sundress, but when he went to reach for her she was gone, running up the lawn. He chased her, her white thighs flashing, dress swishing; it was a hundred yards to the house and she was fast, so that he barely caught her before the edge of the porch. He grabbed her around the hips and she shrieked and they rolled in the grass, laughing, until she was on top, straddling him.

"It's not just the eighth month of the year. You know that, right? It also means respected, illustrious, venerable, *worthy of admiration*." She took one of his hands in both of hers and slid it up under the hem of her dress so it rested on the warm mound of her stomach. "August," she said in that way she had that brooked no argument.

With that settled, they went to the cherry festival street dance. He was twenty-six and she was twenty-one, and they had the very best time of their lives.

I

AUGUST'S FIRST, FULLY ACCESSIBLE memory was of the barn. Riding on his father's shoulders down the hill behind the house, he could see the building ahead of them, its peaked roof and the long, low addition off to the side, faded red with white trim. His father ducking under the door so he wouldn't hit his head, the dull murmur of the milk pump, the cows chewing in the stanchions. Maybe five or six, he was too old to be riding on his father's shoulders, and he didn't want to be there. As soon as he could, he squirmed down and climbed to the haymow. The rungs of the ladder were almost too far spaced, but his father was there at his back in case he slipped.

In the haymow, dusty and dark and warm, his father broke up two bales to make a soft pile, and they had several wrestling matches during which August got repeatedly tossed into the loose hay, a situation he loved more than just about anything. After a time they descended the ladder, and August's father removed and sanitized the milkers while August went around patting each Holstein on the nose. When the milking was done, August helped his father dip the teats of several cows until August dropped the applicator and spilled the iodine solution and his father sat him in the milk room with a mason jar filled fresh from the refrigerator vat to keep him occupied while he finished the chores alone. The milk was full-fat, thick and heavy, cold enough to fog the glass. There was the smell of the cows and straw. The milk room was whitewashed, cobwebs in the old wooden crossbeams, the stainless vat spotless and gleaming. He held the mason jar with both hands, drinking, the milk running down his chin.

Eventually his father came and scooped him up. The cows had been put out to pasture, and the barn was silent. He rode on his father's shoulders back to the house, tired and not protesting now. His mother was at the kitchen table, a dim gray haze of smoke above her head. She had books scattered around her, glasses on, taking notes. He crawled up on her lap and she wrinkled her nose, removing some papers from under one of his grubby hands. The sound of the TV being switched on came from the other room, his father opening a beer.

She closed her books and put them into her backpack. "Looks like study hall is over," she said. "Thanks, *Dad*. Let's get you to the bath."

August was twelve and there were cats in the barn. Litters begetting litters begetting litters—some thin and misshapen with the afflictions of blood too many times remixed.

"Get rid of the damn things," August's father said. "The haymow smells like piss. Take a tire iron or a shovel or whatever tool suits you. You've been after me for school money? I'll give you a dollar a tail. You have your jackknife? You have it sharp? You take their tails and pound them to a board, and then after a few days we'll have a settling up. Small tails worth as much as large tails, it's all the same."

The cats—calicos, tabbies, dirty white, gray, jet black, and tawny—sat among the hay bales scratching and yawning like indolent apes inhabiting the remains of a ruined temple. August had never actually killed a cat before but, like most farm boys, he had engaged in plenty of casual acts of torture. Cats, as a species, retained a feral edge, and as a result were not subject to the rules of husbandry that governed man's relation with horses or cows or dogs. August figured that somewhere along the line cats had struck a bargain—they knew they could expect to feel a man's boot if they came too close; in return, they kept their freedom and nothing much was expected of them.

A dollar a tail. August thought of the severed appendages, pressed and dried, stacking up like currency in the teller drawer of some alien bank. Fifty dollars at least, maybe seventy-five, possibly even a hundred if he was able to track down the newborn litters.

He went to the equipment shed to look for weapons. It was a massive structure, made of metal posts skinned with corrugated sheet metal, large enough to fit a full-sized diesel combine. August liked to go there when it rained. It was like being a small creature deep in the bowels of a percussion instrument. The fat drops of rain would hit the thin metal skin in an infinite drumroll, punctuated by the clash of lightning cymbals and the hollow booming of space.

In the shed there was a long workbench covered in the tangled intestines of machinery: looping coils of compressor hoses, hydraulic arms leaking viscous fluid, batteries squat and heavy, baling twine like ligaments stitching the whole crazy mess together, tongue-and-ball trailer knobs, mason jars of rusting bolts and nuts and screws, a medieval-looking welder's mask, and, interspersed among the other wreckage like crumpled birds, soiled leather gloves in varying degrees of decomposition. August picked up a short length of rusted, heavy-linked logging chain and swung it a few times experimentally before discarding it. He put on a pair of too-large gloves and hefted a broadsword-sized mower blade, slicing slow patterns in the air, before discarding it, too. Then he uncovered a three-foot-long breaker bar wrench with a slim stainless-steel handle that swelled at the other end into a glistening and deadly crescent head. He brought the head down into his glove several times to hear the satisfying whack. He practiced a few death-dealing swing techniques—the sidearm golf follow-through; the overhead back-crushing ax chop; the short, quick line-drive baseball checked swing—the wrench head making ragged divots in the hard-packed dirt floor. He worked up a light sweat and then shouldered his weapon, put the pair of gloves in his back pocket, and went to see his mother.

The old house was set back against a low, rock-plated hill. A year-round spring wept from the face of the rock, and the dampness of it filled the house with the smell of wet leaves and impending rain. The house was a single-level ranch that August's mother's grandparents had built with their own hands and lived in until they died. The old house looked up at the new house, the one August's father had finished the year after August was born. The new house was a tall Victorian with white shutters and a full wraparound porch. August's mother's parents had both died when he was young, and he had no memories of them. After their passing his father convinced his mother to sell the vacation home on Torch Lake. With the money he built the new house and bought eighty head of Holstein-Friesians.

"He feels like it's his own," August's mother had said to him once, smoking in the kitchen of the new house. "His people didn't have much. Everything we got came from my side, you know. He would never admit it in a hundred years, but it bothers him." She coughed. "It's too big. That was my complaint from the get-go. It's hard to heat, too, exposed up on the hill like this; the wind gets in everywhere. My father or grandfather would have never done it like that. They built smart houses for their families, but that's the type of men they were."

August tapped the door a few times with the wrench and went inside. The old house was built by folks interested in efficiency, not landscape, and its windows were few and small. The kitchen was dimly lit by a single shaft of light coming through the window over the sink. The room smelled like frying bacon, and the radio was on. Paul Harvey was extolling the virtues of a Select Comfort Sleep Number Bed. *At my age there are few things I appreciate more than a night of restful sleep. Get this mattress. It was dreamed up by a team of scientists.*

"Augie, my fair son, how does the day find you?"

His mother was at the kitchen table playing solitaire. A pan of thinly sliced potatoes fried with pieces of bacon and onion sat next to her ashtray. She smoked Swisher Sweet cigarillos, and a thin layer of smoke undulated above her head like a smooth gray flying carpet. He'd noticed that she seemed to tune in to Paul Harvey in order to make fun of him, while his father tended to listen to Paul Harvey just to listen.

"I made lunch, and it smelled so good while it was cooking, but now I'm not hungry. I don't know, I may have finally broken through."

August pulled out a chair and sat across from his mother at the small table. "Broken through to what?" he said.

"Oh, I didn't tell you? I've been devoting myself to a new teaching." She stubbed out her cigarillo and shook another from the pack sitting on the table. She lit it, a fine network of lines appearing around her mouth as she pursed her lips. Her nails were long and gray, her finger-tips jaundiced with tobacco stain. "Yeah," she continued, "I'm considering becoming an inediate."

"A what?"

"An inediate—you know, a breatharian?"

"I don't know what that is."

"Air eaters? Sky swallowers? Ether ingesters?"

"Nope."

"You can attune your mind and your body, Augie. Perfectly attune them by healthy living and meditation so that you completely lose the food requirement. I mean, not just that you're no longer hungry—that's not too hard. I'm talking about all you have to do is breathe the air and you're satisfied. You get full and you never have to eat. And you can survive that way, happy as a clam." She took a sip of coffee, smoke dribbling from her nose as she swallowed. "That's what I've been working on."

She pushed the pan of potatoes and bacon toward him, and August ate some even though Lisa had told him she would make him a sandwich when she got up from the barn. The potatoes were greasy and good, the bacon little pieces of semi-charred saltiness. The onions were soft, translucent, and sweet. August ate, then wiped his hands on his jeans and put his wrench on the table for his mother to see.

"Dad gave me a job," he said. "For money."

"Oh, well, I'm proud to hear it. Did you negotiate a contract? Set a salary-review option pending exemplary performance?"

"No, I'm just killing some cats."

"I see. And this is your Excalibur?" She tinked the chrome-handled wrench with her fingernail.

"Yeah. It's a spanner wrench."

She made a low whistle and coughed softly into the back of her hand.

"I'm taking the tails. We're going to settle up at the end of the week."

"That's the kind of work you stand a chance of bringing home with you, if you know what I mean."

"The haymow smells like piss. It's getting real bad."

"Your father. This is gruesome, even for him. Jesus." She looked down blankly at the cards in front of her. "I keep forgetting where I'm at with this. I can get only so far with solitaire before I get stumped. You ever win?"

"I never play."

"I suppose it's a game for old women."

"You're not old."

"If I'm not, then I don't want to feel what old is like."

"Are you ever going to come back to the new house?"

"You can tell him no, if you want. About the cats. You don't have to do it."

"She's been staying over."

"I found all of Grandma's old quilts. They were in a trunk in the back closet. Beautiful things. She made them all; some took her months. All of them hand-stitched. I never had the patience. She used to make me sit there with her for hours, learning the stitches. I'll show them to you if you want."

"Sure. I should get to work now, though."

"Next time, then."

August ate a few more potatoes and then stood up.

"I wish you Godspeed," his mother said, coaxing another cigarillo from the pack with her lips. "May your arrows fly true."

"I don't have any arrows."

"I know. It's just an old Indian saying." She blew smoke at him. "I don't care about the cats, you know," she said. "I look at you and it's clear as day to me that he hasn't won."

The barn was empty. His dad and Lisa were out rounding up the cows for milking. August put on his gloves and wedged the wrench down under his belt and climbed the wooden ladder up to the haymow.

Half-blind in the murk, holding his nose against the burning ammonia stench of cat piss, August crushed the skull of the first pale form that came sidling up to him. He got two more in quick succession, and then there was nothing but hissing from the rafters, green-gold eyes glowing and shifting among the hulking stacks of baled hay. August tried to give chase. He clambered over the bales, scratching his bare arms and filling his eyes and ears and nose with the dusty chaff of old hay. But the cats were always out of reach, darting and leaping from one stack to the next, climbing the joists to the rafters, where they faded into the gloom. August imagined them up there, a seething furry mass, a foul clan of fanged wingless bats clinging to a cave roof. This was going to be harder than he had thought.

August inspected his kills. A full-sized calico and two skinny grays, thin and in bad shape, patches of skin showing through their matted fur. He pitched them down the hay chute and climbed after them. On ground level he breathed deeply of the comparatively sweet manure-scented air and fished his knife from his pocket. He picked up the first cat by the tail and severed it at the base, dropping the carcass onto the cement with a wet thud. He dealt similarly with the other two, pitched them all in the conveyor trough, and went looking for a hammer. By the time he returned to the barn, his father and Lisa had the cows driven in and stanchioned in their stalls. The radio was on, loud enough that Paul Harvey's disembodied voice could be heard over the muttering of the cows and the drone of the compressor. *I don't know about you-all, but I have never seen a monument erected to a pessimist.*

August nailed his three tails onto a long pine board and propped it up in the corner of the barn where it wouldn't get knocked over by cows milling in and out. He passed Lisa on his way out. She was leaning on a shovel and spitting sunflower seeds into the dirt. She had on blue overalls and muck boots, and her frizzy blond hair was tamed into a ponytail that burst through the hole in the rear of her Seedco cap.

"Hi, August," she said. "You didn't come up to the house for lunch."

"Yeah. I ate at the old house with my mom."

"Oh, okay. I'm going to stick around tonight. I think I'll make some tacos for you guys for dinner. Sound good?"

August looked at her face, her round, constantly red cheeks. She called it rosacea, a skin condition. It made her seem to exist in a state of perpetual embarrassment. He wondered if she'd been teased about it at school.

She was only seven years older than he was and had graduated from the high school the previous May. In her senior year August's father had hired her to help him with the milking. She'd worked before school and after school and on weekends. August's father had said that she worked harder than any hired man he'd ever had. Now that she was done with school, she put in full days. She could drive a tractor with a harrow, she could muck out the barn, she could give the antibiotic shots to the cows, and when the calving season came she could plunge her hands in up to her wrists to help a difficult calf come bawling into the world.

"Crunchy shells or soft shells?" August said, knocking at the toes of his boots with the wrench.

"Soft?"

"I like crunchy."

"Well, I'll see what you guys have in the cupboards, but I bought some soft ones already."

"Flour or corn?"

"Flour, I think."

"I like corn." August spat at his feet, but his mouth was dry so the spit trailed out on his chin. He wiped at it with the back of his sleeve.

"I asked your dad what kind he wanted and he said it didn't matter."

"He likes the crunchy shells, too. Trust me. Do you make them with beans or without?"

Lisa hesitated for a moment and tugged at the brim of her cap. "Which do you prefer?" she said.

"Well, that depends."

"I bought some black beans. I usually put some of those in. But I don't have to."

"I like beans. But I don't eat black beans. I think they look like rabbit turds. My dad thinks that, too."

"Okay, I'll leave those out, then. Sound good?" The red on Lisa's cheeks had spread. A crimson blush was leaching down her neck all the way to the collar of her barn overalls. August didn't say anything. "All right, August, see you at dinner. Your dad's probably wondering where I got off to." Lisa headed into the barn, and August wandered out to the back pasture, swinging his wrench at stalks of burdock and thistle, stepping around the thick plots of fresh manure.

He climbed the low hill before the tree line on the property boundary and sat next to the pile of rocks that marked Skyler's grave. Skyler had been his birth dog. His father had brought the tiny six-week-old pup home when August had been out of the hospital less than a week. It was something that August's father had said his own father had done for him. He thought it was good for a boy to have a dog to grow up with. Against August's mother's objections, he put the soft, pug-faced shepherd mix in the crib with August—"to get acquainted," he said. "A boy with a dog is healthier, more active, less inclined to allergy and listlessness." And it seemed true. August had been a particularly healthy baby, a bright, energetic boy with a tongue-lolling, good-natured four-legged shadow.

At twelve, Skyler had been in remarkably good shape, a little stiff in the mornings but by noon harassing the barn cats like a dog half his age. Then, one day after school, August didn't see him anywhere in the barn or yard. He went to the equipment shed and found Skyler, stretched out on his side with a greenish-blue froth discoloring his grayed muzzle. He'd chewed through a gallon jug of antifreeze that August's father had stored under the workbench.

August and his father had carted the body up to the hill and taken turns with the pickax and shovel. When they'd finished they stood and regarded the cairn of rocks they'd stacked over the raw earth to keep the skunks out.

"I guess twelve is as good an age as any," his father had said. At the time, August thought he'd been talking about the dog. Later, he thought that maybe his father had meant that twelve was as good an age as any for a boy to lose a thing he loved for the first time.

. . .

August watched the sky in the west become washed in dusky, pink-tinged clouds. The turning sky made him think, unbidden, of Lisa, the crimson in her cheeks that spread like a hot infection down her neck and shoulders and back and arms, all the way to her legs. This wasn't mere supposition. He'd seen it.

It had been an early dismissal day last fall. August, off the bus and out of his school clothes, eating a piece of cake from the new house, wandered down to the barn, the air sharp with the acrid tang of the oak leaves his father had been burning in the front yard. The pile smoldered; there was no one around. Skyler slept in the shade of a stock tank. The cows were yoked up in their stanchions. The whole barn was full of the low rumble of suction, the automatic milkers chugging away.

And then, through the open doorway of the grain room, there was his father, muck boots on, thrusting behind Lisa, who was bent over a hay bale, her cheek and forearms pressed down into the cut ends of the hay. Their overalls were around their legs like shed exoskeletons, their conjoined bodies larval, soft and pale. August saw the flush of Lisa then, the creeping red that extended all the way down her back to her thick thighs and her spread calves. She had her underwear pulled down, and their brilliant lacy pinkness was a glaring insult to the fly-specked gray and manure brown of the barn.

On his way out, August had turned the barn radio up as loud as it would go. *Golf,* Paul Harvey was saying, *is a game where you yell "Fore," score six, and write down five.*

At the dinner table, Lisa and August's father each had a beer. Lisa cut a lime wedge and jammed it down the neck of her bottle, and August's father said, what the hell, he might try it like that, too. They smiled at each other and clinked their bottles together and drank, and August watched the lime wedges bobbing in their bottles like floats in a level. When they'd finished eating, August's father leaned back in his chair and belched mightily, his rough, callused fingers shredding the paper napkin as he wiped taco juice from his hands.

"Best meal I've had in a while. Thanks, Lisa."

Lisa grinned and said, "You're welcome, Darwin. I'm glad you liked it."

"I got three cats today," August said to break up their stupid smiling competition. "I did it with a wrench. Right in the head. They never knew what happened." Out of the corner of his eye he could see Lisa wrinkle her nose slightly.

His father finished his beer and piled his fork and knife and napkin onto his plate. He was a large man; all his joints seemed too big—hard, knobby wrists and knuckles, his hands darkened from the sun up to the point where his shirt cuffs lay. He was almost forty years old and still had all of his hair, dark brown, just starting to gray at the temples. In the cold months, he liked to wear a bright silk cowboy scarf knotted up around his neck. He smiled at women often, and women often smiled back. His mother used to say that for a guy with manure on his boots he could be fairly charming.

"Come on now, Augie. I gave you a job and I appreciate you getting right down to it. But there's barn talk and there's house talk. I'm sure Lisa wouldn't mind a little house talk now. How about you clear the table and clean up the dishes. And thank Lisa for making that delicious meal. She worked all day and then came up to do that for us."

"Thanks," August said and scooted his chair back loudly. He stacked the dishes into a precarious pile and carried them off to the kitchen. He ran the water until steam rose and squirted in soap until the bubbles grew in great tumorous mounds, and then he did the dishes. Clanking plate against plate, banging pot against pot, running the water unnecessarily, making as much noise as possible to cover the low murmur of Lisa and his father talking in the next room.

Through the kitchen window he could see the murky green cast of the yard light, the hulking form of the barn, and, farther out, the squat shape of the old house, completely dark. When his father came in to get two more beers, August didn't turn around to look at him. He stood next to August at the sink and took the tops off the bottles. He nudged August with an elbow, and August scrubbed at a pan, ignoring him.

"How's your mother?"

August shrugged.

"I'm not going to run her down, Augie, but she's not a woman that will ever give you her true mind. You know what I mean?"

August shrugged.

"She's been disappointed her whole life, probably came out of the womb that way. You don't disappoint her, I know that, but everything else does—me included, always have, always will. She never learned to hold herself accountable. That's the way her parents allowed her to grow up. She's very smart and she thinks she sees things I don't see, but she's wrong, I'll tell you that. I see plenty. You hear me?"

August swirled a cup in the dishwater and didn't say anything. His father slapped him on the back of the head.

"I said, you hear me?"

"Yeah. I hear you." August looked straight ahead out the window.

"Okay then." He reached into the dishwater, came up with a handful of suds, and smeared them on August's cheek. "You're all right," he said. "When you think it's time, you let me know and we'll go find you a pup."

In the morning, the smells of toast and coffee and bacon pulled August from his bed before the sun had even hit the east-facing window. He clumped down the stairs into the kitchen and sat at the table rubbing his eyes. Lisa stood at the stove making eggs. Her feet were bare and she had on the gray long underwear she wore under her barn overalls. They were made for men and tight around her hips, and when she bent over to get the butter out of the refrigerator August could see the faint lines of her panties curving across her full rear.

"Would you like coffee, August?" August nodded, and she put a steaming mug in front of him. "I figure you like it black, like your dad?"

"Sure," he said, taking a sip, trying not to grimace. "Black and strong."

His mother mixed his coffee with hot whole milk, dumping in heaping spoonfuls of sugar. She told him that was how she learned to make it when she'd studied in New Orleans, in another lifetime, before she married his father. August knew that Lisa would never go to New Orleans in a million lifetimes.

His father came from the bedroom. He had a dab of shaving foam under one earlobe. He put his hand on Lisa's waist as he got a coffee mug from the cupboard, and she turned and wiped off the shaving foam with her sleeve.

"How long before the eggs are done?" August asked, tapping his fingers on the tabletop.

"A few minutes. The bacon is almost ready."

August sighed, downed his coffee, and took a piece of toast from the plate on the counter. "Well," he said, "some of us can't sit around. I have to get to work."

He got his wrench from the mudroom and slid on his boots, leaving them unlaced, and walked across the lawn with his boot tongues flapping like dogs breathing in the heat. The cows were milling in the pasture, gathered up close to the gate. They rolled their dumb, baleful eyes at him and lowed, their udders straining and heavy with milk.

"Shut up, you idiots," August said. He picked up a small handful of pebbles and continued to walk, pelting any cow within reach.

Until last year, August had helped with the milking every morning before school and every evening after school, and then his mother forbade it and his father had been forced to hire Lisa full-time.

"Do you like helping your father with the milking?" his mother had asked one evening as they cleaned up the dinner dishes. His father was on the porch listening to a baseball game, and the sound of the play-by-play came through the screen door, garbled and frantic. *A hard line drive, he's going, he's going, he's going.*

"I don't mind it too much," August said, wiping a plate dry. "Most of the time I like it."

"Huh, well, that's a problem," his mother said. She had a cigarette tucked into the corner of her mouth, and ash drifted into the dish-water as she spoke. "You'll be in high school soon, you know. And then there'll be girls. They're going to find you so handsome. And then there'll be college, and then there'll be any life you want after that. This is just a small piece, Augie, and if you hate it then you should know that soon you'll be making your own way."

"But I said I don't hate it, Mom."

"Jesus. I really hope you don't mean that. Getting up early, the shitty cows, the dullness?"

"What about it?"

"My God, Augie, look at me and tell me you don't hate it." She turned to him and held his chin with her soapy hand and her cigarette trembled, and August couldn't tell if she was serious and about to cry, or joking and about to laugh.

"I don't hate anything. It's fine. I like everything fine."

"You're serious?"

"Yes."

"Then I'm disappointed in you," she said, exhaling smoke forcefully through her nose and turning back to the dishes. "But I suppose it's my fault, for letting it go on. I'm going to talk to your father. Your barn days are coming to an end. I'll finish up here. Go listen to the game."

Out on the porch, his father was on the rocker, his legs stretched out long in front of him. He nodded at August as he sat on the step.

We're going into extra innings. Hang on as we pause for station identification. You're not going to want to miss this. The radio crackled and an ad for a used-car lot came on. Bats flew from the eaves, and August threw pebbles to make them dive, and then the game came back on and the Twins' bats got hot and they beat the Tigers by two. August looked at his father. He was slumped in the chair with his eyes closed and his hands clasped together over his chest.

"Night," August said, getting up to go inside.

His father yawned and stretched. "Night," he said.

Later, his parents' arguing had kept him awake, and the next morning his father didn't roust him for the morning milking, and soon after that Lisa was always around, and not long after that his mother had started spending time at the old house. At first, just a few nights a week, and then one morning she didn't come back to make breakfast, and his father burned the toast and slammed the door on his way to the barn.

August tied his boots. He climbed up to the haymow and surprised two cats that had been intently pawing at a dead sparrow on the hay-littered floor. He broke one's back with a quick chop of the wrench and stunned the other one with a jab to the head. The cats were indistinct as they writhed, blurry in the gloom. August silenced their yowling, each with a sharp blow from the wrench, and then gave chase to a few more slinking forms that eluded him by leaping to join their spitting clan in the rafters.

August didn't curse much. His father always said that no one took a man who cursed too much seriously and it was better to be the type of man who, when he *did* curse, made everyone else sit up and take notice.

Now, however, in the dark barn with the hay dander swirling around his face and the cats out of reach above him, he cursed.

"Motherfucker," he said. "Motherfucking, cocksucking, shit-faced goddamn fucking cats."

It was the most curse words he'd ever strung together, and he hoped the cats were sitting up to take notice, trembling in fear at the reign of fire that was about to be visited down upon their mangy heads.

At the old house, his mother had the blinds drawn. She had a large quilt wrapped around her, and the ends dragged over the floor when she got up to let him in. With the shades drawn it was dark, and she had lit an old kerosene lamp. The flame guttered, sending up tendrils of black smoke. She had been playing solitaire. There was a fried pork chop steaming in a pan on the table.

"You want some lunch?" she said, after she had settled herself down in her chair, smoothing the quilt down under her and over her bare legs. "I'm finished. You can have the rest." She slid the pork chop over to August. It hadn't been touched.

He took a bite. It was seared crispy on the outside and juicy and tender on the inside, quick-fried in butter and finished in the oven. That's how she always made pork chops. Lisa wouldn't know how to do this, he thought. His father would get so fed up with Lisa's tough, dried-out pork chops that he'd send her away, and his mother would come back to the new house and he'd start helping his dad with the barn chores again.

"Are you still not eating?" He picked up the pork chop to gnaw at the bone, where the best-tasting meat always lived.

"Augie, that's a common misconception about us breatharians. I eat. Good lord, I eat all the time. Here, actually, let me have one more bite of that." She leaned over and wafted her hand around his pork chop, bringing the smell toward herself, and then took a quick hiccupping little breath and smiled and leaned back in her seat. "Meat from an animal you know always has the best flavor," she said, lighting one of her little cigars. "That's something city people probably don't understand. You remember taking kitchen scraps out to that hog every night after dinner? You fed that animal, and now it feeds you. That lends a certain something to the savor—I'm sure there's a word for it in another language."

She pulled the quilt tighter around her shoulders. "Did you know that, Augie? That there are all sorts of words for things in other languages that we don't have in English? It's like your soul is tongue-tied when that happens, when you have a feeling or experience that you can't explain because there isn't a specific word for it. If you knew all the languages in the world, you could express yourself perfectly, and all experiences would be understandable to you because you would have a word, a perfect word, to attach to any possible occasion. See what I mean?"

August wiped his greasy hands on his jeans. He was pretty sure his mother was naked under her quilt. He wondered if there was a word for that in another language. A word to classify the feeling you get sitting across from your mother, eating a pork chop, with your mother naked under a quilt. She'd made the pork chop for herself, of that he was certain. Also, she had a half-eaten package of Fig Newtons on the counter. He knew she was teasing him about being a breatharian, but he wasn't going to give her the satisfaction of knowing that he didn't understand the joke.

"I don't know," he said. "Just because you have a word to put on something doesn't mean you understand it any better. Does it?"

"Oh, I think so. Definitely. I don't think things really exist until we can name them. Without names, the world is populated by spooks and monsters."

"Just because you give something a name doesn't mean you change what it is. It's still the same thing."

"You couldn't be more wrong, Augie dear. How about death?"

"What about it?"

"What if instead of death everyone called it being born and looked forward to it as the great reward at the end of seventy or so years of slow rot on earth?"

"That doesn't make any sense. Why would anyone look forward to death?"

"Maybe you're too young for this conversation," she said, coughing into the back of her hand. "That's an interesting thought. I bet in some language there is a word for the state you exist in now—the state of being incapable of formulating concepts of, or discussing abstractly, death in all its various forms, due to a lack of experience. You need to have someone you love die, and then you get it. All the understanding of the world comes rushing in on you like a vacuum seal was broken somewhere. I'm not saying you'll ever understand why the world works the way it does, but you'll surely come to the conclusion that it does work, and that, as a result, it will absolutely someday come to a grinding halt, as nothing can work forever. See what I mean?"

"No."

"Well, in time you will. I'm sure."

She picked up her solitaire game and shuffled the cards, splitting the deck, rifling the ends together with a brisk splat and then making the cards bow and bridge and shush back into one. August sat listening, enjoying the sound, thinking, knowing, she was wrong. He *had* loved someone who had died.

"How's the job coming?"

"Not great."

"Motivational issues?"

"No. They're just fast. I've been thinking about a change of tactics."

"Oh yeah?"

"I don't know if it will work. Can I borrow some bowls?"

Lisa stayed for dinner again. August sensed that his life was now split in two distinct pieces. There was the part when Skyler was alive, when his father and mother and he had all lived in the new house, and now there was this part, where things were foggy and indistinct. August twirled Lisa's spaghetti around on his fork and realized, for the very first time, that the whole of his life up until this very point existed in the past, which meant it didn't exist at all, not really. It might as well have been buried right there in the pasture next to Skyler.

It was dark and cool in the barn, and August switched on the radio for company. He hadn't been able to sleep, so he'd risen early, before Lisa, even. He hadn't had breakfast and his stomach rumbled as he climbed the wooden ladder up to the haymow. In the darkness he could see the faint pinpricks of stars through the knotholes and chinks of the barn planks, and then his groping fingers found the pull chain and the haymow was flooded with fluorescent light.

The floor was carpeted with twisted feline forms, tabbies, calicos, some night-black, some pure white, intermingled and lumpy and irrevocably dead. They lay like pieces of dirty laundry where they'd fallen from their perches after the tainted milk had taken its hold on their guts. August coughed and spit, slightly awed, thinking about the night before and the way the antifreeze had turned the bluish-white milk a sickly rotten green. He nudged a few of the still forms with his boot and looked toward the rafters and found them empty except for a calico, its dead claws stuck in the joist so that it dangled there, like a shabby, moth-eaten piñata.

He pulled his shirt cuffs into his gloves against the fleas jumping everywhere and began pitching the cats down the hay chute. As he worked, the voice of Paul Harvey found its way up from the radio on the ground floor.

There's going to be unrest. There's always going to be unrest, but things always get better. Tomorrow will always be better. Just think about it: Is there any time in history in which you'd rather live than now? I'll leave you with that thought. I'm Paul Harvey, and now you know, the rest of the story.

August climbed down the ladder and stepped shin deep into a pile of cats. He got out his jackknife and set to work separating the cats from their tails. He pushed the bodies into the conveyor trough as he worked, and when he was done he flipped the wall switch to set the belt moving. August watched the cats ride the conveyor until all of them went out of sight under the back wall of the barn. Outside, they were falling from the track to the cart on the back of the manure spreader. He didn't go out to look, but he imagined them piling up, covering the dirty straw and cow slop, a stack of soft, lifeless forms. Tomorrow or the next day his father would hook the cart up to the tractor and drive it to the back pasture to spread its strange load across the cow-pocked grass.

It took him a long time to nail the tails to the board, and as he pounded, the last ones were already stiffening. The sky was just starting to take on the milky light of predawn when August carried the board up to the new house. In the mudroom he stopped and listened. There was no sound of his father and Lisa in the kitchen, but he knew they'd be up soon. He leaned his board against the coat rack, directly over his father's barn boots, and regarded his work as it was, totem and trophy, altogether alien against a backdrop of lilac-patterned wallpaper.

August tried to whistle as he walked across the lawn and down the hill to the old house, but the best he could muster was a spit-laced warble. On the porch he wiped at his lips with the back of his sleeve and looked in the window. His mother was at the kitchen table. She held a card in her hand, raised, as if she were deciding her next move, but August could see that the cards in front of her were scattered across the table in disarray, a jumbled mess, as if they'd been thrown there.

It was May 25, the opening day of trout season, and August was riding in the back seat of Vaughn Thompson's long brown Cadillac. August's friend Bob was riding shotgun, because Vaughn was his grandpa and the front seat was his by rights. Bob had been badgering Vaughn every day for a week in the lead-up to the opener, and he'd finally agreed to take them up north to his favorite spots on the Pine River.

Vaughn was a short man, fat, with a fringe of white beard but no mustache. He needed a cane to get around, and August had never seen him wear anything other than massive denim overalls and a buffalo plaid shirt, no matter the season or temperature. He was a heavy-equipment operator. August had asked, but Bob wasn't sure how old Vaughn was. "I don't think he's as old as he looks," Bob said. "He's just fat. At work he has one of the other operators raise him up in an excavator bucket so he can get into his machine without having to climb the ladder."

Vaughn had his cane propped up on the seat between him and Bob. It was made of dense, heavy wood, the handle carved in the shape of a snake's head. He called it his *lickin' stick*. Bob said that you could unscrew the head to unsheathe a long, thin dagger, and August, from his backseat vantage, was trying to determine if such a thing might be possible. From what he could see, the whole cane looked seamless, carved from one solid piece. Bob was probably August's best friend, but he sometimes made things up whole cloth.

Vaughn was an extremely slow driver. He tended to straddle the white line on the road's edge, two tires on pavement, two tires crunching the shoulder gravel. He had a large green Stanley thermos, and he drank coffee and peppermint schnapps from the lid, which doubled as a cup. If he had to piss, a fairly frequent occasion, he did so in a wide-mouthed Gatorade bottle that he kept down by his feet, turning up the radio to mask the sound of his stream, swearing if he missed his target.

The talk at school all week had been about Sam Borden, a kid in August and Bob's class, who'd found a mummy under a brush pile down by the Little Muskegon. He'd told everyone about it, round-eyed, at the back of the morning bus.

"A foot," he said. "That's how I noticed it. A bare foot. Real brown looking with yellow toenails."

"Yellow?"

"Yeah, yellow. I was going fishing out there. I walked over this big brush pile that I usually just go around. I decided to climb over it for some reason, and then there it was."

"Like, the toenails were painted yellow?"

"No, like gross old-person yellow. The foot was all dried-out looking. Like jerky. Just sticking out from under a big log."

"Gross."

"What did the rest of it look like?"

"That was all I saw. I ran home and told my dad."

"You didn't even try to get a better look?"

"Shit. Have you ever seen a dead person's foot? Any of you? That's what I thought. Don't even ask me about why I didn't try to get a better look. I ran out of there as fast as I could, and that's what any of you would've done, too. So shut it."

All the guys had spent time speculating about the origins of the body, and Bob was particularly fixated. He had a theory that he was broaching to his grandpa now as they drove.

"I think it was White Cloud," Bob said. "Chief White Cloud. It just makes sense. Everyone knows he was from around here. He broke out of that reservation back in the day, and then he made his death march all the way back to be buried in his ancient hunting grounds."

Vaughn snorted and poured more coffee into his thermos top, steam rising to fill the car with a vaguely peppermint smell. "Chief White Cloud, my ass," he said.

"I'm serious," Bob said. "Sam Borden said the foot looked like jerky. The toes were like pieces of Slim Jims. That's not just some ordinary body. Right, August? He said that."

August leaned forward, still trying to get a better look at Vaughn's cane. "He did say that. Just like beef jerky."

"See?" Bob said. "That's a mummy. Chief White Cloud is the only thing that makes sense. It's just like the Iceman."

Vaughn sipped his coffee and turned to look at Bob, a single wooly eyebrow raised in a way that August could never duplicate. "The Iceman?" he said.

"Yeah, Ötzi, the Iceman. They found the guy under a glacier in Switzerland or something. He was five thousand years old. Right, August?"

"Yeah. We watched a *National Geographic Explorer* show about it in science class. They said the guy that discovered him got a million dollars."

"If I was Sam I'd be pissed off about that," Bob said. "No one is talking about giving him anything. Chief White Cloud should be worth a thousand bucks at least."

Vaughn shook his head. "The Iceman was under a glacier. Frozen. This asshole your friend found was under a pile of cut brush. I have no idea how he got there, but a mummy he ain't. Hate to break it to you kids. My guess is his name is Tony Spicoli from down in Detroit, and no one that knew him shed a single tear about his disappearance. You boys have breakfast? No? That bag on the seat has donuts, August. Pass me up a powdered sugar."

They ate their donuts in silence, and when Vaughn was done he wiped the powder from his chin with his sleeve and cleared his throat. "Saw a truck was parked at your mom's house this morning, Bobby. That guy still hanging around?"

August saw Bob's shoulders rise and fall. "I guess."

"What's his name again?"

"JT."

"He give you any problems about anything?"

"Nah. He's all right."

Vaughn shook his head. "Your mother. Don't know what it is in her that makes her go after every little thing that seems different from the place she came from. I'm just saying. Down in Detroit, I worked with blacks and Mexicans and red and brown and yellow people, whatever. None of it matters to me as long as you show up to work on time. Still, your mother was my firstborn, and I swear to God she's made it her life's mission to piss me off. First your dad and now this guy. Never mind. Pass me another one, August. Chocolate frosted this time. Chief White Cloud, my ass. Let's go fishing."

Vaughn drove them down a winding gravel road and then finally turned off on an overgrown two-track with fiddlehead ferns and purple skunk cabbage tongues growing up in the center. They went culvert hopping, getting out at every point the road crossed the creek and taking turns dropping their lines from the embankment, sending their hooks, baited with red angleworms, drifting on the slow current. They caught brook trout, mostly hand sized or smaller other than one that Bob hooked, a fifteen-inch standout that made a hard run and jumped to the other side of the culvert. Bob stood on the upstream side with his rod bent double trying to pull the fish back up to him, his grandpa, still sitting behind the wheel with the door open, barking orders.

"Don't horse him, Bobby."

"I'm not horsing him."

"He's going to break you off on the side of that culvert if you're not careful."

"I know. I know."

"You're going to have to do something, Bobby. That fish is kicking your ass."

August had a flash of inspiration. He scrambled down the steep bank and waded out into the bottom of the pool, kicking and thrashing, the trout a dark shape darting this way and that before it shot back up the culvert to the other side where Bob was able to scoop it with Vaughn's old green mesh hand net. Bob hooked a finger through the trout's gills and held it aloft, stern faced, for his grandpa's appraisal.

"I'll be damned, son," Vaughn said. "That is a fine one. You're lucky August is a quick thinker. You boys got your knives? Okay, you know what to do." Vaughn reached over and rustled around in the Cadillac's glove box until he came up with a folded sheaf of newspaper. "Use this," he said. "Do it right on the hood. Make sure to get that line of dark stuff off the backbone, now. Leaving that on there will ruin a trout quick."

"I know," Bob said.

"And make sure you rip the gills out, too. Leaving those in there will make it spoil. Rinse them out in the creek."

"I know how to do it," Bob said. "You taught me last year."

"Believe me, you wouldn't be the first person to forget something I told him how to do." Vaughn nodded at August, standing there wet-legged with a small involuntary shiver starting to brew. "Hurry up, before that kid gets hypothermia."

When the trout were cleaned, they wrapped them in one final piece of newspaper and put them in Vaughn's battered Igloo cooler. August was trembling now, the sun starting to lower behind the tangle of maples and birches. Vaughn had the heat on full blast in the Cadillac, and before he started for home he dug up a Styrofoam cup from under his seat and blew the dust from its interior. He poured a sizable slug of his coffee-schnapps mixture and passed it back to August.

"Your lips are blue, kid," he said. "Drink up. Don't tell your mom on me." Vaughn turned and saw the look Bob was giving him and sighed. He poured his thermos top full and handed it over to him, saying, "And you'd damn well better not tell *your* mom on me." August drank the coffee—only lukewarm now, slightly minty and sharp from the schnapps—and drowsed in the back seat all the way home. Vaughn thumbed through classic-rock stations on the stereo and, with dark coming on, drove even slower.

When Vaughn dropped August off at home, he said his thanks and goodbyes and squelched across the drive in his wet shoes, his rod in one hand, a small, sodden newspaper-wrapped parcel of brook trout in the other. The lights were on in the new house, Lisa's Jeep parked next to his father's F-150. August stomped up the porch steps and opened the door, "I'm home," he shouted into the foyer. "Good night." He slammed the door, stomped back down the stairs, and headed across the yard to the old house.

He sat at the kitchen table while his mother heated oil. At her insistence he'd shed his wet jeans and wrapped his legs up in a quilt. She sprinkled the trout with salt and pepper, and squeezed a lemon. "Look at how pink these are," she said. "There's nothing as good as a wild trout. The ones you buy at the store are all soggy and white. It was nice of Bob's grandpa to take you boys. Did you have a nice time?"

August shrugged. "Sure."

"What did you guys talk about?"

"What do you mean? We talked about fishing."

"Oh geez. That old line. Your grandpa, I wish you could have met him, he was always a big fisherman. When your father and I started dating, my dad took him fishing. My dad had a boat at the time, a Boston Whaler, and they went after lake trout out of Grand Traverse. I remember being so nervous that morning."

"Why were you nervous?" The trout were sputtering in the pan now. She had a piece of paper towel on a screen to keep the grease from popping all over the stove. Her cigarillo had gone out, but the stub of it was still perched between her lips, and when she laughed the ash fell and drifted on her sweatshirt. She wiped at it, frowning slightly. "I was nervous for your father. My dad was . . . formidable. Your father was a kid still, really. All day on the boat together, just the two of them. I didn't sleep a wink the night before, just picturing them out there. What would they talk about? I couldn't even imagine. I thought they might talk about me. And that made me mad, too. I was nervous and mad at the same time. Do you want some toast with this? I could make toast, and I have some cream cheese."

"Sure. Why were you mad?"

"They could have asked me to go fishing."

"Do you even like fishing?"

"Not really, but that's not the point. I was pregnant with you at the time. Just barely. Your father didn't even know yet. I was sick in the morning. I sat home all day and they were on the lake, and when they got home I watched them cleaning the fish on the back porch. They got a few, I remember. Your father caught the biggest one and he was happy about that, trying not to show it. When I finally got him alone, I asked him, I was dying to know: *What did you guys talk about out there, just the two of you together all day?* Your dad looked at me; he was picking at some of the trout scales stuck to his fingers. *We talked about fishing,* he said. *Well, guess what?* I said. *We're pregnant.* That gave him a jolt, that's for sure. Anyway, here you go. Do you want some tea?" She slid a plate in front of him. Three brook trout, the skin browned crisp, heads and tails still on, the eyes crusted over black. Two pieces of wheat toast spread thick with cream cheese.

"No tea," he said. "Thanks. This looks good."

She sat across from him and relit her cigarillo. "You and that Bob are getting to be good friends, aren't you?"

"I guess." He spread one of the trout open with his fork and peeled out the backbone. The delicate rib cage came clean, leaving just the pink flesh there, flattened on the plate. He put the bones aside and flaked some of the fish onto a piece of toast before crunching it down.

"What does his mother do?"

"Works at the bank, I think."

"He doesn't have a relationship with his father?"

"He told me he never met him."

"That must be hard for him."

"Maybe. I don't know."

"How's the fish?"

"Really good. You want some?"

She shook her head, took a drag, and then stubbed the small butt out in the big chipped seashell she'd used as an ashtray for as long as he could remember. "Would you consider Bob to be your best friend?"

"I don't know. Why?"

"I just hope that you're making the sort of friendships that will last a lifetime, that's all."

"How am I supposed to know what friendships are going to last a lifetime?"

"Fair enough. But so much of who we are, and what we become, is dictated by those we surround ourselves with, Augie. We all want to believe we're individuals, but the forces of peer-group persuasion are insidious. For example, when I was twenty, two of my closest friends were already pregnant and engaged to be married."

August wiped his fingers on a paper towel and pushed his empty plate away. "So?" he said.

"I'm just telling you, your life can take a lot of different directions if you let it. But friends are sometimes like hedges. Their presence is comforting, sheltering, but at the same time they're blocking your view of the outside world."

"Bob's not a hedge, Mom."

"I'm not saying he is, necessarily. I'm just rambling. Do you want dessert?"

When Vaughn had a heart attack and died, a year after that fishing trip, Bob inherited his car. He'd been held back in first grade, so he was older than most of the kids in their class. At the time of his grandpa's passing, he'd applied for a hardship permit and taken driver's education. Not quite fifteen yet and he was driving himself to school, picking August up on the way most days. August "helped" Bob with his math homework, and Bob saved him from the various indignities of the school bus. It was a fair trade, and both parties were satisfied. They were planning a trip up north for the trout opener to hit all the spots Vaughn had showed them. Bob had kept everything exactly how it had been in the Cadillac. The snake-head lickin' stick was there. The green Stanley thermos remained in the cup holder, unwashed. And, as Bob showed August, reaching way back under the seat, there was a nearly full bottle of Dr. McGillicuddy's peppermint schnapps. "I haven't touched it," he said solemnly. "Not till the opener."

This was also the year of the Four Mile fights. In the halls during the day, pushing and shoving matches were common. Hormones were released in unstable doses. Grievances were aired by voices that consistently threatened to crack. After Darren Reid and Andy Johnson engaged in ten minutes of epic combat in the hallway between the band room and the gymnasium—leaving the floor tiles splattered with blood and the throngs of student onlookers unable to focus for the rest of the day—the administration cracked down. Any displays of aggression on school grounds, including threats, would result in immediate expulsion. Thus, the settling of scores moved off campus. Four Mile was a narrow gravel road that dead-ended a half a mile from school. There was a turnaround at the road's terminus and a thick screen of poplar and brush. If an argument sprung up in the lunchroom, simply saying the words *Let's go to Four Mile, then, asshole* immediately set the room abuzz with the knowledge of incipient violence. When school let out, some would walk or ride their bikes, and those with cars would load up to maximum capacity, windows down, voices straining to be heard over the music, everyone making their predictions, whipping themselves into a lather.

August had never been in a fight himself. He was vaguely aware that some members of his circle were suspicious of this fact, seeing it as evidence of a certain lack of character on his part. However, he was with Bob more often than not, and Bob got in enough fights that August was generally deemed to be okay, by association. Bob approached fighting the way some guys went at kicking field goals or shooting foul shots. He was methodical, measured. His grandpa had done some amateur boxing and taught him a few things. He kept his hands up and moved in slowly. If a guy rushed him, he'd sidestep and jab at his face. But if a guy tried to play at the same game, Bob would drop his hands and shoot for the takedown, get him straddled and then rain down the punches. In junior high, Bob was unequivocally the toughest kid. That had been settled long ago, and Bob only had to take on the occasional challenger, or, more often, instigate a reluctant would-be challenger, just to keep his hand in.

Fighting other kids in junior high was one thing; fighting high schoolers was quite another. The situation between Bob and Brandt Gidley got its start over a basketball. A few of the guys had gotten in the habit of eating their lunch quickly and then going to the gym to shoot hoops for the rest of the break. They mostly played HORSE, or sometimes twenty-one, not exerting themselves much because no one wanted to go back to class too sweaty. Girls were not into excess perspiration. That was something they'd recently learned. This particular day, Bob and August and a few of the other guys had gotten to the gym early. There were a few good leather basketballs on the rack, amid the ranks of lumpy, worn-out rubber. The leather balls were always in high demand, and, generally, if upperclassmen were present, they claimed them for themselves. On the day of the fight, Brandt came in, found the rack devoid of leather, and tried to make Bob give his up. The game halted. Bob told Brandt to go fuck himself. A tussle ensued in which Brandt threw a ball at Bob's face, prompting Bob to issue the Four Mile challenge.

Brandt Gidley was a huge dude. Captain of the wrestling squad. August thought Bob was out of his mind. No matter how tough you are in seventh grade, a high school junior is a completely different animal. After classes let out, half the school was at Four Mile, it seemed, a ring of people yelling and screaming, and Bob got one good shot in before Brandt wrapped him up and took him down. It was over that fast. One minute Bob was on his feet looking to jab; the next he was flat on his back, his arms twisted up in some kind of agonizing hold, his face contorted with pain.

August was standing right there. He could see Bob's shoulder starting to pull out of its socket, the unnatural hump of it through the thin material of his T-shirt. Brandt had a small, twisted smile on his face, and he lowered his lips to Bob's ear. He spoke quietly, and probably not many people could hear, but August did.

"Does that hurt? If you're done, I'll let you go. All you gotta do is say *My mom's a nigger lover.* Those are the magic words."

"Fuck you." Bob's face was pressed to the gravel, and his voice came through clenched teeth. The one eye August could see was wide and roving; it settled on August for a split second, and later August realized that was when he should have done something. If the tables had been turned, if for some reason it was August getting his arm twisted out of its socket, Bob would have tackled the guy. August knew that, but in the moment he froze. Then Bob tried to buck Brandt off, but Brandt held him down, putting on more pressure until August was certain that something was going to break, but then it seemed that Bob somehow got real calm. He stopped struggling.

"My mom's a nigger lover," Bob said.

"Louder, so everyone can hear."

Bob's eyes were closed now, and he shouted it. The crowd went quiet, and Brandt used Bob's prone body to push himself to his feet. He brushed his jeans clean and turned to a group of his friends, high-fiving. Bob rolled over onto his back. He lay there for a moment, staring straight up, and August started to walk toward him, but then Bob stood suddenly, pushing August aside as he ran to his car. August expected Bob to get behind the wheel and tear away, but instead he was hunched over, digging around under the front seat, and then he was out of the car, striding toward Brandt, who was standing with his back turned, reenacting the move he'd used on Bob with one of his friends, both of them laughing their heads off. Bob had something in his hands, and by the time August realized that it was the snake-head lickin' stick it was too late, because Bob had reached Brandt. In one quick move he unsheathed the long, thin dagger that was hidden in the cane and rammed it into Brandt's back.

There was a noise that came before Brandt's screams. August would remember it for a long time—a hollow, ripping thud as the blade entered. The dagger must have been dull. As a kid he'd carved pumpkins for Halloween with his mom, and the safety knife she gave him made a sound just like that when he sunk it in. Brandt went down, a carnation of red on the back of his white shirt, the blade still there, dangling at a precarious angle while he writhed. Kids were scattering and Bob was gone, his car throwing gravel as he peeled away. August ran.

The fight was all anyone talked about for weeks. The school brought in counselors. There was a police officer on duty now in the lunchroom. When his mother asked, August told her that he wasn't there, that he'd stayed after school to play basketball with some of the guys. He knew she didn't totally buy this, but he also knew her thoughts were else-where. His father had submitted the paperwork for a divorce. One afternoon a furniture truck showed up at the new house and unloaded a brand-new Select Comfort Sleep Number mattress. King-sized. While this was happening, August was in the old house with his mother. Through the blinds they watched the deliverymen unload the base and carry it up the front steps with Lisa holding the door for them. His mother's back was turned to him so he couldn't see her face, but the very next day August returned home from school and there were suitcases on the porch of the old house. His mother was sitting on the front step, smoking, dressed in real clothes—jeans and a flannel shirt.

"You'll not be stepping foot on that particular school bus again," she said, stubbing the cigarillo and standing with a certain crisp, decisive air he'd forgotten she possessed. "Let's get you packed. I've had about enough of this bullshit."

Brandt Gidley nearly died. He had two surgeries in which several feet of his intestine had to be removed, and he missed the rest of the school year. Bob was sent to a facility downstate, and August never saw him again. He'd failed Bob in some essential way, and this was knowledge he felt to the core. He should have stepped in, gotten an arm crooked around Brandt's neck, and squeezed with everything he had.

They were down in Grand Rapids for nearly two years. His mother took online classes to finally finish her degree, and he attended eighth and ninth grade at a large school in which he managed to successfully lose himself. For lack of a better idea, he applied himself to his schoolwork. He and his mother would study together in the living room, silently reading, his mother rising every so often to reheat her tea or smoke a cigarillo on the back porch. They rented a small duplex close to downtown, and for the first time in his life he heard traffic noises at night. His mother rarely went out, and the house often seemed stifling and close.

When it became too much he'd set off with a sandwich in his backpack and walk along the Grand River. In town its banks were straightened, poured concrete—more of a canal than a real river. It ran brown and slow, with the faint odor of sewage. Still, people fished. Below the Sixth Street dam, men in waders drifted salmon roe for steelhead, the huge glass-and-steel Amway skyscraper a strangely alpine urban backdrop. Occasionally there would be fly fishermen wielding large two-handed spey rods, loops of fluorescent line uncoiling, hissing out over the current with a spray of water. Flashy but not very effective. From his observations, August figured the bait fisherman out-caught the fly fisherman three to one. The guys throwing bait tended to be unshaven and camo-clad. They fished with cigarettes dangling from their lips, one hand holding the rod, one hand jammed in a coat pocket, eye on their orange stick bobbers.

August walked everywhere in the city, and he never felt comfortable. There was too much potential, too many options. Twenty restaurants on a single block. A constant stream of faces. He started fishing because at least there, on the artificial banks of a nearly dead river, the ceaseless drone of humanity seemed to recede slightly.

He didn't have waders, so he couldn't get to the best runs. From the concrete wall he pitched small chartreuse jigs tipped with wax worms, and often he'd go days without catching anything. Sometimes he'd catch redhorse suckers. They fought like worn-out tube socks, their slime turning to glue on his hands. He caught only a few steelhead, and he could remember each one, from the moment the bobber dipped to the moment of their release. They were cold and hard, like polished metal cut to the shape of fish.

The biggest was a twelve-pound male, on a miserable rainy day in late March. The steelhead made one tremendous jump and several long runs, and when August was finally able to get the fish near his feet to grab its tail, his hands were shaking at the size of it. He unhooked it, raised its long chrome bulk from the water for a moment to get it more firmly planted in his mind, then released it, watching it until it was just a dark shape finning near the bottom, then gone. He looked around and it was only him there. Usually there were people walking the river path, joggers, other fisherman, bums rifling the garbage cans, but today, nobody. Already the catching of the fish was taking on a dream-like haze. A metro area of over a million goddamn people, humans stacked on top of humans so that you could hardly get away from the throngs, and yet, today, at this moment, the one time he might have liked an audience to something spectacular, he was all alone. It figured. He'd have kept the fish, but no one in their right mind would eat anything that swam in the Grand.

Having left the farm, it seemed that his mother had decided she was no longer going to cook. They ate takeout most nights, and the leftover cartons piled up in the fridge. Foods he'd never had before but his mother seemed to remember fondly from a different life: massaman curry and basil stir-fried beef, pho, laab, gyros and kebabs. In Grand Rapids, a person could get Ethiopian wat and injera delivered at ten o'clock at night and not think twice about it. August didn't mind the strange food. Some of it he liked quite a bit. He also appreciated the fact that it came in disposable containers because, in addition to not cooking, his mother had stopped doing the dishes. Or the laundry. Or tidying the house in any way. Things piled up. It was as if, having moved them to this place, she'd used up all her forward momentum, and now she'd stalled. Eventually, August was forced to do the dishes. He vacuumed; he did his laundry as well as hers. He loaded heaps of clothes in the washing machine, burning with indignation.

The situation in Grand Rapids never seemed permanent, and this was what made it bearable. August slept on an air mattress. They never even got around to fully unpacking. The spare bedroom was full of unopened moving boxes. There was a sense that this was an interim period, a gathering of breath before life would resume. He spent most weekends up at the farm helping his father around the place, wandering the hardwood stands, kicking up grouse and the occasional woodcock, lying in bed in the new house with the sound of the TV coming up the stairs, the dull murmur of his father and Lisa laughing at something Jay Leno had said. He had relinquished the hope that things might go back to how they had been before. He sensed that a new reality was going to emerge, and he walked around most days with a feeling of low-level apprehension, half dreading, half-anxious for whatever was to come.

His mother finished her coursework and got her master's degree in library science. The day it became official, she brought home a large bottle of champagne and let him have a glass with her. She was happy, more animated than he'd seen her in a long time. They had Italian delivered: baked ziti and eggplant parm, garlic bread dripping with melted butter. Halfway through the meal, his mother seemed to lose interest in the food. She poured herself more champagne, looked across the table, and cocked her head, a small, strange smile on her lips. "Do you think maybe it's time for me to start dating?" she said.

August was caught off guard. His face reddened. "None of my business," he said, getting up to clear the dishes. "Do what you want. Are you done with that?"

As the spring came on, she started going for long walks in the evenings. She still didn't cook much, but mercifully she started doing her own laundry. Her squeezed-out tea bags no longer littered the windowsill next to the chair where she read. One day she accompanied him to the river. She brought a book and sat on a bench near where he fished. Although he would barely admit it to himself, he desperately wanted to catch something for her to see. But, as was often the case, he caught nothing. On the walk home she told him she'd had a great time watching him. "You look so serious while you fish," she said. "Deadly serious. Maybe if you smiled you'd catch more." He knew she was making fun of him, and he rolled his eyes at her to let her know that he knew.

His mother was always reading, and at this point she still had hopes that the habit would rub off on him. She started bringing home books that featured fishing. He thought some of the Nick Adams stories were pretty good. Since they were set in Michigan, he could picture the cedar swamps, the clear-cuts, and the colors of the brook trout. He made it through most of *A River Runs Through It* and thought it was okay, if a little fancy at times. She brought him Robert Traver and Tom McGuane and more Hemingway, and while he occasionally sat on the couch with a book for a while to humor her, he knew that she didn't actually understand his relationship with fishing. The thing was, fishing wasn't something he thought about much when he wasn't actually doing it. He didn't have a great desire to learn new tactics or fish new places or read about it in metaphysical terms. Nick Adams fished to forget the parts of the war he'd carried back with him, and August thought that seemed about right. Standing on the banks of the Grand watching a bobber ride a current seam was a magic trick. Fishing allowed him to disappear the city, his mother, his father, his friendless school existence; and while he needed it desperately, he also looked forward to a day when it would no longer be necessary for survival.

At one point during his mother's fishing literature campaign she brought home the movie *A River Runs Through It*. They watched it that night, eating wonton soup and pork buns, leaning over the coffee table so as not to spill on the couch.

"That Brad Pitt," his mother said, slurping her soup. "Such a naughty grin he has."

August decided it was a decent movie. He thought fly-fishing in general was sort of melodramatic. He figured a person might be able to make a movie about bait fishermen, but there was no way they'd put Brad Pitt in it. "God," his mother said. "Look at that scenery. *Montana.* That's not a place you ever really think of, is it? Oh, wow, look at Brad Pitt wading across that river. The way he wears that creel across his chest is just . . . *perfect,* isn't it?"

"Mom. Shut up so I can watch it, please?"

When the movie was over, he went to bed. But before he fell asleep he heard the opening music drifting in from the living room. His mother had started the film over again.

In a million years he never would have guessed that this strange stasis they'd found themselves in would eventually be broken by Brad Pitt, of all things.

Something about Montana, the idea of it, seemed to stick in his mother's head. Now she read books about the Lewis and Clark expedition. She read *Legends of the Fall* by Jim Harrison, and she brought that movie home as well. It seemed like Brad Pitt had a monopoly on all Hollywood renditions of Montana. "That Brad Pitt looks like he has a real firm hand on the reins of his horse," his mother said. "I wonder if he can actually do it like that in real life."

One day he came home from school to find his mother sitting on the couch. She hopped up when he walked through the door. She'd obviously been waiting for him, and he eyed her warily. He went to the kitchen to see if any of the leftovers in the fridge were edible. She followed him, leaning against the doorjamb as he ate cold chicken salad from a carton. "So," she said, "I have some news."

"Yeah?"

"I have a job interview in a couple weeks."

"What job?"

"It's a brand-new library. They just finished building it, and they're going to have two positions available."

"Sounds good," he said. "I'm sure you'll get it."

"Guess where."

"I don't know. Where?"

"Bozeman, Montana." She raised her eyebrows. *"Big sky country."*

There was a brief pause, a forkful of chicken salad stalling en route to mouth, before he recovered. He chewed. Forked up another mound of chicken salad. "Cool," he said, his mouth full.

Later, he found an atlas and did a little research. State animal: grizzly bear. State bird: western meadowlark. State motto: *Oro y plata,* gold and silver. It wasn't much to go off of, but still, the possibilities conjured far outstripped what he'd experienced in Michigan thus far.

. . .

He went up to the farm when his mother flew to Montana, and she called him the evening after her interview. From the tone of her voice he didn't even need to ask. He knew she'd been offered one of the positions. She was talking fast, breathless. "The mountains," she said. "It's unreal. The air smells different, kind of sagey, or maybe it's pine, or juniper, or something, I'm not sure. The building is beautiful, state-of-the-art. The people seem great. I haven't seen Brad Pitt yet, but I'm keeping the faith. Thoughts?"

He was silent for a moment. "Congrats," he said. "I figured you'd get it. You told them yes, didn't you?"

"I did," she said. "Yes, I did."

"Well, then, that's that, I guess."

When she hung up, he went out to watch some TV with his father. He thought he should probably tell him the news, but for some reason he couldn't bring himself to do it. He stared at the TV unseeing, tried to imagine what his life might soon be like.

School let out, and there was a flurry of packing. He went up to the farm one more time before the move. On his last night there, Lisa said she had somewhere to be and so August and his father had dinner, just the two of them—frozen pizza and a salad that neither of them really touched. August's father laughed about that. "If ever you needed proof of a woman's moderating presence in your life, there it is," he said. "She's not even here, and we still make the damn salad. A woman gets to be like your external conscience. That's why you need to make sure you end up with the right one; otherwise you're a rudderless ship. Despite our differences, your mother was always good for me in that way."

"How can someone else be your conscience?"

"Would it make sense to you if I said that I think the best part of a man lives in a woman? Or, maybe, the best part of a man lies in the ideas his woman has about him, what he *could* be or how he *might* act if only she could get him to realize his best self. A good woman might be a man's only hope for salvation on earth. Get me?"

August shrugged. "Not really."

His father wiped pizza grease from his fingers with a napkin and leaned back from the table. "You're just about fifteen now. You'll be having experiences soon. You're going to be moving across the damned country, and we're not going to be seeing each other much for a while. I don't like it, but it is what it is. I feel like it's the appropriate time to give you some advice. I've got two pieces for you. Ready?"

"Sure."

"When it comes to women—this is very important; no one ever told me this and I had to learn the hard way—when it comes to women, you need to be respectful above all, but at the same time you can't let them bend you to their will. Does that make sense? As a man you need to have at least a part of you that's unyielding; if not, you'll get the paper-clip treatment."

"The paper-clip treatment?"

"Yeah, it's just like it sounds. What happens when you bend a paper clip too many times?"

"It breaks."

"Exactly. Keep that in mind. No woman is going to respect a paper-clip man. If you have some unyielding place within you that thwarts her efforts to bend, she may hate you at times. For sure, she will hate you at times. But she will also love you for it, despite herself. Okay, second piece of advice, very important: When you start shaving, don't skimp on razors. Don't go cheap. Also, do the first stroke with the grain, rinse, and then do the second against the grain. Use as hot of water as you can stand when you rinse the razor, then, when it's done, wash your face with as cold as you can stand. It closes the pores and that way you won't get razor burn. Got it?"

"I guess."

"And don't even try to grow any facial hair until you're in your early twenties. Just shave it all off. As much as you think that wispy little mustache makes you look older, it really just alerts everyone to the fact that you're still a punk."

August finished his pizza and sat back, arms crossed over his chest. "Skyler's been gone for over two years," he said. "What if I got a pup now, before I left? I'm not going to know anyone out there."

His father stretched and scooted his chair back. He rose and started gathering up the dishes. "The timing has to be right on these things," he said. "I'm taking you back down to your mom's tomorrow and then you'll be leaving, and having a puppy in the mix for all of that might not be a good idea."

"But I wanted your help deciding. You know more about dogs than I do. You'd make sure I got a good one."

His father stopped gathering the dishes to consider this. He shook his head. "As an adult, dogs come to you," he said. "As a kid, you might have needed my help picking one out, but not anymore. You'll find the dog when it's right. I firmly believe that. At this point, the dog I choose for you probably wouldn't be a good fit. I personally think you should start sniffing one out the minute you get there. But maybe this exact moment is not the best time. See what I mean?"

August shrugged. Picked at something stuck to the tablecloth.

August's father laughed, balled up his napkin, and tossed it at August's head. "Don't be a sad sack. I'm kind of envious. You're about to get turned loose on a new adventure. The Wild West. Going to see things your old man has never seen, that's for sure. Let's get these dishes cleaned up. The Tigers are down in Chicago tonight. I think the game will be on soon."

———

August and his mother left Grand Rapids in a U-Haul with her Nissan trailered on a dolly behind. August thought that if he didn't know her—say, if he just saw her on the street—he would have thought her much too young to be the mother of someone his age. It seemed that the farther she got from the farm, the better her spirits. With Janis Joplin on the CD player and her hair tied back with a scarf, she appeared to be not so much driving westerly as steadily ascending into orbit.

The industrial landscape down through lower Michigan and across

Chicago was uninteresting to him, with the exception of Gary, Indiana, where the smokestacks and power lines and alien-spacecraft refinery complexes were enough to inspire a certain queasy awe. He started on the stack of magazines he'd brought for the journey, and somewhere, on a monotonous tree-confined stretch of Wisconsin highway, he read an article in *National Geographic* about the Iceman. Since their initial discovery, scientists had spent vast amounts of time and energy analyzing everything about him—what he ate, injuries he'd suffered, the state of his molars, the peculiar shape of his tattoos. It wasn't just scientists, though. The Iceman had captured the attention of the world, and the article even mentioned that several women had come forth, volunteering to be made pregnant with his sperm, should any of it still be viable. August figured that this was something Bob would have appreciated and for a while he thought about trying to send the article to him, but he had no idea where Bob was, and anyway, it had been too long since that fishing trip.

Bobby flagged a diesel down, just before it rained, Oh Lord, won't you buy me a Mercedes-Benz, looks like everybody in this whole round world they're down on me. His mother had that Janis Joplin CD on repeat and they listened to it nonstop, until the songs started to lose their individuality, the whole album melting into one long undulating series of pained croons and harsh wails. When they finally crossed the Mississippi near La Crosse, August put the magazines aside and didn't pick them up again for the duration of the trip. Face to the window, he watched the cloistered trees grudgingly give way to the great expanse of grassland. Somewhere in the Dakotas he saw his first antelope. They stopped at a rest area near Theodore Roosevelt National Park, and there was a buffalo grazing on the lawn. He'd never been this far west. He'd never seen a mountain. He and his mother stood together next to the U-Haul, watching the buffalo let loose a prodigious stream of piss, then proceed to drop heavily to the earth and roll in its own urine, emitting deep guttural noises. They were close enough they could feel the ground shaking under their feet. His mother laughed and nudged him with her elbow. "Correct me if I'm wrong," she said, "but that there ain't no Holstein cow."

August's mother had made an offer on a house, sight unseen, after talking on the phone with the owner a few times while they were still back in Michigan. The house was in Livingston, a small town near Bozeman, and his mother was slightly concerned about the commute over a mountain pass, but eventually she decided the deal was too good to pass up. It was a small bungalow, one of four nearly identical homes in a line on the same street. It was almost one hundred years old, but it had been recently refinished so everything still smelled like new paint and fresh laminate flooring.

They'd been there for only a couple of days when August noticed the plaque on a post at the end of the block. It was a national historic registry marker featuring a short description of the town's small red-light district. The four identical homes had been brothels for many years, until the early 1970s, when the prostitutes were forced to move outside the city limits in the lead-up to Montana's outright ban on prostitution.

That night they ate their Chinese takeout sitting cross-legged on the floor amid the stacks of moving boxes. August poked through his cashew chicken, eating around the broccoli. "You know we're living in an old whorehouse, right?" he said.

"Excuse me?" his mother said, chopsticks pausing in mid-arc to her mouth.

"This house was a brothel. Part of the red-light district. It's on the National Register of Historic Places." She insisted that he take her out to see the plaque, and so they went, still holding the take-out cartons. She read, shaking her head, lips pursed. "I'm not a superstitious person," she said. "But, man, talk about bad energy."

"It was a long time ago," August said. "It's all been remodeled anyway."

"Sure. Of course. Nothing exorcises the demons like new stainless steel appliances. Whew. Getting chilly already. Zero humidity here, have you noticed that? So dry. My hair is a damn mess, and I've used a whole tube of lip balm in three days."

"I got a bloody nose yesterday," August said.

"We'll adjust, I'm sure. We're just a couple of old sponges, finally getting that nasty Midwest damp wrung out of us."

The next day, as they were unpacking, his mother burned sweetgrass, a small rope of it smudging and smoking in a bowl on the floor. August made a show of coughing and waving his hand in the air, but really he thought it smelled better than the new paint.

"It's purifying," she said. "Deal with it."

He got his clothes put away and helped her move bookcases and dressers, but when she started unpacking the kitchen she waved him off. "It's a beautiful day," she said. "Get out and explore. The girls and I have things to say to each other that aren't meant for the ears of young men."

"The girls?"

She shrugged, a mixing bowl in each hand. "The painted ladies with whom we're cohabitating."

"I haven't met these ladies."

"Well, they're a hoot, let me tell you. One of them definitely had her eye on you, but I told her that she'd better keep her cold wraith fingers off my darling son."

He snorted and shook his head—the exact way his father did it, on purpose—and then he rode his bike toward the river, the wind flapping his shirt so that he could still smell the sweetgrass smoke. The mountains were a stern, steady presence above town, and he found that they helped him get his bearings. In Michigan the trees obscured everything, but here the town was laid bare. He could ride his bike for ten minutes to the top of the water tower hill, and the whole place was spread out before him: the train yard, the massive ornate depot, the incinerator stack, the false fronts and neon and faded murals of Main Street. He didn't know a single person here other than his mother, and she was already happily communing with ghost prostitutes. He rode down to the river and ditched his bike. He scrambled down the bank, tried unsuccessfully to throw rocks to the other side, and felt quietly, desperately sorry for himself.

Most days his mother came home from the library happy, rushing to tell him about her day or something she'd read. Even her feelings toward the current president, formerly a reliable source of outrage, had shifted into mostly a laughing matter. She was on an email list that sent her a new Bush-ism in the mail every day. "Listen to this one, Augie," she'd say, adopting her version of a Texas drawl. *"Rarely is the question asked: Is our children learning.* You can't make this stuff up. Oh, God, here's another one. Can you believe it? Our dear leader actually said this recently, these words really came out of his mouth: *I know what I believe. I will continue to articulate what I believe and what I believe—I believe what I believe is right."*

She hummed in the mornings while making her coffee before heading to the library. She hung flowers in planters on the back porch and she sat there in the evenings, smoking and reading. The options for takeout were sparse, and so she was cooking again, listening to NPR in the kitchen while she did her best to re-create their favorites from the Grand Rapids days. "The produce lady just looked at me like I had three heads when I asked for lemongrass," she said once after returning from the town's only grocery store. "It's funny the things you miss when you move to the hinterlands." Still, her smile seemed impenetrable, and the few times he tried to puncture her mood to bring her down to his level, he found it impossible.

August took up riding his bike aimlessly, for hours. The roads out of town were lined with sunflowers just past their peak. He pedaled past legions of them, their heavy heads hanging from drying stalks, yellow but starting to fade to brown, petals gone here and there, giving them the look of gap-toothed mouths.

One afternoon he saw kids jumping from the railroad trestle bridge into the river—mostly boys around his age, in cut-off jean shorts, skinny and tan. There was one girl, though, in a yellow one-piece swimsuit. While August watched, she did a front flip and, just before hitting the water, heels first, back perfectly straight, she plugged her nose with her hand—a precise, almost delicate movement. She entered with barely a splash and then bobbed up a short way downstream, arms flashing as she stroked against the current to shore. When she climbed the rocks to get back up to the bridge, her suit bunched in the rear, the pale flesh her suit normally covered bright in the sun. When she gained the trestle platform she removed the offending wedgie with a heart-stopping reach-and-pull-and-wiggle that spread the suit back out. She was short, with blond hair in a wet braid down her back. One of the boys said something to her that August couldn't make out, and then she pushed him off the trestle, laughing, before jumping again herself.

August had ridden for miles in the late-summer sun. His shirt was stuck to his back with sweat, and he knew a different, better, version of himself would go and climb the trestle, introduce himself to the other guys, nod casually at the girl, strip off his shirt, and do a full gainer into a new life where he made friends easily. Instead, he kept riding.

There was a pinch where the mountains on either side of the valley came down close to the river. He'd already noticed that the wind always blew here, the air funneled down and constricted by the ridges. He ducked his head and pedaled hard, airborne grit peppering his cheeks, until he came through and the valley opened before him: Open expanses of pastureland, and hayfields still green from late-summer irrigation water pulled from the river. Not a dairy cow to be seen anywhere. It was all Red or Black Angus here, standing dumb, heads lowered to the grass, sometimes coming to the fence but bolting back walleyed when his bike came too close.

This sort of operation had a certain degree of dignity not found in the milking parlor. These cattle had never felt a stanchion around their necks, had never stood immobile and shitting while a machine sucked away at their teats. They lived a life, short though it may be, out in the elements, free to range, largely unharassed, until, of course, the mo-

ment arrived at which they were loaded up in trucks, bound for slaugh-
ter. A long monotonous life full of swollen udders and indignity, or a
shorter life of relative freedom, albeit one with a certain amount of
inevitable terror and confusion preceding death. It was something to
think about.

Cows weren't people, of course, but August knew that a guy like
Bob, he'd be jumping from that trestle right now instead of sitting out
here alone straddling his bike watching a field full of stupid cattle. He'd
have met the yellow-swimsuit girl. He'd have fought once or twice, and
then the rest of the guys would be his friends. The thing that made him
stab Brandt Gidley and got him sent away was the same thing that
garnered him respect and fear and friendship in quantities much
greater than August had ever enjoyed. August was trying to figure out
whether this quality, whatever it was exactly, was something a person
was born with, or something one developed. One thing he knew without a doubt was that a Holstein cow was born a Holstein cow and
would remain a Holstein cow forever.

He went to the trestle every day for the next week, but he never saw
her there again. Just the boys, yelling and egging one another on into
dives and cannonballs and gainers, frantic with energy, as if they could
already smell the decay on summer's breath and wanted to get in just
one more jump, as if summer couldn't die as long as somewhere, someplace, there was a kid flying out from a trestle, rotating heels overhead,
back arced to meet the river.

When they'd moved in, the house next to theirs had a FOR SALE sign on
the front lawn. Just a few days later the sign had SOLD taped over it, and
a large metal dumpster appeared on the street. Their new neighbor was
a single man, in his late twenties. He drove a newish Ford F-350 with a
toolbox in the bed. The truck was always gone early, before August was
up, and didn't return until sometime just before dark. At that point all
the lights would come on in the house, and because the man didn't
have any curtains or shades and the houses were close, it was easy
enough to see in. He was giving the place a complete remodel. All the

carpet had been ripped up and put in the dumpster, one of the walls in the living room was down to the bare studs, the electrical lines exposed, a light socket hanging, the bare bulb throwing harsh light so that August could see the long, spidery shadow of the man bent over his tools. He worked late into the night, often with the windows open so August could hear classic rock coming from his radio, the snarl of a saw or the whine of a drill.

One night the lights were on as usual, but the classic rock had been replaced with something different: piano, a voice singing in a foreign language, French maybe, no saws, no drills. August could hear a woman's laughter. The man's truck was gone, as usual, by the time August awoke. But as he was pouring himself a bowl of cereal, he saw a woman come out of the front door with a mug. She held it in both hands, the way a child might, and sat cross-legged on the small concrete stoop. She wore a man's flannel shirt, several sizes too big with the sleeves rolled up, and her legs were bare. August ate his cereal, standing at the kitchen sink, watching her. She was in the sun, leaning back against the side of the house with her eyes closed, steam rising from her mug, her hair piled on top of her head in a wild mass. She had a small gold hoop through her left nostril. She didn't move for a long time. Was she asleep? Meditating? There was something interesting about her face at rest, a slackness to her mouth and cheeks that you simply couldn't observe in a person unless they didn't know you were watching. He was so absorbed that, when she suddenly opened her eyes and turned her head to look in his direction, he nearly spilled his cereal milk in his haste to vacate the window.

One day August came home and the woman from next door was sitting in the living room with his mother, drinking tea. Her name was Julie, and she'd recently finished college on the East Coast. Her mother lived in town, so she'd come home for the summer while she tried to figure out her next step.

"Your mom looks just like my aunt Samantha," Julie said. "That's how we met. I ran into her at the grocery store, and I had to do a double take. And then to find out that we're neighbors! I invited myself over for tea to show her the photo." Julie picked up a photograph from the table and held it out. A woman was astride a horse, with a small fluffy dog riding in her lap behind the pommel. She was squinting into the sun.

August had to admit there were some similarities. The same cheeks, the hair at about the right length. He handed the photo back. "Pretty close," he said. "I see it."

He went to the kitchen to make himself a sandwich, but he could still hear the two of them talking. "Ethan thinks I'm crazy," Julie said. "He doesn't care one way or the other about what happened in these houses. He told me about how his grandpa used to catch whitefish out of the river and then ride his bike down here to sell them to the prostitutes for a nickel apiece. He thought they were eating the fish, but they were actually giving them to their cats. I guess they had cats roaming around everywhere. And I personally have seen this one particular cat, like, five times now, that Ethan hasn't seen once. It's a calico. It kind of mews at me and then bolts."

August could hear the click of his mother's lighter. The small noises she made when she was in agreement with something somebody said. "Right off the bat, my first night here, I had the wildest dreams. Women of all kinds, and they were touching me. I mean, these are not the types of dreams I usually have. Maybe a crew of burly fireman, or something like that, but not a bunch of writhing ladies. Burn some sweetgrass. That's my advice. I did that and there's been nothing out of the ordinary since."

"Okay," Julie said. "I'll try it. Can I bum one of those from you? I usually don't smoke, but this is fun. I don't really have any girlfriends around here anymore. And Ethan is, well, I love the guy, but a brilliant conversationalist he ain't." The lighter clicked, a soft cough from Julie. "Whew, I'm out of practice. So, enough talk about ghosts. I want to hear more about these firemen." Peals of laughter. August made haste for his bedroom.

· · ·

Julie started coming around almost every evening. She and his mother would drink wine and smoke on the back porch. The window to his room overlooked the backyard, and with it opened, he could hear most of what the two women said. He was bored, so he listened, and most of what they talked about only bored him further. They spent a lot of time on the current political situation. "I feel like somehow we've become the laughingstock of the world," Julie said. "The guy is so incompetent. It would be funny if it weren't so sad."

His mother and Julie also spent a lot of time discussing Ethan.

"He's very handsome," August's mother said. "So tall. What is he, six foot three, something like that?"

"At least. Maybe even a little taller," Julie said. "Maybe this makes me shallow, but I just could never get with a guy that was my height, or, God forbid, *shorter*. I mean, I'm five nine, and I'm no waif. Ethan makes me feel small, petite almost. It's nice to not feel like a damn giantess all the time."

"I'd hardly call you a giantess. You do have good posture, though, regal almost. I imagine many men are intimidated by that."

"Not Ethan. That's something I noticed right away and liked about him. He's got a natural intelligence, too. I think he could do whatever in the world he wanted to do. Never went to college, but he's much better at math than me. If we go out to eat he can figure out the tip in his head down to the last cent."

"And handy, too, from the looks of it."

"He's always working. He works for a builder up in Big Sky. Gets up at an ungodly hour, drives all the way up there, works all day, drives back, then works on his house. I don't know how he has the energy. When he gets the floors done, I'll have you come over to check it out. Get this, when he pulled the carpets up, in every room, there were these gouges in the wood. We realized each gouge was where the corner of a metal bed frame dug into the wood during—you know." She gave a small laugh. "What would you call that exactly—the point at which prostitution actually happens? Intercourse? Sex? Fucking? These don't seem like exactly what is going on."

"I think I'd call it a transaction," August's mother said.

"Okay, well, a lot of transactions happened in those rooms, apparently, and they all left their mark, and for some reason it affected me strongly. And then Ethan and I got into our very first fight about it."

"What happened? More wine?"

"Yes. Thank you, Bonnie. Basically, he was going to just fill the gouges with wood putty or something, and sand them down so you couldn't even tell that they'd been there. This really bothered me, and I told him that maybe some things you shouldn't just cover up and pretend they didn't happen, and he said, *If I'm going to all the trouble of refinishing the floors, why would I leave these huge divots?* And of course I understand his point of view, but still. Am I crazy? Would you leave them if it were your house?"

"No, you're not crazy. So what happened? Did he sand them out?"

"In the end I persuaded him not to. I guess it really wasn't much of a fight. We don't ever *actually* fight. I'm getting slightly worried about that, to tell you the truth. The things I want to fight about he just acquiesces to me on. It's not fair."

August started working for Ethan after helping him out one Saturday. He'd been mowing the front lawn, and although he hated mowing the lawn back in Michigan, this one wasn't too bad. It was so small he could take his time with it, make it immaculate, give it that baseball-diamond look. Anyway, it was something to do. He was just finishing up when Ethan came to his front porch and waved him over. Ethan was a large human. Coarse black stubble, baseball cap with a carpenter's pencil behind his ear. He wore a ratty old Kenyon Noble Lumber T-shirt, and his biceps strained against the sleeves.

"Hey, bud," he said. "You look strong. Want to make a quick twenty bucks?"

August disliked when people called him *bud* or *guy* or *pal*. It implied a familiarity that wasn't there. He did, however, want to make a quick twenty bucks. Ethan led him behind the house where he'd pulled his truck across the yard, right up to the back door. There was a large white enameled claw-foot bathtub in the bed, secured with ratchet straps.

"This thing is a beast," Ethan said. "I was going to try to just muscle it in with a dolly, but chances are I'd wreck my back or the kitchen floor coming through. You grab that end there and we'll slide it off. Okay, here we go."

The thing really was absurdly heavy. As August shuffle-walked, holding his end, he could feel his arms stretching out of their sockets. They stopped for a rest and a re-grip in the living room and August windmilled his arms, and then they grunted and heaved it to its final resting place in the bathroom. The tile work was all recent, with new stainless fixtures ready to be hooked up. Ethan stretched and shook his head, clapping his hands against his stained jeans, and then dug in his back pocket for his wallet. "The things we do for our ladies, eh? You ever take baths?"

August shook his head. "Nope."

"Me either. Julie loves a bath, though, and so, while she's away this weekend, I'm getting this all set up as a surprise. Anyway, here's your cash. Hey, what are you doing the next couple afternoons? Want to make a little more?"

"I've got nothing going on."

"All right then, come on back here with me. This room here is kind of useless as it is, but I'm going to open up this doorway to make an extension to the kitchen. I'm going to put a bar right here, some stools. You ever see this? It's what they used before Sheetrock. Lath strips with plaster coating. I need it all out of here so I can redo some electrical and put in insulation and then Sheetrock. It's going to be a bit messy. You up for it?"

"I don't really have anything else to do."

"Perfect. Probably the easiest way will be to just smash it up with that sledge. There's a big flat chisel, too. It's nailed in at the studs, so you'll have to pull those out with the hammer. You're a smart guy; I have no doubt you'll figure out the best system. Fill that wheelbarrow and empty it in the dumpster out front. Two hundred bucks? Probably take you two afternoons, but you get the two hundred even if you finish it early. How does that sound?"

"Sounds okay to me."

"All right then, start tomorrow. And, probably best if you didn't come over until sometime around noon. Julie is a late sleeper." He shook his head. "I mean, do what you want, but don't say you weren't warned."

The next afternoon, August let himself in the back door of Ethan's house and got to work. Ethan had left him a note on top of a dust mask. *Wear this or you'll get the black lung and it won't be my fault.*

August put the mask on, and with the first blow of the sledge against the wall was glad he had. The plaster, when pulverized, sent a fine mist of particles in a nasty cloud that immediately coated him in a layer of white. It was clear why Ethan had decided to delegate this particular task; it was going to be a dirty, tedious job. Still, he found demolition to be satisfying work, and he fell into a rhythm. It was gratifying to swing a sledgehammer as hard as he could against a smooth expanse of wall. After a few blows came the more time-consuming business of using the hammer and chisel to break off the lath, then the pry bar to remove protruding nails. When he was standing ankle deep in rubble, he'd scoop the mess into the wheelbarrow and take it out to the dumpster.

After he'd been at it a while, there was a knock on the door separating the back room from the kitchen and Julie stuck her head in, waving her hand in front of her face and wrinkling her nose.

"Jesus Christ," she said. "That is toxic. How are you doing? Can I get you some water or anything?"

Despite the mask August felt like his mouth was coated in a layer of chalk. "Water would be good," he croaked. When she came back with the glass, he stood, gulping, at the edge of the kitchen so as not to track dust in, the mask down around his neck on the elastic band. He wiped his mouth with the back of his hand. Cleared his throat. "Thanks," he said. "I was thirsty."

Julie was looking at him, a smile twitching on her lips. "I wish you could see yourself," she said. "You're, like, Albino Man." She reached over and rubbed his eyebrow, holding her thumb up so he could see how white it was. She was wearing a thin white T-shirt and leggings. No bra. Her hair loose and tangled. She was standing close enough that August could smell sleep on her still.

"I'm going to make some coffee. You want any?"

"I'm okay. I'm just going to get back at it. Thanks for the water."

"Of course. When you want more just come on in and help yourself. Don't be shy. Hey, how old are you?"

"Fifteen."

"Really? That's it? I would have thought older. How tall are you?"

"Over six feet, I guess."

She made a show of looking him up and down. "I'd guess so, too. Are you looking forward to starting school soon? No? Of course not. Stupid question. High school sucks. Okay, I'll stop bothering you. I'm going to make this coffee and then haul my ass to yoga. Tell your mom I'm going to come over tonight, and I'm going to bring a nice salad and some wine and we're going to sit out there and solve many of the world's problems."

"Okay. I'll tell her."

"I just love your mom, by the way. Horrible influence on me, though, with those little cigars. Okay. I'm going to leave you alone now, for real."

August finished the job the next afternoon. He took the last load of broken plaster out to the dumpster and gave the floor a good sweep. He removed his gloves and beat the dust from his jeans with them. As he was putting his tools away, Julie came in and gave a low whistle. "Nice work," she said. "Ethan is going to be happy. He wanted me to give this to you." She handed him an envelope of cash, which he folded and stuck in his pocket. "Thanks," he said.

"You're welcome." She was looking at him unblinking, so that he had to stare down at his boots. "You're kind of quiet, aren't you?"

He shrugged. He hoped the plaster dust on his face was at least doing something to cover the particular shade of red it was turning.

"You remind me of Ethan. You could be his little brother or something. All business. No time for idle chitchat." She was leaning against the doorjamb. One of her legs was crooked up so her foot was propped against her inner thigh, flamingo style, some kind of yoga move, maybe. "Was it tough, your parents getting divorced? Your mom said it was mostly amicable, but I know how those things go; there's no way it didn't get a little sticky at least for a while."

August had his hand still stuffed in his jeans pocket, wrapped around the envelope of cash. "It was okay," he said. "Probably for the best."

"I'm sure you miss your dad, though, right? Your mom said you're going to go back for Thanksgiving?"

August nodded.

"Well, that's good. I know when my parents got divorced it was hard at first but then some positive things actually happened. Before, it had always been the two of them, together, kind of like a unit. And then when they split, I suddenly had two separate individuals, like, now they were able to act differently toward me and didn't have to moderate their behavior to take into account what their partner thought. Anyway, I hope it's going okay for you."

"I'm fifteen," August said. "I'm not a kid. I'll be fine."

"Sure. I know. Hey, what are you doing right now? You hungry? I was going to make some lunch."

"I could eat."

"Of course you could. Your mom tells me you go through a gallon of milk every other day."

"I eat a lot of cereal."

August followed Julie into the kitchen, and she started getting out sandwich fixings. "Wash your hands, you filthy boy," she said. "Ham and Swiss okay?"

August nodded, and went to the sink and washed his hands studiously, probably for longer and more thoroughly than he'd ever done before. When the sandwiches were ready, they ate standing across from each other at the kitchen island. They chewed in silence for a while. "Are you looking for a job?" August said.

Julie put her sandwich down and crunched a chip. "Yes, *Daddd*," she said. "I'm looking for a *jobb*. But the problem is that my skill set, such as it is, is not exactly in high demand around here."

"What's your skill set?"

"Well, my degree is in political science and Spanish. I double majored."

"Oh."

"Yeah. *Oh*. Exactly. So I'm applying for some stuff. Nothing is anywhere near here, though. So that's a whole different sort of problem. My mom says I'm getting too comfortable playing house with Ethan. Maybe she's right, although I'd never give her the satisfaction of hearing me say it. That's why I appreciate your mother so much. She actually gives me advice, not just bitchy judgment."

"She's never afraid to give advice. That's for sure."

"Well, hopefully you're not afraid to take it."

August shrugged. Chewed his sandwich. Tried to hold Julie's gaze but failed. He didn't know much about these sorts of things, but something told him that Ethan was in for a world of hurt.

When August started school, his days took on a more definable shape. Park High was much smaller than the one he'd attended in Grand Rapids, and he immediately realized that it was going to be harder to hide. Mr. Zwicky, the football coach, noticed him in the halls and was on him incessantly to try out for the team. That first practice he didn't even have cleats. He slipped and slid all over the grass in his tennis shoes and felt like an idiot. He'd made up his mind to not come back the next day, but Mr. Zwicky called him into his office in the locker room and told him he liked what he'd seen. "I see potential in you, August," he said. "Can I count on you coming back?" He wore sweatpants and a T-shirt that read PAIN IS MERELY WEAKNESS LEAVING THE BODY.

"I don't know. I guess."

"Good man," he said and then hopped up to dig around in the equipment room for a pair of old cleats.

August showed up for the next practice, and the one after that, and then, somehow, it seemed that he was on the football team. He hadn't played Pop Warner like most of the guys, but he learned quickly, and his size alone got him a starting position on the JV squad. He didn't possess great speed, but he had good hands and long arms and a quick first step. He played both sides of the ball. On offense he was a tight end, and he caught some passes and did a lot of blocking in their run-heavy scheme. Defense was his specialty, though. He liked hitting. As strong side end, as soon as the ball was snapped, he'd use his quick first step to get under the opposing lineman's arms, jam a forearm in his throat under his face mask, and get him stood up and moving back. With the offensive lineman backpedaling, August's attention would then shift toward the quarterback. His favorite moments were when there was a missed assignment and he could come in on the back side and lay into a quarterback with a full head of steam. It was a beautiful thing to put the tip of his shoulder pad square into the back of a quarterback who was scanning downfield for a receiver. To feel the hard woof of breath upon impact, to have the speed and control and strength to keep his legs driving, to feel the other guy's feet leave the ground in that moment before August put him to the turf with every ounce of clean malice in his body. To roll off and stand over a crumpled form and revel in the hurt—that was part of it, too.

August hated practice, though. He hated the locker room and the smell of it. On some level he hated most of his teammates. He hated his coaches. He hated the thought of the games, the slow build of nerves over the week until Friday nights when, on more than one occasion, he found himself in the bathroom before taking the field, dry heaving over the toilet. He hated the fans yelling stupid shit during the on-field warm-ups before the games started. He hated the cheerleaders and the mascot and standing with his hand over his heart for the national anthem. He hated the smell of the whole place, the cut grass, the hot dogs and popcorn from the concession stand, the deeper scent of fall, the early darkness, the leaden pall of incipient snow.

He hated every single thing about football until the long whistle and the thump of the opening kickoff, and then it was pure love. He loved his teammates, their insane yelling and headbutts of congratulation. He loved his coaches, kneeling in the middle of the huddle on a time-out, adult men talking to them as if this moment—down by three but within striking distance and no time-outs left—was the most important thing in the world. He loved the cheerleaders, barelegged in the cold, laughing and doing shitty girl push-ups at every touchdown. He loved the smell, the torn-up sod on the field, and the way the lights made everything outside the realm of the one-hundred-yard field seem irrelevant. He even loved the fans, Ed Gaskill's dad in overalls and stocking cap, booze in his coffee mug, standing against the chain-link fence screaming before the snap, *Crush him, August. Crush him. Come on. Crush him.*

His mother had been uncertain at first. "You do realize that I stopped smoking and drinking completely the whole time I was pregnant with you?" she said.

"And?" he said.

"And, now it pains me to know that you're signing up to voluntarily bludgeon the very brain I've spent years trying to protect."

"There are helmets involved."

"I know. It's just—your father never played football. I understand your desire to fit in at a new school, but do you even enjoy the sport? This seems out of the blue."

After watching his first game, a cold drizzler against Ennis in which he'd recorded three sacks and recovered a fumble for a touchdown, she seemed to have a change of heart. She bought a pair of insulated overalls. Stood silently in the stands with her hands jammed in her pockets. Never clapping. Never cheering. Jaw set. Not sitting down for one single play as long as he was on the field. She said that, on second thought, maybe football was necessary for his development. "You're not my son when you're on that field," she said. "But I realize that that violent guy, wherever he came from, is part of you, too. I just hope he stays right there, wearing the tight pants and the helmet, only smashing into other guys dressed like him who are also taking a hiatus from being their mothers' sons."

"It's just a game, Mom," August said. "Don't make it weird."

The day it happened he'd been in first period at school, study hall, and they had the radio on. It was KPIG out of Billings, and Neil Young was doing the "Rockin' in the Free World"—he'd always remember that. Neil was screaming about a *kinder, gentler, machine gun hand,* when the song just stopped. The DJ came in, his voice halting and unsteady, talking about the reports coming out of New York City. Planes had been flown into the World Trade Center. The Twin Towers had come down. More reports from the Pentagon. Many feared dead. The situation was ongoing.

Everyone should go be with those they love right now. Pray for America.

Of course, normal activities were out of the question for the day. The teachers turned the TVs on to the news and everyone just watched. Some of the girls and female teachers cried, a few of the male teachers as well. None of the boys. Mr. Rogers, the social studies teacher, sat at his desk and shook his head. "We need to turn that whole damn desert to glass," he said. "The gloves are coming off now."

After school, Coach Zwicky called them all into the locker room and sat them down. He looked at them for a long time before saying anything, running his hand several times over his thinning flattop. "None of us will be able to focus on football today. No practice. But I'd like you all to do something together. If you want to go home to be with your family I understand, but maybe you all can get together at someone's house, watch the news as a team. I'll leave that up to you."

He paused again. Cleared his throat. "Things are going to be happening," he said. "I have no doubt some of you will be going. Joining up. I wouldn't even be surprised if they bring the draft back. I'm not trying to scare anyone but you're young men now, and this is a situation that is going to affect your generation. Maybe *the* situation. My friends and I had Vietnam, and this is what you guys are going to get, for better or worse. Now, I realize that for a while your mind is going to be on the events of the day. No way around it. But I want you to get a good night's sleep. Get up tomorrow ready to work. We've got Belgrade on Friday, and I don't need to remind you about the ass-kicking they gave us last year."

They went to Gaskill's house and made nachos. They all sat on the floor and watched the footage—the endless looping sequences of the planes crashing into the towers, the billowing smoke, the panic-stricken people fleeing on the sidewalks. When George W. Bush got on TV, there was a hush. *These acts of mass murder were intended to frighten our nation into chaos and retreat. But they have failed. Our country is strong. A great people has been moved to defend a great nation. Terrorist attacks can shake the foundations of our biggest buildings, but they cannot touch the foundation of America. These acts shatter steel, but they cannot dent the steel of American resolve.* Everyone clapped. August included.

"Rogers is right. We're going to nuke those towelheads," Gaskill said.

"One good thing about living in the middle of nowhere," August said. "Not a single thing here worth crashing a plane into."

"Doesn't matter," Ramsay said. "They might as well have crashed the planes into everyone's living rooms. Nothing is going to be the same after this. You watch."

At the time, August thought this was a bit dramatic. Later he wondered if anyone else remembered Ramsay saying this—tried to determine if he was the only one who'd heard it, or if someone else had said it, or if he'd made it up completely.

After a while he went home and continued to watch the news with his mother. When Bush was on the screen her jaw tightened. "He's going to get free rein now," she said. "The little idiot. Probably the best thing that could have happened to him."

That Friday, when they played Belgrade, the field was decorated with American flags. Over one hundred of them on stakes pounded into the ground on the sidelines. Both teams had American-flag stickers on their helmets. When "The Star-Spangled Banner" was played, the teams stood together in the middle of the field, players intermixed, arms linked. Belgrade won by three touchdowns, and most of their starters were sitting by halftime. It appeared that some things would remain the same after all.

One morning August woke to find the mountains covered in snow, a low line of intermittent clouds clinging to the peaks above town. The cottonwoods along the river were shedding their leaves, and the black bears were moving close to town to feed, becoming bold in their all-consuming search for calories to get them through winter. He told his father about this when he called.

"I went outside the other morning," he said, "and it was garbage day, so everyone on the street has their bin out on the curb, and I looked down the block and every bin had been tipped over. It was a bear for sure. We had one up in a tree behind school the other day."

"No shit? Right in the middle of the day? In town?"

"Yep. Just after lunch. It had climbed this crab apple tree right next to a house, and it was eating the fruit that had fallen into the gutters."

"Well, I'll be damned. Has it been getting cold out there yet?"

"Snow in the mountains just the other day. None of it is sticking in town. It's been really windy. How's it been there?"

"Not too bad. We've had some cold rain. Leaves are turning. Nice time of year here—well, you know how it is. School going okay?"

"School is going fine."

"How's your mother?"

"I think she's doing okay."

"Looking forward to seeing you for Thanksgiving. Lisa is going to be with her folks, so most of the time it will just be you and me. We can get up early and sit in the blind, see if anything comes along. I've been spotting a nice one occasionally, running the back fence in the morning. An eight-point at least, real heavy, kind of a wide spread, would be real good next year, but if I don't shoot it you know damn well the

Amish will, so there's no sense waiting. I went and bought a big old stainless-steel pot and a propane burner. I'm going to get a bunch of peanut oil and we're going to deep-fry a turkey. And then watch the Lions get their ass beat by whoever they're playing. How's that sound?"

"You're going to deep-fry a turkey? Seriously?"

"Sure. I did it once. Might have been before you were born or too young to remember it. Turned out real good. You have to do it outside, though. Maybe we'll do it in the garage. Or we could just do it in the yard and make a fire and throw a ball around a little, if it's not too cold. Okay, I guess those cows aren't going to milk themselves. About time to head to the barn. I'll be talking to you."

His mother and Julie continued their evening talks on the back porch, often wrapped in blankets now because the nights were cold. He kept his window closed and didn't listen as much anymore, but on one particular night Julie came over with two bottles of champagne. He was in the kitchen cleaning up the dinner dishes when she swooped in. She was flushed, laughing, and she gave him a wet kiss on the cheek as she went by. He made a show of grimacing and wiping it away, but when she'd waltzed out to the porch he was still rubbing his fingers together, her saliva there slick and warm.

He finished putting the dishes away and went upstairs to do some anatomy and physiology homework. By the end of the term he needed to have all the bones in the human body memorized. At his desk he opened the window, the cold air coming in sharp; he flipped idly through his flash cards, paying more attention to what Julie was saying.

"I can hardly believe it," she said. "Africa! I'm going to be in Gaborone, the capital of Botswana, and then probably a smaller village at some point. Two years! Maybe it's naïve of me, but I could really make a small bit of difference in some people's lives. Botswana is just devastated by AIDS. And the Peace Corps looks good on a résumé, no matter what I end up doing after that. I'm so excited, and nervous. So nervous."

"Cheers to you," August's mother said. "I'm so proud of you. I'd considered the Peace Corps myself a long, long time ago. I know what a demanding process it is. They don't just accept anyone that applies. And of course you're nervous. I'm a bit nervous for you. *Botswana.* It really doesn't get more foreign. But so beautiful, too. You're going to come back a different person. It makes an old woman jealous, looking at you, about to just shoot out into the world and discover yourself. I'm being sentimental." August heard a rustling sound as the women scooted their chairs together and hugged.

August wondered if the Peace Corps idea was something Julie had dreamed up while soaking in the claw-foot tub, and what sort of regrets Ethan might be feeling. Ethan's house only had that one bathroom, and when Julie was gone, Ethan would no doubt be reminded of her every morning, stepping up over the high side, soaping up, watching the water swirl down the drain. That damn thing must have weighed five hundred pounds.

Julie didn't leave for her assignment for almost six months, but, as far as August could tell, she and Ethan lasted only a few weeks after she'd received the news. For a while she was on the back porch frequently. Tears and wine, endless looping conversations. Eventually she moved back in with her mother, and her visits became less frequent, but before she left, she came over for dinner, and August eavesdropped for a while afterward. "We never had much to talk about," she said. "Do you know that one John Prine song—'Angel from Montgomery'? *How the hell can a person go to work in the morning and come home in the evening and have nothing to say?* That's Ethan. My heart is ripping out. I wish I was just gone. This in-between time is killing me."

"You need someone emotionally and intellectually compatible with you. Trust me, I learned the hard way. The man that makes your womb glow is not necessarily the one you should end up with in the long run. Our biological impulses sometimes lead us off the cliff. Two years of delirious passion followed by thirteen years of annoyance and frustrations that eventually blossomed into full-blown disgust—that's what I had with Augie's father. Flee to Africa and fulfill your potential and find some wild-eyed Peace Corps poet that makes both your womb *and* your mind glow, and then write me lots of letters telling me all about it. Deal?"

Julie sniffed loudly. She gave a weak laugh. "Deal," she said.

August flipped his flash cards without reading them. He wasn't entirely sure how one went about making a woman's womb glow. Anyway, the fact that this ability alone would not be enough to satisfy a woman such as Julie—or his mother, for that matter—was rather terrifying.

For two weekends August helped Ethan strip old wooden siding from the exterior of his house. His plan, once the old siding was removed, was to put up Tyvek and then new vinyl siding. "The house will be much more energy efficient after that," Ethan said. "This place is so old and drafty. Right now, I'm pretty much paying money to heat the outside. I'm going to get this exterior wrapped up while it's not too cold and then spend the rest of the winter finishing the inside, and then I'm going to flip it. Possibly buy another one and do the same thing. Now that she's gone I'll have more time to work. I'll get things done faster."

August nodded. "Having to wait till noon to get to work every day probably really slowed you down," he said.

Ethan laughed and shook his head. "Actually, now that she's gone I find myself spinning out more easily. Kind of like, what's the point? You know? I'm doing all this work, trying to make all this money, and for what? Money or working hard doesn't get you a woman like her."

"What gets you a woman like her?"

"Very good question. Luck, maybe. And now I feel like mine's run out. Before her I dated a bank teller, a nurse, a dental hygienist, and a single mom whose ex-husband was wealthy enough that she didn't need to get a job. None of these women made me feel lucky or unlucky. After her I can hardly remember what their faces looked like."

They were working on the back wall, a tarp spread along the foundation to catch the pulled nails and strips of splintered hardwood siding. "Damn, but she could be difficult," Ethan said. "She cried a lot. None of those other girls I dated cried, unless we were drunk and got in a fight about something and then in the morning it was usually all forgotten. Most of those girls I felt comfortable with. I never felt comfortable with Julie. Maybe I should have recognized that was a problem. I introduced her to my dad once. He told me that she reminded him of a female English setter he had one time. A real expensive bird dog, fancy lineage and all of that. Beautiful dog. Great hunter, too. Except that one day the dog started licking her front leg. And didn't stop. Couldn't stop. She licked through her fur, her skin. There was a big wound, and the dog just kept licking. He'd bandage it and she'd chew the bandage off. In the field he'd lose her. She wouldn't come to his whistle, and when he finally tracked her down she'd just be on the ground licking like crazy, whining because it hurt, but she was unable to quit for some reason. She licked her leg all the way down to the bone." Ethan stopped, shook his head, and took a big sniff of air. Someone was burning leaves, a gray day in November, a low ceiling of clouds. "Well, it is what it is," he said. "I'm going to stop bitching and moaning. Let's get back at it, or else I'll be out here trying to put the new siding on in a goddamn blizzard."

August worked his pry bar under a piece of siding and hammered on the other end to get it to pop, nails coming loose with a satisfying shriek. "What did your dad end up doing with that dog?" he said.

Ethan was scooping up fallen siding, tossing it into the wheelbarrow for a trip to the dumpster. "He took her out to the woods behind the house and shot her. Buried her deep and put a pile of rocks on her grave. Always said that she was the very best dog he'd ever owned, until she wasn't. And then she was the very worst. My dad can be a real bastard."

August was called up to varsity for the final game of the season. It was in Bozeman, and it snowed so hard they had to shovel the lines on the field at the end of each quarter. August saw limited action and they lost the game, although toward the end, when it was obviously hopeless, the coach sent him and a few of the other young guys in to give them a taste of what it was like at the next level. August nearly got to the quarterback once and then did get there another time, but a split second too late, driving the Bozeman backup quarterback to the ground just as he completed handing off the ball. That was it, and soon they were on the bus for the slow drive over the whiteout pass to home. For the seniors it was the last game of the season and the final of their life. A few of them wiped at tears as they slumped on the bus. The end of the game. It meant something that the thought of impending graduation didn't.

August flew back to Michigan for Thanksgiving. It was his first time on an airplane, and even though he tried to be nonchalant about it, he held his breath during takeoff and let it out loud enough after they were finally airborne that his seatmate looked at him sidelong. His father met him at the airport in Grand Rapids. He shook August's hand and threw his bag in the back of his truck, and they started the drive north.

Everything seemed drab; August noticed that right away. The bare trees, the sky a cement sort of gray. Drab and flat. "No snow yet," he said.

His father shook his head. "Nah. Some in the forecast for next week, maybe. Lots of rain, though. Looks like you've grown three damn inches since I've seen you last, kid."

August shrugged. "I don't know about that. I think I'm still about the same height."

"Could have fooled me."

August watched his father out of the corner of his eye as he drove. He tried to assess whether he seemed different in any way, older, skinnier, fatter, happier—but it was impossible to tell. Anyway, he'd been gone for only a few months. There was no reason for anyone to have changed that much at all.

"Saw that buck again yesterday morning. I'm surprised the Amish haven't gotten him yet. You know how they are—if it's brown it's down."

"When's the last time we went hunting?"

"Oh man, it's been a while hasn't it? I was never too caught up in it. I mostly like sitting out there and seeing what there is to see. I guess you're the same way."

August nodded.

"The great thing about hunting is getting up early and then watching it get light from the blind. Waiting for something to show up, drinking coffee, being quiet, all of that. What I don't like about hunting is what comes after you actually shoot something. Field dressing it, dragging it out, hanging it up, processing it—that starts to look a lot like working on your day off, if you ask me. And these people that are really into hunting, I don't get it. If you were hungry, then that's a different deal. But all these fat Texans decked out with fancy gear on these hunting shows? I just want to say, *Look at yourself, man, killing something from half a mile away with a high-powered rifle doesn't make you an alpha predator.* Your mother's father was that way. Quite the sportsman."

"I remember we went, maybe four years ago, for opening day. We never saw a single deer. I think that was the last time we did it."

"You might be right about that. That definitely seems right."

Since August had been gone, his father had put a small TV on the kitchen table. It was on now, low volume, a local channel doing the weather. August knew that his father had always liked to drink his coffee and eat his eggs watching the news. His mother said that a TV in the kitchen or dining room was barbaric, and so for as long as August could remember, his father had eaten breakfast on the couch in the living room, hunched awkwardly over the coffee table, trying not to spill coffee or drop eggs on the carpet. Now he had the little TV right there and he no doubt ate comfortably in the mornings, the coffee-pot within easy reach, happily watching the weather girl move across her green screen. To August it pointed to a reality he hadn't much considered—no doubt there were elements of this new childless, wifeless life that his father preferred.

There was something else. Something about the interior of the house seemed different. He couldn't place it for the first day he was there. It wasn't anything tangible. Other than the new TV, the furniture was mostly the same, his father's barn clothes still hung on the hooks in the mudroom, the dining room was still painted pale yellow, the living room walls were still rough-textured plaster. It was the next morning, still dark, half-asleep in the kitchen, his father pouring coffee for them both, that he realized what it was. The smell. Even after she'd moved to the new house there had always been a certain odor, his mother's sweet cigarillos gone slightly stale, the linen bags of lavender she scattered around to cover it up. Now his mother's smoke was gone. The house just smelled of freshly wiped-clean surfaces or whatever was being cooked. Right now it was his father's standard—over-easy eggs, a stack of heavily buttered white toast, bacon popping in the cast iron. His father was already dressed for hunting, long underwear under his camouflage overalls. He normally shaved before heading to the barn for chores, but this morning his face was rough with stubble, more gray than black, August realized.

August had his head propped on his hand at the table. The coffee was hot and he couldn't drink it as fast as he'd like; his father, though, slurped it down like it was lukewarm.

"I see you're on the hard stuff now," his father said.

"Huh?" August had started to doze sitting up, and his father's words jolted him back.

"I said, you're taking it black these days," his father pointed his bacon fork at August's coffee. He shook his head. "Go away for a little while and he comes back six inches taller and drinking coffee like a man."

August shook his head and sat up a little straighter. "I'm not six inches taller." He took a sip and tried not to make a face as it scalded his mouth. "It smells different in here," he said. "Better, actually."

His father loaded a piece of toast with eggs and crunched it down. "Is your mom still chain-smoking those nasty things?"

"Not as many, maybe. Still doing it, though. She mostly goes out to the back porch to smoke these days."

"Well, that's good. Lisa and I both just kind of got sick of the smell and so we took a whole day, rented a steam cleaner for the carpet, took down all the curtains, bleached the walls, everything. Made a big difference. You get enough food? Okay then, let me fill up a thermos and we'll head out."

"Chores?"

"Lisa is coming over this morning to get them done. Day off for me. She said she'd make us some brunch, too, when we're back from the woods, before she heads to her folks' house."

"Brunch?"

"I know. I'm not exactly sure what that entails, either. I'll probably just be ready for a ham sandwich by that point, but whatever. We humor them, August. That's something you realize as you get older. A woman can use brunch like a wrecking ball."

They were on the porch, slipping on their boots in the dark, their breath coming out in blooming white clouds. "I know a guy whose girlfriend really liked taking baths but his house only had a shower, so while she was gone one weekend he put in a big old claw-foot tub. I helped him carry it in. It was really nice and then maybe only a couple months after this, his girlfriend got accepted into the Peace Corps, broke up with him, and left for Africa. I mean, he didn't care about baths. He just takes showers like a normal person."

August's father laughed softly and rubbed his face with one hand, his palm making a coarse sandpapery sound against the stubble. "I bet that was a learning experience for the guy, for sure. Of course, you can't go through life without making any gestures at all—that's no way to live—but you need to be real careful who you reveal yourself to. You make a gesture, open yourself up like that to a woman, and then she knows right away that she's got you, hook, line, and sinker. How'd you meet this guy? Mr. Claw-Foot Tub?"

"He's our neighbor. His girlfriend—ex-girlfriend, I guess—is real good friends with Mom. They sit outside and smoke and drink wine all the time."

"Well, that makes sense. Poor fucker."

They walked out through the back pasture, the dead grass silvered with frost. Then through the row of white pines, grown tight together so they had to push branches away from their faces, fingers sticky with pitch, up a small rise into the hardwood stand, impossible to walk quietly now, dead leaves crunching underfoot.

The blind was on top of the hill, a shallow dugout area around which August's father had arranged logs and cut branches for concealment. They sat with their backs against sugar maples and watched the woods around them awaken with dawn. August's father had only one gun. It was old, a Japanese 7.7 mm Arisaka with open sights, and a chrysanthemum stamped on the receiver. August's grandfather, a marine, had brought it back with him from the South Pacific. He had died when August was young, and August had no memories of him. As the day gained strength around them, August watched his father's eyes droop, then close completely. He had the gun cradled in his lap and gave a small, halting snore. August's father had never been a marine. For most of Vietnam, he was just slightly too young, and then when he turned eighteen his number had never been called. August looked at him now and was simultaneously glad and disappointed to not be the son of a soldier.

August was starting to doze off himself when the rustle of leaves brought him back. He moved his head slowly, trying to see where the noise was coming from. He thought it might be a squirrel running back to its acorn stash under an oak, but then his eyes registered a larger brown shape moving just within his periphery. He shifted slowly to get a better look and he saw it, a buck, no doubt the one his father had mentioned. It was a big-bodied animal, neck thick and swollen with the rut. A good set of antlers, heavy and brown at the base, gleaming ivory at the tips, polished from rubbing on trees and sparring with other males. August reached his leg out and prodded his father with his boot. His father's eyes opened quickly and August nodded to his left. The deer was sixty yards away, moving steadily, its head down, probably following the scent of doe in estrus. They watched the deer coming, disappearing and reappearing between the trunks of beech and oak and maple. His father was whispering something that August couldn't make out, so he leaned closer. It sounded a lot like "I forgot to load the gun."

"What?"

"The box of cartridges on the table at home. No bullets. Gun empty." He shrugged.

August was stiff from sitting on the cold ground. He reached for the gun and then stood, lining up the iron sights, the buck slowing as it sensed something was not right. "Bang," August said. And then the buck bounded away, the white flag of its tail receding through the brush. His father laughed and reached out his hand, and August helped him to his feet. He stretched and shook his legs out. "My fault," he said. "Rookie move."

"Nah, it's fine. Easier this way. Probably I'd have missed anyway."

"I guess now we'll never know. Hell of a nice deer, though. What do you say? Brunch?"

When they got back they kicked off their boots and hung up their jackets in the entryway. Lisa was in the kitchen, her blond hair pulled back into a tight ponytail. She wore a Detroit Lions sweatshirt and men's Carhartt pants. She gave August a hug. She smelled like flour and cinnamon, and also of the barn.

"It's great to see you, August. Do you like eggs Benedict?" she said.

August settled into a chair. The TV was on, NFL pregame. In several hours the Lions would start the inevitable process of losing to the Bears. It was Thanksgiving. "Sure," he said. "I like eggs Benedict just fine."

After eating, August did the dishes, and Lisa and his father went to the living room. He could hear them talking but couldn't make out the words, just the cadence, a measured give-and-take. Lisa would say something and then his father would respond, followed by periods of quiet in which neither said anything. He had no way of knowing what they were saying, but it sounded like the conversation of two people in perfect agreement. Or, just as likely, two people engaged in a tired disagreement. Before leaving for her parents' house, Lisa gave August another hug. "You used to be just about my height," she said. "Now here I am, craning my head looking up at you. Don't let your dad eat all those cinnamon rolls. I made those for you."

After Lisa left, August took the garbage out to the bin and kept walking down to the barn. He tried to put himself in his father's shoes; he tried to imagine seeing Lisa, and then his mother, through his father's eyes. He could get a fair picture of Lisa this way, how his father might see her strong, chapped hands, her Carhartts stretched over her thick thighs, an early riser, red-faced and pleasant. His mother, though, she shifted, a husky voice and a wry smile, a specter, mostly obscured by a cloud of smoke. He hadn't put a coat on and his arms goose-fleshed in the cold. In the barn it was warmer but empty and quiet, the cows all out to pasture. He wandered past the rows of stanchions, letting a hand trail along them, the inner wooden yokes varnished smooth by the rub and push of countless bovine necks dumbly enduring the suck of the milker, reaching out for feed.

Out of habit, on his way toward the haymow ladder, he flicked the radio on. It was the same old fly-specked Sony with the antenna extension his father had fashioned from a coat hanger. After an ad for Marvel Quality Used Cars, Paul Harvey's voice came on.

On Thanksgiving Day it seems especially important to honor the good folks that help this great land produce her bounty. Here's a tribute to all the farmers out there.

August climbed the ladder and stuck his head up into the haymow. Shafts of light found their way through the knotholes and gaps between the barn boards. Dust and chaff swirled in these bands of light, and he sat with his feet dangling down. There was a soft rustling in the loose hay at August's back and then a gray cat stepped into view. It was large, a tom from the looks of it, one of his ears torn from fighting.

August clucked his tongue and the cat came sidling up, arching its back, rubbing against August's boot.

Paul Harvey was reading his "So God Made a Farmer" speech. August had heard it years before, and he could remember feeling something then—a "Star-Spangled-Banner"-before-kickoff sort of upwelling. *A farmer,* Paul Harvey was saying, *is someone strong enough to clear trees. Who will stop his mower for an hour to splint the broken leg of a meadowlark.*

August snorted. "A meadowlark's broken leg, my ass," he said. The cat tensed at August's voice, crouching slightly. When August reached out his hand, the cat sprang away, hay skittering out from under his scrambling paws. August climbed back down to the milking floor and, before he switched off the radio, stood, arms crossed over his chest, listening to Harvey finish.

August tried to imagine what his mother would say about this homey little soliloquy. He tried to envision his mother and Paul Harvey engaging in a discussion. His mother's eyes narrowing to slits, a soft cough and an exhale of smoke before she eviscerated him. He could picture Paul Harvey's rheumy old-man eyes clouding over in confusion and then outright fear. It wouldn't be fair.

On his way out, August flicked off the light and closed the big swinging double doors behind him. He walked back up to the house. In the mudroom, while removing his boots, he reached in the pocket of his father's neon orange hunting vest. There were a half dozen long-nosed brass cartridges there, cool and heavy in his hand. They'd been there the whole time. August had thought he'd heard them, clinking softly as his father walked.

He'd left Montana when it was late fall and when he returned, less than a week later, it appeared that full-on winter had set in. There'd been a storm. The town was coated in a thick layer of white, with gray chimney smoke hanging in a low inversion cloud. August went back to school, just about fell into a rhythm, and then it was Christmas break and his days were empty again. His mother got him a pair of cross-country skis, and as the snow continued to pile up he started taking them on silent tours through town. He'd set out in the evening, already dark at five P.M., the streetlights glowing orange, snow blowing through like TV static. He liked making fresh tracks right down the middle of the road like he owned the place, like he was the sole occupant of a universe where cars no longer had the right-of-way.

———

Ethan had managed to get only half of his house sided before the storms hit. The lights were rarely on, and August almost never saw Ethan himself. Sometime in late February a FOR SALE sign appeared in the dirty snow pile in Ethan's front yard. The wind had started up by then, picking away at the unfinished siding, loosening the strips so they bent and sagged and eventually broke away, toppling the FOR SALE sign, which was never righted.

On one occasion the highway patrol closed the highway and routed traffic through town after a semi tipped over and smashed a car. August had no idea a place as windy as this could exist or, maybe more accurately, that people could exist in a place as windy as this.

Eventually spring did set in, an extended mud season when people tromped around in muck boots and turned their faces gratefully to the sun when it showed. School let out in late May, and not long afterward August flew back to spend the summer with his father on the farm.

The first morning, August came downstairs to the smell of coffee, the sound of bacon popping, and his father, hands flour-white to the wrist, kneading biscuit dough. The TV was on with the sound off, and the weather lady was moving across the screen, gesturing in a muted meteorological dance. After eating egg, cheese, and bacon sandwiches, August thought they'd head to the barn for chores and was surprised when his father made another full pot of coffee and settled back down in his chair. "How's it feel to be home?" his father said.

August wiped crumbs from the tablecloth into his cupped hand and emptied them onto his plate. He shrugged. "Good. I never knew you could make biscuits like that."

His father laughed. "Did I ever tell you about my first job? No? I was about your age, maybe a little younger. My uncle had that logging camp up by Kalkaska, and I was too small to really go out in the woods and work, but I helped the cook. Wayne was his name. Only guy I've ever seen that had hairs growing on his nose. Not out of his nostrils. I mean right here, on the bridge of his nose. He was that hairy. A Sicilian guy, I think. A vodka-and-orange-juice-for-breakfast kind of guy. But he made the best biscuits I've ever had, and he showed me the trick."

"What's the trick?"

"Cold butter. Chunk it up small and don't overmix. Butter has to be real cold. That's how you get that nice flaky texture. Ol' Wayne. Haven't thought about him in a long time. My uncle had to close the camp. I wanted to log more than anything when I was your age, but it all just kind of ran out of steam before my time. Speaking of jobs, I've got a proposition to run by you. You're of an age now where you could use some income. Gas and hamburger money. I want to hire you for the summer. I'll pay you hourly, six-fifty cash. That's a buck over minimum wage and you won't have to report it to Uncle Sam. What do you think?"

"Gas money?" August said. "I don't even have a car."

His father finished his coffee and put the mug in the sink. He had his back to August but August could tell he was smiling, trying to hide it. "We'll go get the chores done and then hammer out the particulars later."

When the cows had been milked and kicked back out to pasture, the milking parlor floor scraped clean of shit and swept, August's father said, "Let's go up to the shed and take a look at something." He slid open the big double doors and flicked on the overhead lights, then stood to the side and swept his arms open. "Surprise," he said. "She's not a thing of beauty, but the engine's rebuilt and she runs strong."

It was a small pickup truck, a Ford Ranger, at least ten years old, white but pintoed with brown rust spots. "New tires, too," his father said. "It had some pretty bad baloney skins before, but I coughed up for some new rubber. What do you think?"

"Seriously?" August said. "It's mine?"

"All yours. I insured it under my name because that will be cheaper than you trying to do it yourself. I got the first six months covered. I'll let you know what the rest of the year comes to and you can just pay me. Your mom told me you did driver's ed this spring. A guy your age needs wheels for the summer, no way around it. I figured I was either going to have to let you borrow my truck, or I could get you something of your own and save us both a bit of hassle."

Early July with windows down, the washboard rumble riding up the old truck's blown shocks. Fields of corn, the plants knee high and spreading, the damp moisture-hogging smell of them in the evening air. August, done with chores, took the back roads to town. His father liked him to stay for dinner, but on the weekends he begged off and he figured his father understood. "A pocketful of cash and some wheels," he said. "Those were the days. Get out of here and be safe."

There was nothing much to do. August had been gone three years, long enough to recognize that he was no longer a part of it in any meaningful way. He'd left right before childhood friendships forged into lasting relationships. He saw people around, kids he'd gone to school with. *Oh, hey, Augie,* they'd say. *Back visiting for a while? Where are you living now, Colorado?* Having left—having seen the mountains, having seen the bears ambling through town and the wind-driven snow piling to the eaves—August felt a certain superiority. People here talked as if their noses were plugged, a nasal drone—his father, even. Now, when he listened to his father speak, the sound of it was strange, hokey. The trees crowded in and the dark green of the woods choked the road edges. There was a deep-seated flatness here, and people weren't raised to crave any sort of vantage point. August realized that a landscape could shape your hopes and expectations for what life might possibly have to offer. There were trailer houses dotting the unkempt fields along the back roads, driveways choked with weeds, plastic swimming pools, trampolines broken down and fading under the sun. August saw them all as if for the first time.

On Fridays and Saturdays he'd generally go to the Moe-Z-Inn and get a burger and a Coke and sit on the back deck overlooking the Morley Pond. It was a stagnant, dammed section of the Little Muskegon River, and in early summer it was already choked with algal bloom. As a minor, August could stay until eight o'clock. He usually lingered right up until the place shifted from restaurant to bar and a different crowd started rolling in, guys he vaguely recognized as being a few years ahead of him at school. Construction workers mostly, still in their boots and jeans, sleeveless shirts, and sunglasses pushed back on the tops of their heads. They crowded around the bar and talked loudly, got the jukebox going with Guns N' Roses and Mötley Crüe. Eventually the girlfriends filtered in—sundresses and teased hair, crop tops and pierced navels, tribal tattoos scrawled across lower backs. August sat in the shadows on the deck, nursing his Coke, picking at his french fries. Sometimes he thought he could probably get away with staying past eight—no one ever made a move to kick him out—but he never tried. When the time came, he'd put his money down and walk back through the bar, swing into his truck, and drive the back roads slowly to the farm, not ready yet to go home but with no other idea for something else he might do.

Lisa was around only on weekends. She was taking summer classes at Central Michigan, studying to be a vet tech. She'd show up on Friday evening with grocery bags and a backpack full of textbooks. August thought she looked older. Her face less round. Once he went into his father's bathroom looking for toothpaste and saw a dripping line of her just-washed bras and panties hanging from the shower stall, like tropical fruit. Occasionally, on the weekends, midday after chores were done, the door to their bedroom would close and the house would take on a heavy silence. August never heard a single thing. Not one thing. And in this absence of sound, it was too easy to imagine it all with a burning clarity, until he had to leave, slam the door behind him, take the truck out to Brockway Lake, jump from the dock, and sink past the thermocline to the cold mud bottom, holding his breath until his lungs were screaming.

During the week it was just him and his father. The repetitive cycle of chores. The cows as shit-covered and dumb as ever. They got a load of hay delivered, and his father sent the bales up the conveyor while August stacked them. It was hot in the haymow, chaff sticking to the sweat on his face, his bare arms prickly from hay-scratch. It took most of the afternoon, and when they finally quit, the bales were stacked to the rafters. They ate fried chicken from the Town and Country deli counter and drank sun tea with lemon wedges on the porch as the evening finally cooled. His father turned on the radio for the game. Fireflies rose, blinking, from the lawn in the darkness, strange constellations of them shifting and reforming.

"Don't have those in Montana," August said. "I've never seen them, anyway."

"Really?" His father said. "That's too bad. Wouldn't seem like summer to me without fireflies. And baseball. No pro teams in Montana, right? I guess you could find some college ball, or something. Speaking of, wish I could have seen you play this season. It'll be varsity next year, eh?"

August nodded.

His father whistled through his teeth. "I was always more of a baseball guy, but I can still appreciate football."

August rubbed the insides of his arms. The sting of hay rash still hadn't gone away after a cold shower. "I'd love to see you play," his father said. "I'm going to try to get out there for a game next year. Your mom seems surprised at the way you took to it. I guess she has some ideas about how you are, and football doesn't necessarily jibe with those ideas."

"She came to every game. Even when we played Havre. That was like a six-hour drive."

"Your mom has it in her to be supportive. Although I sometimes think she just likes to pretend interest so she can pass judgment in a more informed manner."

"She bought overalls. I think she likes it."

His father laughed and rocked back in his chair. "It's possible," he said. "I guess that could be. *Varsity,*" he said, whistling again, shaking his head. "Be careful they don't elect you homecoming king. You don't want to peak too early."

Sometimes his mother called him. The jangle of the old kitchen phone, the cord stretched so he could sit at the table. "I sort of feel like I'm a teenager again," she said.

"Why is that?"

"Trying to screw up the nerve to call a boy that may or may not even want to talk to me. You could call your mother sometimes, you know? I shouldn't have to feel like I'm courting my own son."

"That's weird, Mom. I've just been busy."

"Busy with what?"

"Nothing that interesting. Chores. Hay. Listening to some baseball with dad. Driving around."

"You're not driving like an idiot, are you?"

"I'm not driving like an idiot. What have you been up to?" There was silence on the line for a moment, and then his mother laughed. "The weather has been so nice here," she said. "I've been meaning to plant some flowers in that little raised bed next to the house. Coffee on the porch has been pleasant. I played five games of solitaire this morning and made a deal with myself—if I won a single game without cheating it would mean that I probably wouldn't die alone."

August twisted the cord and looked out the kitchen window. He could see his truck parked in the driveway. The keys were in the cup holder. He could drive into town and get a big fountain soda and take it to Brockway Lake, swim out to the floating dock, and lie on the boards till he was hot and dry before swimming back. "Did you win?" he said.

"I won three games. But I cheated a little every time. I'm looking forward to your return, Augie."

In early August, Lisa finished her coursework and was around more during the week. She spent most nights, and in the morning would pad around flat-footed in the kitchen wearing cutoffs and one of his father's white T-shirts. Sometimes in the afternoons she would lie out on the back deck in her bikini with a bottle of baby oil, the radio on. She'd never struck him as a woman who'd be in possession of a bikini. But there she was, stretched out on a towel, flipping a magazine, glistening with oil, her pale skin the sort that never tanned properly, her breasts large, blue-veined, pooling heavily off to her sides.

August started sleeping at the old house. He told his father it was cooler at night and that he slept better. His father looked at him with his eyebrows raised. "There's air-conditioning in the new house," he said. "How can you tell me that old dump is cooler?"

August shrugged. "Seems like it is."

His father looked off over August's shoulder toward the old house, and his eyes were flat. "Some winter after we get a new snow I'm going to burn that place down," he said. "I'll call the fire department to get a permit. Kerosene on the carpet. Kerosene on the curtains. One nice little match. When it's done I'll rent a bulldozer and plow the foundation over, and I'll plant some corn for silage right on top of the ashes."

Solitary coffee in the early-morning gray before chores. August found he enjoyed this time. At the new house, his father, a naturally early riser, tended to be jocular and loud first thing. Teasing Lisa, making cracks at August before he was even awake enough to respond. At the old house, August eased into the day, made his breakfast the way he liked it, yolks firm, toast not too crispy. He usually had the radio on,

NPR from Grand Rapids, *Morning Edition.* He didn't pay much attention to the news itself, but the dull murmur of voices was companionable. He did his dishes right away after eating. Wiped down the counters. Turned off the coffee maker. This way of living, having a whole house to himself, it felt like something he'd been wanting all his life and just hadn't known it. He couldn't imagine why his mother would spend a single moment worrying about being alone. Breakfast just the way he liked it and not having to speak a word to anyone until he was good and ready. Adulthood meant he wouldn't have to suffer anyone else's company unless he chose to. He could see it coming and he was ready.

A steady progression of long summer days. Soon, football practices would be starting, and his return flight was rapidly approaching. One night, after dinner, he got up to do the dishes. "I was thinking, I might just drive the truck back to Montana," he said. His father was at the table, his checkbook out, paying bills. He tapped his pen on the table a few times and shook his head. "Probably not," he said. "We bought you a round-trip ticket. It's too long of a haul for that old thing anyway."

August was rinsing plates, stacking them in the drying rack. "The engine's rebuilt. It runs strong. New tires. You said it yourself."

"It's too far. It's a drive-around-the-county sort of truck. Not a drive-across-the-country sort of truck. You'll fly. The truck stays here."

August drained the water. He wiped his hands on the towel. "What's the use of giving me a truck if I can't drive it where I want to go?"

"Well, son, I hate to say it, but if you were living here you could drive it to your heart's content."

August hung the towel carefully on the hook above the sink. He slammed the door on the way out as hard as he could. He could hear his father shout something, but he was already striding toward the old house, barefoot, through the dew-wet grass.

Later, August put the truck keys on the kitchen counter in the new house and didn't touch them for the last few days of his stay. At the airport, on the morning of his flight, they shook hands wordlessly. August shouldered his bag and headed into the terminal.

The waning days of summer. The hillsides a parched brown, only a few scraps of snow clinging to the shaded couloirs on the Beartooths. They had a week of no-contact conditioning practice—endless laps around the baseball diamond, stretching and drills in the rock-strewn practice field, Coach Zwicky blowing his whistle with random outrage. Just when August thought he couldn't take it anymore, they donned the pads and had their first full-contact practice, and for the next week August hit so hard he could feel the echoes of it in his sleep. He had lumps on his forearms from bashing against face masks. His face broke out in painful blackheads where his helmet's chinstrap rubbed. Then school started and he was tired all the time, moving slowly from class to class, gingerly easing in and out of the desks.

The girls had all turned beautiful somehow, seemingly all at once. Summer tan, pushing the dress code to its very outer limits. They'd walk together in the halls, perfumed and laughing, hair tossing. August went to class, went to practice, did his homework. Every night he showered, long and hot, leaning with his back against the tile, and all the girls from school passing like a procession behind his closed eyes. Lisa was there sometimes. Julie. Faceless women he'd never met, too. What swirled down the shower drain started to look a lot like despair. Before getting out he ran the water as cold as it would go and stood there for as long as he could bear.

His mother bought him a used Subaru wagon, and while he was grateful for the car he missed his truck, rust spots and all. There were bonfires on logging roads after the games; kids got beer from older siblings or from raiding their parents' liquor cabinets. The cops sometimes showed up, and everyone scattered like quail.

At the homecoming game against Townsend, August took a shot from their cannonball-shaped fullback that made him leave his body for a moment, a helmet-to-helmet collision that turned things black around the edges, something within him rising up so he could see himself on hands and knees, slack-jawed after the whistle, his mouth guard lying on the grass, a line of spit trailing down to it, trying to stand but falling on rubber legs. A couple of the guys helped him to the sideline, and he eventually went back in to play the final quarter. Apparently he recorded a few tackles, one for a loss, but he couldn't recall much of it. Everything was hazy until the bus ride back home, when he started to come out of the fog.

They made the playoffs that year, but lost in the first round to Browning—Blackfeet boys, some with tattoos already, some with long black hair streaming from under their helmets. After the second snap August realized that while everyone was ostensibly playing the same game, the Browning team was playing for some other set of stakes that he couldn't quite fathom. Down in the pile, elbows flew, fingers jabbed through face masks poking for eyes; shoving matches after every down. They had a rangy halfback who torched the field for over a hundred yards. When it was done, both coaches, fearing blood, decided to forgo the customary end-of-game team handshake.

And then the season was over and August didn't mind. He'd been getting headaches. Dull, throbbing pain behind his eyes. He didn't tell his mother, and as winter set in they receded and he felt fine.

On Christmas Day, August called his father.

"Merry Christmas, Dad," he said. "Thanks for the card and the check. I appreciate it."

"Oh, sure. I figured you could find some use for it."

"I'm going to use part of it to get a new windshield for my truck. I was behind a plow the other day and a rock kicked up. I've got a huge crack."

"Truck? What happened to the Subaru?"

"I sold it. There was a guy down the street selling an F-150. So I sold the Subaru and bought the truck and still had some left over."

"How'd your mom feel about that?"

"She told me that she'd given me the Subaru, and I could do what I wanted with it. I mean, she wasn't exactly happy, but she told me it was my decision to make."

"I see."

"The truck's a little newer than the Ranger you got me. No rust, either. They don't use salt on the roads out here, just sand. That's why all the older cars in Michigan are so rusty, all the salt. Out here, an old car can sometimes still be in pretty good shape."

"Interesting. I didn't know that. I wish you could have made it back home for the holidays. We missed out on hunting this year."

"Have you been seeing any nice ones?"

"Not really. I think the Amish must have gotten that eight-point. No sign of it since last year. There's a bunch of does and a few scrub bucks. I haven't really had time to sit in the blind. Anyway, too bad I didn't make it out there to see you play. Sounds like you had a great season. All-conference first team, eh? That's great."

"It was okay. We lost bad to Browning, and they went on to take state. They blew us out of the water. What are you up to today? Is there snow on the ground?"

"There was, but then it all melted. It's a brown Christmas this year. I'm just loafing around. Lisa will be over this evening, and we'll have some dinner. Nothing too exciting. Maybe I'll look at plane tickets for you soon. You're still planning on coming out for the summer, aren't you? I could use your help. I figure I can pony up a raise for you. Seven-fifty. Does that work?"

It had started to spit snow. August was lying on the couch, and he could see two jays sparring over the suet in the feeder. His mother was in the kitchen, whistling off-key along with a Mannheim Steamroller album. "Yeah," August said, finally. "I'll be coming back. Seven-fifty works for me."

"That's great. I'm looking forward to having you around. I changed the oil in your truck the other day. Took it for a little spin. She's running like a top."

That spring, August took the SAT and did well enough. It wasn't long before the college brochures started flooding the mailbox. He didn't give them much more than a glance, but one morning he came downstairs before school and found his mother flipping through the pile, drinking her coffee. "Oh, look at this one, St. Lawrence University, in upstate New York; it looks beautiful. Or how about the University of California, in Santa Cruz? Right in the redwoods, maybe you could learn how to surf. Oh, hey, here's Dartmouth, that's flattering, I mean, *Ivy League,* Augie, wouldn't that be something?"

"Just because they sent me a brochure doesn't mean they would actually let me in. Surfing," he shook his head. "I don't see it."

"This summer we need to visit a school or two, at the very least. It's hard to get a feel for these places unless you walk the campus, see the lay of the land, meet some students. I think it will be fun."

August was at the sink pouring cereal into a bowl. "I told Dad I'd come work for him again this summer," he said. He went to the fridge for the milk, not looking at his mother. She was silent, and he didn't have to look at her to know her face: jaw set, eyes narrowed. He started to eat, still standing with his back to her, feeling her stare.

"What?" he said. "I told him I'd come back to work, and he's counting on it. I can't change my mind at the last second."

His mother rose and walked over to stand next to him. She put her mug in the sink, and he could smell the coffee on her breath, smoke from her morning cigarillo in her hair. "Your father doesn't need your help in that goddamn barn," she said. "He needs you around so he can feel like his life hasn't been a complete waste. I'm going to work now, but we're not done discussing this."

There were many more discussions. Fights. Long spells where he and his mother barely exchanged words. And, in the end, there was one more humid green Michigan summer. A summer tallied in fountain

Cokes and the slow accumulation of $7.50 hours. Cicadas droning in the poplars, sticky nights with the windows open, the heat lightning crackling the black eggshell of sky. All the girls in town and none of them his. The stink of manure, hay itch, the sharp line of tanned skin right at the point his short sleeves stopped. Baseball and sun tea. His father and Lisa argued occasionally now, some new threshold in their relationship reached. She sometimes made dinner with her mouth pressed in a tight line, pans slamming on the cooktop. There were no college visits.

At the airport, the day of his departure, his father shook his hand and heaved his bag out of the back of the truck. "Thanks for all the help this summer," he said. "Couldn't have done it without you. Senior year," he said, giving a low whistle. "Hard to imagine. Enjoy it. Next summer we'll talk about bringing you on board on a more permanent basis. No more hourly wage. I was thinking more of a partnership, a profit-sharing kind of deal—what do you think?"

August shouldered his bag, watched a jet taxiing down the runway behind his father's shoulder.

"Sure," he said. "Yeah, maybe. We'll see what happens."

When he returned to Montana he told his mother he'd apply to Montana State in Bozeman for next year. He'd thought about it over the summer. He knew he could get a good scholarship, and he didn't want to accumulate debt. She told him that she respected his decision. "MSU is not a bad school at all, and you'll be close, so that will be nice. I kind of like having you around."

Gaskill's dad had a raft, and on the last weekend before school started a few of the guys planned an overnight float on the river. Originally it was going to be Ramsay, Gaskill, Veldtkamp, and Richards, but then Richards's grandmother died in a car accident in Gallatin Canyon and he had to go to the funeral. With Richards out, August got the invite.

They launched in the early afternoon below the railroad bridge east of town. It was a hot day, and before they set off they all climbed the trestle to jump into the river. Halfway up the embankment, Veldtkamp turned around and ran back to the raft. When he returned, his hands were full of Coors Light cans. They stood side by side, bare feet on the tracks on the edge of the rusted iron bridge. Veldtkamp punched holes in the cans with his pocket knife, the beer spraying a fine golden mist on their arms and chests. He handed the beers around and then raised his toward Ramsay. "Here's to Private First Class Ramsay. Here's to Mon-fucking-tana. And here's to honor. Get on her. Stay on her. If you can't cum in her, cum on her. Cheers, boys." They tilted their heads and popped the tabs to shotgun their beers, then released a chorus of belches and launched themselves from the trestle, hitting the river in a ragged line, coming up splashing and hooting. They swam to the raft, kicked it away, and they were off.

The river was wide here, slow, midsummer low with mats of electric-green algae furring the rocks. They turned lazy circles in the middle of the current; occasionally one of them would pick up a paddle and make a few strokes to keep them away from the bank. They drank beer, hanging off the sides of the raft, trailing limbs in the water to cool down.

"Too bad ol' Richards couldn't make it," Veldtkamp said. "I mean, I'm glad to have you along, Augie, but that Richards is such a funny bastard. He could do stand-up."

"Too bad about his grandma," Ramsay said. He was fair skinned, hair so blond it was almost white. He'd slathered zinc sunscreen across his cheeks in thick splotches. He was older than the rest of them, and after graduating last year he'd joined the National Guard. He was back from Fort Benning for a visit, and in less than a week he was going to be deployed.

"I heard it was a drunk driver that ran her off the road," Gaskill said.

"Nah," Ramsay said. "I heard from Richards himself. His grandma was epileptic and had a seizure while driving. At least they think that's what it was." He was silent for a moment, and then he cleared his throat. "I wish that would happen to my grandma sometime."

"Oh, Christ," Veldtkamp said, rolling his eyes.

Gaskill was conspicuously looking away, rubbing the back of his neck.

"What?" Ramsay said, his eyes moving back and forth between them. "*What?* My grandma is a raging cunt, and she deserves to die. She's the main reason my mom is so fucked up, and anyone that did what she did to me and my brothers should be locked away."

"We know, dude. Milky. We've heard this. Many, many times," Veldtkamp said.

"What are you guys talking about?" August said. "What's milky?"

Ramsay shifted on his perch in the raft to face him. He took a long drink of beer and belched. "I never told you about Milky?" he said.

Veldtkamp sighed and dunked his hat in the river so that when he put it back on, water drained across his face and chest. "I'm really missing Richards right now. He would've nipped this right in the butt."

Ramsay leaned over and tried to kick river water at Veldtkamp. "I bet you'd like it if Richards nipped *you* in the butt. It's supposed to be *bud.* I've heard you say *nipped in the butt* for years and let it slide, but you're pissing me off now."

"Sorry, dude, we've just heard the story about Milky literally millions of times."

"Who was Milky?" August said.

Ramsay drained his beer, crunched the can on his thigh, and tossed it in the bottom of the raft. "Milky was my pet calf," he said. There were simultaneous groans from Gaskill and Veldtkamp, which Ramsay didn't acknowledge. "My mom's mom is a really rich lady. A horse lady. Her second husband left her a bunch of money when he croaked. She bought one of those fancy horse trailer rigs with the little camper up front and stalls for the horses in the back, and she drives it all over the country. A hundred-thousand-dollar trailer, at least. She has a big house down in Santa Fe, too. I've never seen it in person, but she used to send us a Christmas card and a smoked turkey every year, even though she had disowned us. She'd send us a card with a picture of her and her two dogs in front of her house, a big fountain, the whole deal. And that turkey. I always liked it a lot. It was real smoky tasting, and it came from someplace in Texas.

"Anyway, she never liked my dad, and when my mom and him got married that was it. She disowned my mom. I'd never even seen her until the spring when I was ten. It was around Easter, and I think she'd started going to church, or was feeling guilty, or something, so she packed her horse trailer and drove up from Santa Fe unannounced. I remember her just showing up on the doorstep; we were living in View Vista still. All the way in the back, the crappiest cat-piss-smelling brown trailer in the place. This was before my dad started driving trucks and we moved out into the valley. Anyway, my mom went to the door and about collapsed when she opened it. My grandma was there with a big smile. She had on a black hat and black jeans and long gray hair and wore that stupid turquoise and silver jewelry all the rich old people down there wear, and she gave my mom a hug and told her that she looked like she'd gained about fifty pounds since she'd seen her last, and then bent down to shake me and my brother's hands.

"We were being shy, but she was acting all excited and pretty much dragged us out to her horse trailer and had us get up in the back stall with her and she had a little brown and white calf in there with a red halter on it. Brown body, white face. Real small still. She said she'd brought it for us to raise, as a present, and told us to play with him in the yard while she talked to our mom in the house.

"We walked the calf around the park for a while, showing him off, then we started building a little corral for it out of some boards and stuff my dad had laying around. I don't remember why, but we decided to call him Milky. After a while he laid down in the yard and let us pet him and then fell asleep. We were just hanging with him there when my grandma comes storming back out. She pulls Milky up by the halter and drags him back to the horse trailer. The calf is bawling now and we're confused and asking her what she's doing, but she just says that our mother is impossible and that she tried to do something nice and this was all she got in return and it would be the last time she tried anything like this again. And then she got into her rig, drove away, and I haven't seen her since.

"I found out later that she'd been in there trying to convince my mom to leave my dad. To pack us up and move down to Santa Fe with her. At the time, though, I was just mad at my mom for making my grandma take Milky away. I told her that she'd probably gained more like a hundred pounds and then she slapped me off the porch and I ran away, but it was March and cold as shit so I only lasted for a few hours after it got dark and came back with my tail tucked. She made me a burrito and didn't say anything about any of it."

Ramsay rummaged in the cooler for another beer, cracked it, and drank long and deep. He looked out over the Bridgers in the far distance. "Ol' Milky," he said. "He'd follow you around like a dog. Barely had him for an afternoon, but you could tell he was a good one. That was the only time my mom ever hit me. Not the case with the old man, of course, but she only did it that one time and I guess I deserved it, so it is what it is. Whatever. It was a long time ago."

"Sure was," Veldtkamp said, rousing himself from where he'd slumped at the bottom of the raft. "You boys remember that time we floated down to Big Timber and caught up to all the girls from the MSU soccer team on inner tubes?"

"So, Ramsay, that's it?" August said. "She took your pet calf that you had for half a day?"

"You're killing me, Augie," Veldtkamp said. "Goddamn, we need Richards here."

"No, Augie," Ramsay said. "Actually that wasn't it. At Christmas, Grandma sent us the usual package. She always addressed the box to us boys and because I was the oldest I got to unwrap it, and even though I knew what it was I still got kind of excited about it because I really liked when my mom sliced the turkey up and made sandwiches. We're all sitting around in our pajamas, Christmas morning in that shitty View Vista trailer, and I open up the turkey box and instead of a turkey there's about ten packages wrapped in white butcher paper all soggy and leaking blood. There was a note on top that said, *Merry Xmas. I hope you like my present better this time. XO Gram.*"

"You're shitting me," August said. "Seriously? *Milky*?"

Ramsay shrugged. "Part of him at least."

They were silent for a moment and Veldtkamp was doing something, covering his face. A snicker finally broke through and then a full-on guffaw. Ramsay didn't look at him.

"I'm sorry," Veldtkamp said, holding up his hands. "That last bit about *XO Gram* just gets me every time. I mean, it's sort of hilarious." Veldtkamp was laughing uncontrollably now, and soon enough Gaskill caught it. Both of them were down in the bottom of the raft, guts heaving, slapping their legs, the raft, each other.

Ramsay was shaking his head, looking off toward the mountains, jaw clenched, and August found himself laughing, too.

At the first sound of this, Ramsay turned sharply. "What's funny, August?" he said. Suddenly no one was laughing anymore. Gaskill and Veldtkamp stopped clowning and straightened themselves up.

"Huh?" August said. "I thought you guys were joking. That didn't actually happen, did it?"

"I went to Veldtkamp's house that day. I puked, and then I ran all the way across town in my pajamas and stayed at his house on Christmas because I hated my family. His mom cleaned me up and gave me one of his presents so I'd have something to open and wouldn't feel left out. He and that other laughing asshole over there have known this shit since we were kids, but you don't have that with me. So stuff it."

August looked at Ramsay, trying to determine if he was being serious or not. He gave one more small experimental chuckle and Ramsay reached out, surprisingly fast, and gave him a hard slap on the side of the head.

"Shit, man," August said. "We're just joking." Gaskill gave August a nudge with his knee and shook his head.

Ramsay's face had gone red under his layer of zinc, and his fists were balled up at his sides. "I don't care if you are bigger than me. You're soft and everyone knows it. I will tear you down."

August shrugged, stumbled out an apology. He thought Ramsay might really hit him, but then Veldtkamp submerged his head in the water and came up shaking like a dog to get them all wet. "And that, my friends, is why we don't talk about Milky," he said. "It never goes well. I think it's about time to shotgun another one of those beers.

What do you say, champ?" he said, sliding up next to Ramsay until their bare legs were touching.

Ramsay pushed him away. "God, I hate all you fuckers," he said. But he took the beer he was offered, and not long after he was laughing with Veldtkamp, telling the story about the time they tipped Zwicky over when he was in the port-a-john behind the practice field taking a shit.

They floated. Chewed the stringy elk jerky Gaskill had brought. Drank beers. Jumped from outcropping ledges into deep emerald pools and then draped themselves on the hot rubber tubes of the raft to dry. "How was basic, Ramsay?" Veldtkamp said.

Ramsay shrugged. "Humid and shitty. Not much worse than two-a-days, though."

"Two-a-days sucked this year," Gaskill said. "Zwicky is a damn Nazi. He was only giving us two water breaks a session. One of these years someone's going to get heatstroke and die, and it'll be his fault."

"At basic, did they make you take those pills to stop you from getting boners?" Veldtkamp said.

"What?" Ramsay said.

"My cousin signed up, and he said they made them take these pills. Saltpeter. Keeps you from getting boners. He said the whole time he was there he didn't get one single hard-on. No morning wood or nothing."

"I don't know about that," Ramsay said. "You don't get boners in basic because you're dog-tired all the time and people are yelling at you constantly and you're surrounded by dudes. I mean, why the fuck would you expect to get an erection in that sort of situation?"

"Erections just happen," Veldtkamp said. "Doesn't depend too much on your surroundings, in my experience. Did you get boners at basic, or not?"

"I don't really remember. I was too tired to give a damn."

"It's that saltpeter. My cousin told me at some places they just put it in the water, so you don't even know."

"Whatever," Ramsay said. He was looking over their heads at the slow scrawl of the riverbank passing by. "I've got an idea," he said. "Tonight, we should find an island with a big pile of driftwood and torch the whole thing."

"I like the way you think," Veldtkamp said. "Do we have lighter fluid?"

"I brought a little can of diesel," Gaskill said.

"Good man."

"There's burn restrictions in place right now," August said. "Someone might call the fire department."

"Fuck those fire department queers. I'm going to Afghanistan," Ramsay said.

"Fair enough," August said. He realized now that he should have immediately punched Ramsay in the face when he'd called him soft. Ramsay might have said the words, but it was August's inaction that rendered them true.

When the sun started to dip toward the rimrock they found their island. It was a several-hundred-yard expanse of mid-river gravel, dotted with willows, and a huge, jackstrawed tangle of dead cottonwoods and gnarled root wads sitting on the upstream side, remnants from spring high water.

They unrolled their sleeping bags and didn't bother with the tent because the night was clear. The river was loud around them. They made a small fire and roasted brats on willow sticks, waiting for it to get dark. When it was time, they let Ramsay do the honors. He emptied the can of diesel on one of the sun-dried root wads and got it going with his lighter. It didn't take long before the flames were shooting up, crackling over their heads, the stink of diesel fading, sparks drifting out over the river.

"Always wanted to do that," Ramsay said, raising his hands to the blaze.

"When that big cottonwood log in there gets going it's probably going to burn for two days," Veldtkamp said. They'd gone through all the beer and were now passing around the bottle of Jack Daniel's that Gaskill had procured, at a highly inflated rate, from his older brother. They were silent, and the rush of the gathering fire joined the rush of the river, a great hollowing torrent of sound. They were in the middle of the current and somehow it seemed that they were in the middle of the fire as well, some middle place of the universe in general. "They've got spiders over there," Ramsay said. "Camel spiders. They're about a foot long and can run fast as a dog. Saw pictures of them on the Internet."

"Seriously?" Gaskill said.

"Dead serious. Pass me that whiskey."

They lurched and staggered. There were boasts and oaths. They were going to Vegas first thing when Ramsay got back. Burn that town to the ground. There were fist bumps and claps on the backs and eventually just silent contemplation, the clear wash of stars, tears that threatened to spill but never could. August was not really a part of it. He drank and tended the blaze. He knew Richards should have been there, not him, and he wished he wouldn't have come. Eventually he pretended he was drunker than he was and stumbled away to sleep.

When he got up to piss, sometime in the early hours, Ramsay was still awake, back against a log, watching the fire. August sat next to him. Veldtkamp was passed out in the sand, snoring loudly.

"You good, man?"

"I'm fine. Can't sleep." Ramsay laughed, short and dry. "My mom told me she had a dream. The dream was that I come back from overseas, and I go on to get my law degree. I turn into a judge and then I get elected as a senator. My main campaign promise is that I'll push for healthcare reform. Cheaper prescriptions."

"She saw all of that in the same dream?"

"I guess it was a long one. My mom puts a lot of stake in dreams. She has eight prescriptions. I think she needs *less* prescriptions, personally. Not cheaper ones."

"Well, I'd vote for you, man. If you ran, I'd help you put up signs and stuff."

"Gee, thanks, pal. I had a dream, too. I dreamt I was in a giant canopy bed with seven black-haired virgins swarming all over me. Seven of the hottest virgins you've ever seen. Tits and ass everywhere, just smothering me."

"Isn't that what they believe? When they blow themselves up or whatever? They become martyrs and then they go to heaven and get a certain number of virgins?"

"Exactly. I dreamed a jihadist's dream. If that's not fucked up, I don't know what is. Now I feel like he's out there, dreaming my dreams, and when we meet over there one of us is going to have to kill the other to get things back to how they should be."

"It's just a dream. Probably doesn't mean anything at all. How'd you know they were virgins?"

"They told me so. They said they'd been waiting forever, saving themselves, just for me. Scared me shitless, and now I can't sleep."

With football, the headaches resumed. On the second game of the year versus Big Timber, August covered the kick returner, the two of them meeting near the middle of the field at the point of top speed. There was an explosion of light and the clap of pads, then the returner, a small, quick kid, flopping on the turf like a carp, out cold and in the throes of seizure. Play was halted and the Big Timber team took a knee. A stretcher materialized, and although the kid was awake enough now to sit up, they still carted him away, ambulance lights flashing down the road toward the clinic. Coach Zwicky was incensed, ecstatic, red-faced, with spit flying. *"That was a hit!"* he screamed, grabbing August's face mask. *"That was a goddamn hit, son. Jesus Christ! That kid's mother felt that. The whole town felt that!"* August looked at the big lights above the field and saw tracers, black spots swirling.

That night there was a bonfire after the game, but his head was pounding and he left early. When he got home the house was empty, and he was glad. That fall his mother had started dating a man she'd met at work. A teacher. He lived in Bozeman, and often on the weekends she would stay over with him. August had only met him once. He wore glasses and had longish graying hair. He'd moved to Montana from Southern California, and he had August's mother taking yoga classes with him. She was trying to quit smoking, supposedly.

August took a long shower, gingerly probing all the lumps and scrapes and sore spots on his arms and shins. He was lying on the couch in his boxers, half drowsing in front of the TV, when the doorbell rang. August sat up, moved the curtain aside to see who it was. In his surprise, he opened the door before really thinking it through. He realized he should have gone and put some pants on, but it was too late and he stood there awkwardly in the threshold.

"Julie?" he said.

She'd cut her hair shorter, and she looked slightly heavier than the last time he'd seen her. She wore a sundress, although it was a cool evening, and she was holding a bag of fried chicken in one hand and a bottle of Cook's champagne in the other. She was smiling, but it was obvious that she had just finished crying. She made a show of squinting at him, stepping back as if to get a better look. "Is that Augie?" she said. "Jesus Christ, you turned into a giant."

He opened the door all the way, and she gave him a hug as she came in. It was a substantial hug, her arms across his bare back, fingers digging in. He could feel his face reddening. "Am I interrupting?" she said, already settling on the couch. He shook his head, mumbled something about putting some clothes on, and headed to the bedroom. "Don't feel like you have to get dressed up on my account," she said with a laugh. When he came back in jeans and a T-shirt, he sat on the opposite side of the couch from her. She told him that she'd come to see Ethan, that she'd finished her Peace Corps assignment and the whole time she'd been gone they'd been writing each other. "He told me all the stuff he was doing to the house. He said he got the new siding finished just before winter hit and that he was going to put in a hammered-copper countertop because he saw one in a house he was working on in Big Sky and he thought it looked really good. He said he couldn't wait to see me and to show me all the stuff he was doing. He said he was putting French doors out to the patio. He was going to do some landscaping in the backyard this summer."

She shook her head. Sniffed, and then sat up a little straighter on the couch. She tore the foil from the champagne bottle and popped the cork so it shot out and bounced off the ceiling. "So, I show up," she said. She drank directly from the bottle. "I wanted to surprise him. The first time we ever met, when he'd just bought the house, I came over and I brought fried chicken and Cook's champagne. Tonight I did that again because it was such a good memory. I was coming down the street, and I was so excited to see him. And then I get here and it looks like the place has been abandoned. The siding's falling off. There's a FOR SALE sign down in the mud. He was sending me these complete bullshit emails, for two years, and I don't even understand why. It just seems vindictive. Cruel. Weird." She had her legs crossed. Thick thighs. Long, bare legs with a few red bumps near her ankles. Bug-bite scars, he thought. African mosquito bites.

"My mom isn't here," he said. "She's staying over at her boyfriend's house tonight."

"Oh, I know. I talked to her this morning, actually. She seems happy with Art. It's nice that she's found someone that she can relate to. Apparently he's really smart."

August shrugged. "Kind of a hippie," he said. He was trying to figure out why exactly Julie had knocked on the door if she knew his mother wasn't there.

"Am I bothering you?" she said. "I don't want to be a nuisance. It looks like you were getting relaxed."

"I had a game tonight. I was just watching some TV. You're not interrupting."

"That's right, your mom told me that you've turned into a jock."

"I don't know about that. I like football okay. How was Africa?"

Julie had opened the bag of chicken and was eating a drumstick. She sucked chicken grease from her fingers and leaned back on the couch, closing her eyes. "Botswana was . . . Botswana. I don't even know where to start, really. There's this saying Peace Corps people always use: *Life begins at the end of your comfort zone.* You can get used to just about anything. That's something I learned. What you think is normal can shift in much less time than you might think."

"Makes sense. I think Ethan is up in Alaska, working on a pipeline.

I haven't seen him in a long time. The place was for sale, but the bank might own it now. I'm not sure."

Julie drank more without opening her eyes. "I'll be fine. I've got a job in New York that I'm starting after Christmas. I wasn't going to be staying here anyways. Still, all those emails. I was telling him my thoughts, writing to him about how I was feeling and what I was seeing and he was sending me, I don't know, *fiction*. That's fucked up. You want some chicken?"

"Already ate. Thanks, though."

"You want some champagne?"

He took the bottle and swigged, passing it back, fighting down a belch as the warm bubbles hit his gut. "Ethan told me a story one time about a dog his dad had. A real good bird dog for a couple years, and then all of a sudden it started licking its leg and couldn't stop. It licked right down to the bone, stopped hunting, even, so his dad ended up shooting it. He told me his dad was a real asshole."

"That's a horrible story," Julie said. "I'm not surprised. I met his father once. Maybe that's just how it works. Everyone's father is an asshole. Daughters shrink from it or rebel against it, but sons absorb it, pass it on to the next generation, ensuring that, outside of a certain amount of necessary biological attraction, men and women will continue to be incompatible. Just how tall are you, anyway? Your mom told me you'd sprung up." Julie paused, smiling, and tilted the bottle toward him. "As I was walking tonight I realized how much I missed the dry air here. That's something about Africa I never enjoyed, the humidity. In bed it always seemed like I was sweating. Do you want to go for a walk or something? It really is a beautiful evening. If you're busy, I'll take off and leave you alone."

As she was talking she was moving closer to him on the couch. They were hip to hip now and he could smell her, fried chicken, champagne, a tendril of perfume. She had her hand on his arm. "Are those bruises?" she said. "You're all banged up, aren't you? Maybe we shouldn't go for a walk." And then she swung her leg over and she was straddling him. She pulled the top of her dress down and her breasts were loose, large and pale in his face. He put his mouth to her nipples, left then right;

her fingers were raking his hair. He'd run out of ideas and wasn't sure what to do next. Eventually she took his hands, placed them where she wanted them.

She stayed the whole night. They lay in the tangle of sheets, and in the morning he woke up to the shift of her weight leaving the mattress. He watched her slip her sundress back over her head, then come to sit next to him.

"I'm a mess," she said. "I don't know what's wrong with me. That was the first time for you, wasn't it?"

For a moment August thought about lying but figured she already knew. "I guess," he said.

Julie rubbed her eyes. "I was in a weird place last night. That was not rational thinking."

August couldn't think of anything to say. He had an image of her splayed on her back on the couch. *I need your tongue right there,* she'd said, hands on the back of his head, pushing him down. "In fact," she continued, "not only was that ill-advised, but I think it was illegal. You're in high school."

"I'm a senior," he said, realizing how stupid it sounded the moment it was uttered. He put his hand on her leg, tried to move it further up her thigh, but she shook her head and stood. "I've got to get going," she said, shouldering her purse. "I'll let myself out." She didn't move to leave, though. She was looking at him, a small smile threatening to emerge. Abruptly she reached and ripped the sheets off him. He lay naked while she appraised him seriously.

"You don't have to go. My mom usually stays over in Bozeman until Sunday."

At this Julie released a small squeal. "*Your mom,*" she said. "I can't even think about her right now. I'm leaving. Bye."

And then she was gone, and August lay there for a long time. Trying to remember everything exactly how it had happened. Panic setting in as he realized that some of the particulars were already starting to blur. Eventually he got up and ate three full bowls of cereal.

The next week at school his mind couldn't stop returning to her, on the couch, on the bed, on the floor. That slightly terrifying low moan she'd made. When the bell rang, he'd have to carry his books in front to hide his erection. Football practice seemed interminable. He didn't know when he was going to see her again, and this worried him almost as much as thinking about what he might say or do when he eventually did.

After practice on Wednesday he came home and she was in the kitchen talking with his mother, both of them holding glasses of wine. He was still in his football pants, sweat-soaked undershirt, and dirty socks. He said, "Hi, Julie," and she said, "Hi, August." Her look gave him absolutely nothing.

"We're going to make a little chicken salad, Augie," his mother said. "Hit the shower and then come eat with us."

"Yeah, hit the shower, you stinky boy," Julie said.

His face burned. He left the room.

At the dinner table he mumbled responses, picked at the salad, tried to catch her eye several times to no avail. She and his mother were laughing and chattering like usual, and he wanted to get up and leave, but he also found it very necessary to look at her. The fine hair on her arms caught the light when she picked up her wine. She had delicate ears, dry patches of skin at her elbows, a small, regular blue vein pulsing in the pit where her neck met her collarbone. When he said good night the women opened another bottle of wine and retired to the porch.

He went to bed, and at some point despair finally turned to sleep. Much later, when she woke him, he wasn't sure if he was dreaming. She was slipping under the covers, kissing his chest, her hands cold at first and then warming. "I got a little too drunk to drive," she whispered into his ear. "On purpose. So I'm sleeping in the spare bedroom right now."

It was real. No dream. She was astride him, and it was the sound of it, the wet rhythmic beat that inflamed him maybe more than anything else. After dinner he'd convinced himself that the first time had only been her making a mistake. But now here she was, driving him into the mattress, breath coming in quick bursts, her hands clenching his, pinning them to the pillow above his head. Her breasts swung like pendulums, brushing his face, and he felt like laughing, a great feeling of relief. She'd come back and now he knew that this was going to continue in some way.

He became worthless to anything in the world that wasn't her. He walked the hallways at school in a fog. Girls he'd formerly lusted after now looked like children. Their arms too thin, no hips, their stomachs not rounded enough, their breasts too small. Football was torture. The guys, the stupid locker-room pranks. The way they talked about the girls they knew, girls they'd like to know. *You have no idea,* he wanted to say. *You idiots don't even have the slightest idea what it can be like.* He endured the days between Wednesdays and Fridays because he had to, but if there'd been some way to fast-forward through time, he'd have done it in a heartbeat, even if it meant his life was shortened exponentially. Most Wednesdays she'd come for dinner but not always, and the times she didn't he was despondent.

"Your mom's going to start thinking I've got a drinking problem," she said one night as she hurried to undress at the side of his bed. "I can't keep getting too drunk to drive. No more Wednesdays after this for a while."

"But Friday, still? After my game?" He knew he sounded worried, but he couldn't keep the notes of it out of his voice. She had him in her mouth now. She nodded yes. Instant relief. A whole week without her would be intolerable. Fridays were the best because they had the whole night, the whole house, and the morning, too. His mother was still coming to his games. Sometimes she brought Art along and they stood side by side on the bleachers, laughing and shouting along with the cheerleaders. Had it been his father in the stands with his mother there would have been no cheesy, excessive cheering. This observation seemed to bring to light some slippery truth about the underlying natures of both these partnerships, but it was hard to pin down, and mostly he tried to ignore his mother and focus on the game.

He hadn't been playing well. Part of it was that his mind was else-where; part of it was the fact that his temples pounded every time he made hard contact. After that hit in Big Timber, it felt like something had come unattached in his brain. He knew that probably this wasn't possible, but still, he started to hold back.

On Friday nights, after the game, the guys would try to get him to go to some bonfire or another and he would say maybe he'd show up, but he never did, and eventually they stopped asking. He would go home and take a shower, letting the hot water pummel whatever part of him hurt the most. After, he'd wait on the couch until she appeared. Sometimes she wanted to get right to it, sometimes she wanted to drink wine and talk first. He didn't always enjoy the talking, and after half a glass of wine his tongue felt thick and slow. Of course, this had something to do with Julie herself. She tended to speak in paragraphs. He was constantly on edge, trying not to say anything that might give him away. She liked discussing politics, and his basic strategy was to agree with everything she said.

Once, while walking around the living room, wineglass in hand, rattling off a list of American atrocities committed in the Middle East, she'd stopped abruptly in the middle of a sentence. She shook her head as if coming out of a reverie. She finished her wine in one gulp, then pulled her shirt over her head and slid her leggings off so she was standing in her bra and panties, her thighs goose-fleshed. "I some-times forget that you're seventeen," she'd said, crossing to him. "I need to keep this grounded in some sort of reality."

She liked certain things that he would have never considered. She moved his wrist so his hand was around her throat. "Squeeze," she said, grabbing his hair and pulling his head down to where he could use his tongue. "Harder."

"You actually like that?" he said afterward.

She laughed. "Wasn't it obvious?"

"I guess. I don't get it."

. . .

Most Fridays she came by, but on several occasions she didn't. These nights he lay awake until the early hours, half hoping she'd still show, imagining in searing detail all the possible things she might be doing instead and with whom.

Julie worried constantly that his mother would find them out. "Your mother is one of my very good friends," she said. "I feel like I'm stealing."

"How would she find out?" he said. "There's no way."

"I don't know," she said. "I kind of feel like she already thinks something is up."

"What do you mean? I hardly even look at you when you come over for dinner anymore."

"Exactly. You stumble around like a dork. At this point I think she just thinks you have a crush on me, and that's okay. She can't find out, though. I would die."

Julie was moving to New York at the end of November and it was already mid-October. He was agitated and restless when he wasn't with her, and even when he was with her, he wasn't comfortable. He'd counted the nights they had left, and the number was piercingly small. Now she talked excitedly about her new job, the apartment she was hoping to get in Brooklyn. All the kinds of food she was going to eat when she finally got to the city. He tried not to mope. He tried to be noncommittal. He now knew exactly when she was almost there. He'd tighten his grip and her face would go an unattractive mottled red and she'd wheeze, her eyes wide open but somewhere far away.

They played Ennis. A home game, an unseasonably warm night. August battled with the Ennis end all game. He was huge, six six at least and not skinny, either. The rumor was that he'd had offers from D-1 teams, and all night he thwarted August's efforts to penetrate the line. Late in the third quarter the fullback broke through a hole and sprinted down the left sideline for a touchdown. August, away from the play, saw the giant end loping down the field, already celebrating his team's score. August had the angle. He came from ten yards away and blindsided him, sending him sprawling into the bench on his team's sideline.

There was a whistle. August got an unsportsmanlike conduct penalty. Coach Zwicky pulled him off the field. Grabbed him by the face mask. "I appreciate the energy," he said. "But that's not how we do things here and you know it, son. Go back in the next series and do it the right way."

August went back in and the Ennis tight end owned him for the rest of the game. The guy was huge, and now he was pissed off. Afterward, August sat in the locker room taking his pads off slowly, the stiffness already coming on. He felt like he'd been trampled by an angry crowd.

That night Julie came over. When he was on top of her he felt an extra slickness: a coppery smell filled the room. She was on her period, and as he looked down he saw the sides of her thighs were smeared with it. "Is it okay?" he said, slowing, causing her to clench her legs, her heels hooking around his buttocks, drawing him deeper. "If you stop now I'm going to kill you," she said. Afterward they took a shower and did it again, standing, the water running pink down the drain. They threw the sheets on the floor and slept rolled up in the comforter. And that was the last time.

In the morning, Julie left early, as she normally did. August ate half a box of cereal and watched some TV. He was coming down the stairs, heading to the laundry room with his arms full of blood-stained bedding, when his mother came through the door. He tried to turn but there was no way to hide it. "Jesus," she said. "What happened on your bed?"

He could think of nothing immediately. "I cut myself," he said finally. He walked past her to the laundry room and he could feel her watching him. He started the machine, and when he came out to the kitchen she was sitting at the table, arms crossed over her chest.

"Kind of a cheap shot you gave that guy last night," she said.

August shrugged. "The guy was a giant. I couldn't do anything with him. I thought I might shake him up. Didn't work. You saw it. He kicked my ass for the rest of the game, so he got the last laugh, I guess."

"Okay," his mother said. "Fair enough. Where'd you cut yourself?" She was staring at him. Unblinking. He went to the sink for a glass of water to break her gaze. He looked out the window and drained his glass. "Don't worry about it," he said. "Not a big deal."

"You didn't cut yourself."

"I did, actually."

"I know exactly what it was on those sheets. You can't even look at me."

"It's really none of your business. Live your life. I'm doing fine in mine."

"This can't continue," she said. "I will be calling her."

"Calling who? Okay, so what? I had a girl over last night. It's someone from school. We hang out occasionally. It's life. People have sex."

"It is life, you're exactly right. And if I thought it was someone from school I wouldn't be all that concerned, or even surprised. But I know damn well who it is, so we can just stop pretending. Listen, Augie, I'm not mad at you at all. You've done what probably every seventeen-year-old boy in the world would do if given the chance. The problem is not you. The problem is her. She's closer to thirty than she is twenty. She does not need to be messing around with high schoolers. Not my son, anyway. You're not playing on the same level. You may think you are, but you're not. Trust me."

"What? You mean, you think it was Julie? Is that what you're saying? You're crazy."

"Stop it." She stood, came to him, reaching for his hand. Her voice was soft now. "I'm not mad. I love you more than anything, and that's why I have to step in here. It's not right. It just really isn't. Not her with you. It will only end one way."

August pulled his hand away. "She's leaving anyway. What does it matter? We like each other. So what?"

"Oh, Augie. She and I talk all the time. She tells me things. Her *guys.*

That's what she calls them. One in Bozeman, a lawyer. There's a bartender here in town, maybe another one occasionally, he's a fishing guide, I think. What she does is her business. I don't judge her; she's casual and having fun and that's fine, but when it involves my underage son it's different. I'm going to call her right now. This is done."

August knew she was lying. She was saying these things to him as a way to break them up. He was out the door, slamming into his pickup, burning out the driveway, knowing for sure that it was probably all true.

He didn't speak to his mother for days and then, for a long time after that, nothing more than necessary. She told him that Julie had left early for New York. "She called to apologize to me, and I suggested it to her," she said. "She told me to tell you that she had shown some bad judgment, and she hopes you don't think badly of her." August turned and walked out of the room without acknowledging her words.

She was on him constantly to complete his application to Montana State. Because he wouldn't do it himself, she filled out the paperwork so all he had to do was sign. Every morning there was an argument, and finally he acquiesced. He signed all the forms. He took the envelope to the post office and he threw it away.

Football wound down. He started attending the postgame bonfires, drinking whatever booze the guys had managed to procure. He'd ended up having a decent season but not the one his coaches had hoped for based on his junior year. The team finished with a losing record, and on the last bus ride home after the final game, all he felt was relief that from now on he wouldn't have to suit up for practice or smell the rancid interior of the boys' locker room.

For most of his school career he'd gotten comfortable Bs and As without trying too hard. His senior year he pulled a few Cs intermixed with his Bs. Possibly this was due to Julie or the fact that high school was all but over, or that when he tried to do the reading his eyes tended to swim and the slow pulse of a headache would build.

He occasionally had dreams about playing still, scrabbling toward a quarterback who remained just out of reach, the field shifting and unsteady under his feet. Mostly he had dreams about her. Winter came, and it seemed that since she'd left, a certain quality of light had been bled from the world.

II

T O AUGUST, THE FACT that he was born in the Midwest was starting to lose its importance. At some point, the place you're from takes on an abstract quality. Maybe those were the formative years, but they seem less and less real. He'd always heard that the human body is 70 percent water. When he looked at his hand, he couldn't see evidence of that any more than he could consider his childhood and determine what effect it had on the current shape of his life.

Whenever his father called, he made sure to let August know that if he didn't go to college he'd need to be finding a job, and that he had plenty of work for him if he decided to come back. He never came right out and said that he was struggling to get everything done around the place, but August could tell that he wanted him to think that was the case.

Of course, August knew his father wasn't all alone back there. Once when he called, August heard a woman's voice in the background. It was almost ten at night, and he could picture his father sitting in the kitchen, the old yellow phone's cord stretched all the way over to the table. He could picture the room exactly. What he couldn't picture was the woman. It wasn't Lisa, or at least it didn't sound like her. He heard her speak briefly in the background. She'd said, *Babe, do you want it with butter, or plain?* August considered himself an adult, basically, and it didn't bother him too much. But still, his father had a woman he'd never met making him his popcorn, calling him *babe*.

August was starting to think people were inscrutable at heart. He hadn't forgiven his mother for running Julie off, but eventually they reached a sort of uneasy truce that allowed them to live together. It was easy to think that, because they birth you, you get some sort of access to their inner life. If anything, August thought the opposite was more true. He'd spent nine months next to her heart, and now it seemed like she was going to live the rest of her life with a faint air of embarrassment, covering her tracks, worried about what he might have heard in there.

August was still fighting with her about college. At this point, continuing with school seemed like handing his mother a victory in the ill-defined battle they'd been engaged in since Julie left. She'd called the Montana State registrar and was furious when they told her no application had been filed under his name. He'd instead decided that he wanted to be a wildlands firefighter or possibly go work in the Wyoming oil fields, like Gaskill's older brother, who'd returned to town with a brand-new truck. Said he was going back and could get August on.

This was two years after 9/11 and the military recruiters still came to August's high school at least once a week, smelling blood. As a senior August could sign up for the National Guard and they'd give him four thousand dollars just as soon as he passed the test. *Put your time in,* they'd say, *just a few years, and then when you get out we'll pay for your school. You want to go to college, son, don't you? Of course you do. But how are you going to pay for that? You're an upstanding young man, I can tell. You expect your parents to foot the bill? Are you going to take out loans?*

August saw through that whole game pretty quickly. Probably thanks to his mother, he had to admit. She still spent weekends with Art, but on weeknights she made August watch Bill O'Reilly with her. She'd sit on the couch, smoking, emitting a small noise of disgust with each drag. When the show was over, she'd switch off the TV, mix herself a drink, and tune in the radio to the NPR station out of Billings.

They'd sit in silence and listen to the BBC World News. She never said anything, allowing him to formulate his own opinions.

August didn't figure that there was much formulating in him at all until Ramsay got blown up. He had four younger brothers. His mother weighed three hundred pounds and hardly ever left the house. His old man drove long-haul trucks, only came home every couple of weeks. Ramsay had been smart enough to go to college anywhere, for free, probably, but he had to do the weekly grocery shopping for his mom, had to clean up after his brothers. In other words, he wasn't listening to BBC World News on NPR. He'd taken the four thousand dollars. He'd come back from that first deployment with burns over 70 percent of his body and died at a military hospital somewhere in Texas. August still couldn't quite figure out what exact part of a National Guardsman's duty involved riding in a Hummer in Afghanistan. The brochures the recruiting officers gave out showed smiling young men and women in fatigues handing one another sandbags while flood-stricken locals stood by, gratitude written all over their faces.

After Ramsay, everything seemed desperate somehow. It was as if August and all the guys he knew had caught something. One of their own would never be coming back, and that first encounter with the enemy, that taste of mortality, had left everyone a bit unhinged.

***

August never really knew June that well, but she seemed to exist on some higher plane than everyone else in school. Maybe she wasn't a knockout beauty—she didn't have one of those austere faces that you see in magazines. She was, however, extraordinarily cute. Small, blond, upturned nose, huge blue eyes. And her voice: not high and girly like you might think from looking at her. It was kind of raspy, soft, but rough somehow. Like she got her full-grown woman's voice early. She was smart, too, but different from Ramsay, in that she took it seriously. She was valedictorian, and everyone knew that was going to be the case from about the second day of freshman year.

She might have been small, but she was immaculately formed. She was on the volleyball team, and they wore those spandex shorts. August remembered seeing an unusual number of local guys around for home games, dudes who couldn't tell you the difference between a set and a spike. They ate popcorn and made jokes about the kneepads while watching June flip her long hair out of her face brusquely and squat low, swaying side to side a little, waiting for the serve.

At the end of their senior year, she got accepted into Brown. No one was completely sure where Brown was, but there was the general sense that it was prestigious. Most people who were going to college were heading to the state schools in Bozeman or Missoula. But June, she was going to Brown. At one point August looked it up. Rhode Island. A state hardly even as big as Sweet Grass County. She never made a big deal out of it, but it was one of those things that took her out of the town's stratosphere, placed her in slightly more rarified air.

People used to call him Augie, but as of late he'd been discouraging it, because he thought it sounded like something you might name a small puppy that will grow up to be a useless dog. His mother still called him Augie. His father had always called him August. In a roundabout way, his name was the way he finally met June.

As far as he knew, he'd been in school for two years before she knew he existed. He was walking back to the locker room from football practice, and she was in her car about to leave. She had a red Mazda Miata. Her dad was part owner of a car dealership in Billings and got it for her on her sixteenth birthday. She had the window down, and when August walked by she whistled to get his attention.

"Hey," she said. "August, right? Too bad your name's not July." These were literally the first words she'd ever spoken to him.

"Yeah?" he said. "Why?"

"Then maybe I'd let you come after me."

And then she drove off, a little blond girl in a little red car, hair whipping out the window, laughing hysterically.

No one would say that June was a complete good girl. There were rumors. Her parents were strict Catholics, and, of course, she was saving herself for marriage. But she had the Catholic knack for finding loopholes.

"She gives blow jobs," Gaskill said once while he and August were drinking warm beer, stolen from Old Man Gaskill, sitting on his dropped tailgate by the river. "I've confirmed it."

"Yeah, who says?"

"My cousin goes to school down at MSU. I guess she's been around a little bit down there. College dudes. They don't put up with that I'm-waiting-for-marriage bullshit. You know what else I heard?"

"What?"

"Just because the front door is locked doesn't mean the back door isn't wide open."

"No way."

"Seriously. I heard that. She's still a virgin, though, technically. It doesn't count."

"Oh, come on."

"No shit."

August didn't believe him, not really, but still. He'd see her—walking the halls, her girlfriends around her like a protective shell, or at volleyball practice when he was heading out to the football field—and he'd wonder.

What happened was, they had a party for Ramsay. On a weekend, not long after graduation, they draped his casket with the flag and lowered his remains into the ground, and that night there was a bonfire by the river. Gaskill's dad worked for the phone company and always had chunks of telephone pole lying around. Telephone poles soaked in creosote—there was not much better for building a monumental bonfire. They made a scaffold of poles that was fifteen feet high, and the whole time they worked they didn't once mention Ramsay. August didn't know what the other guys were thinking. Personally, he was trying to remember the last thing he'd ever said to Ramsay, but he couldn't. For some reason August thought that maybe if he could just remember the final words to ever pass between them, he'd be better able to classify what Ramsay's death meant. Because, as it was, he didn't know what to think.

He wasn't going around saying that Ramsay had been his best friend or anything like that—unlike some other people. After this whole thing, he'd have to say that nothing increased your popularity like dying. What did he know about Ramsay, really, when it came down to it? He was a tall, skinny kid. So pale his nickname had been Casper. He'd been on the football team, a mediocre wideout. He'd run track, too, and had been better at that. The truth was, Ramsay and August had just hung out together occasionally. It might have been easier if they had been close; at least then August wouldn't have had to wonder how much grief was enough.

At the time, their telephone-pole monument seemed like an appropriate act of memorial to their friend. Everyone agreed that Ramsay had always loved setting shit on fire. They waited till dark, doused it with gasoline, and then torched it. The blaze came up taller than the cottonwoods, and people couldn't stand within twenty feet of the thing without the heat curling their hair. Flames licked at the treetops, toxic clouds of creosote smoke shifted and pulsed—it was magnificent.

Everyone came. Kids no one even knew were there. It was the only party August could remember from that summer where the cops didn't show up to harass them. It was like the town itself had decided to let the kids get Ramsay out of their systems the only way they knew how. And they did some of that, August figured, but mostly everyone just got drunk as monkeys.

Veldtkamp was back from summer practices in Missoula—he'd gotten a full-ride scholarship to U of M. He was staggering around with a bottle of Jack Daniel's, shouting, "Calvin Ramsay was an American hero." Trying to fight several people who didn't display what he thought was a proper level of enthusiastic agreement.

Richards burned the shit out of himself trying to jump over the flames shooting from a fallen pole, and some guys had to tackle him to put out the fire that blossomed on his shirt.

It was sometime during this that June showed up. She was with a guy no one recognized. He was older, midtwenties at least. He had a faint look of disdain on his face and refused to shotgun a beer, and it wasn't long before the taillights of his car were seen fading down the river road.

But June stayed. She was wearing a dress and her bare legs were tan, red-brown in the firelight. August watched her standing there with some of her girlfriends. They were all laughing and talking loud, everyone was; the fire burned with a low roar that people had to shout over to be heard. But even so, it seemed that June was overdoing it somehow. Her laughs were the loudest, lasted the longest.

"What the fuck?" he heard her say once, her head thrown back and her eyes half-closed, an incredulous look. "I mean, really, what the *fuck*?"

A few guys had gone in on a half gallon of Southern Comfort one hundred proof. They filled a cooler with ice and dumped in the whiskey and mixed in a few cans of pineapple juice. Gaskill stole his mother's turkey baster, and he and August walked around the party with the cooler, offering up shots.

They got to June's group, and the girls tilted their heads back one after another so Eddy could shoot a turkey baster's worth of the booze down their throats. Laughing, coughing, swearing. Everyone sticky with pineapple juice. When it was June's turn, she said, "For Ramsay," the way everyone had been doing all night long. *For Ramsay, for Ramsay, for Ramsay.* It was a mantra, a chant, a motto, a rallying cry, a failed attempt to raise the dead. August had taken the baster from Gaskill so he could do June, and she tilted her head back and he could see the cords of her throat work as he squeezed the bulb. Her head was at his shoulder, her hair full of static, reaching out, clinging to the hair on his arm.

When it was done she wiped at her mouth with the back of her hand. "One more," she said, smiling, juice glistening on her chin.

There was drunkenness, screaming, laughing, dancing. Dust rose and swirled in angry red columns across the fire. In the general devolution that followed, August saw June kiss one of her girlfriends, on the lips, while everyone watched. Then a while later she kissed Veldtkamp, then Richards, then Gaskill, and then Veldtkamp again. By now her girlfriends had faded away. She was sitting on the ground, laughing maybe, or crying. No, definitely laughing. And then Veldtkamp had her over his shoulder, and she was giggling, and then she was limp, her hair almost dragging into the dirt.

The fire was at the back now. They were underneath the cottonwoods, the soft midnight sounds that cicadas make. August could smell the river moving out in the darkness, damp and black. Veldtkamp had lifted June and just started walking, and a few guys were following, and then he swore and dropped her. August could see a yellow line of her vomit trailing down his back. He took off his shirt and threw it into the bushes.

She was sitting, legs spread, her hair in her eyes. Her dress was pushed all the way up on her thighs, one of the straps fallen off her shoulder. The guys all stood around her. August was there, too. She was making a noise, moving a little, scooting, maybe trying to get up. Veldtkamp knelt next to her, bare chested, weight-room-inflated muscles popping out all over the place. He pulled the top of her dress down and exposed her breasts. There was nervous laughter.

"Holy shit," someone said.

June made no move to cover herself. She wiped at her mouth with the inside of her elbow, said something unintelligible. Veldtkamp was still crouching next to her. His hand was up under her dress, moving between her thighs, and she groaned and slumped so she was leaning back on her elbows. And then Veldtkamp was standing unsteadily. Looking around as if noticing the spectators for the first time. He weaved a little and fumbled with his zipper.

"Well? How about it? For our boy Ramsay," he said.

For Ramsay. Someone else said it, and then someone after that. Jostling. Laughter. August was at the back but eventually he was at the front. The group had shifted to circle her and everyone who was there was there all the way. June in the dirt. Swaying on hands and knees, back arched with a moan, eyes closed, cheek pressed to the leaves.

When it was August's turn, June had gone silent; no longer able to maintain hands and knees she slumped to her side. She'd vomited again and he could smell it on his hands, and at this he faltered.

"Looks like Augie's got himself a case of the whiskey dick," someone said. August wiped his palms on his jeans and finally June rolled onto her back and spit, badly, so most of it glistened down her chin and neck. She opened her eyes and looked at him. She laughed. And then her whole body convulsed in a dry heave. August broke away, hobbling at first, hitching his pants, running headlong into the dark, the cotton-wood branches clutching at him. He ran until he tripped and fell. He was far out, away from the party that was all but done anyway. He couldn't hear voices. He could see the vague outlines of the trees, and he could still see the fire.

For some reason, lying there was where it came to him. The last thing he'd ever said to Ramsay. It had been after that float trip. They'd come back to town and stopped for burgers at Mark's In and Out. They were sitting at a picnic table outside bullshitting, as usual, but Ramsay wasn't really talking. He was tapping his fork on the table, staring at it. Someone threw an empty fry container at him to get him to stop, and he kind of shook his head and came to. Up until this point everyone had been talking about girls or football or something. But Ramsay looked around, his hand still rapping his fork on the table like he couldn't stop himself.

"If you could do this an infinite number of times," he said, "eventually it would fall right through to the other side. We learned about it in physics last year. I was just thinking about it for some reason."

Everyone was looking at him, wondering what in the hell he was talking about.

"Yeah," he said, dropping the fork. "It has to do with the vibration of particles. Everything vibrates, and if all the particles making up this fork were to zig when the particles of the table were zagging, *bam*. Fork right through table."

"Oh, bullshit," August had said. "No way. What keeps us from falling right through the earth?"

Then Ramsay lowered his sunglasses and looked over the rims. "It's theoretical, dumbass." And then he looked over August's shoulder. "Speaking of ass," he said. And everyone turned to watch Ms. Moore, the new gym teacher, jogging down the sidewalk in her yoga pants, headphones on. After that they went their separate ways. Ramsay walked off down the street, out of Montana, and, after a certain length of time, onto an IED.

That was what it was, and there'd never be a chance for revision. The permanent stupidity of this made August's eyes water. From where he'd fallen he watched as the scaffold of telephone poles collapsed, sending a billowing cloud of sparks two stories high.

The morning after the party, August and a few of the guys went for breakfast. They sat in the truck-stop diner, hungover, eating biscuits and gravy. Not talking, other than to ask for the salt or pepper or butter, and even this was oddly formal. Some of the guys had known one another since birth practically, and this morning they ate like strangers.

"That damn Southern Comfort," someone said. "I feel like shit." Everyone groaned, as if that was the real source of the problem. There was a *Billings Gazette* in the booth, and August flipped through it. On the second page was a picture of June's father. He had just been indicted for allegedly embezzling close to half a million dollars from his partner in the car dealership. He passed it around.

"Jesus," he said. "No wonder she got so wasted last night. She must have just found out about it."

Everyone nodded, shook their heads. It all kind of made sense.

August didn't see June again for the rest of that summer. No one did, really. He got a job out at the Heart K Ranch, doing grunt work around the place. A lot of fencing. He'd set out on the four-wheeler and be gone all day, twisting broken wire back together, resetting posts. He was still living at home but was hardly there. Most of the time he'd get done working and crash on a cot in the back of the tack room.

His mother had been bringing Art around more often. August had the general sense that she was trying to press the three of them into some sort of familial unit. She had Art over for dinner frequently and she always invited August to stay, but he'd make up excuses to be gone. Sometimes, seeing Art's car in the driveway, August would just turn around and go back to the Heart K—lie down on his cot and breathe in the smell of leather and horse sweat leaking from the saddles.

August called his father to tell him that he'd found a job.

"It's been a hot one, this summer," his father said. "We had a week straight of midnineties. You been getting that out there?"

"Not that bad. People are worried about how dry it is, though. Feels like the whole place could go up in smoke at any minute. The place I'm working has me cutting brush away from the buildings, cutting the tall grass. We've got hoses ready in case we have to wet down the roofs. There's a lot of outbuildings, though. It's a pretty big spread."

"Oh yeah? A *spread*. Sounds better than a little old farm."

"It's different out here."

"I wouldn't know. It might not be a *spread*, but you've got a place back here. Seems ridiculous to be working for another man when you could be part owner of something that's rightfully yours. Am I that bad?"

August wanted to tell him about the silent presence of the mountains, about going out to work every day under a great blue shifting tarp of sky. Instead, he told his father he had a girlfriend. It seemed like something he'd be more likely to understand.

"Well, shit," he said, his voice changing. "Why didn't you just say so? I guess I'm not surprised. You have yourself a little cowgirl?"

"Something like that."

"What's her name?"

"June."

He laughed. "Well, if you get married and have a few girls you can name them April, May, and July and you'll have all the pleasant months covered."

"I don't think that's going to happen anytime soon."

"Well, be smart. That's all I'm going to say. And you could come back for a visit, you know? I'll send you money for a plane ticket this fall. We could go hunting. Maybe Thanksgiving?"

August told him sure, and when he hung up he realized he hadn't really asked his father anything about *him*. This was a relatively new thing, the knowledge that his father was something other than just his father. He had a separate life, a unique existence, one that August might inquire about. He couldn't say for sure what had done it but there had been a shift, and for the first time August knew he would never go back to stay.

August kept busy at the ranch and didn't see his old crew too much, but even so, he couldn't help but hear things. Toward September, word was that June had just resurfaced. August saw her once. He was driving through town and she was walking into the movie theater, with Veldtkamp of all people. He couldn't believe it. He braked so hard the car behind him almost hit his bumper. He saw her for only a second, and she was turning away. Veldtkamp had his hand on her waist.

August found out later that they were dating. He also heard that Veldtkamp had fought and successfully beat up every other guy that had been there that night. And that he was looking for August.

In a small town a person could run for only so long. August knew that if Veldtkamp was dead set on it, he'd catch him eventually. If it was just a matter of taking a minor ass-beating, August might have come out some night when there was a party. Let him puff and blow for a bit in front of everyone; take a few shots before the guys dragged him off. It would be worth it to just have the whole thing finished. The problem was that August was the last one. Once Veldtkamp settled with August, possibly he'd be able to put it to rest in his mind. This was what bothered August the most. The fact that, after punching him out, Veldtkamp might just be able to forget about the whole thing.

Veldtkamp was saying August wouldn't even come into town because he was so scared. August didn't try to explain himself. Even to

Gaskill, who tried to give August some boxing pointers that he'd learned from his dad, who'd won a Golden Gloves tournament in Helena twenty-some years ago. "Just jab with the left," he said. "Jab-jab-jab, to set up the distance, and drop the right. That's the finisher."

"All right, Tyson," August said. "Is that what you did when he called *you* out?"

"Tried. He just body-slammed me. You can't let it ruin your life, man. Take a couple swings. Maybe you'll get a black eye. It's not that big of a deal."

The day August found the buffalo jump was the same one that Veldtkamp finally caught up to him. He'd been out on the backside of Baldy, riding the fence line, when he came across it. No one on the ranch ever told him it was there. He felt like, at the very least, he'd rediscovered it for his generation, and that gave him some sort of ownership. Just from walking around he could get a pretty good sense of how it worked. They had rocks and sticks and stuff piled up so it was like a funnel. This was what caught August's attention at first. It was all still there—two parallel lines of stones and bleached-out juniper stumps, tightening in, narrower and narrower the closer you got to the lip. The Crow would get up there on top of the butte and hide under buffalo skins, waiting to chase the herd over the edge.

August parked his four-wheeler and scrambled around the sagebrush to the steep face of the butte. The buffalo bones were thick, sun-bleached white. He could see butcher marks on some of them, the places where the knife had scraped the flesh loose. There were scapulae as big as shovel blades, ribs like scattered parentheses. Mostly, though, just countless unidentifiable broken bits and pieces. He kicked his way through the rubble on his way up to the top, a hollow clacking sound, bone against bone, grinding under his boots, the sound of it rising up against the face of the cliff, magnifying somehow, until it seemed that the buffalo had risen, were coming down the hill again, a skeleton herd racing toward doom with the wind whistling through the empty sockets of their skulls.

When he got all the way up to where it was grassy and flat, he sat with his legs kicking over the edge, looking down at the white jumble of old buffalo parts below him. It was like death's own mosaic down there. He squinted for a long time, trying to find a pattern in all the nonsense. He thought that if he could just see June and talk to her. If he could just ask her something. He'd say, *Did you used to have a yellow one-piece swimsuit? Did you ever do flips off the railroad trestle into the river? Did your hair ever come down to your lower back, and did you wear it in a braid? Do you know that I saw you and I'm sorry?*

He made up his mind right then that he was going to leave. It was hard to explain, but he got a real strong feeling that he'd just stumbled onto the last thing in this country worth discovering, and he might stay around for the rest of his life and he wouldn't happen upon anything even half as good.

The sun was setting by the time he made it back to the pole barn at the ranch. He parked the four-wheeler and threw his gear into the truck. It was a decent enough evening to part ways with the Heart K, he thought. The sky, like a tangerine had split and was leaking all over it; the windmill clattering in the breeze, a couple of the horses rolling in the dust of the corral. He'd be happy to find another job like it, exactly the same, just somewhere else.

Veldtkamp was waiting for August at the end of the ranch driveway. His Camaro was parked next to the cattle guard. A purple Camaro. Rear-wheel drive in a state where the snow was ass-deep by Thanksgiving. He was out leaning against the door and straightened up at the sight of August's truck. When August rolled to a stop he was at the window.

"Get out so we can talk," he said.

"I guess we can talk just like this."

"You holier-than-thou little shit. Just because you ran off doesn't mean you're above it all."

"It was your idea."

"Get out."

"I'm not getting out."

Veldtkamp started to try to drag August from the truck. His hands found August's shoulder and the collar of his jacket. August pulled away just enough that Veldtkamp's head was almost inside the cab of the truck, and then he punched the gas. For a moment Veldtkamp was clutching August's arm, and then his feet got tangled and he went down and there was a thump, the back of the truck jumping like August had hit a pothole, except it wasn't a pothole, because Veldtkamp screamed. August didn't look in the rearview. He went home to pack a bag.

When August came down the stairs from his room, his mother was sitting at the kitchen table. She'd made him a sandwich. It was there on the table, chips, a pickle, the whole nine yards. August was itching to be gone. He could still feel that thump—could hear Veldtkamp scream. His leg for sure. Maybe his knee. He'd been one of the first guys to be decent to August when he'd moved to town. They used to go out at lunch and throw the football around. Veldtkamp had earned that full ride.

August put his bag down and sat. His boot was tapping on the floor. He'd make it stop and then it would start again without him even realizing it.

"Are you going somewhere?"

He'd planned on telling her that he was just taking some clothes and stuff over to the ranch. But he'd never lied much to his mom. "I guess so," he said.

"Are you going back to be with your dad?"

August could see how much it took for her to ask this question. "Nah. I think I'm going in the other direction."

"Okay. Because I'd understand if you wanted to do that. I'm not saying you shouldn't."

"It's fine, Mom. I'm not going back there."

"What about school this fall?"

"I don't think it's for me."

"So you've thought about it, really thought about it?"

"I have. Seems like something people do to put off actually doing something."

"And that's your conclusion?"

"For now."

"Eat your sandwich before the mustard makes the bread soggy."

August did, and she sat watching him, smoking. When he got up to leave she went to the fridge, came back with a grocery bag full of individually foil-wrapped sandwiches. She must have heard him packing and known all along he was leaving. She'd used up a whole loaf of bread. She gave them to him with a hug. "Goddamn it, Augie," she said. "You had better remember to call your mother."

After two cold, monotonous months on a rig outside of Casper, August quit without giving notice. Forfeited a small amount of due pay. Just drove. For a while he found temporary work on a ranch near Buffalo. It was a small place at the foot of the Bighorns. The foreman had broken his leg in a car accident, and he needed help getting things done. It was midwinter now, short days, the wind punching sharp and metallic from the high country. In the mornings August took the tractor out to spread last summer's alfalfa hay in long rows on the wind-scoured winter pasture. The cattle gathering to feed, the gray fog of the tractor's exhaust, the gray fog of the cattle's breath, the gray fog strung along the cottonwoods that hid the river. In a sophomore English class he'd taken at Park High, Mrs. Defrain was always going on about the objective correlative. As far as he could tell, it was just a fancy-sounding name for a trick writers used to portray a mood in their characters. August was starting to think that whoever was penning his life's plot needed to experiment with a different tactic. Maybe some magical realism. June sprouting the wings of a dove, flying low to him so her feathers ruffled his hair. Maybe Julie rising from the ashes of a cold, dead fire to roll with him in snow that melted under the heat of their conjoined bodies, the sun finally rising, the water flowing warm as blood, yet barely able to slake the ravenous thirst of the flowering love trees that were taking root, growing, blossoming, enveloping them.

When the ranch foreman had mended enough to climb up on the tractor, August collected his pay and headed back to his mother's for the holidays. He kept to himself. Slept late and ate too much, spent the afternoons scanning the classifieds. Not long after the new year, he drove north toward Great Falls, passing through all the dead and dying little towns—Clyde Park, Wilsall, Ringling. Towns in the sense that the signs proclaiming their existence were still standing, if nothing much else. Shells of crumbling houses, train depots, grain elevators with pigeons wheeling from under the eaves.

In the back of his truck August had two duffel bags full of clothes, and on the seat next to him he had another sack of foil-wrapped sandwiches from his mother. Ham and cheese and raw onion on wheat with Dijon. He'd eaten two of them already and drained a thermos of coffee. Willie Nelson on the radio coming slightly scratchy from a Billings station.

He had the directions to the Virostok Ranch written down and he read them just to hear the sound out loud. "*On 89, head north to 294, then take 294 until you get to Martinsdale. In Martinsdale, hang a left at the blinking light and go five miles until you see the turnoff for Old Smith Road. Go right on Old Smith Road. It turns to gravel in a mile, and then after that go eight more miles. Crest a big hill, and just after, hang a left at the Virostok Angus sign. Head on up to the main house.*"

Nearly twenty miles out of town on dirt roads. And Martinsdale, the nearest town, wasn't much of a town to begin with. He tried to sing along with Willie but his voice cracked like always, and so he unwrapped another sandwich, wishing he had more coffee.

The Virostok ranch house was tucked back into a small depression in the hills. A white two-story Victorian with a wraparound porch, one winter away from needing a new coat of paint. Off to the side of the house there was a pole barn and a corral with a big chestnut gelding standing swaybacked in the weak sun. There was an older Subaru wagon in the driveway. An unstacked pile of firewood with a splitting maul stuck in a big cottonwood round. August parked next to the

Subaru and got out, stretching. Smoke was rising from the chimney of the house in a gray pillar. There was no doorbell, so August stood on the slightly warped boards of the porch and knocked. He could hear music coming from inside. It was faint, but it sounded like rap, lots of bass.

After another few knocks the door opened and a woman stepped out onto the porch. She was wearing workout clothes—black leggings and a purple tank top. Her sandy-blond hair was held back by a head-band. She had wide hips, a small bust, almost no taper at the waist—a sturdy keg of a woman, approaching forty years old by the looks of it, with a fine layer of sweat on her bare arms, droplets clinging to downy hairs on her upper lip.

"Oh, hey," she said. "Sorry. I was on the elliptical and didn't hear you at first." She held out her hand. "I'm Kim, Ancient's fiancée. He had to go to the hardware store but he told me the new hand might be pulling in soon. August, right?"

"Yep."

"You find the place all right?"

"No problems. Easy enough."

"Where you from, August?"

"I drove up from Livingston. That's where I've been living for a few years. But I'm from Michigan, originally."

"Oh, Livingston's a nice little town. I almost moved down there years ago to get my master's at MSU. That place is crazy about fishing. It's amazing how people travel from all over the world to go to Yellow-stone to catch a dinky trout and put it back. You like fishing?"

"It's okay. I go sometimes."

She laughed. "Well, we got the Musselshell up here. In the spring it's a muddy mess, in the summer it's pretty much dry, in the winter it's frozen. Someone told me there's fish in it, but I'm not sure how."

"Probably some catfish, at least. A catfish can pretty much live in anything."

Kim was looking past August, and he could see the distance her eyes traveled, over his shoulder, over the brown fields, out to the low moun-tain range to the south.

"I guess if you don't have a little catfish in you you're bound for misery up here," she said, shaking her head. "Let me get my boots on and I'll walk you over to your room." She went back inside and reemerged in rubber muck boots and a down jacket. August got his bags from the truck and followed her across the yard to the pole barn. In the back there was an apartment with a couple of small windows, a patio made of flat cement pavers, and a gas grill.

She flicked on the fluorescent lights. There was a bunk bed along one wall. Concrete floors with an assortment of carpet remnants for rugs. A sink and a small set of cupboards. A two-burner hot plate and a half-sized refrigerator/freezer. There was a round table with a single chair. The walls were fresh white, unadorned except for a calendar from Western LP Gas, from last year, and a framed cross-stitch that read IF YOU'RE NOT GOD OR GEORGE STRAIT, TAKE YOUR BOOTS OFF!

"No frills," Kim said. "But it's comfortable enough. Feel free to do whatever you want to make it yours. Paint, or get a couch, or hang stuff up, or whatever."

August dropped his two duffels. "I'm not too picky. Looks fine to me as is," he said.

"No TV," she said. "I'm not sure if Ancient told you that when you talked to him."

"I'll survive."

"I guess you and Ancient will hit it off, then. He doesn't care about TV one way or another. His idea of entertainment is changing the oil on a tractor. He wanted me to get you started on that pile of firewood out front. I told him that you'd probably want to take a little rest and relax when you got here, but he said it wasn't like you'd caught a redeye from Tokyo. Working for him can be a real treat," she said. "You'll find that out, I imagine."

"He's paying me to work," August said. "I've got nothing else to do. Where does he want it stacked?"

"There's a spot around the side of the house, a lean-to with a concrete pad. You'll see it. There's a wheelbarrow there, too."

"Okay, I'll just get my stuff straightened out and I'll get to it."

"Well, there's no hurry, I'm sure. Oh, and I'll be making some dinner tonight. Why don't you come up to the house around six? Usually you'll be on your own for food, and God knows you'll be happy enough to get a break from Ancient's cantankerous ass, but since it's your first day I thought it would be nice to have a little get-to-know-you meal. Pork chops and green beans, salad and some cornbread."

"Sounds good. Thank you."

"All right then, I'll leave you to it. Going to get my butt back on the elliptical." She paused with her hand on the doorknob and didn't say anything for a moment. "You got a girlfriend back home?"

"Nope. Haven't found the time recently."

"I doubt you'll find many alluring prospects up here. Does Livingston still have all the trains coming through? I remember how loud that was. They'd blow their horn three times at the crossing, and it was enough to rattle your fillings if you happened to be standing out on the street."

"Yeah, that's still going on. More than ever. They got coal trains heading to Portland now. Seems like a constant stream of them."

"That must be pretty special."

"You get used to it."

"Well, that's how it is up here, too. Except for it's not trains, it's silence. I've been up here for a year now, and it's like the Grand Central Station of silence. I'm sure I'll get used to it at some point, but I'm still waiting."

When Kim left, August unpacked his jeans and shirts and refolded them into the dresser drawers. He hung his lined Carhartt jacket on the rack next to the door and dug through the smaller pockets of his duffel for his deerskin work gloves. He sat on the bottom bunk for a moment and then leaned back, fingers laced behind his head. He was over six feet tall and several inches of him hung over the foot of the bed, but the mattress was firm and felt new. The top blanket was wool, a diamond Indian-style pattern on it. There were two pillows. They were crisp and felt new as well. He heaved to his feet, and before heading out the door, he took down the UNLESS YOU'RE GOD OR GEORGE cross-stitch and slid it under the bottom bunk. He put the outdated Western LP Gas calendar in the trash. The walls were blank now save for the two nails. He went out and got to work.

The logs were already cut to stove length; they just needed to be split. It was pine of some kind, straight grained and sticky with pitch. They were quick to cleave, flying apart with a satisfying crack at the head of the maul. August fell into an easy rhythm, warming a little with the exertion, rolling the sleeves of his flannel up over his elbows.

He split two wheelbarrows full and carted them over to the lean-to. He made square end-stacks and then started filling in between them. He'd worked his way through half the woodpile when a flatbed Ford pulled in and parked next to the Subaru. The man who got out wore jeans and a fleece-lined jean jacket, a silk scarf knotted up at his throat and a battered wool Stormy Kromer hat. He was younger than August had imagined he would be—midthirties at the oldest. August took off his gloves and leaned the maul against his knee.

"Unless you're the firewood fairy, I'm going to guess that you're August?" August nodded, and they shook hands. "I'm Ancient Virostok," the man said. "Welcome aboard the good ship Virostok. As of this moment we're managing to stay above water." Ancient regarded the pile of split wood and nudged a piece with his boot. "Looks like Kim got you lined out on the firewood. I appreciate you getting right to it."

August shrugged. "I've never minded splitting firewood."

"I hear you there. That's a task that I almost hate to delegate. You know what they say about splitting firewood?"

"Maybe."

"It warms you twice."

"My old man always says that."

"Sounds like an intelligent person. You told me when we talked on the phone, you're originally from the Midwest somewhere, right? Wisconsin?"

"Michigan. Pretty much the same."

"Your old man's got a little spread back there, you said?"

"Farm. He does dairy."

"I hope you don't think it's me prying, but I'm just curious. Seems funny to work on another man's place when you got one in the family. You and the old man at odds?"

"Some. I don't much like dairy. And I like it out here." August gestured vaguely behind him at the hills. "Sun comes out more." He nodded at the woodpile. "We don't burn pine back there. It's all oak and maple. Hardwood. Crooked grain. Hard on tools."

"I've never been to Michigan. Been to Minnesota one time, though." Ancient took his cap off, scratched his scalp, and then settled it back down firmly. "Rochester, Minnesota. Wasn't there long enough to really give me the lay of the land, though."

"What were you doing down there?"

"Mayo Clinic. Took my dad a couple years ago. The fact that he wasn't the one who hired you will tell you all you need to know about how that whole deal turned out."

"Sorry to hear that."

"Well, we were on the outs a lot. But I never did go off to work anywhere else, though I definitely thought about it. Three generations of Virostoks, right here. My mom named me Ancient because when I came out in the hospital my face was all scrunched up and small. She said I looked one hundred years old as a baby. Now I suppose I look about thirty-five, and I only feel like I'm one hundred."

August didn't say anything and leaned on the ax handle.

Ancient crossed his arms over his chest and said, "We're running three hundred head, give or take. One thousand deeded acres. Access to another five hundred of BLM, and we just picked up another piece, I'm happy to say. Decent grass and we got it pretty cheap. We've got water rights on the Musselshell and the North Fork and two good wells. We've had half a dozen serious offers to sell in the past few years, but I told them all thanks but no thanks, and that's how it will be until it hurts too bad to get out of bed. My dad was a mean old son of a bitch but fair and hardworking, and that's who I model myself after. I'm not saying all this to brag myself and the place up, just want you to have a sense of who and what you're working for, that's all."

August nodded. "Sounds good."

"I guess I told you most of that on the phone, didn't I?" Ancient said.

"Pretty much."

"Something tells me you just want to get back to work and don't want to hear a bunch of rambling from me."

August shrugged.

"Kim's always telling me that I repeat myself. I've spent a fair amount of time alone, and so when I talk I'm not always as concerned about my audience as I should be. Kim tells me that, too. You got a lady friend back home, August?"

"Haven't had time recently."

"Jesus Christ. At your age I didn't have time for much else."

August put his gloves back on and hefted the maul. "I've been working a lot."

"I guess you and I will get along, then," Ancient said. "I'll let you get back to it. Dinner in an hour."

Dinner was dry pork chops, dry cornbread, mushy canned green beans. They sat at the rectangular dining room table, Kim and Ancient across from August. There was no music or TV, and the sound of cutlery on plates was very much in the room.

"This is a delicious meal," August said. "Thanks, Kim."

"Oh, sure," she said. "Glad to do it. I came to cooking late in life. Up until recently I just really couldn't be bothered. I was addicted to those Healthy Choice microwave meals. Busy with work, busy with school. Food was just kind of a means to an end. Being up here with Ancient, though, I've had more time. And it's more fun to cook for an appreciative audience. Ancient is so hungry by dinner I could probably serve him shit on a shingle and he'd love it."

Ancient shrugged and smiled. He'd picked up his chop and was gnawing the meat from the bone.

"God, Ancient," Kim said, laughing. "You're a savage."

"In Asia, if you don't belch after your meal you're considered a rude dinner guest," Ancient said, putting the bone down and wiping his mouth with his napkin.

"So?" Kim said.

"So, it's a similar concept. I'm trying to get every scrap of meat off this thing, and you should take it as a compliment." Ancient smiled and winked at August. "And you know what they say—the sweetest meat is closest to the bone."

"Oh, really? Is that what they say?"

"Sure, but I've always been a more-cushion-for-the-pushin' sort of guy."

"Keep digging yourself in, pal. How about we change the subject? August, what sort of things do you like to do in your free time?"

August was trying to cut the remaining meat from the pork chop bone, but the knife wasn't sharp enough and the pork chop kept sliding on his plate. "Oh, you know," he said. "Stuff with my friends. We do a lot of driving around."

"Fishing?" Kim said. "Didn't you say you like fishing?"

"Sure. I like to go fishing sometimes."

"I remember when I had time to go fishing," Ancient said. "Nineteen eighty-nine, I think it was."

"Oh, bull crap, Ancient. I bet you could never sit still long enough to fish in the first place, no matter what. I love you, but patient you ain't."

"I have patience," Ancient said. "Just not a leisurely sort of patience, is all. Anyway, fishing is for people who don't have to work."

"Well, maybe I should take it up, then," Kim said, putting her fork into a pile of disintegrating green beans, tightening her mouth—not quite a frown, but a tightening nonetheless.

"You said you went for a master's degree?" August said.

"Almost. I was going to, but ended up not."

"For what?"

"Education. I'm a teacher. But not currently. I was teaching high school English in Boise before I came here. I still love it. I love the kids. It's just the parents."

"You should hear the shit she had to put up with from these parents," Ancient said. "It would boggle your mind. It's no wonder kids in Asia do better on all the tests and things. Their parents aren't coming into the school to whine to the principal if little Junior gets a bad grade. When I was a kid, ol' Mr. Rodabaugh would lay into you with a yardstick if you weren't acting right. I guarantee every D I got in math I damn well earned."

"Who wants dessert?" Kim said, rolling her eyes. "I've got a frozen chocolate cream pie. It's store-bought but it should still be pretty good."

August was in the Two Dot Bar, waiting on his hamburger. The bartender was a large older woman wearing a Montana State Bobcats sweatshirt and a baseball cap emblazoned with a rhinestone cross. "Whatcha drinking?" she said, putting a napkin down.

"Bud," he said.

"I don't recognize you," she said. "You old enough?"

August looked around the empty place and put his wallet on the bar. "I'm old enough," he said.

"Bottle or draft, then?"

"Bottle."

There was a single small TV hanging over the backbar, a basketball game on. San Antonio playing L.A. August drank his beer and watched without much interest. From where he sat he could see into the kitchen, the large, stained, apron-covered gut of the cook leaning against the grill. There was a blast of cold air at his back as the door opened and closed and a man walked in. August watched in the cracked mirror as he crossed the room and pulled up a stool at the other end of the bar. He was stocky, with a thick black beard, a red silk scarf, and a wide flat-brimmed vaquero hat.

The bartender sighed. "Timmy," she said. "Coors?" The man nodded, and when she put the bottle in front of him he drank half of it in one long pull and then belched. He took his hat off and set it on the stool next to him, rubbing his scalp, his thick black hair sticking up in greasy spikes. August's burger came out, and the bartender slid it over.

One skinny patty, a whitish piece of iceberg lettuce, some onion, and a pale-pink tomato surrounded by a pile of soggy French fries. August doused the burger with mustard and salted the fries liberally. He could feel the man at the end of the bar looking at him as he started to eat.

"You're pretty brave," the man said.

August dunked a fry in ketchup. "Yeah? Why's that?"

The man jerked his head at the kitchen. "I heard the county health inspector went back there once. No one's heard from him since."

"Oh, shut up, Timmy," the bartender said. She waved her hand at him and slid August another beer. "Don't listen to that idiot. He's been coming in here since he was about sixteen, driving me crazy."

"It's because I love you, Theresa. I kid because I love you. But I'm serious about that food." He shook his head and pointed his beer at the burger. "Here we are, surrounded by prime beef and homegrown potatoes, and Theresa still gets the frozen patties from Sysco. The fries they poop out into a mold from processed potato goop."

"Maybe you should start a restaurant, then, hotshot," the bartender said.

"Maybe I will. This would be a good place to start one. And a bar, too." He wagged his empty Coors. "How's that burger, man? Be honest."

"Timmy, let the guy eat in peace."

"I'm just asking."

"It's okay," August said. "I was hungry. Better than I'd make at home, that's for sure."

"What an endorsement. I'd like you to envision a thick quarter-pound patty. Fresh, never frozen. Grass-fed beef from prime Angus that were born and raised happy their whole life, just down the road from here on the Duncan Hanging R Ranch."

"I never knew a cow that seemed super happy," August said.

"I beg to differ. Because my family and I raise them, and I know them all intimately. Well, maybe not *intimately*, but enough to know that there's not a sad one in the whole bunch." The man slid over a few stools and reached out his hand for a shake. "Tim Duncan," he said. "Glad to meet you." The man's hand was hanging there between them, and eventually August put down his burger, wiped his fingers on his napkin, and shook. "I'm August," he said.

"You're Virostok's new guy right? I recognize your truck. Our place is just on the other side of the river. Well, used to be some on your side of the river, too, but that's a whole different story. Anyway. I've seen you driving around. How's that miserable cocksucker Ancient?"

"He seems all right. I haven't been up here too long. Ancient and I get along fine. It's work."

"We all go way back. It's been Duncans and Virostoks up here since the beginning of time, practically. Ancient's old man was a stand-up character for sure." Tim rose abruptly, and his stool skated loudly on the floor tiles. He jammed his hat back on his head and said, "That's it. I can't stand it, you, a newcomer to the valley, sitting here eating beef-flavored soybean-cardboard in this tomb that Theresa calls a bar. As your neighbor I'm insisting that you ride with me down to Martins-dale, where there are several fine establishments that treat their valued customers to Duncan beef and where there may even be members of the opposite sex under sixty. No offense, Theresa."

"Go to hell, Timmy. You're obnoxious. I'm not going to buy your overpriced beef. And you piss me off, so it's on principle now."

"I'm not giving up on you, Theresa. I'll see you next week."

"I sincerely hope not."

August was bringing his half-finished burger up to his mouth for a bite when Tim reached over and plucked it from his hands. He leaned over the bar and dropped it in the garbage. "There. It's where it belongs now." He threw a twenty on the bar and said, "Come on, August. It's Friday night. The bright lights and fleshpots of Martinsdale await." He headed out the door without looking back. August pushed his plate across the bar and stood up. He shrugged. "Sorry," he said. The bartender waved him away, shaking her head.

In the parking lot, Tim's diesel was running, the exhaust pooling white and thick in the cold. August got in and Tim handed him a beer from the half-empty twelve-pack on the floorboard, and then they were spinning in a circle, snow and gravel flying from beneath the truck tires, squealing out onto the pavement toward Martinsdale.

. . .

At the Mint Bar they each got a shot of Jim Beam with a PBR back, and before long, large plates with thick-cut golden fries falling off the edges were pushed across the bar at them. The burgers were massive, the meat perfectly cooked, the center a delicious medium pink. When August bit into his, the juice ran down his chin.

"Eh?" Tim said, punching him on the shoulder. "How about that for a burger? I don't even need to tell you I told you so, because you know it already. That's correctly done right there."

"That's your happy beef, huh?"

"Damn straight. Every place around here besides the Dippy Whip and Theresa's Two Dot Bar buy their beef from us. I gave up on the Dippy Whip; they're corporate. Theresa is just old and crotchety. I also think that her and my old man had some sort of falling-out way back in prehistoric times, and she hasn't gotten over it. I'm still working on her, though."

"I saw that."

"She's been on the verge of going under for years. I'm not too worried about it either way. I just like giving her shit." Tim looked around. There were three men sitting on padded high-back chairs playing video keno. A few more at a table in the rear playing poker. "Pretty dead in here," he said.

"Is it ever not dead?" August said.

"Fourth of July gets pretty rowdy. Rodeo is in town then. Sometimes random nights this time of year girls from Bozeman or Great Falls wander in on their way to the hot springs. That can be fun."

"Hot springs?"

"You haven't been? Shit, that's what we should do after this. Probably be a bikini or two at the very least. You got a girlfriend, August?"

"Haven't had the time for it lately."

Tim took a pull from his beer and laughed. "Time? Time has nothing to do with it up here. You could have all the time in the world and it wouldn't make two shits of a difference. Unless you mean time enough to go somewhere else, like Austin, Texas. You ever make it down there?"

"Nope."

"Let me tell you, it's a world apart. I went a couple times to visit my older brother, Weston. He was going to school down there. I was just a little guy then, and the girls were all into him because he was a roper and could play the guitar, too. They didn't give me the time of day. But I never saw so many boots and skirts. Bikinis on the lawn. Legs for days. Something like that ruins your sense of reality." Tim shook his head. "*Man*tana—where the men are men, and so are the women."

"And the sheep are nervous. I've heard that one before," August said.

"Yeah, well, it applies."

"Maybe you should go to school down there, with your brother, in Austin. You could be a ladies' man."

Tim crumpled his napkin and pushed his empty plate away. He drained his beer and belched long and loud so that even the keno players looked up from their blinking machines. "Can't do that, because my brother Wes was driving to San Antonio from a little rodeo outside of some town called Bandera and a van load of illegals crossed the center line. They had a head-on collision and he died. The guy driving fell asleep, apparently. He died, too. Three or four other wetbacks survived. It was like a clown car full of them, I guess."

"That's tough. I'm sorry."

"It about derailed my dad. He started applying for paperwork to go be a border patrol agent. He hates Mexicans more than any man alive. He says we should just shoot them when they try to cross. Let them fuck up their own country."

August made rings on his napkin with his beer, scraped the PBR label with his thumbnail.

"I'm not saying that I say that. That's just what he says. You know what I say?"

"What?"

"Life's a bitch and then you die."

"I've definitely heard that."

"You've heard all of them, haven't you?"

August shrugged. A TV above the bar was showing the same basketball game he'd been half watching before. "Speaking of San Antonio," he said, nodding up at the TV. "Did you know there's a basketball player on the Spurs that's got your name? Tim Duncan. He just made both his free throws there."

"I was named after him."

"Really?"

"Yeah, my dad was hoping I'd come out tall and black and be really good at dribbling."

"Something tells me you were a disappointment."

Tim laughed. "My grandfather's name was Timothy. My dad's name is Timothy. I'm Timothy. No one gives a damn about basketball. You about done with that beer? Let's get the hell out of here. Watching dudes play video poker depresses me."

The moon was up, and the steam coming off the hot springs roiled alabaster against the black hills. There was a small hotel there, and Tim and August went in to pay their four dollars and get towels. August didn't have trunks, and so for another two dollars he rented a pair from the front desk.

Tim had filled a plastic garbage bag with snow from the parking lot to make a cooler for their beer. August slid into the hot spring gingerly, the water stinging his cold feet and legs. The pool was concrete, lined with thick cedar log slabs. The wood was furred and slick with a thin layer of algae, and the water smelled of sulfur. August floated on his back with his beer propped on his chest and considered the stars appearing and disappearing in the wash of steam passing over like clouds. He had never been in water like this. He rubbed his fingers together, and it was as if he could feel the mineral content, silky and viscous, more watery, somehow, than just plain water.

"What do you think?" Tim said. "They say it has medicinal properties. There's old Swedes up here that drink the stuff and swear it's the fountain of youth."

"You ever drink it?"

"No way. Smelling it is bad enough."

"That's what I was thinking. Rotten eggs."

"I do think there's something to it, though. Everyone up here soaks this time of year. It does something for your bones. Even my old man, a guy who doesn't believe in anything, still comes here a couple times a week while it's cold."

There were other people sitting at the far end of the pool, August realized. He caught small snatches of conversation, could just barely make out whites of eyes and teeth across the expanse of steaming water. "What do you mean your old man doesn't believe in anything?"

"Oh, you know, isn't your old man that way? Seems like dads just get to a certain point and it's like they're incapable of believing in a single goddamn thing unless they came up with it themselves."

"Ha," August said, sipping his beer, now rapidly warming and taking on a slightly sulfurous tinge. "I thought that was just mine."

"Nah, it's universal. For example, I wanted to go into the marines. I was going to do my years and then hire on with one of those government military contracting companies and make bank doing security and stuff. A guy I went to school with did that and now he's loaded. He goes over to Iraq for a couple months at a time and guards a pump station or something, works out a lot, and makes six digits. His wife has fake boobs, and he's got two Harleys."

"I highly doubt that is as fun as it sounds."

Tim heaved himself out onto the side of the pool, and white wings of steam rose from his shoulders. "You think this is fun? Mucking around in the cow shit in the same crap town I've lived in for twenty-two years? I realize you're new, but come on. This place isn't that great."

"Better than getting shot at."

"Is it? I mean really? It comes down to risk versus reward, man."

August shook his head and back-paddled so he was leaning against the pool wall. "I had a friend that joined the National Guard after school. They sent him over there and he got blown up. He just wanted to get his college paid for."

"I'm sorry to hear that."

"It would be one thing if it was something I believed in, fighting Nazis, or whatever. I mean, what is terrorism? Who is terrorism? Your six-figure salary is the only honest reason to do it, in my mind, and it's not enough for me." August raised his arms from the water, cupping each palm and letting streams of it run through. "Plus, I like it out here. Better than Michigan. You don't even know that you've got it pretty good."

"That's what everyone who isn't from Montana says about Montana. If you're from here and not into the big-money shit like skiing and fly-fishing, it's a suckhole."

"Then go drive to Austin if it's so great. You have a truck and free will, right?"

Tim crunched his empty beer can on the pool side and tossed it in the trash bag, fishing out another while he was at it. "Unfortunately, it's not that easy," he said. "I'm stuck. After my brother's deal, no way. It's me and the old man and my younger brother, and just between me and you, my younger brother is not meant to fit in around here. He's fifteen and about two years from taking off and never coming back."

"What do you mean?"

"He's got half his head with long hair and the other half shaved. He wore eye makeup and a pink dress, like a tutu kind of thing with ruffles, to prom. They didn't want to let him in to the dance, but he threatened to sue and the superintendent backed down. My old man used to beat his ass so bad. Hasn't done it in a while, and it never really made much of a difference anyway. That kid gives so few fucks it's almost scary. Looks like a fairy most of the time, but everyone in his class at school is scared of him. No one even picks on him as far as I know. It's like he's transcended it somehow. He and I can't even speak the same language. Only one he ever listened to was Weston. Him and Weston were the same in some ways. Weston was a three-dimensional person, and so is Avery. A lot of people you meet are only two-dimensional but both my brothers are three-dimensional, just in real different ways."

"He wore a tutu?"

"With ripped black stockings. And that's basically why I'm stuck here. Blah blah. Sob story, cue the tiny violins. I've been scoping it out, and there's not one single bikini in this place, is there?"

"Doesn't look like it. Just us and those guys over there. Why are they all wearing those T-shirts?"

"Hoots," Tim said, lowering his voice. "Hutterites. You know about the Hoots?"

"A little. Kind of like Amish, right?"

"Yeah. They're an interesting crew for sure. Some of their women are decent-looking. Those little bonnet things they wear do it for me."

"Jesus."

"I'm serious. You never see them at the hot spring, though, unfortunately. Something to do with their religion. Only the men can come here, and even they have to cover up with those T-shirts. Things would be more interesting around here, though, if there were a bunch of hot-to-trot Hoot girls splashing around."

"You are insane."

"You think I'm kidding? Those girls all grow up on the farm. They've been seeing cows and pigs and horses and chickens getting it on from a young age, and so they're not prudes like most city girls you run into. They tend to be a little thicker on average, but that's because they're real healthy and have appetites, unlike skinny models who just want to be looked at but not touched."

"Have you ever even spoken to a Hutterite woman?"

"Not much. I tend to just admire from afar. It's hard to get through the force field of elders, but there is a way."

"Yeah?"

Tim lowered his voice further and slid a little closer. "Sometimes they look for studs."

"Studs?"

"Studs. The perils of inbreeding are real, pal. Sometimes they find dudes from outside the colony to do the deed with some of their unattached women."

"Oh, fuck you."

"I'm not even joking a little bit. My brother Wes and one of his friends did it the summer before they went off to college. That's the only reason I know about it. My brother's friend Cale got to know some of the old Hutterite boys somehow, and one day he went out there to go antelope hunting and they brought him up to the house and fed him a bunch of rhubarb wine, and over the course of the evening the Hoots told him that if he'd come back with proof of a clean VD check then he could do some *good bucking*. That's what they call it. *How'd you like to come down to the colony and do some good bucking, young man?*"

August looked across the pool at the hulking shapes of large Hutterite men sitting on the hot-spring bench, intermittently visible in the steam, sopping black T-shirts plastered to rounded bellies. "You are so full of shit."

"Look at me, I'm not joking. Cale told the Hoots that he had a friend that might be down, too, and the Hoots said the more the merrier. Now, Cale and my brother were always messing with each other, pulling jokes and stuff. So the way my brother told it is that Cale went to the clinic, got tested. Then made a copy, did a little work with some Wite-Out, and forged one for Wes. Cale took Wes to the bar, bought him a few beers, drove around a little, and then headed down to the colony.

"Cale had the whole thing set up, of course. The Hoots were ready for them, and they had a bunch of wine. The women made a big feast. They had some live Hoot music, not sure what that sounds like, really, but there was some dancing. The girls were out in the mix. I guess there were three or four that were looking for seed."

August threw his empty beer can so it bounced off Tim's head. "Seed, my ass. You're ridiculous."

"Let me finish—this is all a true story. So one of the Hoot elders asks to see the paperwork, and Cale whips out the test reports, and at this point my brother is kind of like, *Huh?* He's got a Hoot gal sitting next to him, rubbing his shoulder, pouring him wine. Cale is like, *Yep, happy early b-day, son. I told them you're the biggest stud around.* At first, Wes says, *No way,* and Cale has to talk some sense into him. They're in this room full of huge Hoot dudes. Probably some of them aren't super happy about what was about to go down, because these are girls they've grown up with, and they have to just sit there while the elders let these outsiders dip their wicks. Tensions were high, that's what I'm saying. Wes is saying, *No fucking way, man.* And Cale turns to the elder and says that his friend is having some second thoughts about procreation and maybe needs some persuasion. The Hoot elder says, *We can offer a side of beef, a whole full-size butchered hog, or a fifteen-year-old Ford F-150 that still runs okay but probably will need a new transmission soon.* The Hoots pretty much only bargain. They're not big on actually buying things with money."

Tim reached into the trash bag, came up with another beer, cracked it, and took a long drink. "So, Wes has been on the rhubarb wine heavily at this point and knows that Cale is going to give him endless amounts of shit about this if he backs down. Also, Wes was always up for stuff. You couldn't hardly ever out-weird him. That was one of his dimensions. So, he grabs one of the eligible bachelorettes and takes her for a spin around the dance floor. Apparently Hoot women don't get to drink too much, but in this situation they're all knocking back the rhubarb hooch and Wes said she was downright aggressive. Took him by the hand. Dragged him into this little room they had set up off the back of the place.

"Okay, now, this is the part where I knew it was all truth when Wes told me. I mean, at first I was skeptical, too, but then he got to this part and I knew he hadn't made it up. The Hoot gal pulls him into the bedroom and he sits on the edge of the bed. She sits next to him and then she reaches under the bed and pulls out a big white sheet. She says, *I'm supposed to put this over my top to cover myself from you. Okay,* Wes says. *We don't have to do a damn thing if you don't want to.* The girl looked at Wes, looked at the sheet, and then laughed. She threw the sheet on the floor and pulled the dress over her head and that was that."

"So, why exactly did that make you know he wasn't lying?"

"Okay, well, Wes had this real funny thing—he liked women to have a lot of hair down there, like a real big bush."

"Weird."

"I know. It was his thing. I have no idea why. Anyway, he told me that he was kind of disappointed because this Hoot girl was completely shaved! Can you believe that? He said, after, they got to talking a little and he asked her about it, kind of teasing. And she got shy and said she'd heard that men outside the colony liked it bald and so she'd done it that morning, and Wes said he had to laugh at the irony of it all."

"So that's why you're convinced he wasn't bullshitting you?"

"Pretty much—it's just too strange of a detail for him to make up. Also, when he talked about it, he got kind of serious. I mean, he would be joking about Cale setting him up and all of that, but when we got to that end part of the story he was serious. Wes didn't take much serious, but he said that the Hoot gal was nicer and funnier than pretty much any girl he'd known, and I think he kind of regretted the whole thing. He came at me with this story out of nowhere, too. It wasn't like he was looking for a way to fuck with me. We were just driving somewhere and he came out with it like it was bothering him. He also said that after it was over she said that she was supposed to lay on her back and put her knees up to her chin and wait for thirty minutes, but instead of doing that she just went to the bathroom and got dressed and said she'd let the chips fall where they would. And, there's one more reason I know it's true."

"Yeah?"

"He showed up one day with a whole butchered hog. Told our parents that he'd helped the Hoots put up a bunch of hay over the weekend and that's how they'd paid him. I know for a fact that my brother Weston never helped no Hoots with no hay. He hated doing hay more than anything. Always got all sneezy and itchy."

"That's quite a story."

"For a fact. How about you?"

"What about me?"

"The wick, son. Have you ever dipped the wick?"

"Oh, Jesus, who cares?"

"Well, have you?"

"Yes. I've dipped."

"I don't believe you. What was her name?"

"It doesn't matter."

"That's because, like as not, she's a figment. No shame in it, pal. Maybe we can go down to Billings one of these weekends and shed you of the great weight of your virginity. That's why you're so serious, I bet. You dip the wick and all your troubles melt away and you're reborn a man."

"That hasn't been my experience."

"I'm serious. There's a reason why men have been fighting and dying for it since the beginning of time. Okay, I can tell you're getting embarrassed. We're about out of beer, and soaking in a hot tub with nothing but dudes depresses me. Let's get the hell out of here."

Near midnight now, snow starting to fall, the wind punching it sideways across the shafts of Tim's headlights. The Qwikstop was still open, and they pulled in for more beer. August stayed in the truck, and Tim came running back with a case and a foil package of Backwoods. He handed August a beer and a cigar. He pulled his hat a little lower down on his head, lit his Backwoods, clenched it between his teeth, and tossed August the lighter. He cracked his beer and raised it toward August. "Here's to Clint Eastwood," he said, dropping the truck into gear and roaring out of the parking lot. Everything silent under the snow. No signs of life on the streets of Martinsdale. No footprints on the sidewalks. No TVs glowing blue through living room windows. Tim barreled through the single red light. "Welcome to the great Western apocalypse," he said.

August blew a line of smoke out the slightly opened window. "I was thinking about your brother and the Hutterite girl," he said.

"Oh yeah? You thinking about going down to the colony and signing up for some good bucking?"

"Not really. I was thinking that the Hutterites wouldn't have just given your brother that butchered hog for no reason."

"I know. That's what I was saying. I'm not bullshitting you about the story."

"No. I mean the Hutterites wouldn't give your brother a hog unless he fulfilled his end of the bargain, see what I'm saying?"

"I know, man. He did it, I'm sure of it."

"Tim, what I'm saying is that unless he actually knocked her up, there's no way they'd just give him a hog. They weren't bargaining with him about the sex. It's clearly about the sperm to them. Same as when you have an AI guy come and do your heifers. They wouldn't come through with the hog unless it took, and she got pregnant. You probably have a nephew or a niece out there. That's what I'm saying. Uncle Timmy."

Tim nodded, sucked deep so his cigar cherry glowed angry. He exhaled through his nose and said, "Yeah, I've considered it. A little. The kid would be two or three years old now. Half-Hoot, half-Duncan. I mean, half-Hoot, sure. But half-*Duncan,* too. I've been thinking, maybe soon it'll be time to swoop in. Get the kid back into the fold of his family. Kid needs its mom up until a certain point. But a Duncan living like a Hoot? If my old man knew he would rupture." Tim drank, tipped his ash into an empty can in the cup holder. He hunched down a little in his seat to get a better look outside. "What a night," he said. "What a mystery. Ever think about it? How the blackest sky can make the whitest snow?"

"Huh?" August said.

"Let's go get him. Tonight."

"Him?"

"My brother's son. I guess it could be a daughter, but I feel that it's a son. Tonight's the night. I'm glad you brought it up. Suddenly I feel ready." Tim was driving on the river road now, the Musselshell out there somewhere, cracked and frozen under a crooked line of midnight trees. It was snowing harder now, so that it seemed to come from the earth as much as the air, an upwelling of particles, white sky, white ground, headlights breaking against a swirling white wall, the truck plunging.

"I wasn't suggesting anything," August said.

"No, you said it yourself. He got the hog because *it took.* And pretty soon now my father's grandson is going to be speaking German and wearing pilgrim clothes. Ain't happening. For so long, I've been the only one that knows, and now you know, and here we are together, on our way, taking action." The truck fishtailed slightly around a corner and Tim howled, pushing the button to lower both of their windows. He crammed his hat down against the rush of air, snow coming in, dusting their coats, sticking in eyebrows and eyelashes, snow behind the windshield and outside it, no separation from the gusts. They were in the blizzard's belly now, a part of it, no longer just traveling through.

"Maybe you want to slow down," August said.

Tim didn't turn to look at him. Eyes lost in the whitewash, the barest hint of dark that implied the road's shoulder. "Like I haven't driven this exact way every day of my life," he said. "All roads lead to the one you're on at any given moment. Right? Isn't that the saying?"

"I'm not totally sure on that."

"Oh, you haven't heard that one? Thought you'd heard them all."

Without slowing, Tim jerked the wheel to the left and they bounced over a cattle guard and down a rutted, snow-covered drive. There were vapor lights, downcast and glowing green, barely illuminating the shapes of outbuildings. They were approaching the colony, the truck lurching, Tim punching the gas to make the diesel rev. Long, dark dormitory buildings loomed ahead and Tim slowed the truck and let it idle. The headlights were blazing into a lace-curtained window. Someone's kitchen, maybe. Tim lit another Backwoods and sucked deep, his cheeks caving. He wedged the cigar in the corner of his mouth. "Hang on, kid," he said, then cranked the wheel, laid on the horn, and popped the clutch. The truck, light in the back, did a fast donut, tires burning through the snow, headlights whipping around. Doors and windows, a child's swing set, a pump house, a basketball hoop. August was clinging to the oh-shit handle with everything he had, snow in his face, the smell of rubber melting against the frozen ground. Tim kept it hammered wide open, horn blaring, windows and doors, the swing set, the pump house, the basketball hoop. Lights were coming on in the dorms, and still they were spinning. The windows the doors the swing set the pump house the basketball hoop a dark figure holding something, backlit in a doorway.

"Gun!" August yelled. "Guy's got a gun."

Tim's jaw was tight. He slowed, straightening the wheel, plowing them through a drift up and onto the driveway, the lights of the colony behind them now, fading, as they crashed over the cattle guard and hit the river road.

"Holy shit," August said, punching at Tim's leg. "That was crazy. They probably have no idea what just happened. That dude had a shotgun, I swear. I didn't know Hutterites even had guns. I didn't know they played basketball, either."

Tim was driving slowly now. He rolled the windows up and cranked the heater. "Any more beer left?" he said. After a while he parked at a turnoff overlooking the river. They each had a beer and August tipped his can toward Tim. "To your brother Weston," he said. "RIP."

Tim nodded, took a long drink, and belched. "You ever hear stories about people who are drunk surviving accidents? Like, all the time how drunk people in car wrecks survive when all the sober people die. Right? You've heard that, haven't you?"

"Yeah, I guess."

"Why is that? I've never really figured it out."

"I guess it's because when you're drunk your muscles are looser, and so you are more able to absorb impact, or something."

"Maybe that's it. Anyway, that wasn't the case with my brother. Ol' Weston got piss drunk after that rodeo and drove and crossed a center line and he ran head-on into a van, and the van was driven by a guy with his wife and two kids in the back and everyone died except one of the kids, and the kid, a girl, was mangled, and my old man went broke paying her medical bills. That's how it actually went down. They were Mexicans. Illegals. Shoot them at the border, my dad says. Then he sells our best section of river-bottom pasture to your boss, Ancient Virostok, to pay for the kid's surgeries. No one made him do it. He did that on his own."

"Shit, man. That's bad."

Tim was staring straight out the windshield. Snow falling, melting on the warm glass. "Hutterites and Mexicans and my brother Weston. It's like an unholy trinity. I was never religious, but then he died and I sort of figured some things out. You can't believe anything that anyone tells you; that's for starters. A man can only believe himself and only the things that come to him in dreams, because that's where the will of the world is pure."

"I never remember my dreams," August said. "They say everyone dreams, but every morning I wake up blank."

Tim turned to look at August, and there was no recognition there. "Who are you, and why are you even here?"

August was going to say something, make a joke, but the look in Tim's eyes was withering. August backed out the truck door, turning up the collar of his coat.

"I don't even know who you are," Tim said. "You're a figment."

August was walking now, hands jammed into his pockets. At least three miles to the Two Dot Bar and his truck. He'd be very cold when he arrived.

⸻

The bunkhouse phone rang, and it was August's father. August was heating a bowl of chili in the microwave. Only four-thirty but already dark. A hollow banging as the wind picked at a loose piece of aluminum sheeting on the shop roof.

"I got your number from your mother."

"I was meaning to give you a call."

"Yeah, that's okay. I imagine you're busy."

"Just doing odds and ends around the place right now. Getting ready for calving, though."

"Fun. Fun."

"What's new back there? How are things? Is Lisa still there?"

"Things are all right. Lisa was gone for a while, but she's back now and we're doing better. Been having a bad winter, and that's hard for everyone. It's almost like when I was a kid. Don't know if you've seen it on the news, but we've been getting the lake-effect storms just about every week. I had to get up on the milking shed and cut the snow off in big chunks with a spade. I thought the roof was going to buckle."

"That's a pretty sturdy roof, though."

"It was wet snow. I didn't want to take any chances. You been getting snow out there?"

"Not a lot. It's been windy."

"Cold?"

"It was twenty below the other morning."

"How does it feel? It's that dry cold, right? Not as bad as it gets back here with the damp?"

"I guess that's true. Twenty below is still pretty damn cold."

"That's a fact."

"But the sun comes out more here, so it doesn't seem so bad. It's not so gray all the time."

"I guess I've been here long enough I'm used to the clouds. Wouldn't know how to take it if it were any other way."

"It's not too hard. Sunshine's not too hard to take, really." The microwave dinged, and August pinned the phone between his shoulder and ear. He removed the bowl from the microwave, gingerly. Steam rose from the rim and he dunked a spoon, blew over it a few times, and took a cautious slurp. It was scalding, and he spit, swearing, and nearly dropping the phone.

"You all right there?"

"Hot chili," August said. "Trying to eat."

"Oh, I didn't want to interrupt your dinner. Just checking in to make sure you're doing all right."

"It's fine. I'm all right."

"Okay then. I'm signing off."

"I didn't mean—"

"Have a good one, son."

"Night, Dad."

August had been sleeping for hours. The sound of voices from the yard woke him. A yellow beam from the headlights pointing toward the bunkhouse cleaved the room. He shuffled across the cold concrete floor and stood with the door cracked, listening to Ancient and Kim argue. Kim was behind the wheel of her Subaru and Ancient was outside the car, leaning against the frame of the driver's side so she couldn't close the door.

"What?" Ancient was saying loudly. "What did you expect? Huh? What did you think?"

Kim said something August couldn't hear, and Ancient barked a laugh. "Surrre," he said. "That's rich. That's a good one." He pounded the roof of the Subaru with his fist, and then the car started moving so he had to twist awkwardly to avoid getting run over. There was the scrabbling sound of Kim's tires tossing gravel as she pulled away fast, her lights red and dimming as she turned out onto the road. Ancient was down on his back in the driveway, and when he tried to get to his feet he stumbled. He wasn't wearing a belt, and his jeans had slid down his hips. August could clearly see the dingy white of his underwear as he made his way across the yard, hitching his pants with each step.

A week later they were fixing a fence at the back of Ancient's newly acquired piece of pasture, and they'd gotten their truck stuck. There'd been a weeklong thaw that had softened the frozen two-track into a thick red gumbo. Ancient had been driving, and they'd slipped and skidded down a small hill, coming to rest on the rise that hid the Musselshell River. They got out of the truck, and Ancient bent to inspect the tires, caked over with clay. They both looked back at the hill they'd have to climb to get out of the field. Ancient removed his hat and ran his hands through his hair before jamming it back down. After backing the truck all the way up to the very edge of the new fence, Ancient told August to sit on the bed, for more weight over the back wheels, and he gunned it, trying to build as much speed as possible. They made it less than halfway up the hill before the wheels started spinning, throwing up greasy clods of red clay. The truck fishtailed to a stop, and Ancient backed it down. They tried three more times until finally they were dug in so deep that he was unable to move at all and they were stuck. They tried rocking it, with August pushing from the front. Then they tried putting alder limbs from the riverbank under the tires, and that didn't work either.

The pasture was not attached to the main Virostok ranch holdings, and so they were more than five miles from the house and a tractor they might use to pull them out. Ancient sighed and spit into the mud. He shaded his eyes with his hand and looked off across the river, where the slowly rotating turbines of the Hutterite colony's wind farm were just visible. "Well, fuck," he said. "I guess we'll go talk to the Hoots."

They set out walking across the rutted pasture, a few of Virostok's Red Angus watching them balefully. At the top of the hill they angled across the field and ducked under the fence that separated Virostok's section from the Hutterite land. They climbed the rise, and the windmills loomed before them, three stories high, their brilliant white turbine blades turning lazily. August could feel only the slightest breeze and was surprised that it was enough to move the windmills.

Both of them stopped walking, and craned their necks up; the blades in front of the sun draped great dagger-shaped shadows across the brown fields.

"I watched them put those things up," Ancient said. "The blades came in from Seattle, I think. Two flatbed railcars for each one. They had to truck them up the last leg here from Livingston. I remember seeing them coming up the highway, bigger than seemed possible."

"I heard that eagles and hawks sometimes run into windmills and get killed," August said. "But from here it looks like they're moving so slow I don't see how that could be true."

"I'm not sure about that," Ancient said. "I do know the Hoots are making a killing on the deal, though. The company that put them up leased the land, and I guess the colony gets some kind of percentage of the profits. It's been five years, and I've been noticing they've got a bunch of new trucks on their place. Giant new chicken barn, too. You ever been down into the colony?"

August shook his head. "Kind of. Not really."

"Well, you're in for an experience."

From the hill they could see down into the Hutterite compound. "Doesn't look like anyone's around," August said.

Ancient looked at his watch. "Probably dinnertime. Don't worry, they'll come out of the woodwork when we go down there. They're always around."

August and Ancient headed down the hill, crossed the small bridge over the Musselshell, and continued behind the large, dormant gardens into the colony itself. The whole place was exceedingly neat. No trash or junk. A wooden fence circled the main yard and it was a brilliant, freshly painted white. The dorm buildings were long and low, with many separate entrances on each sidewall. Every doorway had a small poured-concrete stoop upon which rested a metal-wheeled cart. Probably thirty doorways, August guessed, between the two buildings. Thirty evenly spaced doors, thirty stoops, thirty carts. No decorations of any kind, every door a clean, freshly painted white.

"Kind of creepy," August said.

Ancient laughed. "Oh, come on. They're God-fearing Americans, just like you and me." He reached around in his back pocket and pulled out his dip can, thwacking it a few times against his thigh before packing his bottom lip. "But seriously," he said. "All these people think radicals are only living in hippie towns on the coast. Berkeley or Brooklyn or whatever. These people right here are the straight-up most radical group of people I've ever heard of. At some point they said, *Fuck society. We're going to go out to the middle of nowhere, Montana, and live our goddamn lives. We're going to raise our chickens and wear our little homemade outfits and the rest of the world can burn itself to the ground for all we care.*"

Before long a man emerged, wiping his hands with a rag. He wore the standard Hutterite garb—a black broad-brimmed Stetson and a dark blue pearl-snap shirt tucked into black Wrangler jeans. Black boots covered in mud. He had blondish-red muttonchops, his belly strained the front of his shirt, and his red face was split in a big smile.

"Hey, John, how's it going? Long time no see." Ancient and the Hutterite shook hands; the Hutterite's were huge and grease stained.

"Okay," the Hutterite said. "Sure has been a long time." He put his hands in his pants pockets, rocking back a little on his heels. "Remind me of your name again," he said.

"I'm Ancient Virostok. That's me over there." Ancient pointed in the direction of the pasture. "Remember, I gave you and your boy a lift from Livingston a few years ago when your truck broke down?"

The Hutterite nodded and rocked a little more on his heels. "I don't have a son," he said. "Maybe that was my cousin, John Daniel. I'm John Rile. I've got three daughters. John Daniel has a son, though. Probably you gave him and his boy a ride, because he's the fowl boss and he gets down there to town for deliveries. I'm the farm boss, though, so I mostly stay around. That John Daniel, though, he gets down there to town as much as he can. He's always going to the Taco Time drive-through and getting those chalupas with the hot taco sauce. He loves spicy. We don't get much of it up here. I don't really like spicy. What can we do for you, then?" the Hutterite said. "Want to buy some fryers?"

"Well," Ancient said, "the thing is, we're stuck. Got our truck bogged down in the pasture on the river back there, and we'd be super obliged if you could give us a hand." While Ancient spoke, dormitory doors were opening. Kids stepped out into the yard, the boys dressed in home-sewn dark blue pants and shirts, the girls in dark blue or dark green dresses, hair covered by black-and-white polka-dotted kerchiefs. They stood quietly at the edge of the yard, watching.

"Real muddy out there, eh?" John Rile said. "I bet. I'll drive the Kubota up there, should do the trick. No problem. Maybe you want some fryers, though, since you came all this way? Nice fresh ones right now, all wrapped up and ready to go."

Ancient shrugged. "Sure," he said. "My fiancée will be happy about that." He pulled out his wallet. "How about three?"

John Rile nodded and looked at August. "And you?"

"I don't know," August said, looking at Ancient. "I'm sorry, I don't even know what we're talking about. What's a fryer?"

John Rile blinked and wiped at his mouth with the back of one hand. "Poultry, boy," he said. "A nice young fryer. You must not be married. You probably like our rhubarb wine, though, eh?"

"I don't know," August said. "Never come across it before." August could see Ancient trying to hide his smile, looking down at the ground and kicking at something with the toe of his boot. "How you set for cash, August?" Ancient said.

August patted his jean pocket and shrugged. "I guess I got like twenty bucks."

"Whelp," Ancient said. "Bust it out and pay the man for your booze."

John Rile was smiling again, holding the twenty Ancient had given him for the fryers. August dug out his wallet and handed over his money.

"Good deal," John Rile said. "I'll get Ma to box up the fryers and set up your jug. You have a chain?"

"I've got a tow strap," Ancient said.

John Rile stuffed the two twenties in his pocket and said, "We're in business, then." He turned to the gaggle of kids and yelled, "Tell Ma Sal three fryers and a jug, hurry up."

John Rile drove the Kubota out of the colony with August and Ancient riding perched on the fenders, and the box containing the fryers and rhubarb wine resting in the tractor's front bucket. The kids followed, running silently behind the tractor, and a gray-muzzled heeler trotted behind them, tongue lolling.

It was nearly dark by the time they got the truck up the hill and out of the pasture, and everyone involved was very much splattered with mud. After extended thanks and goodbyes to the Hutterite clan, they headed out, with Ancient at the wheel. The box of fryers sat between them on the bench seat. The rhubarb wine was in a plastic milk jug, and August twisted off the cap and sniffed.

"Ever had that before?" Ancient said.

August shook his head and took an experimental sip. It was golden in color, sweet and syrupy—not too bad, but tasted faintly of the milk jug's plastic. He offered the wine to Ancient, who shook his head.

"Had plenty when I was younger. Just tastes like a hangover to me."

August recapped the jug and put it at his feet. "I heard a thing about the Hoots the other day," he said. "Probably not true. But I heard that they sometimes get guys from outside the colony to come sleep with their women, like, as a stud service."

Ancient was shaking his head, laughing. "That old line. Guys have been saying that around here for thirty years. I don't know one single person that has actually ever done it, though. Just wishful thinking by a bunch of sad-ass bachelor ranchers."

"That's pretty much what I thought. I met a guy the other night that was giving me a big story about it."

"Who was that?"

"Guy named Tim Duncan. I guess you probably know him."

Ancient started to say something, then stopped. Shook his head. "I've known that kid since he was a toddler. They've had a tough go of it over there for a while. Timmy's dad, Big Tim, is, well, I don't know. He used to be all right. You ever drive by their place? It's on the back way to town on Dry Creek. All those signs out by the road?"

August shook his head.

"Yeah, it's kind of out-of-the-way. No real reason to go that direction."

"What kind of signs?"

"Conspiracy theory shit. About how 9/11 was a cover-up and Bible verses and Nazi-type stuff. Your basic standard-issue right-wing lunacy."

"Tim told me his brother died a few years ago."

"Yeah. I knew Wes, too. Good kid. Everyone liked Wes. Hell of a natural athlete. Did rodeo and pitched in high school and probably could have just walked on anywhere, but I guess he went down to college and got distracted so that he didn't care too much about sports. Can't blame him there."

"Tim said he was drunk and got in a wreck."

"That's the long and short of it. We've all been there. Bad luck. Big Tim's screwiness seemed a little more harmless before Wes died. But that's no real surprise. You lose a kid like that and all the normal anger within a person gets the heat turned up on it. Timmy's not a bad kid."

"He said you bought some land off his dad."

Ancient nodded. "For more than a fair price at that. He say that I took advantage, or ripped them off, or anything like that?"

"Nothing like that."

Ancient looked out the window and tapped his fingers on the steering wheel. "People around here, I don't know. Everyone's all neighborly, and then you find out that people you've known for decades have been secretly holding their breath, waiting for your downfall. Timmy say anything about Kim?"

"Kim? No. Why?"

Ancient shrugged. "People are nosy."

"Where is Kim, anyway? I haven't seen her in a while."

They were home now, sitting in the driveway. Ancient turned the truck off, and the diesel ticked. They sat there looking at the house, no lights on because there was no one there.

"Give me that jug," Ancient said. August handed it over and Ancient tilted it back, his Adam's apple bobbing twice. "Goddamn, but that's bad," he said, coughing. "I don't know what it would do to you first, get you drunk or give you a cavity." Ancient was sitting behind the wheel looking straight ahead. He had the jug on his lap and was turning the cap over in his fingers. He was a small man, high cheekbones perennially red and chapped. Tangled blond hair flaring from under his dirty cap. "Sometimes when your fiancée says she's going downstate to visit her sister, it means that she's going downstate to visit her sister. Apparently, though, it can also mean that her return is questionable."

After two months of unrelenting cold, in early March, just in time for calving, the warm winds started coming down from the north. August and Ancient patrolled the herd, cutting out the heavies and moving them into the small corral near the calving shed. Ancient was on his big geriatric gelding, Chief, the only horse left on the ranch, and August drove the four-wheeler. It was a fifty-fifty day, as Ancient termed it. Fifty degrees and blowing fifty miles an hour. Snow melting, the knobby four-wheeler tires throwing big clods of wet mud.

They got a half dozen of the cows that seemed closest to being ready separated from the herd, and then they stopped to eat their sandwiches, hunkering down on the lee side of the calving shed. In this patch of calm, the sun warmed them and August leaned back against the boards of the shed and closed his eyes. They were halfway through calving, and the long days and nights had started to take their toll. He hadn't had an uninterrupted night of sleep in a week. Ancient, some-how, didn't seem tired. He chewed his sandwich loudly, crunched his chips. "Check out ol' Chief," he said, nudging August's leg. August opened his eyes. Chief had wandered to the wind block as well. He stood next to them, asleep on his feet, reins trailing in the dirt. "I swear that horse is part dog. He'd follow me into the house if I let him. You want to hop on his back this afternoon? He pretty much drives him-self. If he had thumbs he could probably run this ranch better than me."

August shook his head. "I'll stick with the four-wheeler."

"Suit yourself. My dad was a hell of a horseman. Chief was his last. Started him as a green broke colt. He always said the only reason he messed with cattle at all was to keep his horses exercised. He hated the four-wheeler. Of course, he wasn't dumb; he recognized how useful they are. But he used them for doing the irrigation only. It was like a religion for him. Money only factored in when it was scarce and he never set himself up to make more of it. Poverty and a pasture full of horses eating new grass—that was his idea of heaven. You have horses on your place growing up?"

August closed his eyes again. Shook his head. "Dairy cows. They pretty much come when you call them. No need for horses."

"Dairy," Ancient said, as if trying it on for size.

"One hundred acres," August said.

"One hundred acres?"

"That's it."

"My old man and I probably would have killed each other if we were cooped up on one hundred acres."

"There you go," August said. "Instead of that I came out here."

Ancient nodded and balled his sandwich foil. He thwacked his chew can a few times and packed his lip. "My old man could be a funny dude. The first four-wheeler we got was a Honda. He always called it the Jap quarter horse."

"Good one."

"He had a lot of good ones. Kim only met him at the end, when he was already half out of it. She'd chopped her hair so it was even shorter than it is now, and the old boy thought that was something. He told her that the West was won by women with men's haircuts. She laughed. I think they liked each other okay."

August didn't say anything and the wind picked up for a moment, the gust sending up a howl as it was cleaved by the single strand of electric wire strung up on posts to the shed.

"Yep, when ol' Chief kicks the bucket it's going to be the end of an era. It'll just be me, Ancient, the poor orphan boy. The only one left who remembers how it used to be." Ancient grunted, heaved to his feet, and stepped around the side of the shed. "The divine wind," he yelled. "The Chinook. The snow eater." He turned his back and unzipped, sending a plume of wind-driven piss flying for nearly thirty feet.

August took the Dry Creek cutoff, pausing for a moment on the old single-lane iron bridge over the Musselshell. He could see down into the water; it was clear enough to make out the rocks of the streambed, and he watched for a while but couldn't see any trout. He clattered over the bridge timbers and headed toward town, driving slowly on the heavily rutted road, passing a field of winter wheat and a group of crows, shards of scattered iridescent black against electric-green new growth. The field was fenced, and there were signs on the posts running along the barrow pit. They were hand-painted, thick black letters against whitewashed plywood: KEEP AMERICA FOR AMERICANS! JEWS ARE THE TERRORISTS—MOSSAD DID 9/11! BUSH KNEW! Some of the letters had dripped, lending their messages an air of fresh fevered intensity.

August was creeping along, reading, when a truck rumbled around the corner and slowed. It was Tim. He braked next to August and rolled his window down. August rolled his down as well, and Tim nodded at the signs. "You taking some time to get educated?" he said.

"I don't know about that," August said.

"There's a lot of shit that don't make sense about 9/11."

"Like what?"

"Like the fact that there were unidentified explosions that came from the ground floors. It wasn't just from the planes. And—" Tim paused, rubbed his face, spat out the window. "You know what? It don't matter. It's not my deal. My dad's always going on about it. Talk to him if you want all the info. I'm just living. How's it going? How's that dick Ancient?"

"Going fine. Ancient's fine, I guess."

"Does he pay you to drive around admiring the scenery, or what?"

"He had to go to Billings. I'm headed to town to get some stuff from the Feed-n-Need."

"What kind of stuff?"

"Some big stainless lag bolts. Rehanging a gate that ripped out of a post. It was just screwed in at the hinges before."

"Yeah, that'll happen. If you want to make it last, you have to drill a hole through and then bolt it."

"That's what I'm going to do."

"Smart."

"I guess."

"So if you're going to town, why'd you come this way? It's going to take you about twenty minutes longer."

"Never been back here before. Ancient told me Dry Creek would pop you out in town. Just decided to go for a drive."

"Probably he told you to come check out crazy Duncan's place, didn't he?"

August shook his head. "He didn't say anything about it."

"Uh-huh." Tim looked off. "I was thinking. You and me should get dogs. Pups. Raise them up. It's nice to have a dog around. If we got them at the same time they'd grow up together and learn things from each other, and maybe we could get a two-for-one kind of deal from a breeder. Something smart and trainable, like an Aussie. Maybe a heeler, but then heelers are always so standoffish and weird. I've been bit by three dogs, and they've all been heelers. What do you think?"

"About getting a dog? I'd have to think about it. Not sure that it's the right time."

"Hell, the timing is never exactly right to get a dog. You just have to get one and then arrange your life accordingly. That's the point of it. Having a dog makes you act more responsibly."

"I'll consider it. I like dogs."

"Of course you do. If you didn't they'd have stopped you at the border."

"What border?"

"It's just a turn of phrase. I'm just bullshitting you."

"How about the other night? About your brother. Was that bullshit?"

"No bullshit, man. Sorry about all the stuff at the end there. Things are a bit fuzzy, to tell the truth. I'd been putting them back pretty steady all day. I sometimes turn to black. I should never have had the whiskey at the Mint. That's what did it. If I just stick to beer, I'm fine. Get me on the whiskey, though, I turn right into ol' black Tim. It's a known fact about myself, and I apologize." Tim reached out his window, his hand in a fist. "We cool?" he said.

"Sure."

"Well, then, don't leave me hanging. Give me a bump, pal."

August reached out and knocked his fist against Tim's.

"Good man," Tim said. "Don't forget about the dog." Then he drove off, tires spinning, leaving August there with his arm outstretched.

August kept on toward town. The signs continued for a half mile. A NATION BEGET BY SIN WILL REAP ITS OWN DISASTER! A MAN SHALL NOT LAY WITH ANOTHER MAN, IT IS AN ABOMINATION! A MAN SHALL RETAIN THE RIGHT TO KEEP AND BEAR ARMS! 9/11 WAS AN INSIDE JOB! SHEEPLE WAKE UP!

August got a pot of canned chicken noodle going on the hot plate. When it was bubbling he didn't bother with a bowl, just crushed a handful of saltines in and started spooning it out. He was finishing when his father called.

"How'd calving go?"

"Pretty good. We lost one, but other than that it went all right. Not a lot of sleep for a while, that's for sure."

"Well, that's calving for you. Always hard when one doesn't pull through."

"It was that. For sure."

"I was looking at your weather. Looks like you've been getting a little warm-up the last few days."

"It's been decent. Super windy, though. Ancient calls it the Chinook wind. Comes down from Canada this time of year. Melting the snow in a hurry."

"From Canada?"

"Supposedly."

"Seems like if it came from Canada this time of year, it would be a colder wind. Wouldn't it?"

"I'm not totally sure. That's just what he said."

"Well, I'm sure he knows the weather in his neck of the woods. I don't doubt him. Just seems a little counterintuitive."

"I think the mountains have something to do with it. They stall the weather patterns out in certain ways."

"That could be. I've never seen the Rocky Mountains. I guess I'm probably getting too old for it to make much difference. It seems like it's a young man's country out there."

"I don't really see how you could be too old to see the mountains. You just look at them, and there they are."

"I don't mean I'm too old to look at them. What I mean is, I'm too old to *see* them, you know what I mean? I could drive through the Yellowstone National Park and look at Old Faithful or whatever, but the time for me to tackle the landscape head-on has come and gone."

"Well, you could still come and visit sometime."

"Yeah, I'll just punch the autopilot button on the place here and take off for vacation."

"I was just saying."

"I know what you were saying, but some of us have to work and can't just take off whenever the mood strikes."

"Never mind. Has it been starting to warm up there at all?"

"Not a tremendous amount. We had a decent little stretch last month, but I didn't put the long johns away. Had a bad ice storm last week. All the kids around here got school off for a few days. We didn't have power until yesterday."

"Good thing you've got generators."

"Lisa was making candlelit dinners every night anyway. She's a hard worker, but damned if she isn't still a woman all the way through."

"Isn't that the point?"

"What do you mean?"

"If she wasn't all woman, she'd just be your hired hand still. Right?"

There was a soft laugh. "She sometimes seems to forget that she was my hired hand at all. Anyway. You don't really get ice storms out there in Montana, do you?"

"I've never seen one. Too cold, I think. It just snows and blows and drifts."

"I'd take some drifts over an ice storm any day. With an ice storm you almost always lose power."

"I used to like ice storms when I was little. That was the best sledding. Remember that metal saucer we had, and how you sprayed it down with silicone, and I made it from the hill all the way to the road before I stopped?"

"I remember. That was a hell of a storm. That ice was about an inch thick over everything. You were just a little shit then, and you could just walk right on top of the snow. I, of course, broke through the ice crust with every step. Wore my ass out carting you up that hill."

"I don't remember that. I thought I walked myself. I guess all I really remember is flying down the hill."

"Isn't that the way of it? For every child's fond sledding memories there's the forgotten parent who lugs him up the hill. It's all right, though. Probably in order to be your own man you have to forget certain things about the one that made you."

"I'm not trying to forget anything."

"No, I know. Well I'm about cashed in. Talk to you later."

A cup of coffee down before it was even light, the second cup as the gray dawn solidified into golden morning. August toasted two pieces of white bread. He slathered them with butter and then sliced bananas, carefully arranging them like pale coins. He drizzled a precise zigzag of honey over the bananas and he ate, sitting on his small porch, his hood up against the chill, inhaling the steam coming off his mug. From where he sat he could see the light on in Ancient Virostok's kitchen. Occasionally Ancient was visible, alone, moving across the window, filling the coffee carafe with water, rinsing out a travel mug, washing his hands after peeling strips of bacon into the skillet. August finished his whole pot of coffee before Ancient emerged from his house. When he did finally step outside, he stood on the porch and stretched and yawned.

"What a morning," he yelled. He gave August a little salute. "You coffee'd up?" he said. "Let's go deal with that son of a bitch of a tree."

With Ancient driving they headed out the rutted drive and turned east, toward the river. The radio was on low; August could just make out the song, Doc Watson doing "Tennessee Stud." Ancient was thumping his thumbs on the steering wheel in time, and the truck smelled of coffee and mouthwash covering last night's alcohol.

"Billings," he said, shaking his head. "What a shithole. You spent much time there?"

"Not much."

"Well, good for you. I'll be happy to not step foot in that cesspool for a while. They got the reservation right there and that's always been bad enough, but now they got the oil fields and that's even worse. Only thing worse than a drunk Indian is a drunk roughneck with a pay-check burning a hole in his pocket. You told me you did a stint down in Wyoming, right?"

"I don't claim it. Just a couple months. Long enough to figure out it wasn't for me."

"Good money, though, I bet."

"Paid out most of it in rent."

"Yeah, that's what I've heard. Nowhere to live. I also heard prosti-tutes from Vegas fly in and out every weekend. Absolutely raking it in."

"Maybe. I have no idea."

"I've never paid for it, myself. I have nothing morally against it. But it doesn't do it for me, knowing that the woman, no matter how hot she may be, is just at work, probably thinking about what she's going to have for dinner later or something. She could care less about you, and if that's the case then what's the point? Might as well save some money and jack it. Same with titty bars. Never saw the logic of spending a bunch of money to sit next to other dudes drooling over bored single mothers who fundamentally hate you."

"They do this thing on the rigs. We worked really long hours. Some of the guys would buy a bunch of those energy drinks and open them up and let them sit overnight so the carbonation goes flat. They'd use it to brew the coffee with. One morning I got up and drank a cup of that. I was going to lace up my boots, and I was leaning over and I just threw it all up. I vomited on my boots. I couldn't get all the puke out of the laces and I could smell it all morning when I was working, and so when I took lunch break I just went to where I was staying and packed up my things. Left my boots there. Drove away barefoot. Some people can stand the smell of puke. I can't."

"My God. What that must do to your guts," Ancient said. "You were smart to get out of that. My old man might have been right about some things. Poverty on a ranch is still better than a lot of situations. Like living in Billings, for example. Jesus. The women aren't even good-looking down there. Big hair. Thick ankles."

"Did you see Kim?"

With the flat of his palm, Ancient rubbed his chin. Unshaven, it scratched against his chapped hand. "Yeah, I saw her. People always run their mouths about out-of-towners that move here. Good-looking girl like Kim takes up with Ancient, and then everyone starts their sniping."

"I haven't heard anything."

"I suppose not. People know that you and I work close so whatever comes to you will come to me eventually. And you're not from around here either, so there's that."

"Maybe people are talking about me," August said.

Ancient looked at him and took a sip of coffee. He shook his head. "No one is talking about you, cowboy. Hate to burst your bubble."

. . .

Ancient and August stood on the bank of the Musselshell and regarded the problem. A giant cottonwood had fallen and come to rest directly against the headgate that fed the irrigation ditch that watered the hayfield. The cottonwood's massive trunk was wedged in such a way that raising or lowering the steel gate was impossible. It was stuck closed, and until they were able to get it open, no water was going to find its way out to the thirsty alfalfa.

The river was up, flowing brown and cold. The pressure of the water was forcing the tree hard against the gate. Ancient's plan was to get a rope around one of the tree's upper limbs and use the truck on the bank to pull it up and away. To facilitate this process he had come to the conclusion that they ought to cut away as many of the tree's thick branches as possible, streamlining the whole mess and making it more likely to come free under the force of the truck.

Ancient was messing with the chainsaw, and August could smell gas. The sound of the river was a constant dull hum; the chainsaw was chugging but wouldn't start. "Goddamn this thing," Ancient said. He was dropping the saw with his left hand and pulling the cord in his right with everything he had, over and over, grunting with every stroke, the old grease-coated Stihl growling a little but stubbornly refusing to fire.

August stood on the edge of the concrete that held the headgate and looked over at the tree, sticking like a knife in the cold meat of the current. The only way to reach the limbs that needed to be cut was to climb out onto the tree itself. Water was cresting on the lower end of the trunk, and the deep furrows of the cottonwood bark were black and slick looking. There was a chug and a cough and then a snarl as Ancient finally brought the saw to life. He revved the motor a few times and brought the chain to a high whine before backing off and letting it idle.

"All right, she's purring like a kitty now," he said. "Hop on out there and I'll hand it to you."

August looked at the saw, looked back at the cottonwood bucking in the current. "Maybe we should just give it a shot with the truck first," he said.

Ancient gave the saw a goose and shook his head. "Won't work," he said. "That limb there and that limb there have got to go. If we pull on it like it is we're just going to be wedging it further up in there. That or maybe we'll fuck the gate up beyond all repair. Come on. We'll just have you hop out there and then I'll hand you the saw and zip-zip you're done."

"Right," August said. "Zip-zip." He stepped off the concrete wall to the cottonwood trunk, gingerly finding purchase, his boots squelching on the wet bark. He could feel the river under his feet. August steadied himself with one hand on a limb, and Ancient stretched out with the saw until August could grab it. The heavy saw unbalanced August. He knelt and went to work on the first limb. The chain flung chunks of bark and then hummed into the pulpwood, sending out a rooster tail of white, sappy, wet sawdust. The first limb went easily. The saw was sharp and the cottonwood was soft. In a few moments, August kicked the limb away and it bobbed off downstream, turning slowly in the roiling water. He changed positions and started on the second limb. This one was trickier; the river was pushing on it in such a way that the saw kept binding. Finally, as it neared the center of the limb, as big around as his thigh, the saw ran to a stop completely. He tried to jerk it clear but the bar was wedged, the current pushing the limb back on itself as if trying to heal the cut.

"Is it stuck?" Ancient said.

"Looks like it, doesn't it?"

"Can you wiggle it out?"

"I'm trying."

"Maybe if you step out on the limb and push it down that will release that pressure?"

"Jesus Christ." August slid one foot around the stuck saw so that he could put his weight on the stubborn branch. He gave a hop, and when his weight fell on the limb he pulled on the saw and he felt it budge slightly. He repeated the hop-and-pull maneuver and was able to get the saw free.

"You're going to have to try to cut it from the other side," Ancient said. "It's just going to bind again if you go at it the same way."

"I know," August said.

"Okay, just pointing out things as I see them here from mission control."

August changed angles and started the saw on the upstream side of the limb. Now the current was pushing the branch away from the saw, and the wood ripped eagerly under the chain. Too eagerly. Before August was ready there was a sharp crack and the limb broke free. Swinging up and over the cottonwood trunk, the butt of the limb knocked into the bar of the Stihl so quickly that August still had the saw running wide-open when it bit into his boot with a whine. Leather and rubber vaporized instantly. In the shock of it, he dropped the saw, slipped from the log, and met the water with his back.

He was fully submerged. For a second he could hear the saw running underwater and then that was gone. He couldn't feel pain yet, but he was certain that in the split second the saw had smashed into his boot it had chewed all the way through. He struggled toward shore, his jeans and denim jacket weighing him down. Ancient yelling, cursing, running down the bank.

August got a hold of an overhanging Russian olive and pulled himself out of the water, gasping. His foot still didn't hurt, but he was scared to look. He wrestled himself into a sitting position, expecting to see blood and gore. As it turned out, the saw had cut through the leather of his boot upper so that a stripe of his white sock was visible, but that was it. He'd been a sock's thickness away from having the chain tear into him. He collapsed onto his back and listened to Ancient crashing through the brush toward him.

They eventually looped a length of rope around the top of the tree and, with the truck, were able to shift it enough that the current washed it out downstream. Then Ancient cranked up the steel gate and sent a tongue of tea-colored water probing down the dry irrigation channel.

Driving back to the house, Ancient said, "I had that saw for damn near twenty years. Not your fault, obviously, but I'll miss it. Never gave me any problems. Stihl makes a good product."

"Too bad," August said. His clothes were still soaked, and he had to force away a shiver.

"I should have had you tie a rope to the handle. That was my fault."

"That probably would have been the smart thing."

"But don't worry about it. Could have happened to anyone. I just want you to know that I don't blame you for dropping the saw like you did."

"I could have cut my foot off," August said.

"Oh, come on. Five white monkeys could have flown out of my ass, too. Neither of those things happened, though, so it doesn't make much sense to worry about it."

"Easy for you to say."

"Oh, I get it. You're pissed at me."

"The whole thing was stupid. There could have been some better way to go about it."

"Let's hear it, then. How should we have done it?"

"Forget it."

"No, I want to know. I'm all ears."

"You're right. We should have tied a rope to the saw. That's what we should have done." August leaned his head against the window and closed his eyes for the rest of the ride.

That night August stood under the shower until the hot water ran out. Afterward, somehow still cold, he took the wool blanket off the bed, wrapped it around himself, and called his mother.

"Augie, what a nice surprise," she said. "I was just thinking about you."

"Oh yeah? What were you thinking?"

"Nothing specific, really. I was just having a general Augie thought cloud. And then you called. It's like I summoned you." She laughed and he could hear her inhale, taking a drag from her cigarillo. "How's life on the ranch?" she said.

"Oh, it's okay. They've got Hutterites up here. They're kind of like the Amish back home but not quite as strict. They've got trucks and electricity and stuff."

"Well, that's interesting. I'm glad you're getting some culture."

"What have you been up to?"

"Oh, you know me. Just continuing on the long path to self-betterment. For every hour of confusion and doubt I experience I'm trying to devote at least ten minutes to positive self-talk and self-love."

"*Self-talk?* What does that mean?"

"The specifics are between me, myself, and I. But in general it's combating the hostile babble of the world with some highly directed inward praise."

"How can you praise yourself and have it do any good?"

"It's possible, it just takes some practice."

"Seems like trying to tell yourself a joke to make yourself laugh when you already know the punch line."

"Well, that would be the cynic's response. Speaking of, have you been talking to your father?"

"Not in a while."

"That's what he said. I called him recently."

"I didn't know you guys were talking these days."

"Not much but here and there, mostly in regards to you."

"Me?"

"Specifically about your decision to not attend college this year. I know that you know that your father didn't go to college. However, I feel that you're processing this information incorrectly. Instead of understanding that your father wants a better life for you than the one he had, I think you believe that because he didn't attend, you yourself needn't."

"It has nothing to do with him. We've been over all of this."

"Okay. It sounds like you're really *thriving* up there. But, you know, you could probably get into MSU next semester with no trouble and still get a decent scholarship even."

"I fell off a tree into the river today and almost cut my foot off with a chainsaw. I'm fine, don't worry. I wasn't even going to tell you, but to be honest, I'd rather do that every day of the week than go sit in a classroom down in Bozeman."

August's mother was silent for a moment. An inhale and long exhale, a soft cough. "You brought that up to make me worry, and that's unkind."

"I was just trying to make a point. I didn't mean it like that. Never mind. Are you still getting those Bush-isms sent to you every day? I heard a good one the other day, and I wrote it down because I knew you'd like it. Hang on, I've got it here somewhere. Okay, here we go: *There's an old saying in Tennessee—I know it's in Texas, probably in Tennessee—that says, fool me once, shame on—shame on you. Fool me—you can't get fooled again.*"

He thought she might laugh, but she didn't. He heard the click of her lighter. "I'm having a harder and harder time finding the humor in our current situation," she said.

August and Tim Duncan were set up on the long, sloping flank of Antelope Butte shooting gophers, sitting in the back of Tim's truck, using the side for a rifle rest. They'd been at it for a while, and the truck bed was littered with spent shells. The field in front of them was dotted with small lumps of dead gopher, and the surviving gophers were hunkered down in their holes, not showing themselves. August and Tim waited. The sun was a benevolent presence in the sky, the scent of cottonwoods budding down by the river on the wind like a gift.

"Okay, okay, here we go." August could hear Tim expelling his breath in one long rush and then the pausing at the bottom of the exhale, that moment of stillness where the trigger was best squeezed. The rifle cracked, and Tim clucked his tongue. "Gotcha," he said. "Check it out. That used to gross me out so bad when I was a kid."

August shielded his eyes against the sun. He could barely make out a dead gopher and another live gopher doing something with the carcass.

"Wes always told me that gophers were cannibals. Just waiting for one of their pals to go down so that they can munch on their flesh. But that's not it."

"Hand me that," August said. "I can't really see."

Tim passed him the rifle and August tracked with the scope until he found the gopher Tim had just shot. Under magnification, he could see the living gopher chewing through the hole that Tim's .22 round had blown in the dead gopher's belly. The gopher stopped what it was doing and looked up. August could make out its snout clearly, covered in blood, its eyes black shards.

"That's disgusting," August said. "I thought gophers only ate seeds and berries and stuff."

"Well," Tim said, "that's actually what's going on. Basically, I shot the guts out of that first one, and the second one is in there eating the undigested contents of its pal's stomach. That's the survival instinct at its finest right there." Tim took the rifle back from August and worked a shell into the chamber. He settled down in his shooting stance and scanned the field until he found his target. "Hope that last meal was a good one, little buddy," he said.

With the light going gold and then orange and then pink over the top of Antelope Butte, Tim emptied his clip. He ran an oiled rag along the Marlin's blued barrel and worn stock, taking care to wipe the areas around the trigger and bolt. "Hey," he said. "I never asked you, but what's up with you having the day off? I mean, I have the day off, but that's because it's Sunday and that day still means something in the Duncan household. I know for a fact that Virostok doesn't keep the Sabbath holy."

"He just gave me the afternoon off," August said. "He does that sometimes."

"Nah," Tim said. "You're his only hand. I got my brother and so we switch off doing chores on Sundays and it happens to be my Sunday off is all. But if I'm Virostok and I got you on the payroll, then you don't get any extra days off." He held the Marlin up and huffed a fog on each lens of his scope, wiping the lens clean carefully with the tail of his shirt. He slid the rifle back into its fleece-lined case and zipped it up before leaning back against the cab, stretching his arms up, and interlacing his fingers behind his head. "Don't tell me if you don't want to, but something's up."

"I don't think it's any big deal," August said. "He went down to Bill-ings again."

"I drive by the place almost every day. I haven't seen Kim's car there in, since I can't even remember when."

"She's down in Billings visiting her sister, I guess. That's what An-cient told me."

"So then why'd he go down to Billings? If he needed something from there, he could've just had her pick it up. Why do you need to visit your own fiancée?"

"I don't really know, man. I got the afternoon off. I don't care. None of my business."

"Uh-huh." Tim fiddled with the zipper on his gun case, zipping and unzipping in rhythm. "Did you know that you can look up registered sex offenders on the Internet? Just type in your zip code, and it shows all the perverts in your neighborhood."

"So?"

"Do you have a computer at Virostok's?"

"No. No Internet in the bunkhouse, either."

"Well, you could go to the library or something if you wanted to check it out."

"Why would I want to check it out? Why don't you just come out and say whatever you're trying to say?"

"I'm not the type of guy that talks about folks behind their backs. I'm just saying that if you're in the mood for some interesting reading, you could check out the sex offender registry."

"I think that's probably the last place I would go for some interesting reading."

"Suit yourself."

"I aim to."

"Fine. Then forget I mentioned it. I was thinking. It's almost rodeo season, and you know what that means, right?"

"What does it mean?"

"Cowgirls, and wannabe cowgirls, which are better in my opinion. You dance?"

"No."

"Seriously?"

"I don't give a damn about dancing. You do?"

"Not about dancing by itself, but if you mean dancing as a way of meeting young ladies, then the answer is hell yes. All the girls that show up for rodeos can dance, or want to. If you can't two-step or jitterbug, at least a little, you're going to be sidelined, bud."

"I couldn't care less."

"The dudes dance, too."

"So?"

"So, I'm saying that if girls aren't really your thing, you'll still need to dance to pick up men. Either way, there's no avoiding it."

"Fuck you."

"No judgment here, pal. It's the twenty-first century. If you're into cowboys, I'll still be your friend."

"I'm not gay."

"Then you should probably let me show you the basic moves. You don't need to be Travolta out there; you just need a couple standby maneuvers to get things flowing."

"I have absolutely no interest in learning how to dance."

"I told you, it's not about the dancing; it's about the women. A means to an end. Do you want to meet women, yes or no?"

"Not particularly right now. I just don't want the hassle."

"The hassle? Dude. Life is the hassle. Women are the only thing that make the hassle worth enduring half the time."

"Do you want to go get a beer, or what?"

"Does the pope shit in the woods? Let's get the hell out of here."

Tim drove, windows down, although it was evening now and getting cool. "My theory is that you're nursing a little broken heart. Am I right? Some girly do you wrong and send you packing with a bad taste in your mouth and your feelers hurt?"

August shrugged. "Something like that," he said. "I don't want to talk about it."

"Okay. Okay. I understand. I'll just say one thing, and then I'll shut up about it. Best way to get over an old lover is to get under a new one. That's all I'm saying."

"Good one."

August was done with work for the day. He had a package of Virostok's ground beef thawing in a bowl on his kitchen counter. Before firing up the grill he called his mother.

When she answered he could hear music in the background. That one CD she always played when she was cooking dinner for someone. It was the old Cuban guys, Buena Vista Social Club. When that was on in the kitchen, she was preparing to not dine alone.

"Augie!" she said. "How are you?" He could hear the sound of her earring scraping across the phone receiver and then a wooden spoon banging several times on the edge of a pan.

"I'm okay. You cooking?"

"I'm making spaghetti and meatballs. Art was telling me he hasn't had a good meatball in ages, and that got me thinking. My mom had a great meatball recipe so I dug it up. Good Italian-seasoned bread crumbs are the key, and little chunks of fresh mozzarella that get all melty."

"Oh, Art's there. I don't want to keep you. I was just about to make some dinner myself, and I was calling to ask what you put in the hamburgers you make. I've made them a few times, but they haven't turned out as good as yours."

"Art's not here yet. You're cooking? Wonders never cease. I'd imagined you up there on a steady diet of Cup O' Noodles and Frosted Mini-Wheats."

"I've been doing a fair amount of that. But Ancient gave me a freezer full of beef, so I figured I might as well start using it. So far I've done tacos and burgers. Fair to medium results, but it's just me so it's not like anyone is complaining."

"I'm glad you're cooking. When you meet a girl you like it's always nice to be able to make her something. It's cheaper than going out all the time, and I've always said that the way to a girl's heart, or whatever you're trying to get to, is through her stomach. Shit, my marinara is bubbling over and I think Art just pulled in. I'm going to let you go, Augie. The secret to my hamburgers is Lipton's French onion soup mix and Worcestershire sauce and an egg to hold it all together. Good luck, dear, I've got to let you go."

August heard a clunk as she dropped the phone on the counter without hanging up. Buena Vista Social Club, indistinct muttering from his mother, the sounds of a spoon against a metal pan. A male voice. He heard his mom say something about a wine opener. August pressed his ear to the phone. It was silent now except for the music. What were they doing? He hung up before something happened that he couldn't unhear.

He sat for a moment regarding the package of half-frozen beef and then looked in the small set of cupboards about the sink. Salt, pepper, garlic, Tabasco. Nothing even closely resembling Lipton's French onion soup mix or Worcestershire sauce. In the end he put the meat in the fridge, changed his shirt, and headed to town.

Tending the Two Dot Bar was a tall, slope-shouldered man, not tremendously older than August, sandy hair and a tucked-in pearl-snap shirt. He slid a coaster across the bar and gave a nod of his head.

"Bud," August said.

"You old enough? I don't recognize you."

August put his wallet on the bar. Looked around. There were two women working the keno machines at the back; other than that the place was empty. "I'm old enough," August said.

The man shrugged. Twisted the cap off a Budweiser bottle and put it down.

"I've actually been in here a few times," August said. "Usually it's Theresa behind the bar."

The bartender leaned against the beer cooler and wiped his hands on his towel. "That's my aunt. It's her place. She's having migraines lately so I've been helping out. She never has migraines on Fourth of July weekend when I could actually stand to make some money in here. Always she gets the migraines on Tuesday nights in the off-season when she wants to go up to Great Falls with her girlfriends for the karaoke contests."

"Karaoke contests?"

"Yeah, there's some bar up there that has a contest every month. Theresa thinks she's Shania Twain or something. She trucks up there with her little gaggle of divorced friends to get shitty in a town where no one knows who they are and they can just go wild."

"I never really understood karaoke," August said.

"I hear you there. You want a food menu?"

"I know what I'm going to get."

"Shoot."

"Small Caesar salad and small pizza. Pepperoni, mushrooms, and green olives."

The bartender put the food order in, and when he returned he fished out another beer for August and got one for himself. "I figure that by closing time tonight I'll have pulled down, in tips, just slightly more than the gas money it takes me to drive over here. I feel that I'm entitled to make up some of my pay in Aunt Theresa's booze."

"Seems fair," August said.

"So, what brings you to town?"

"I'm out working at the Virostok place. Been here a couple months."

"Oh, sure. Ancient used to come in here quite a bit. Haven't seen him in a while. How's he doing?"

"Good, I guess. Fine. He's got a fiancée."

The bartender rolled his eyes and took a drink. "I know how that goes. A fiancée will definitely infringe on a guy's bar time." He wiped his hand on his rag and extended it across the bar. "I'm Cale, by the way."

"August."

"Like the month?"

"The one after July."

"Huh. I never met an August before. Is that a family name?"

"Not a family name. My mom's a librarian. She got it from a book."

"Like a book of baby names?"

"No, it was a novel she liked, I think."

"You haven't read it?"

August shook his head. "Nah."

"If it were me, I think I'd read it. I'd be curious."

"Maybe someday I will."

"My parents named me Cale after my mom's favorite uncle. It's a Jewish name. I'm not Jewish, but somewhere back in my family they must have been. It means *brave dog.*"

"Seriously?"

"Yep. My mom always told me that, and then I looked it up one time. It's true."

"That's a pretty good meaning for a name."

"I've always thought so. There's a lot worse you can do than *brave dog*. I think a man that knows what his name means does his best to live up to it. That's why I think you should figure out where yours comes from."

When August's food came, he sprinkled dried Parmesan and red pepper flakes over his pizza and let it cool, starting in on the salad. It was iceberg lettuce, swimming in thick Caesar dressing, croutons already soggy. Cale watched August eat. "Not too many people go for the salad here," he said. "Or the pizza. Our burgers are pretty good, though."

August shrugged. "I've got a freezer full of beef at home."

"You and everyone else. The question is, do you have someone at home to turn that beef into a hamburger while you sit and drink a beer? I thought not. And that's why this place has a crew of regulars. The food has nothing to do with it."

"Is Tim Duncan a regular?"

Cale flicked his rag at something on the bar. "Oh, sure, all the Duncans used to come in a lot. Tim's brother Weston was my best friend. Big Tim used to be in here damn near every night just to talk to Theresa. I haven't seen him in a long time."

"I've been running around with Tim a little bit," August said. "He seems like a good enough guy." August took a bit of pizza, strings of melting cheese stretching out long on his chin. "But I guess I'm actually not one hundred percent on that."

Cale drained his beer and threw it in the trash. It broke against the bottles already in there, loud enough that one of the ladies playing keno said "Goddamn" and turned to look, her glasses low on her nose. Cale opened more beer for both of them. "Timmy can be a bit of a wild card," he said. "No way to deny it. Avoid giving him hard liquor. I learned that lesson. Get some of the high octane in him and he goes off the rails."

"I did notice that."

"I think his heart is in the right place. But Wes was a beautiful person, and I don't care who hears me say. Loved him like a brother. I'm getting married in a few months. Supposed to be a real big happy day in my life. I've got my drunk uncle Dwight as my best man. Should be Wes. He never met Noelle. She moved here right after he left for school, and that's a weird thing. I've got this woman I'm going to spend the rest of my life with, and she never met the person that meant the most to me. Almost doesn't seem right somehow, but that's not something a woman wants to hear about." Cale sniffed and rubbed at his nose with the back of his hand.

August finished his last slice of pizza and pushed the plate away. "So, this may sound weird," he said. "But when you said your name I actually kind of knew who you were, because Tim told me a crazy story the other night and you were in it."

Cale crossed his arms over his chest and laughed. "Uh-oh," he said.

"It was mostly about his brother, something you and Wes did down at the Hutterite colony."

Cale frowned, shook his head. "What did we do at the Hutterite colony? I've only been down there once or twice to get turkeys for my mom around the holidays."

"I figured it was a bullshit story. Tim was drunk. Never mind."

"No, what did he say? I'm curious."

"That you got a VD check and then took Wes down there to the colony to be, like, studs, because the Hutterites were looking to get some of their women pregnant. Tim said his brother told him about it."

Cale shook his head. "Fucking Wes. Still messing with me from the grave, I swear to God. First off, I'm not the one that was banging a

Hoot. Second, stud service? That's just a myth dudes are always talking about up here. Never happened." Cale stopped. Twirled his beer bottle a few times on the bar. "I maybe shouldn't say anymore, but fuck it. It's not like Wes is going to get pissed at me. It's a hell of a story, way better than that stud nonsense. You like fishing?"

"It's all right. I used to do more of it when I was a kid."

"Wes loved it. Hardly anyone fishes the Musselshell, but he had some spots where he pulled out huge brown trout. Seriously, some of them were as long as your leg."

"People are always saying that. I've never seen a trout as long as my leg."

"I'm telling you. He didn't catch a lot of them, but when he did, they were giant. Believe me or not, I don't care. The size of the fish isn't the point. One of the spots Weston would go to was in the middle of the Hoot colony. He'd hop in at the bridge in Two Dot and just wade downstream for miles. The Hoots don't give a shit about fishing as far as I know, so the trout are just hanging out there, dying of old age.

"That summer before Wes left for college he was going fishing, like, every day. He'd get done with his chores and he'd be fishing. Early morning. Sometimes staying out past dark. I was hardly seeing the guy, and he wasn't showing me pictures of the trout he'd been catching either. I finally pinned him down about it. He was like, *Don't laugh, but I've been spending a lot of time with Sarah Jane.* And I'm like, *Who the hell is Sarah Jane—is that, like, a euphemism for something? Are you doing meth, brother?* But no. Sarah Jane was a Hoot girl. I, of course, started giving him a ton of shit about this but he didn't laugh. He said that he'd been fishing on the river way down there in Hoot land, a nice warm day in spring, and he came around the bend and there was a girl laid out on a rock, reading, blond and butt-ass naked. He surprised her and she got embarrassed and covered herself up, but they started talking and I guess you can figure out the rest. That was Sarah Jane. She was only sixteen, and she somehow turned Wes into an idiot."

"She was a Hutterite? And she was sunbathing naked?"

"I know. I never really met her, but apparently she was not your average Hoot gal. She had this spot down there where no one from the colony would ever see her, a cliff that she scrambled around somehow. The only way anyone could come up on her was from the river."

"I've never come across anything that interesting while fishing."

"Yeah, me neither. Weston was always lucky that way. Until he wasn't. For a while, though, he was head over heels. Before he left for Austin, he and I were drinking some beers one night and he told me he was thinking about saying fuck it and not going. Said he and Sarah Jane might just take off somewhere for a little while and see how it all panned out. I remember exactly what I told him. I said, *Wes, look at me. That is a horrible idea. You're thinking with your dick. You're going to college. There's going to be a million girls in Austin, and all of this will seem ridiculous.* And after a while he said, *You're right. I don't know what I'm thinking about. Of course I'm going to go.* And then he went. And look what happened."

Cale had been polishing a glass, but now the rag in his hand had stopped and he was looking over August's shoulder at the door as if expecting someone to come in.

"Everyone you meet, their lives can hinge on the words that come out of your mouth. You ever consider that? You can just say a few sentences and then your best friend dies. We just walk around all day putting words on people, sowing the seeds of disaster. He could be set up right now, a little place of his own with Sarah Jane, helping run the cattle on his family place. Happy and in love. That's the alternate universe that occurs if I don't open my mouth."

August turned to see what Cale was looking at, but there was no one at the door. They were silent for a few moments, and then August drained his beer. "You look at the extended forecast lately?" he said. "Is it supposed to stay mild like this for a while?"

Cale cleared August's dishes and brought him his change from the twenty he'd put down. "I'm not sure. But you know what they always say about Montana weather: If you don't like it, just wait ten minutes and it will change."

"They say that about the weather everywhere."

"I heard about a place in Africa where it hasn't rained in one hundred years."

"Yeah?"

"I bet they don't say that about the weather there."

"I guess you got me. See you around."

As August was making his way out the door, one of the keno machines went off, lights flashing. The gray-haired lady in front of it had her arms raised over her head, fists clenched in victory. "Sadie, you lucky bitch," her friend said. "You've hit twice this week. Why does God hate me?"

After picking up several gallon jugs of weed spray at the Feed-n-Need, August swung by the Martinsdale Carnegie Library and signed up for a library card. The librarian wrote down his information from his driver's license on a small green piece of paper that she then ran through a laminating machine. She trimmed the plastic edges and slid it over the counter at him, her nose wrinkling slightly. He'd been helping Ancient all morning with his old baler. It had been spewing hydraulic fuel, and haying season was right around the corner. Mostly, Ancient was doing the work and August was getting him the tools he asked for, holding things, shining the flashlight on grease-coated fittings in the dim interior of the shed. Ancient had one CD in the old stereo in the shop. It was Jimmy Buffett, and it was on constant repeat. Although he wasn't under the machine, wrenching, August still managed to get himself coated with grease and fluid. His jeans had long black smears, and even after multiple washings with GOJO in the shop sink his hands were still stained, dark crescents under each fingernail. Worst of all, he had Buffett stuck in his head. Jangly steel drums.

After some browsing August selected a large tome from the "Regional Interest" section entitled *The Hutterites: A People's History*. Before leaving the library he sat down at one of the public computers and connected to the Internet. He found the Montana sex offender registry website, typed in the Virostok Ranch's address, and in less than a minute was looking at a picture of Kim Meyers. Deep purple bags under her eyes, her hair shorter and dyed peroxide blond. Below the picture was a short list of information.

36-year-old female. Level 1 offender. Registering offense (Idaho):
   Sexual acts with a minor. Victim: 15-year-old female. Vehicle:
   1999 Subaru Forester.

Further down the pages was a definition list.

Note: 46-23-509 MCA provides for sex offenders to be designated a
   level 1, 2 or 3. Under this law, the following definitions apply to
   sex offender designations:
Level 1—The risk of a repeat sexual offense is low.
Level 2—The risk of a repeat sexual offense is moderate.
Level 3—The risk of a repeat sexual offense is high, there is a threat
   to public safety, and the sexual offender evaluator believes that
   the offender is a sexually violent predator.

August scrolled through the list of all the offenders in Meagher
County, Kim the only woman among a sad lineup of twisted gray
beards, slumped shoulders, gaping jaws. One guy was near August's
age. Shaved head, glasses making his eyes look as if they were disembodied and swimming.

Desmond Swandel. 21-year-old male. Level 2 offender. Registering
   offense (Montana, Yellowstone County): Sexual acts with a
   minor. Victim: 8-year-old male. Vehicle: None.

August looked at Desmond Swandel long enough to notice that he'd
shaved badly before the photo was taken. A patch of reddish stubble
was visible on his lower chin. He closed the browser, checked out his
book, thanked the librarian for her time, and drove home on the river
road. He had the window down to erase the public-library smell from
his nose, and he could hear the prehistoric sounds of sandhill cranes,
paired up for mating, calling out from the greening fields.

The phone in the bunkhouse rang, and August let it go for a while before he picked it up.

"Catch you at a bad time?" his father said.

"No, not really. Just thinking about making some dinner."

"Seems like I'm always calling you at mealtime."

"It's okay."

"What are you having?"

"Ramen."

"Really?"

"I'm putting some vegetables and shrimp in it."

"Well, that's a little better than just plain. But I guess you inherited my culinary skills."

"I fenced all day. I really don't care what it is."

"Don't have to explain it to me. I hear you loud and clear. If it weren't for Lisa, I'd probably be asking you for your recipe. She made beef Stroganoff the other night. When's the last time you had that? That's a meal you forget about, but when you have it you're always reminded how good it is."

"Never cared for it much myself."

"Really? How not?"

"It's gray. I don't like gray food."

"Huh. Lisa's is actually more of a light brown. I bet you'd like it."

"I doubt it."

"Well. I saw one of your mom's daffodils poking up next to the house last week. Then last night we got two inches of snow. Typical March weather. You know what they say—in like a lion, out like a lamb."

"Seems like it doesn't finally start going out like a lamb until sometime around June here."

"Everything's bigger and badder out there, eh? Speaking of June, though. You haven't mentioned your gal friend recently. What's up with that?"

"She's out on the East Coast for school. She's coming back for spring break, though. We talk on the phone all the time."

"That long-distance thing, I don't know. Maybe it's a blessing in disguise. In my opinion, as a young buck, you should play the field. Makes things a little easier if you decide to settle down later. A *little* easier. I don't think it's ever actually *easy*, as long as you still got blood pumping in your veins. The struggle of modern man."

"What's that?"

"Settling down."

"Last I checked it's a free world. No one is making you do anything."

"Maybe not. We're on the edge of a new humanity. I feel that way. I do. Pretty soon society is going to be run by women, and I don't know that it's necessarily a bad thing, just that you and I are going to be obsolete."

"How so?"

"We're entering the age of cooperation. The age of teamwork. The age of feelings and equality. The only reason they're still allowing boys to be born is because there's other nations out there not advanced enough to look down their nose at war. As long as you got people being born into dirt-floor huts wanting something they haven't got, you're going to need boys to hold guns. From hero, to necessary evil, to relic of our barbarian past—that's the fate of man in the arc of time."

"You told me once that a good woman is man's only hope for salvation on earth."

"That doesn't sound like me."

"Pretty sure you did. Doesn't matter."

"Let me put it real simple: Men will ruin the world. Women can save the world, but they'll ruin men in the process. Get me?"

"I guess." They fell silent for a moment and then August said, "They clocked the wind at seventy-one miles per hour at the little airstrip up here last week. An RV heading down 89 flipped and rolled twice, but I guess no one died. Seventy-one is almost hurricane strength."

"Doesn't it have to be sustained to be considered hurricane strength—not just a gust? I mean, that's still a strong wind, of course."

"Not sure on that. Maybe. They said that on the news, about the hurricane strength. It wasn't just something I made up."

"No, of course not. I don't doubt it. I was just not totally sure about what exactly constitutes hurricane strength, you know? Shrimp, you said? Never would have thought it to put that in ramen myself. You getting it frozen, I take it?"

"Yeah, frozen."

"Already cooked, though, right?"

"They're cooked."

"Peeled?"

"The tail is still on there."

"So, do you thaw them out and then take the tail off and then put them in the ramen, or do you just put them in frozen?"

"I usually just get the water boiling and then put in the broccoli and carrots or whatever and that's when I put the shrimp in. Frozen. It works fine. You just take the tails off as you eat them."

"Well, that sounds pretty easy. Healthy, too, I imagine. Maybe I'll try it some night when I'm baching it. Okay. I'll let you get to it. You're probably hungry. Nice talking to you."

Late June, with the shadows of the clouds making calico patterns on the hills. August rode shotgun in Tim's truck on their way down to Wilsall for the first rodeo of the year. Tim tossed August a shooter of Beam and handed him a can of Bud. "Put them down fast, pal," he said. August downed the Beam and sipped from the beer. He looked over at Tim. He was dolled up. Clean summer Stetson. Pale pink pearl-snap tucked into freshly ironed Wranglers. His boots were wet-looking, devoid of mud and manure. "You're not drinking?" August said.

"Oh, I will. Plenty. I'm not the one that needs to get loosened up, though."

"What?"

"Yep. Get loose."

"Why? What are you talking about?"

Tim laughed, pulled his truck off the road, drove into a flat rocky pasture, and parked. He fiddled with his CD player and Johnny Cash doing "Cocaine Blues" came on. He turned it up. "Here we go," he said hopping out. "The Tim Duncan five-minute crash dance course. Let's get to it."

"I'm not dancing. Let it rest."

Tim hooked his fingers in his belt loops and rocked back on his heels. "You can just start walking from right here, then. You go to the rodeo with me and you're going to dance. Bottom line. I've got a reputation to uphold. I've got a gal coming from Bozeman with a friend, and I told her I'd have a tall, good-looking cowboy with me that would be happy to twirl her girlfriend around. If you're the tool standing there against the wall, it makes me look bad, understand? Relax, you're not going to be out there doing the fox-trot or the tango or whatever. A girl just wants to be spun a little." Tim tapped his boot on the ground and whistled along out of tune. "Don't be nervous. It's easy."

"I'm not nervous. This is ridiculous."

August stood in front of Tim, and Tim grabbed his hand and pulled him close. "Okay. I'm going to be you. Meaning, I'm going to lead. As a man, you lead. It doesn't really matter too much what you do, as long as you do it with conviction. This is your basic western swing, or jitterbug, or whatever you want to call it. Works better with the faster songs, it's kind of flashy, you get the lady twirling, which is what they all want. The basic spin is here. Twirl, dumbass. Okay, you see how I kept my right hand on your sexy midsection while you spun? That's key. Dancing is foreplay, pal. No other way around it; that's why it hasn't gone out of fashion and never will. I leave my hand on your hip right there and as you spin it travels around, stomach, to lower back and that's where it rests. Enough pressure so that she can feel it, not enough to be the creepy guy copping a feel. After the spin you're in close. Two-stepping. The footwork can be a little tricky but it's *short, short, looong*. So, two shorts left, one long right. Yep, like that. If you're in doubt, just shuffle a little. See, I'm a good leader so it just comes natural for you to follow like that. If you can do it like I'm doing it, the girl kind of naturally falls into step.

"Couple more little things. Girls get wet for the pretzel. Even if it goes wrong and you get all tangled up, just laugh about it. It looks complicated but it's not too hard. My left hand is going behind my back. See how I'm looking back at it? That lets the girl know she's supposed to grab it. *Grab it, jackass.* Okay, now I bring it up and over.

Damn it, don't let go. Try it again. Okay, grip tight, it's coming up and over and you're spinning, good. Just watch the elbows and go a little slower than the music. That's the key. You see these asshole guys from Bozeman or Billings, and they're dancing flat out no matter what the song is, jerking the gal around like a rag doll. Keep it slow and tight. Pull the lady to you. Okay, nice, now back to home base. There you go. Spin me out. Perfect, now grab that one there and lead me through the pretzel. Fuckin'-A, man. You're a natural."

"Oh, shut up," August said, dropping Tim's hands and stepping back. "There's been three trucks that have gone by and seen us out here."

"Why are you so uptight? My dad taught me and my brothers how to dance just like that. It's no different than learning how to drive. It's basic knowledge you got to have. Okay, that's good enough; the rest you'll figure out on the fly. You Michigan people are a trip. You remind me of a guy I knew in high school that moved here from the Upper Peninsula, Gerald Priest was his name. If he wasn't sure about something he'd say, *Well, Tim, you know, I don't know, you know?* Used to just kill me every time. I haven't thought about him for a long while now. Wonder whatever happened to that guy. I think he was at graduation, then he disappeared. *You know, I don't know, you know?* Funniest thing ever."

Wilsall was besieged by pickup trucks. Stock trailers parked at haphazard angles around the rodeo grounds. The Bank Bar had a crowd of people spilling out onto the street, everyone holding beers or red plastic cups of mixed drinks. Tim drove slowly through the throng, windows down. "Goddamn, would you look at that," he said. "So much ass. Those look sprayed on. Do they have like some sort of tool they use to get into them things? It's going to be a good night, pal."

Tim parked, and they dropped the tailgate of his truck and sat, drinking beers from the cooler they'd packed earlier, watching the procession of women in tight Levi's and sundresses with boots.

"Are we going to go get a seat?" August said. "Might be getting pretty full."

"What do you mean? We have our seat right here."

"Aren't we going to go watch the rodeo?"

Tim went wide-eyed. "Are you serious? You want to go watch dudes get bucked off bulls when we have a front-row seat to a parade of Western femininity at its finest?"

August laughed. "I've been to the rodeo down in Livingston. I guess I don't really care about it one way or the other."

"Of course you don't. You're like me, you work on a ranch. You don't need to waste your free time watching a rhinestone-bedazzled mockery of the shit you do every day."

As if on cue a man walked by wearing a gold belt buckle the size of a dinner plate. Spurs on his boots jangling with every step. Tim and August wordlessly stared at him, and when he'd passed Tim slurped on his beer and belched. "Too easy," he said. "I'm not even going to comment."

"I'll start watching rodeos when they feature a fence-post-driving competition," August said.

"Exactly. Or shit mucking. But until then, we'll sit out here and take advantage of the sights. When the actual thing gets going we'll make our way into the bar and get set up before it turns into an absolute zoo."

By the time the rodeo finally let out, August and Tim had staked out a prime spot at the bar, close to the dance floor and the stage where the band was getting warmed up. People kept streaming in, and the whole place filled with a dull roar. Tim ordered them both shots and beers, and not long after they'd slammed their empty glasses down on the bar, a group of women materialized from the crowd near them. It seemed that Tim knew some of them and soon he was leading a short, busty blonde out onto the dance floor. A tall brunette with a rash of freckles across her cheeks and the bridge of her nose looked at August, smiled and shrugged, extended her hand.

August tried to keep Tim's instructions in mind, but *short, short, looong* was immediately lost in the mass of people twirling on the dance floor. August pulled the girl in close, and she had a tangible heat, his hand on her lower back feeling the twin bands of muscle there. They rotated slowly and he spun her, and as she went he could see the white of her smile, her long hair splaying out around her face; could smell her citrus shampoo clear through the bar-sweat beer smell. There were elbows in his back, hats and hair in a kaleidoscopic twirl. He pulled her back in. He shuffled and was surprised to find that she seemed to mostly be in step with him. She put her mouth up to his ear, shouting over the band. "I'm Maya. Thanks for dancing with me. I love it, but I'm not very good."

"I'm August," he said. And then he spun her again and the talking was done. Before the song's end their random progress around the dance floor brought them near Tim and his partner. Tim was leading the blonde through an intricate series of moves—her face flushed and happy, their arms a blur, both of them laughing. When the song ended, Tim dipped his partner low so that her head nearly hit the ground and then swung her back up. She gave a little jump and straddled his hips with her arms around his neck. He walked her to the bar that way, running blindly into people with his face buried in her cleavage.

August danced with freckled Maya; he danced with Christi, Tim's partner; he danced with a procession of other women, their faces and bodies running together. The room was stifling, and he had sweat rolling down his temples. He did the few moves Tim had taught him, and he learned a few more from watching other couples. The band kept everything going, and he went from one partner to the next with hardly enough time in between to get a drink at the bar. For the most part, the women did the asking.

When the band stopped, Tim and Christi were deep in conversation at the bar. August ordered one more beer and finally sat, glad for the rest after what seemed like hours of frantic movement. People were trickling out now, and the bartenders were shouting about last call. August felt a warm hand on the back of his neck, and freckled Maya plopped down on the stool next to him. Earlier she'd been wearing a plaid shirt tied up at the midriff but that was gone now and she was in her tank top and Levi's. Her arms were covered with the same spray of freckles that crossed her nose. There was a dark spot on her tank top at her lower back where her sweat had soaked through under the various hands of all the night's dance partners.

"Whew," she said. "I'm about danced out." She laughed and nodded down at Tim and Christi. "Looks like those two are getting along well." She turned her eyes on August and smiled. "I had fun dancing with you," she said. "I tried to get back to you, but it seemed like every time I looked you had your hands full."

August shrugged. "You'd get bored dancing with me more than a few times anyway. I only know, like, three moves. I was just doing them in different orders and hoping the song would finish before it became obvious that I'm clueless."

Maya laughed and then her hand was on his arm. "I know what you mean. Have you ever watched an older couple dance? Sometimes they're just so good, like they can predict each other's movements perfectly."

"Must take a long time to get that way."

"Probably. I like to think that some of these old-time dancers started out like us."

"Seems like dancing with the same person for years and years might get boring."

"Dancing with the same person isn't boring if you're always trying new things. And maybe you take little breaks occasionally and have a quick dance with someone else just to reaffirm that dancing with your old partner is still the best." She reached over and took a long drink of his beer, her eyes on his the whole time.

Eventually Tim and Christi broke their huddle and came over, and before long they were all out in the back of Tim's pickup. Only a few hours until dawn, the air cool, the occasional shouts of the diehards still standing around outside the bar. Tim had blankets, and the girls were wrapped up in them. They drank the remaining beers in the cooler, and before long Tim and Christi moved to the cab of the truck. Maya rose up, the blanket over her shoulders, raised her arms out like wings, and settled herself down over August. She laid her head on his chest. There was a soft laugh from the cab of the truck, then a differently pitched sound, and soon the whole truck was rocking unmistakably.

Maya snorted. "God, that didn't take long," she said. "Christi is such a tramp." Maya was moving against him and August was fumbling with her belt, her zipper. She wasn't exactly making it easy for him, but she wasn't telling him to stop, either. When he started to pull her jeans off, she wriggled to help, both of them laughing when they got hung up around her ankles. Her panties soon followed and he moved down, starting with his tongue the way Julie had always liked it, slow at first. Maya's hips were going, but where Julie would seem to ascend Maya actually started to slow. Eventually she was still, and so August tried harder. He moved his hand up until he could feel the soft cords of her throat; he clenched. She made a startled squawk, pulled his hand off her, and wriggled away. "*What was that?*" she said. "No more of that. I'm not into that." He tried for a while longer, but something had been put off. Her legs were rigid now, she made no sounds, and eventually he just rolled away and lay on his back.

There were muffled yips from Christi in the cab. Maya groaned and turned on her side, facing away from him. It was quiet except for the soft squeaking of the truck's suspension. "I don't know how for some people it seems to be so easy," she said. "I'm sorry. I just can't get into it until I'm comfortable. That's just the way I'm wired."

"It's fine. I'm tired, anyway."

"Me, too. You can still put your arm around me if you want."

Before long Maya was giving soft, halting snores and August lay there with his arm going numb underneath her. There were some decent stars, and he searched for a constellation in the shape of how stupid he felt.

He was awake to witness the dawn, and he disentangled himself from Maya and stepped softly from the truck. He was waiting on the porch when the cook came in to open the Wilsall Diner.

"Coffee?" he said.

"Yeah, you and every other person in this hungover town," the cook said. "You can sit and wait. It's going to be a few minutes."

When August returned to the truck with two steaming Styrofoam cups, Tim was sitting on the tailgate and the girls were gone. Tim had found a beer somewhere and was drinking, not even trying to keep the smile off his face.

"Hair of the dog?" he said.

"Ugh. I might hurl if I tried that."

"Suit yourself. It's the best thing, really. You a little hungover, son?"

"Little bit."

"Well, I feel great." Tim gave a shout and stretched. "Good morning to be alive."

"You're probably still drunk."

"I could still be. Whew. What a night, eh? Goddamn rodeo season. Best time of year. We've got at least a couple of these things a month through September. Buck up, pardner. It's going to be a hell of a ride. So what was the deal with that Mayra?"

"Maya."

"Maya. What kind of name is that, anyway? She was smoking. How'd that go for you? Does she have those freckles everywhere?"

"We only messed around a little. Nice girl."

"Like, you mean she was a *good* girl kind of nice girl?"

"Pretty much."

"Well, that's not all bad. You laid the foundation, right? Usually the good ones it takes a bit of groundwork. That's how the game is played. And, was I right about dancing, eh? *Eh?*"

"It's all right."

"Just all right? I saw you out there twirling them like a champ. It's amazing they weren't getting all tangled up and tripping, that's how fast their panties were dropping."

"Not quite."

"Nah, you were doing good. But seriously, it's better than actually talking to them to break the ice, isn't it? I mean you had your hands on, like, twenty attractive, slightly sweaty young ladies last night and how many sentences did you actually have to come out with?"

August laughed and nodded. "You're right about that. It's usually never that easy for me."

"Allow me one big fat *I told you so*. I've got a whole theory about it. You can pretty much tell if you'll have good sex with a girl based on how you dance together. If everything is all awkward and jerky out there, that's how the sex will be. If you just start flowing right out of the gate, then that's how it will be when you get horizontal. Tim's theory of attraction. Keep it in mind."

"Looked like you and Christi were dancing pretty good."

Tim finished his beer and flopped back into the bed of the truck. "You know who is definitely *not* a *good* girl?"

"I have an idea."

"She's not good, but she might be perfect. Little Timmy is in love."

August worked the come-along on the final strand of wire, and when it was tight he made a double wrap around the corner post and stapled it in place. He wound the tag end of the wire around the standing end with his pliers, and when it was secured he removed the come-along and the fence was done. He plucked the top strand a couple times with a gloved finger, and it thrummed satisfactorily. He sighted down the wire. Despite the roughness of the ground, his posts ran mostly clean and straight.

Ancient was down in Billings getting parts for the baler and seeing Kim. It was just midmorning, and August was done for the day. He tossed his gear in the milk crate lashed to the back of the four-wheeler and headed back down the hill to the house. In his room he stood with the door to the small fridge open, drinking orange juice from the carton. He washed his coffee mug and spoon and bowl from breakfast, dried them, and put them away. There was a broom in the small closet, and he used it on the kitchen floor. When he was done he examined the contents of the dustpan—they were negligible—then spent ten minutes leaning back on his bunk contemplating the underside of the box spring above him. Silence above and silence below, silence to his right and left. He heaved to his feet and headed to town.

. . .

At the Feed-n-Need he perused the small selection of fishing tackle. He settled on a six-foot ultra-light Ugly Stik and a Zebco 202. He picked up a small plastic divider box and a handful of Mepps and Blue Fox spinners, a canvas-insulated creel with a shoulder strap, and, as an afterthought, a wide-brimmed straw hat.

The man behind the cash register had a full gray beard with a brown stain at the corner of his mouth from tobacco spit. "Going fishing?" he said, raising his coffee mug to his lips, making no effort to start ringing August up.

"I was considering it," August said.

"Where you going to go?"

"Probably just go mess around on the Musselshell."

"Used to be good. You're about twenty years too late on that one."

"Yeah?"

"It's these pivot lines these ranchers are using, and the stuff they spray on their fields for the grasshoppers. People want to tell me that that stuff is only toxic to bugs, and I say, What do you think trout eat?"

"I can see your point there."

"Not a real popular opinion to have around here, but the cow sultans and their minions are ruining the fishing in this state. What these guys don't realize is that their days are numbered."

August adjusted his items on the counter. Looked at the cash register. Rocked a little on his heels. "Oh yeah?" he said.

"Definitely. This way of raising meat isn't going to be viable in another fifteen, twenty years. Soon we're going to be a nation of vegetarians. Not because we want to be, but out of necessity."

"Are you saying because of global warming?"

"Not directly, but as a result. Only the elite are going to be able to afford Montana beef. The rest of us are going to be scrounging. I'm not saying it's going to be completely apocalyptic, but it will be a lesser doomsday, at the very least."

"Well, that sounds bad."

"Everything seems normal now but we're on the cusp." The cashier waved his finger in a circular motion. "Feel lucky that you live out here. It could be a lot worse. Imagine being in New York City."

"I really can't."

"Think 9/11 times a thousand. I'm preparing. Every time I go to the grocery store I get a dozen or so extra canned goods. I've got a big root cellar under my house, and I've got shelves of beans, water, blankets, candles, stuff like that."

"Can't hurt to be ready, I guess."

"Damn straight. Nice choice on the pole there. An Ugly Stik is real durable. Should last you a good long time. Want my advice?"

"Sure."

"Forget the Musselshell. Go to Martinsdale Reservoir and walk around the edge of the reeds on the south side and throw off to the middle. There's a nice little ledge out there, and the rainbows will be hanging next to the deeper water. The state stocks ten thousand rainbows annually and usually you get your limit in an hour." The cashier picked up the Ugly Stik and wiggled it a few times. "Oh yeah," he said. "Should be able to toss those spinners a mile. I'm jealous. I'll be stuck in here. Wishin' I was fishin'. Story of my life. Do me a favor?"

"Yeah?"

"Come back in and let me know how it goes. If you do good I might get up there this weekend. Always nice to have a recent report."

"Okay," August said. "Will do."

On the way out of town, August hit the Qwikstop. The skinny guy with FUCK LOVE tattooed on his knuckles was behind the counter. Apparently he'd been in school with Tim, and he never asked for ID. August got a six-pack and a bag of ice. He loaded his creel with Pabst, packed the ice around it, and headed out away from Martinsdale toward Two Dot. The hayfields were a ripe green, heavy with a damp heat that he could smell. They'd be cutting this week, and this was probably his last day off for quite some time. He parked off to the side of the road near the bridge in Two Dot. Sun warm on his neck, he strung up the rod, tied on a silver Blue Fox, put the treble hook through the hook keeper, and cranked the reel until the line went taut. He donned his new hat, slung the beer creel over his shoulder, and scrambled down the steep bank.

The rocks at the river's edge were covered with a dried layer of silt, and the low branches of the Russian olives and alders were plastered with hardened gray muck and leaves where the water had receded following spring runoff. August walked downstream on the bank, and when the vegetation got too tangled, he was forced to step into the Musselshell's flow. The rocks were snot-slick underwater, and his old tennis shoes offered little traction. He proceeded slowly, the rounded river stones slipping and rolling underfoot. At a likely-looking pool he flipped the bail on the reel and tossed a cast toward the far bank. It had been a long time since he'd fished, and it showed. His finger came off the line too late and the lure plopped in the water only a few feet away, a silver tangle of backlashed monofilament forming on the spool of his reel. As he teased the coils out of the line before it could tighten into an impossible knot, he felt like his fingers had thickened somehow since he'd last done this. The hand adapts itself to the tool most held. He could wield fencing pliers and a come-along all day, but now the soft new cork of the fishing rod felt foreign, the light six-pound monofilament as difficult to grasp as gossamer.

After clearing the tangle August made a few passable casts, the lure sweeping through the pool; he could feel its fluttering pulse in the taut line under his finger. Half a dozen uninterrupted casts and swings later, August gave up and reeled in, continuing on downstream. He passed under a low timber-frame bridge, squadrons of cliff swallows darting out of their mud-daubed nests. He could make out the roofline of one of the Hutterites' outbuildings in the distance and he debated turning around, but kept going. He stopped and fished at several more pools with no luck. The sun was starting to slope in the west, the hottest part of the day, and he was glad for his hat. He kicked through the streamside grass, the grasshoppers jumping and bursting into flight, striated black and yellow wings clacking. At a point a mile or so from the Hutterite bridge, the bank shot way up, a sheer cliff wall of yellow sandstone that forced August to backtrack and drop down into the river. The water was moving quickly here, hip deep and racing. With every step he took, the current threatened to push him off his feet, and eventually he went down. Half swimming, half stumbling, he was pushed around the bend and onto a sloping gravel beach, sheltered by an overhang of rock from the cliff above.

He pulled himself out, his T-shirt and jeans plastered to his body. He noticed, too late, that his two remaining beers had fallen out of his creel, and he watched them bob off downstream, followed by the four crushed empties, all of them in a line like a little family of aluminum ducklings. August dropped his rod and creel and removed his dripping hat. The cliff wall stretched over twenty feet above him, the face slightly concave with a ledge sticking out. The declivity in the rock extended back a few yards, and at the base of the cliff was a jumble of large chunks of sandstone. The small beach was protected from the wind on three sides; the sun lowering over the hills in the west seemed to focus its energy, the cream cliff walls reflecting its light and heat. August peeled his shirt over his head and shrugged off his jeans. He walked gingerly up the small pebbled beach to lay his clothing over the rocks to dry, and it was behind one of them that he found a blue plastic tarp.

Underneath the tarp was a cushion, like what might be found on a reclining beach chair, a down pillow, and a white sheet, folded into a neat rectangle. August moved these aside and found a grain sack. In the sack: a pair of imitation Ray-Ban sunglasses; several tubes of Blistex SPF 15 lip ointment; a small bottle of baby oil, greasy and half-empty; two packs of Marlboro Lights, one unopened, the other with only a few cigarettes left; a purple plastic Bic lighter; and a small black plastic portable radio with an extendable antenna, batteries dead.

August spread the cushion out and lay back with his head on the pillow. Out of the corner of his eye he spotted a single long blond hair on the white cotton pillowcase, and he plucked it up and held it to the sky. The sun illuminated the strand; it shone a clear glassine honey. He brought it close to his nose, and of course there was no scent. A single strand of hair was not enough to retain the odor of shampoo, smoke, sweat, perfume. Probably not two strands, either, or three or even four. But, at some point, gather enough strands and you had something discernibly human.

August blew the hair away and reached for the cigarettes. After several flicks, the lighter caught and he leaned back, puffing a stale-tasting Marlboro Light, already feeling the tingle as the intense sun started to burn his pale bare chest and limbs. He tried, unsuccessfully, to blow smoke rings. He tried to take a nap but couldn't. He wished he hadn't lost his beer. While fishing out another Marlboro, he noticed something tucked away behind the remaining cigarettes. It was a Polaroid of a couple, about August's age by the looks of it. They were sitting on one of the sandstone rocks in this very place, both of them sun-browned and blond, squinting into the camera that the man had obviously held at arm's length. He had his free arm around the girl's bare shoulder, both of them shirtless; naked probably—although their lower bodies weren't in the frame, their faces seemed like those of naked people, somehow. The woman's hair long and blond and loose, flowing down past her small breasts. Her erect nipples parted the gold current on both sides, pinkish and pointing out slightly. The boy had shaggy hair, disheveled like he'd just taken off his hat or maybe the girl had just run her fingers through it. They wore cheesy smiles, mugging for the camera. They could have been free-loving hippies, a Woodstock photo, or a California surf couple circa 1960.

August looked at the picture for a long time. Trying to imagine himself inhabiting a moment in such a way, at ease with a woman like that.

He flicked his butt into the Musselshell and shrugged back into his still-damp clothes. He repacked the grain bag, folded the cushion, and covered the whole thing with the tarp, like he'd found it. Then he tucked the Polaroid into his T-shirt pocket, where it wouldn't get wet during the many stream crossings to come as he made his way back to the truck.

"You're wearing that?"

August looked down at his shirt. "So what?"

"It's like tropical birds, man. You can't go to a rodeo in a dingy-ass gray shirt. You need plumage. Hold on. I'll be back."

August sat with his truck idling while Tim ran back inside his house.

In a few moments he came out, then stopped on the porch, the screen door open behind him. August had the windows down, and he could hear Tim talking to someone in the house. "I said I'll be back early, and I'll be back, fuck. Lay off me." He let the door slam behind him and came off the porch shaking his head, a grin on his face. He swung into the truck and threw a shirt in August's lap. August held it up. It was a silk pearl-snap, a blue-and-white paisley design. "Are you kidding?" August said. "It's like a clown shirt."

"Trust me. It's going to fit you like a glove. And you're going to have to fight off the buckle bunnies with a stick. The arms are too long for me, and you see how jacked I am. If I flexed I'd blow the buttons out. It was Wes's—better you have it than letting it go to waste in the closet. You can thank me later. Let's get the hell out of here before my old man starts in on some more of his bullshit."

The rodeo was in Gardiner, and August drove south while Tim opened their beers. The two-lane highway was clogged with motor homes and RVs, impatient tourists in rental cars trying to pass on blind curves.

"I never understood the passing thing," August said. "You nearly kill yourself to do it and then you pretty much always get stuck behind another RV. Like that BMW asshole right there. I guarantee he doesn't get to Gardiner more than three minutes faster than us."

"It's not really about getting there faster," Tim said. "It's about getting there on your own terms. Fighting against the slow hordes. These motor homes make me crazy. And you drive like a grandpa."

"Fifty-five, stay alive," August said, tipping his beer in Tim's direction.

They pulled into Gardiner, and there was a solid line of traffic heading to the rodeo grounds. The BMW that had barely avoided a head-on collision was four cars ahead of them in line. A small herd of scraggly elk stood on the high school football field, and people had their car windows down, snapping pictures. August finally found a parking spot and maneuvered his truck in. Tim dropped the tailgate and brought the cooler within easy reach, and they settled back to pregame.

"You going to put that shirt on or what?" Tim said.

August shrugged. "I don't know if it will fit."

"You're pretty much the exact same size as my bro before he went down and gained the freshman fifteen. Just try it on and see."

"I don't know."

"Oh, because he's dead? Putting on a dead guy's shirt freaks you out, is that it?"

"A little. What if I get it dirty, or rip it or something?"

"It's a shirt. Not a relic. Wes had a million of the damn things. He was kind of a dude that way. Liked to get all fancied up. I already tossed out, like, twenty of them. You could get in a knife fight in the damn thing for all I care. Just put the stupid thing on and get loose."

August shrugged the shirt on and buttoned it up. He smoothed it over his chest. "I've never worn a silk shirt before," he said.

"Tuck it in, you heathen."

August tucked the shirt in, and Tim handed him a beer. "My bro would be proud. And your girl is probably going to get all swoony just looking at you."

"My girl?"

"Mayra."

"Maya?"

"Yeah, her."

"She's going to be here?"

"Of course."

"How do you know?"

"I've been talking to Christi. She wants round number two, no surprise. Anyway, she says Maya has been asking about you. Apparently you didn't get her phone number? Amateur move, pal. Or maybe you're dumb like a fox. A woman who knows you like her will ignore you quicker than shit."

"Dumb like a fox," August said. "Yeah, that's definitely it."

"Well, whatever it is, I'm a results-oriented man myself, doesn't matter. She's into you, and she's smoking hot. Since you kind of ditched her last time you're going to have to apply a little more pressure tonight. The old hard-to-get routine works for only so long, and then they just give up and take up with the next swinging dick. That's some advice Wes gave me. There's always another one of you out there, so don't go getting it in your head that you're special. Men are expendable. It's like evolution. It's like hunting season. The draft."

"Hunting season?"

"Yeah. Why is it that you can shoot your limit of rooster pheasants or drake mallards or whatever, but there's always a restriction on the female side of things?"

"People want trophies?"

"Well, maybe that makes sense for elk, but for all the other stuff, not so much. You just don't need as many males around. Genetically speaking. One weenie can service many wombs. Ladies have an innate understanding of this reality, and so they don't need to put up with a bunch of bullshit from any one dude. Hear me?"

"Interesting theory."

"Keep hanging around me, pal. You're bound to learn."

August tugged at his collar and held an arm out. "I feel ridiculous in this thing."

"Shut up. You're a magnificent peacock; spread your feathers. Here come the ladies."

Christi wore a man's Wrangler shirt tied up at her midriff, jean shorts cut off so high the crease where her buttocks joined her thigh was clearly visible. Maya wore a pale yellow sundress that hugged her hips and flared at the upper thigh, her legs long and bare. Devoid of freckles, he noticed. Tim let out a low whistle and swooped Christi up into a kiss.

Maya shook her head and rolled her eyes and hopped up to sit on the truck tailgate next to August. She took the sleeve of his shirt between her fingers and rubbed. "Wow," she said.

"I know. It's ridiculous. Tim made me wear it."

"No, it's amazing. That's silk, isn't it?"

"Afraid so."

"So soft. It must feel great. You look great. It's nice to see you, by the way."

"You look great, too."

Maya laughed and tossed her hair dramatically. "Well, aren't we just *great!*" She looked at Tim and Christi, embracing next to the truck, whispering things into each other's ears and laughing. Tim had a hand firmly clenched on each of Christi's partially exposed ass cheeks.

"Not as great as those two, apparently. Are you going to offer a girl a beer, or what?"

The post-rodeo dance was held at the Blue Goose. The crowd of people spilled out of the open doors onto the street, and August and Tim followed the girls as they made their way through the tightly packed throng. At the edge of the stage, Christi produced a silver flask from her tight back pocket, unscrewed the cap, took a long slug, and then passed it. The flask was body-hot and the whiskey burned. August coughed and passed it back to Christi, and then Maya was grabbing his hand and pulling him out on to the dance floor.

It was so crowded that actual dancing was mostly out of the question. Maya pressed against him and they just revolved. He tried to spin her but there was no room, and she came back to him, laughing, after bouncing off a wall of bodies. She had her thigh fit in between his, and he could feel the firmness of her breasts pushing tight below his sternum.

When the song ended, Maya said she had to go to the bathroom and headed off through the crowd. August looked around for Tim and Christi, but they were nowhere to be seen. He worked his way toward the bar, and when he was finally able to belly up he found himself wedged between a crew of guys about his age, summer Stetsons and fresh-pressed jeans, boots with a level of shine he'd never attempted to achieve. Their shirts were a riot of colors. August would have thought it impossible, but the blue-and-white paisley number he was sporting looked almost inconspicuous next to theirs. They were talking about the rodeo. Apparently, a bull rider had been thrown and had landed awkwardly. The sound of his leg breaking had been audible in the grandstands.

"Could you hear it from where you were sitting, man?" a guy in a fuchsia shirt with embroidered stars over the pockets said. August realized he was talking to him and shook his head. "When I go to the rodeo, I don't actually go to the rodeo," August said. "I just go to the bar." The guys all laughed at this and then they were ordering shots and the bartender was setting them up on the bar: Jägermeister, black and evil-looking in the glass. One of the crew pressed a shot into August's hand, and they all tossed them back. August felt the Jägermeister settle on top of the whiskey in a less than pleasant manner. He tried, unsuccessfully, to get one of the bartenders' attention to ask for a beer and a glass of water. In the mirror of the backbar, he saw Maya coming through the crowd. He was turning to suggest they step outside for some air, when he saw her reach for a hand and lead the fuchsia shirt out onto the dance floor.

August watched for a moment. Maya had her leg fit in between fuchsia shirt's legs. She was right up against him, and they found a pocket of open space and he spun her, rotated and caught her hands behind his back in a move that August didn't know. He didn't have to watch long to realize fuchsia shirt was a much better dancer than him. Maya was smiling from ear to ear. Her freckles glowing, hair tossing around her face, her dress rising as she spun, a momentary blurred hint of white panties.

"Goddamn, Trey has a live one there," one of the guys said and nodded at Maya.

August turned back to the bar. "Let's do more shots," he said.

By the time August finally punched fuchsia shirt, the Blue Goose had long been a carnival fun house of faces and hats, belt buckles and barstools; he'd already been to the bathroom and heaved the contents of his stomach. He swished his mouth out at the sink and wiped his face with paper towels. He stumbled through the crowd and saw Maya leaning into fuchsia shirt at the bar. He had his arm around her. He was saying something into her ear and she was laughing, and August pulled him around by his shoulder. Fuchsia shirt said something like,

"Hey, dick, watch out." August saw Maya's look of surprise, and then he tried to give fuchsia shirt everything he had to the side of the head.

August's aim was slightly off and his fist only glanced off the back of fuchsia shirt's head, sending his hat flying. Fuchsia shirt still went down, dazed, hands on knees, and August was going for the choke hold when someone hit him from behind. He crashed into fuchsia shirt, and they went down in a heap. He saw the pale yellow of Maya's dress sprawling toward the floor and then it was a melee of faceless limbs, disembodied fists. He took a knee to the face and there was an immediate spill of blood from his nose. His eyes puddled and blurred with tears. Someone was punching him repeatedly in the ribs, and then that person was gone and August got his forearm around fuchsia shirt's neck and he could clearly feel the coarse stubble of his jaw through the silk and he was trying to get a deeper purchase when there were hands on his shoulders pulling him back and Tim's voice saying, "We're done, we're done. Stop, August, you fucker."

He let Tim yank him to his feet, and together they stumbled out through the overturned barstools and spilled drinks, August trying to wipe his face, spitting blood.

They sat in August's truck, Tim behind the wheel. "Well, that got Western," Tim said. "You're shit-faced, aren't you?"

August didn't say anything. Pressed his face to the cool glass of the truck window.

"I was out back having a cigarette with Christi and then we come inside and it's a free-for-all. What did that asshole say to you, anyway?"

"I don't know. It was all just stupid. Maya was there, and I punched him."

"I *see*. It was that kind of deal. I did notice them dancing. I'd like to be able to tell you that getting in a brawl will impress her, but I honestly don't really think that's going to be the case, Hoss."

"It was stupid."

"You were trying to squeeze that dude's head off. Bunch of frat boys.

That one that was whaling on you from behind—I dotted him good. He's probably in there looking for his teeth." Tim sucked on the bleeding knuckles of his right hand. "Well, I suppose we should get out of here before those assholes regroup. Or the cops show up. Keys?"

"I can drive."

"I don't think so."

"I'm fine."

"Keys." Tim stretched out his hand, palm up. "Come on, cough 'em up, Rocky." August gave him the keys and they were starting to pull away when the girls appeared in the headlights. Maya was at the window. "What's your problem, August?" she said.

"Sorry," August said. "I don't know."

"I think everyone's a little drunk," Tim said.

"I'm not drunk at all. Look at my leg," Maya raised her leg and even in the dim streetlight glow the large bruise on her thigh was already visible. "Who gets in fights over dancing? What are you, twelve? Say something."

"Sorry. I don't know."

"God. You're so weird." Maya turned and strode away, pulling Christi with her by the hand.

Tim drove the winding road through Yankee Jim Canyon, the big river down there—a churning mass of boulder-strewn rapids. The headlights lit the white memorial crosses on the curves—a deadly stretch of road—and Tim drove with two fingers on the wheel. He'd procured a beer somewhere, and he had it jammed between his legs, swigging occasionally. No music on, just the rush of air from the lowered windows. August pressed his nose on either side, feeling the crusted blood there.

"That thing broken?" Tim said.

"Not sure. Doesn't feel good."

"I think if it's broken you know in a hurry. I think you might need an alignment."

"Huh?"

"Your truck. It's pulling a little left. I think it's out of alignment."

"Maybe. I don't know."

"When's the last time you rotated your tires?"

"I have no idea."

"Sometimes they do it when you get an oil change. When did you get an oil change last?"

"I can't remember right now."

"Don't you put the receipt in your glove box? We could probably figure it out."

"Tim, I don't really give a shit."

"Okay, fine. I'm just trying to make conversation."

"Well, don't feel like you have to on my account."

"Okay. Fine."

They were silent for a few miles. And then August said, "You ever see a buffalo jump?"

"I thought we weren't talking."

"Have you?"

"Jump over what? Like, have I seen a buffalo jump over a fence?"

"No, I mean an old Indian buffalo jump. A place where they used to run them over a cliff. I found one way back in the hills on a place I used to work. Bunch of broken skulls and stuff. You could see where they'd come over the edge and then where they'd land on the rocks below. Must have been a hell of a thing to see. A whole herd coming over like that."

"Yeah? And?"

"And, that's it. I was just thinking about it. Buffalo herds have a lead bull and the Indians would get that one spooked and running and the rest would just follow him right over the edge."

"Dumb animals if you ask me. You probably couldn't get cattle to stampede over a hill. And they're plenty dumb, so that's saying something."

"I was thinking that when there's a stampede going, at some point, the buffalo have to realize what's going on. Most of them just follow blindly, but then when enough of them have jumped off into space, one of the guys in the back must be kind of like, *Well, wait a minute, I see what's going on here. Maybe I'll just run in a different direction.* And then, when he starts off, some of the others start following him and then just like that they're all running behind him and he's leading them off to safety. And since the old lead bull is down at the bottom of a ravine getting butchered, does that mean the new guy takes his spot?"

"I don't think buffalo hold elections or anything like that. So yeah, probably he's the man now."

"What I was thinking was that at some point in the future, the Indians will come up on them again and get the stampede going and the new lead bull will do the same damn thing as the one before him. See what I mean? It's just a cycle of stampedes. One animal following another, off the cliff or to safety, it doesn't really matter. No heroes. We go around all day on the earth, one direction to the next, just following the ass in front of us. Like with women. Right about when you start thinking you're the lead bull, that's when the earth comes out from under your feet. You'd think we'd learn, but there hasn't been an original idea in the world since Adam first stuck it to Eve. Probably the best way to go about things is to just live out your days solitary and then, when it's time, go wander off into the brush to die."

"Sounds lonely."

"At least it's dignified."

"This is getting pretty metaphysical. You got your cage rattled, didn't you?"

"Sorry I got blood all over your shirt."

Tim looked over at August. He flicked on the dome light and shook his head. "It's ruined. How could you?" he said. "That was my last link to my beloved dead brother and now I have nothing to remember him by. I used to smell it every night before saying my prayers." He flicked off the dome light and laughed. "No heroes? You're just now coming to that conclusion? Welcome to the planet the rest of us have been living on, pal."

―――

It was early evening when August drove the four-wheeler into the shop. He'd been out setting new fence posts on the high ground above the ranch house. Jimmy Buffett was blaring from the fly-specked ste-reo. *To be a cheeseburger in paradise / I'm just a cheeseburger in para-dise.* Ancient was there, ducked up under the cowl of the round baler.

"Fuck," he said. "Fucking cunt-nut. Get the fuck on there, you motherfucking fuck." He pulled his head out, nodded at August, and threw the wrench he'd been holding so it banged hollowly on the sheet metal on the opposite side of the shed. He wiped his forehead with the back of his sleeve. "How'd your day go?" he said quietly.

"All right," August said. "Got a few more posts to set tomorrow and then I can start stringing up the new wire." August topped off the four-wheeler with gas. Ancient, watching him, raised his eyebrows at the sight of August's still-swollen nose and cheek, but didn't say anything. "That hill is steep up there," August said. "I feel like one of my legs is shorter than the other."

"Yep," Ancient said. "That'll happen." He'd ducked under the baler again, and then he came up suddenly with another wrench that he gave the same treatment as the first. After hitting the side of the shed it clinked to the cement floor and Ancient shook his head. Wiped the grease from his hands on a rag. He punched a button on the radio, si-lencing Buffett. "That has to be the stupidest song in the world. You look like you could use a beer, and this baler is shortening my life ex-pectancy every time I look at it. I'm sick of feeling sober. Let's go to town."

As Ancient drove he thwacked his chew can on his thigh and packed a large dip in his lower lip. "Grass is looking decent," he said, nodding at the glistening-wet field, a rainbow forming in the spray of the big irrigation pivot. "We'll be doing first cutting before you know it."

"Looks like it."

"You ever go to the Big Hole Valley? Down by Wisdom?"

"Wisdom?"

"Yeah, that's the town name. Wisdom. Hardly anything there. A bar. Maybe a post office. They still do hay the old way over there, with a beaver slide. You ever see that? Crazy thing. They've got this wooden contraption, kind of like a big scaffold ramp with a sliding platform. Some of the old boys still use horses with a buck rake. They push the hay onto the platform, and then they have another team that's hooked up to pull the platform. The hay goes up the ramp, and when it hits the top all the hay flips off onto the pile. There's a couple guys up on top with hayforks tamping everything down and evening it out."

"So, no bales?"

"Nope. You just get a giant stack, like thirty feet high. Only works in real dry places, because a big pile like that is prone to rot. But just think of it—no goddamn baling machines to ruin your life."

"You'd have to deal with horses, though."

"Some guys just use tractors to run the slide."

"Well, maybe we should build one and give it a try."

Ancient laughed and shook his head. "Wouldn't that be funny? The looks I'd get from the old codgers around here if I threw up a giant haystack."

"It's dry enough up here, isn't it?"

"Yeah, but when the wind gets going in the winter that whole stack would vaporize."

"I hadn't considered that."

"It's nice to think about, though. Just hooking up the team and going to work. Of course, it would take about four people and a couple days to finish a field that a single guy with a tractor and baler could do in a few hours." Ancient parked across the street from the Mint and shut the truck off, the diesel ticking. "The good old days," he said, shaking his head. "Nostalgia ain't what it used to be."

Ancient was drinking his beers two to one ahead of August. He put five bucks in a keno machine and won fifty, and so then they were doing shots of whiskey. He loaded up the jukebox and came back to his stool next to August. "I haven't tied on a daytime buzz in a long time," he said. "Can't even remember when. Pre-Kim, that's for sure."

"How's that going, anyway? Kim?"

Ancient shrugged. "She's down in Billings. She's got it in her head that she can't live up here, it's too small, nothing for her to do."

"But didn't she know that going in? You own a ranch. Wasn't like you pulled a bait and switch on her."

"I guess. Truth be told, it's not so much that she doesn't like the ranch. When we were first dating we'd go on hikes all over, and she'd go on and on about how beautiful it was and how she'd love to just live in a place away from everything else. She likes the ranch. And she likes me well enough. Me and the ranch aren't the problem."

"What's the problem, then?"

Ancient took his hat off and scratched his head, settled it back down, spun his bottle on the bar a few times. "There's some people around here that just can't mind their own business. People that have some kind of grudge against me for one reason or another, and instead of approaching me about it man to man, they decide to slander my fiancée and leave shitty little notes in the mailbox and things like that."

"Notes in the mailbox?"

"Yeah, can you believe it? How can you call yourself a man if you're going around slipping notes to people in their mailboxes?"

"What kind of notes?"

Ancient looked at August narrowing his eyes. "Are you telling me you have no idea what I'm talking about? You haven't heard anything about Kim? You've been hanging out with Timmy. I have a real hard time believing that he hasn't talked some shit."

August scratched at the label on his beer. "I don't know."

"What don't you know?"

"I don't know."

"I know you know. You acting like you don't know is just going to set me off. Tell me what you heard and then we can go from there." Ancient had both his hands balled on his thighs. He was leaning back on his stool, not taking his eyes from August.

"Tim told me one time that I ought to check out the sex offender registry in Meagher County. That's it."

"He just told you to check it out, didn't tell you why?"

"He said he wasn't going to talk about anyone behind their back."

"And you went and looked."

August shrugged.

"Did you go and look it up or not? Tell me flat out."

"I looked."

"You were curious."

"I guess."

"Sure, a guy tells you to check out the sex offender list and doesn't tell you why—of course you're going to look. It's human nature. Hey." Ancient reached over and slapped August's leg. "I'm not pissed at you. You're a good guy and you mind your business, I know that. But you read what you read in that registry, and now you've got questions."

"You don't have to tell me anything."

Ancient finished his beer and set it down hard on the bar top. "Hell, I know that," he said. "I don't need you telling me what I don't have to tell you."

"Okay then."

"*Okay then.* Look at you, Mr. Cool. Acting like you weren't foaming at the mouth to find out just who was the pervert on the list. Were you surprised it was Kim? Did you think it was going to be me?"

"I didn't think anything. It was Tim that brought it up."

"That I don't doubt. That little shit. I don't know who did it, him or his dad, but I guarantee it was one of those two. My bet is on Big Tim, because he's twisted and he spends all his time looking up conspiracy theories on the Internet when he should be out handling his business. He's a piss-poor cattleman, always was. I bought that chunk of pasture from him at a fair price rather than let the bank take it from him, and he acts like I stole it. And then Kim finds a little anonymous note in the mailbox. Calling her a pervert and a pedophile and a dyke and what-ever. She moved up here in the first place to get away from all that noise. She thought this was a place where she could go about her life and people would leave her alone. You know what she did? Her big crime? I'll just tell you flat out. She was a student teacher—"

"I really don't care. I don't even really want to know."

"You don't want to know?" Ancient laughed and shook his head. "I could almost believe that's true. You've been working for me for a while now, and I pretty much don't know a damn thing about you. I get the sense that's how you want it, and that's all well and good. But Kim and I are decent people and you're going to know the root of this thing whether you want it or not, because I'm going to tell you and you're going to listen. Kim was a student teacher. Twenty-three years old, at a high school in Boise. She was also helping out with the girls' volleyball team and one of the girls got infatuated with her. Fifteen or sixteen years old, a high school junior.

"Now, Kim is the first person to admit that she showed some bad judgment. Okay? She knows she messed up, but Jesus Christ, she's been branded some kind of predator for the rest of her life. She and this girl got close and they took a couple showers together, or whatever. Doesn't really matter. Kim realized it had gone a little too far and so she cut it off, and then the girl got all mental. She acted like a jilted lover. Started calling Kim and showing up at her house at all hours, and then when Kim kept turning her away she went to her parents and said that her teacher had touched her inappropriately in the shower, and of course one thing led to another. You're trying to tell me that a twenty-three-year-old woman soaping up with a very consenting fifteen-year-old girl is the same thing as some defect molesting his ten-year-old niece? It's ridiculous. And then to have a puke like Duncan putting his little notes in your mailbox when you're just trying to live your life? I don't really blame her for taking off. Anyway, let me pay for these." Ancient looked at his watch. "Feed-n-Need will still be open if we hustle. I've got a purchase I've been meaning to make."

On the short drive across town, Ancient said, "Remember that time you dropped my chainsaw into the river?"

August shook his head.

"No? You don't remember that?"

"I remember it a little different."

"What's the saying? *History is just the memories of the victors*? Something like that. We're all pretty much constantly victorious in our own minds."

"You had me out on a sketchy tree in the middle of a river, and I slipped and nearly cut my foot off."

"Don't get all huffy. I'm just needling you. That thing was older than the hills anyway."

At the Feed-n-Need, Ancient bought a brand-new Stihl MS 311 with an eighteen-inch bar. It came with a spare chain and a heavy-duty orange plastic case. The Feed-n-Need employee threw in a gallon can of gas, a pair of safety goggles, and ear plugs. It was the same old-timer with the tobacco-stained beard, and when he recognized August he pointed and said, "The fisherman returns. How was your luck?"

"Not too good. I got skunked."

"Did you do like I told you and go to Martinsdale and cast off the reeds at the south side?"

"I just went down to the Musselshell."

"Well, shit. No wonder." He shook his head and smiled, winking at Ancient. "You try to help out the youth, and it's like their ears are deaf to the words coming out of your mouth. You give a kid a hot tip, and he goes and fishes where there aren't any fish."

Ancient signed his receipt and hefted his saw. "I've always preferred going fishing where there's no fish. Your naps don't get interrupted as much that way."

"You know the saying. Give a man a fish, he'll eat for a day. Teach a man to fish and he'll be a bum for the rest of his life."

"Good one," August said.

Tobacco beard hooked his thumb in August's direction and spoke to Ancient. "This one's not overly impressed with my humor."

"Don't take it personal," Ancient said. "I saw him smile once. I think."

In the parking lot, Ancient put the saw and gas in the back of his truck, slammed up the tailgate, and slapped his hands together. "Now, that's shopping," he said. "Get in and get out. A purchase a man can feel good about. A lot of money to shell out, but I'll have that saw for fifteen years, if I can keep it out of your hands." Ancient laughed. "Your face. It's just too easy."

On the road home, dark now, with a half-moon hanging over the valley, the irrigation lines spraying silver under its light, Ancient rolled his window down and took a big breath, letting it out in a long whistle. "Goddamn," he said. "There's something about coming into possession of a new chainsaw that makes a man eager to cut something down. I've just had a brilliant idea."

Ancient took the Dry Creek cutoff road and they rattled over a cattle guard, off the pavement, the truck light in the back, skittering over the washboards. They were nearing the Duncan place, and when the first sign loomed white in the headlights Ancient slowed, put the truck in park, and hopped out. August turned in the seat to watch. Ancient had the saw out and was tipping up the gas can, his face glowing red in the taillights. He pulled the cord twice, adjusted the choke, pulled it once more, and the saw roared to life. He revved it a few times and stepped off the road into the ditch. The saw hardly paused as he ran it through the first two-by-four signpost.

"Hoo boy, that's a sharp saw," he yelled. "Come on. Slide over behind the wheel and drive me up the road. I'll be in the back. We're getting all these stupid things." Ancient tossed the sign in the truck bed and sat on the tailgate, the saw idling next to him. August drove and they progressed this way—Ancient hopping out to cut the signs, the pile of them in the back of the truck growing—until they reached the head of the Duncans' driveway.

Ancient had August back the truck in, and he kicked and slid the signs out of the bed onto the driveway, over a dozen of them, a pile hip high. Ancient put the saw back in its case and then emptied the gas can over the signs. He put the can in the truck and produced a book of matches from his pocket. The match popped to life in his hand, and when he dropped it the signs erupted with a deep thump of blue-orange flame. From the truck August could just make out the lettering on the top sign—PREVENT WHITE GENOCIDE!—the paint beginning to bubble and melt.

Ancient swung into the cab and August accelerated away, the bonfire fading in the rearview. Ancient wasn't saying anything, and August could smell chainsaw gas. When they got home—the engine ticking, the house in front of them empty and black—Ancient finally laughed. He took off his hat and rubbed his head and opened his door. He paused with his foot on the running board.

"I bought me and Kim tickets to Jamaica for our honeymoon. We were going to go this fall."

"Jamaica. Really?"

"She said she wanted to go one time when we were first dating. She really likes coffee. They have the best coffee in the world there. Blue Mountain. And, believe it or not, I like the marijuana smoke occasionally. They've got the best of that, too. And beaches. I've always wanted to go scuba diving."

"You still think you'll go?"

"Hard to say."

"Probably expensive tickets."

"I bought traveler's insurance. They recommended I do that. Especially because it was a honeymoon trip. The travel agent I used said that it would definitely be a good idea, because *things happen.* I asked her what she meant by *things happen,* and she said that people have been known to change their minds. Also, hurricanes. I told myself I bought it because of the hurricanes. I think she threw that in there for that very reason. No one wants to believe their honeymoon won't happen. Getting traveler's insurance for something like that is kind of like going the prenup route. You know it's a smart idea, but it's sort of like setting yourself up to fail. Anyway, if Timmy comes asking you about the signs, you can straight-up tell him I did it."

"I'm not going to say anything."

"You don't have to lie for me."

"Okay."

"Shoot. I guess I got a little excited tonight. I might live to have regrets about this. Big Tim is generally not one to let things lie."

August filled a large bowl with Frosted Shredded Wheat and poured in milk. There was a sunset happening, and he ate his cereal on the small concrete patio behind the bunkhouse, watching it go. Darkness fell, with the first stars coming in like pinpricks, small holes, a buckshot pattern fired into the black sky. August slurped his milk from the bowl and went inside to call his mother.

"Augie!" she said. "It's great to hear your voice. I was just thinking about you."

"You always say that."

"Because it's always true."

"Do you really think about me that much, or do I just happen to call when you are?"

"It's like breathing. Probably is the same for all mothers."

"Meaning?"

"I don't make an effort to think about you; it's just going on constantly in the background. Inhale, exhale. Like that."

"That's kind of creepy."

"And that, in a nutshell, is the plight of mothers everywhere. I don't know why we continue to put ourselves through it. Anyway, how'd those hamburgers turn out?"

"Hamburgers?"

"Last time we talked you said you were making hamburgers."

"Oh yeah. They were decent. Not as good as yours."

"That's right. And they never will be. Don't you forget it. What else have you been up to?"

"Mostly just work."

"Your father's son. I sometimes think he works so much because it's easier than coming up with something else he might actually *like* to do. Be careful about that."

"I went fishing."

"Oh? Good for you. Were they biting?"

"Not really. Was nice to get out, though." There was silence on the line for a moment. And then August could hear a clicking, her lighter, the sharp inhale as she sucked on her Swisher. "So," she said. "The reason I called you was that Art asked me to marry him, and I just wanted to let you know. I said yes, of course."

"You didn't call me," August said. "I called you."

"We're not going to have a ceremony. He's not religious, either, and we've both been through this before. We'll just go down to the courthouse and then have a party after. I'd like to have a little dinner. Just you, me, and Art. He wants to get to know you better, and I'm certain you two will hit it off if you just give him the time of day. And—this is exciting—Art wants to go on a trip somewhere. The word *honeymoon* seems a little ridiculous, but there you have it. He's thinking Greece, and I have to say that I like that idea. He's big on history. And I'm big on beaches and baklava and spanakopita. So I think both of us will be happy. I haven't been on a vacation in forever."

"Vacation. Must be nice."

"Don't act like your blind pursuit of work is a virtue. Your father always did that, and it annoyed the hell out of me. When I was a little younger than you, I studied abroad in France and Germany. You could easily do the same if you applied yourself. And anyway, I'm old. I've earned a vacation."

"Well, I hope you get travel insurance." He could hear her long exhale, could easily picture the fine network of lines around her lips as she pursed them, cigarillo smoldering in her forked fingers. She laughed. "Travel insurance? Why do you say that?"

"Probably an expensive ticket. And things can happen."

"When you say *things,* do you have something in particular in mind?"

"I don't know, Mom. Maybe a hurricane. How long have you and this guy been dating, anyway? It seems kind of drastic."

"It's the Mediterranean, hon. They don't have hurricanes. And at my age it gets increasingly harder to do anything that someone your age might call drastic. So I'm just going to take that as a compliment. How about you? You find any interesting cowgirls up there?"

"Mom."

"What? You're always so secretive. Every once and a while you could let me in on some things going on in your life."

"What do you mean? I wake up, I go to work, I do that all day, and then I go home and go to bed. That's pretty much it."

"I don't buy it. Even your father could only do so much nose-to-the-grindstone before he'd have to go out and blow off some steam. With a waitress, or a hairdresser, or Lisa the milkmaid, or whomever."

"Jesus, Mom."

"Well, I'm sorry. It is what it is. I'm not even mad at him anymore. We just got started too young. And we had a lot of fun. I just want you to have a fulfilling life and not have strange hang-ups. Okay? And don't just knock up the first rancher's daughter that comes along. These are the thoughts that keep your mother up at night."

"Thank you. Really appreciate that advice. Stay away from fertile ranchers' daughters. Check."

"We moved right during your high school years; I know that wasn't easy for you. You never took anyone to prom. You never really brought anyone around. And then all that stuff happened with *her*. I'm not worried, I just, I don't know. I feel like you're such an honorable, not to mention good-looking, young man, and you'd have a lot to share with someone. I hope you are having experiences. If you were in college you'd be surrounded, I mean—well, you know how I feel about it. I'll stop harping."

"I learned how to dance the other day."

"You kid."

"Serious. My friend Tim taught me. We went to a rodeo, and he told me that if I didn't dance I'd make him look bad and so he showed me a few moves beforehand and it was pretty fun, actually. Not too hard. I danced with ranchers' daughters of all shapes and sizes."

"Well, I'm glad. I bet you're a great dancer. Your dad was rather light on his feet, believe it or not. We'd go to polka parties in Grand Rapids on the weekends when we were first dating. He had the girls lined up around the block. He made me so nervous."

"Polka parties?"

"Yes indeed. Mostly ironic, but still. Wild times. Well, I'm glad to hear you're making friends and mingling. Was that so hard? Just a little insight into what exactly you're up to, and I'm much less worried."

"There's no need to be worried. I'm fine."

"Inhale, exhale, hon. I'll stop the worrying when I stop the breathing."

August was at the bottom of an irrigation ditch hauling a ripped section of orange poly tarp out of the mud when Ancient rode up on Chief. He leaned over in the saddle, squinting down at August. "Should have worn your muck boots," Ancient said. "You're going to be all squelchy for the rest of the day."

"Don't have any muck boots."

"Feel free to borrow mine next time."

"I've got size thirteen feet."

"Well, that's a problem then."

"This mud smells like ass."

"That's a fact. I don't know how many hours of my life has been spent shuffling those stupid dams around. We used to do all of it with flood, back in the day. We'll get this switched over to the pivot at some point. When the money comes in. No way to deny it's more efficient." Chief stood dumb still except for an occasional tail swish at a buzzing fly. Ancient raked his hat back on his head and sighed. "Yes, sir. Long-term plans are a bitch," he said. "Owning some ground gets a man looking ahead, balancing the improvements he'd like to make against the things that will realistically show fruit in his life span. And then from there it's a short trip to thoughts of legacy. You get this land, and then you start realizing that there's only so much you can do with your allotted time."

August had the ripped tarp up on the bank now. He was coated in mud to midcalf. "Yeah?" he grunted. "Legacy?"

"Definitely. Three generations of Virostoks right here," he said, making a circling motion with his hand. "Three generations, and sometimes I think that, for all our striving, what we've managed is just a flesh wound on a very small patch of the earth's hide. There could be three more generations and still we wouldn't have dug in deep enough to leave a scar worth noticing. When my old man was alive? I never once had thoughts like this." Ancient lifted his nose and made an exaggerated sniff. "Love the smell of cottonwood in the spring."

August had the new tarp in place now and was using the shovel to set the cross brace in the soil so it wouldn't shift when he opened the gate and sent the water flowing down the ditch.

"Cottonwood gives me allergies," he said, stomping the loose dirt to tamp everything down.

"My old man had the allergies bad. Hay always got him, and cats, too. If he so much as came into a room where a cat had been, his eyes would get all red and he'd start hacking and coughing and sneezing." Ancient had a small soft cooler tied up on the back of his saddle, and he turned and unzipped it. He pulled out two cold cans of Pabst and reached one down toward August. "Getting hot out here," he said. "Take a breather and have a beer with me."

August clapped the dirt off his gloves, leaned on his shovel, hawked, and spit into the dirt at his feet. "It sounds good," he said. "But if I drink one now I'll just get tired. I've still got those three tarps to move and set on the east side."

"It's just one beer." Ancient tossed the can so August had no choice but to catch it. "It's my old man's birthday today. He would have been eighty-four. That's why I'm out exercising this old bag of bones here." Ancient slapped Chief's haunch, and Chief, unconcerned, continued pulling up mouthfuls of the long grass at the ditch's edge.

August cracked the beer and it foamed up through the mouth of the can, spilling down his wrist. He took a drink, shoved the spade head-down into the soft dirt, and leaned against the parked four-wheeler.

"You see that up there?" Ancient pointed up toward a low hill at the back of the field, half a mile distant. "That juniper tree sticking up from the ledge rock?"

August shaded his eyes from the sun. "That little one by itself, all twisted up and gnarly looking?"

Ancient nodded. "That's the one. My old man wanted his ashes buried up there, under that tree."

"Ashes buried?"

"Yeah. Most people that get cremated want their ashes scattered, I know. My old man wanted to get cremated, but he wanted his ashes buried. I don't think he liked the idea of his parts just scattering out willy-nilly. Wanted everything to be contained in one area. I go to the funeral parlor and they've got his remains in this little cardboard box. They tried to sell me all sorts of urns and things, but I said nah. My old man had a thermos. A big Stanley, all beat up and dented. I don't think he ever washed it out, not once. He brought that thing with him everywhere. I took the cardboard box home and I got a funnel from the shop and I funneled my old man's ashes into the coffee thermos, screwed the cap on tight, and Chief and I rode him up to that little rise with the little juniper tree. I had a shovel with me, thinking I was going to bury the thermos, but when I made it all the way up there I found out that the tree is growing out of a crack in bare rock. It's the only tree around because there's nothing but sandstone except for one crack, and that's where its roots had gotten their hold. So I ended up just wedging the thermos down in the crack and piling up some rocks around it. Seemed to work out okay. Every year on his birthday I go up and check on it."

August wiped the sweat beading on his forehead with the back of his sleeve and settled his cap down. "Most likely, buried under rocks way up there, nothing would mess with it."

"I suppose not. That thermos with my old man's ashes will definitely outlast me and my time. If I ever had kids, probably theirs, too."

"Those Stanleys are bombproof. What's that thing they were always saying in science class—matter can't be created or destroyed, just changed. Right?"

"That seems familiar. Apply that to a person and you might be tempted to call it immortality."

"Or eternal imprisonment," August said.

Ancient drained his beer and crunched the can against the pommel. "All of that depends on what side of the bed you woke up on in the morning, I guess."

"Probably true."

They didn't say anything for a moment, and in this period of quiet Chief released a burst of wet flatulence. Ancient laughed and shook his head. "That's what ol' Chief thinks about our philosophizing. You done with that? Hand me the can. Okay. Well, I've got to get on. I'm headed up to that rise to sit for a spell with my back to the juniper tree, ponder eternity, and survey my holdings. Keep up the good work."

Later that night August made tacos. He stirred a packet of store-bought taco seasoning into a pan of ground beef and waited for it to brown. He chopped a small white onion and put a stack of soft corn tortillas in the microwave. It was a mild evening, and he had the bunkhouse window open, hoping to hear the yodeling of the coyote pack that seemed to hunt frequently in the low hills behind the house. When the meat was ready he spooned it onto the tortillas and sprinkled on the raw onion, eating standing over the stove so that whatever fell from the tortilla landed back in the pan. He'd forgotten to buy salsa or cheese, and the tacos were dry and bland. He ate because he was hungry, but when he was full he considered the ground beef left in the pan and tried to imagine it reincarnated as leftovers. He ended up scraping the whole mess into the trash. When he was at the sink washing his dishes in front of the open window, he heard a voice, indistinct and soft, coming from the corral.

He opened the bunkhouse door slowly, wiping his hands dry on his jeans, stepping barefoot out onto the small patio. Standing at the corner of the bunkhouse he could see around to the far edge of the corral. Ancient was there, sitting on the top fence rail, facing away from August. He wore a white undershirt and jeans. He sat with slumped shoulders, his back curved in an unnatural arc, the knobby ridge of his spine protruding. A sickle moon cast the yard in dim light, everything matte, monochromatic, except for the bottle of vodka—on a post next to Ancient's right hand—which glowed as if lit from within. Chief was standing close and Ancient was reaching to stroke his muzzle.

Ancient was talking, but August couldn't make out the words. The horse was making a strange grumbling whinny and nodding its head, reaching for the apple half Ancient had in his outstretched palm. There was the sound of appreciative horsey chewing, then Chief blowing and shaking out his mane. Ancient tipped the bottle so that, from where August stood, it appeared that the moon had become imprisoned within the glass itself and Ancient's drinking was nothing more than an attempt to reach it—as if, when he finally gulped the moon to his lips, he was going to take it in his mouth and spit it back to its rightful place in the sky.

August was done for the day. He was drinking a beer on the porch when his father called.

"You finally thawing a bit out there?" his father said.

"Yeah, it's been nice."

"You got a cold? Your nose sounds stuffed up or something."

"Allergies, I think. The cottonwoods by the river are putting out a lot of pollen."

"You taking an antihistamine?"

"I haven't been."

"Well, you probably should. You can get the twenty-four-hour stuff over the counter now. Generic so it's not too expensive."

"I'll check it out."

"We didn't get the rain we normally get in April. I'm a little worried about what that's going to mean come summer. But then again I've seen it warm and dry in April and then rain every day in May and June; you never really know."

"Yeah, you can never tell."

"I put a new coat of paint on the barn and milking parlor. Haven't done that since probably before you were born."

"What color?"

"Barn is red. Milking parlor is white."

"So, exactly the same as before?"

"Same as before. Just freshened it up a little. It was Lisa's idea. Nice bright white trim on the barn. I didn't think it looked too bad, but now that it's done I guess I can see her point. She says that if your work environment is attractive to the eye then you go about your day a little jauntier. That may or may not be true. But take it from me, if your girl-friend is happy you're bound to be a little jauntier yourself."

"I talked to Mom the other day. She says her boyfriend proposed. They're going to get married. Did she tell you?"

There was a pause. A low whistle. A soft laugh. "No, I guess my in-vite got lost in the mail."

"She said they're not going to go have a church ceremony or any-thing. Just go to the courthouse and then have a little party after. She wants me to come down for dinner to *get to know* her boyfriend."

"Well, of course."

"Pretty soon we're going to be smack in the middle of haying. An-cient isn't going to be impressed with me asking for time off."

"I'm sure you could get away for an evening."

"You know how haying is, though. Sometimes you have to just work until it's done or else you'll be stuck with it laying down when it rains."

"Oh, you don't have to tell me. Once when I was about your age I was helping my dad put up hay in a section we were leasing over in Mecosta. We had the whole field cut and we were just starting to bale. We had this old John Deere round baler, and the hydraulic pump that runs the little arm that feeds out the twine was on the fritz. We messed around with it and my dad finally got so pissed that we called it a day and were going to come back in the morning and get it straightened out. We'd put up about two bales out of a forty-some-bale field. That night it started to rain and it didn't stop for nearly three weeks and everything just rotted where it lay. I think Dad was bitter about that until his death. We could have just kept filling the pump with fluid and limped it along. An expensive way to learn a lesson for sure. I hadn't realized your mom and that guy were getting all that serious. Seems kind of sudden if you ask me."

"It's been over a year."

"That long? Is he a good guy? What's your impression of him?"

"I hardly know him. She met him at the library."

"He works there?"

"No, I think he works over at the university. He was just coming into the library a lot or something."

"I see. Well, I looked at your extended forecast out there and they're calling for a slightly cooler than average summer with average to slightly above average precipitation."

"Yeah?"

"That's what it said. So as long as you guys get your hay up it should be pleasant and not too hot. But you never know. I've seen those long-range forecasts be so wrong it's not even funny. I didn't even realize that they were living together."

"They're not. I don't think. At least not full time, anyway. He's got a place over in Bozeman."

"So is she going to sell hers and move in with him?"

"I really have no idea."

"Probably she'll just keep hers and rent it out. Or, depending on what his place is like, he'll move in with her and then they'll rent out his. That's what I'd do. Having some rental income is a great way to go. Okay, well, nice talking to you, son. Keep your nose clean."

"Night, Dad."

It was around noon, and August took the four-wheeler back to the house for lunch. He was standing in front of his sink eating a ham and cheese sandwich and drinking a Coke when he saw the truck come barreling up the drive, veer around the corral, and keep going, cross-country, through the pasture behind the house.

It was an older Chevy flatbed with a green HANGING R logo on the side. August walked out the door and around the shop, and from there, he could see the truck had come to a stop at the fence line near the top of the hill. A man was out, doing something at the back. The man got back into his truck, pointed it back down the hill, and accelerated. The truck paused for a second and then came down the grade, something silver flashing in its wake. It took August a moment, but he realized that the truck had been hooked up to one of his new corner posts. The driver was roaring down the hill towing thirty yards of fence. T-posts were flopping and falling; the big pressure-treated corner post was bouncing over rocks, the wire strands singing wickedly, screeching and popping. The truck was coming fast toward the yard, and August, still holding his sandwich, ducked back into the shop. From the window, he watched as the truck came to a gravel-crunching stop in the driveway. The man hopped out, his beard a thick gray-black. Short and stocky in a baseball cap, jeans, and grimy white tennis shoes, he moved unhurriedly to the back of his truck and unhooked a tow chain from the corner post. He threw the chain into the bed of his truck, wiped his hands on his jeans, and swung back into the cab. He drove away and August watched the ragged cloud of dust follow his path all the way out the road. He called Ancient from the phone in the bunkhouse. He got voicemail once. He tried again and this time left a message.

"It's August," he said. "Not sure if you're still in Billings, or on your way back, or what. I'm at the house. I think Tim Duncan, Big Tim, just came and pulled out all the fence I built going up the hill behind the shop. Hooked it up to his truck and dragged it. Not sure what you want me to do. I'll hang around for a while to see if you call back. Okay, bye."

It was well past dark when August heard Ancient's pickup come up the drive and then keep going past the house. August stepped out to watch Ancient's taillights bouncing up the rough track to the upper pasture. When the truck stopped and the door opened, August could see Ancient's form crossing the headlights. He stood there, illuminated, his hands on his hips, inspecting the line of downed fence. There were coyotes singing in the draw by the creek. Ancient put his head back and let out a howl, and the coyotes went quiet. He howled again, and then a solitary coyote called back, and then another. Ancient kept it up until it sounded like the whole pack was letting loose in a frenzy of yips and yodels. August returned to his bunk, but he could hear the coyotes going for quite some time. There'd been occasions where he'd tried to join the coyotes like Ancient had, but August could never make the right sound, and so he'd always stop, feeling ridiculous.

August had the coffee maker set on a timer, and he came awake slowly to the pissy trickling sound of the pot filling. He slipped on the same jeans he'd worn the day before, three days past due for washing, and poured himself a cup. He took a leak outside, his feet bare, the grass dew-wet, daylight just gaining strength. Back inside he put two pieces of bread down in the toaster and switched on the small radio he kept on the counter. KPIG out of Billings came in, only slightly scratchy. They did the weather; this early in the day it was a mechanized voice reading the report. More sun, no clouds forecasted. No surprise. The first song after the weather was John Mellencamp's "Jack and Diane," and August slathered peanut butter on his toast—wishing for jam— and ate it dry and sticky standing at the sink. He'd pinned the Polaroid from the Musselshell up on the wall there and Mellencamp was singing about *two American kids growing up in the heartland,* and August was looking right at them. Jack and Diane. *Two 'merican kids doin' the best they can.* He poured the rest of the coffee from the pot into his travel mug, switched off the radio, slipped on his boots, and went out to gas up the four-wheeler. He had a whole line of dragged fence to rebuild.

Another afternoon under the sun. Rebuilding something that had been torn down was never as satisfying as making new. The first fence had been truer, but in the end he was satisfied. When he came back down the hill in the evening, Kim's Subaru was parked in the drive. Ancient's truck was gone, but lights were on in the house. August put the four-wheeler away in the shop. He was walking across the yard to the bunkhouse when Kim stepped out onto the porch and waved him over. She was wearing overalls and yellow rubber cleaning gloves, and had a red paisley handkerchief tied around her head. "Hey, August," she said, smiling and taking off a glove to shake his hand. "How are things?"

"Good," August said. "Things are fine. Just finishing up for the day."

"Great. Well, I'm here for the night. I had to come up and get a few things, and I decided I'd give the house a nice deep clean. Leave Ancient by himself for just a little while and it looks like a bomb erupted. He had to go up to Helena to a breeder to take a look at a bull he might lease. He's going to be back sometime tomorrow. He told me to tell you that."

"Sounds good."

"Hey, would you mind giving me a hand here for a minute? I was hoping to get this elliptical machine on top of my Subaru. It will be a little cumbersome but shouldn't be too heavy. Maybe you can help me get it secured?"

August followed her into the house, and together they carried the machine, rearranging themselves a couple of different ways to get it out the door and hoisted onto the low roof of the Subaru. She had ratchet straps, and August went to work getting the bulky thing secured. When he was done he gave it a hard shove, and it didn't budge. "I guess that will do it," he said. "I'd probably keep it under a hundred on the highway, though."

"I'll definitely do that. Thanks for your help. I'm going to make some dinner soon. You probably want to get washed up, but after that, come on up to the house and eat with me."

"Oh, that's okay," August said. "You don't have to go to any trouble for me. I've got stuff I can eat in the bunkhouse."

"It's no trouble. I'm cooking anyway. We both need to eat; no sense in doing it separately when we can share. It'll be ready in about an hour."

Dinner was overcooked boneless, skinless chicken breasts. Undercooked baked potatoes. Canned green beans.

"Thanks for doing this, Kim," August said. "The chicken is great."

"Happy to do it. I marinate the chicken in Wish-Bone Italian dressing. That's the secret. Gives it a really nice flavor, I think."

"Never would've thought of that." They were sitting across from each other at the large dining room table. The house was silent around them, empty, with shadows gathering. She'd turned the chandelier lights lower. "Mood lighting," she'd said with a laugh. She opened a bottle of wine and the room was dim. He'd have preferred it to be brighter.

"So," she said. "How are you liking it up here? I haven't seen you in a while."

"I like it. It's beautiful country."

"I can't argue with that. The country is impeccable. Have you been meeting any of the locals?"

He chewed his chicken. Kept chewing. Chased the swallow with water. "A few," he said. "People are pretty nice around here, mostly. I think they kind of keep to themselves. Everyone's got a lot of work to do."

"I suppose. It's funny; for how empty and vast it is up here, it can really feel pretty damn crowded sometimes. I've actually been surprised by how much I've come to enjoy Billings. I'm not going to get into things with me and Ancient. I'm sure you really don't care about it anyway. But living up here, I'd have to drive a hundred miles to go to a damn yoga class, or get a decent piece of pizza, or see a show. Everything is so far."

"There's good things about that, though. No traffic. You don't have to lock your doors."

"Sure. I appreciate those things. When I moved here I was looking for some out-of-the-way place where I could just live my life. And then I met Ancient, and he is different from some of the people around here, in a good way. But he's also one of them, too. Do you admire him? Just a question. I'm curious what you think of him."

"Ancient is fine. I like him fine. He's good with cattle. Good at what he does." August was trying to eat more quickly. He wanted this, whatever this was, to wrap up. He longed for the simple, empty confines of the bunkhouse.

"Sure, but what do you think of him as a person? Is he someone you might ever model yourself after?"

August said nothing. He gave a small shrug and focused his attention on his potato.

"I'm sorry. I guess that's not really a fair question. He's your boss. It is what it is." Kim had refilled her wineglass several times. Her chicken was still mostly intact. "Let's change the subject," she said brightly. "So, tell me, have you ever been in love?"

August's every inclination was telling him to shrug and be noncommittal. To dodge and mumble his way out of this meal, out of this dining room, and out from under this awkward woman's inquisition. He'd worked all day and he was tired. Instead, he found himself putting his knife and fork down on the plate loudly. "I have," he said. "Have you?" He looked at her directly for the first time. Something on his face seemed to make her smile falter. She sipped her wine.

"Tell me about her," she said.

August was very aware of his hands, splayed on the tablecloth. Tanned dark. A dry crack on his thumb. Dirt under the nails, thick veins leading to his wrist. As he spoke he looked at them. "She was my mother's friend. My last year of high school."

"So she was much older?"

"Twenty-seven. Ten years older than me at the time."

"What did she look like? Was she beautiful?"

"She's tall. Blond. Not skinny. But not fat, either. There's just lots of her, and it's not mushy but it's soft."

"I can imagine her perfectly. I know that type. And she broke your heart, right?"

"Maybe."

Kim nodded as if this had confirmed something she'd thought all along. "Are you to the stage yet where you appreciate the experience for what it was? Because you were young and you learned, right? She taught you things?"

August was looking over her shoulder now. Out the window behind her he could see the yard light blink on, glowing green. "She taught me about her. That's it. And so far, I don't see how that knowledge could be useful in the future. Because she's gone. It's useless knowledge."

They'd finished the bottle, glasses empty, food cold. "What do you mean? You don't think all women are fundamentally similar?"

"I couldn't say."

"Maybe you haven't had a large enough sampling size yet to draw conclusions."

"She's not like you. I know that much."

Kim gave a dry laugh. "Outside of being one, I've had some experiences with women. Men like to make out that there's some big mystery there, but it's not true. You ever hear about something called *the sacred feminine*?"

August shrugged. "No."

"It's basically a theory about how all life on earth flows through the female form. And that women are closer to the sacred than men because they can give birth. It's supposed to be about female empowerment, but I guarantee the concept was dreamed up by a man. Men want to believe that a woman embodies something essential about the universe, and so they tend to get all worked up over us. Most women won't admit it, even to themselves, but deep down we know it's all bullshit. A woman is like a knot. A knot isn't sacred. A knot isn't profound or evil or virtuous because it's intricate. Once you've untangled a knot it disappears."

"So?"

"All I'm saying is that you should forget her. If you don't, she'll be like black paint on your hands, and it will stain everything you touch for the rest of your life." She cleared her throat and stood up, her chair making a loud noise on the floor tiles. "Help me clear this stuff away. No dessert tonight, sorry."

He helped her scrape the plates and left her there in the empty kitchen, leaning against the counter with her arms crossed over her chest.

———

Coming back from town, August pulled off at the Hutterite farm stand that had just opened for the season. It was a small whitewashed plywood structure with a corrugated metal roof and awning. Behind a low counter were racks of jars: apple butter and strawberry-rhubarb jam, pickled asparagus and green beans and cucumbers. Shelves of baked goods, pies, and loaves of white bread. There were large plastic bins stacked for the eventual produce that wasn't yet ready for harvest and a hand-lettered sign: SELF-SERVE. PUT CASH IN THE BOX. FOR FRYERS DRIVE TO COLONY. NO SUNDAY SALES.

August stood considering the jars of jam and preserves. Chokecherry jam. He'd never seen that before. It was a warm day, and the pies seemed to glisten and sweat under the plastic wrap. He picked out a loaf of plain white and a loaf of sourdough and a jar of apple butter and a jar of the chokecherry. He was digging through his wallet for correct change when a Hutterite girl came up from the colony, towing a wheeled metal cart. From the cart she lifted a large box full of baked goods. She smiled at August and began restocking the shelves. August watched her, blond hair, a few tendrils escaping the polka-dot kerchief she wore over her head. A dark-green dress with a black apron, her feet bare, soles dirty as she raised up on her tiptoes to reach the top shelf. She was humming.

"This chokecherry jam," August said. His voice seemed loud, bouncing around under the tin roof of the shed. The girl turned, startled. "What's it like?" he said, quieter.

"Like?" she said.

"How does it taste?"

"It's sweet," she said. "Chokecherries are really sour, so we add lots of sugar."

She had just the faintest hint of accent. German, August figured. She had a small mole on her right nostril. He thought she was probably fourteen or fifteen years old. "Okay," he said. "How about the apple butter? How's that taste?"

She looked at him, eyebrows raised. "You've never had apple butter?"

"Maybe, but it's been a long time."

"It's sweet," she said. "We boil down lots of apples with cinnamon and sugar. Everyone likes it. I'm sure you'll like it."

"Okay. Well, I think I'll get one of each and these loaves of bread, too."

She gave him a small smile. Pointed at the sign, then tapped a finger on the slotted cashbox bolted to the counter. "Go ahead and just slide your money in here and help yourself," she said.

August had his wallet out. "Is there any way I could get change? All I've got is a twenty." He waved the bill slightly, as if to provide evidence.

She produced a key from her apron and unlocked the cashbox.

Apparently it had been a slow day. It contained a lone twenty. She shrugged. "I guess that doesn't help much. I could run back to the house?"

"I don't want to put you out. I'll just pick up some more stuff, I guess. A few more jars of jam, maybe. I could give them to my mom or something, because I probably won't eat it all."

"Well, that's nice. Jams make great gifts." She turned back to her work, organizing the pies, taking one out of circulation that seemed to not pass inspection.

"How about this strawberry-rhubarb?" he said. "Is that pretty good?"

She didn't turn around. "It *is* good," she said. "All of it is pretty good, actually."

"What's your favorite?"

She was humming again and her response came in a short, melodious burst. "Strawberry-and-butter-and-sourdough-toast," she sang, laughing. "I like that for dessert."

August laughed, too. He picked up a jar of strawberry and another jar of apple butter and set them next to his loaves of bread. Emboldened, he said, "Are you related to a girl named Sarah Jane, by any chance?"

She had a broom and was starting to sweep the leaves and grass dander from the floor of the shed. She stopped, no longer humming. "SJ?" she said.

"Yeah. SJ. I was just curious. A friend of mine knew her, I think. A few years back. I think she lived here."

The girl was looking in his direction, not quite at him, somewhere off above his shoulder, eyes narrowed slightly. "SJ is my second-oldest sister," she said.

"I thought you looked like her," August said. "That's why I asked."

"How do you know what she looks like?"

"A picture. My friend showed me."

"Graven image."

"Huh?"

The girl was sweeping furiously now. Ramming the broom into the corners so hard, pieces of straw were breaking off. "Thou shalt make no graven image," she said. "Excuse me." August stepped to the side so she could sweep past his feet.

"Does she still live here?"

The girl gave one firm shake of her head. Paused her sweeping for a moment to slam the cashbox closed and fasten the lock. "Arm River," she said. "Up in Saskatchewan. I haven't seen her in almost two years. And she hardly ever calls."

"Does she have children?"

"Why do you care?"

"I'm asking for my friend, that's all. He wanted to know."

She was sweeping again, angrily. Broom-straw shrapnel flying, making more of a mess than she was cleaning up. "She only just got engaged last month. So how could she have children? Didn't even tell me herself, just sent a letter in the mail. Will you be needing anything else? Because I'd like to finish cleaning this."

August gathered up his jam and bread and retreated from the stand, the girl sweeping him out the door as he went.

It was late afternoon, and the sun was stalled at a wicked angle. August was wrapping up his near-daily battle with the irrigation dams, sweat plastering his shirt to his back. Ancient drove up on the four-wheeler and helped him get the last poly tarp in place. "Hot bitch today," Ancient said. He stood with a grass stem between his teeth regarding the rising water. "Killed a rattlesnake out behind the house earlier. Was laying all stretched out big as you please, right across the path going to the shed. Didn't even move when I came up and got him with the shovel. It was like he wasn't concerned about me at all. Big sucker. Cut this off him." Ancient reached into his pocket and opened his palm to show August the segmented rattle, nearly as long as his pinky.

"Damn," August said. "That is a big one."

Ancient shook the rattle to make it buzz, then put it back in his pocket. "Might make me a key chain out of it or something. Some guys think a rattlesnake rattle is good luck. My old man got bit one time.

His leg swole up like a tree trunk. He wanted to wait it out, but I made him go down to Billings to get the shot. He bitched the whole time about how much it was going to cost and was out messing around with the horses again at dawn the next day. Tough old buzzard. They don't really make them like that anymore." He cleared his throat. "You been around me a fair bit these past months. Feel free to tell me straight up. You think I have a drinking problem?"

August wiped his forehead with his shirtsleeve and settled his hat back on. "What does that even mean?" he said. "A drinking *problem*."

"Exactly. That's what I told Kim. I said, I might have a drinking habit but that don't necessarily mean it's a *problem*. She loves yoga, right? She always calls it her *practice*. Well, I told her that my practice is drinking. It's something I engage in. It's not something that runs my life. She thinks my behavior has been getting erratic, and if I want her to come back I'll have to go to at least one AA meeting. That's her condition."

"Just one?"

"That's what she says. But I get the feeling that we're playing a game, and she's the one that gets to make all the rules. I go to an AA meeting and what's next? It's a slippery slope. Do you think I've been acting *erratic*?"

"Do you want her to come back?"

"Of course. That's what all this is about. You're evading the question. Have I been erratic?"

"Maybe you should just do it. If it makes her happy. A good woman might be a man's only hope for salvation on earth."

Ancient looked at August. Blinked.

"I heard a guy say that one time."

Ancient laughed, spit his grass stem into the ditch, and straddled the four-wheeler. "I might have to ponder that one for a bit," he said. He looked at August for a long moment. Shook his head. Fired up the four-wheeler and drove away.

August took the back way home from town. It was early evening, and he had a rotisserie chicken from the IGA steaming in a paper bag next to him on the seat of the truck. He had a side of potato salad and a peach iced tea and a six-pack of Bud. He slowed as he passed the Duncan place. There were new signs, the paint still glistening a fresh and urgent black. They had been installed on two-by-fours as before, but something looked different now and August slowed further, craning out the truck window to get a better look. Each two-by-four was backed by a chainsaw-wrecking metal T-post.

August drove the rest of the way home and sat on the porch to eat. He read some of his Hutterite book, his chicken-grease-coated fingers smearing the pages. It didn't seem the sort of book that one needed to read from cover to cover in any particular order, so he just opened to a random spot and started in. He learned that the Hutterites were devoted to pacifism and that, during World War I, numerous Hutterite men were imprisoned for not complying with the draft. Two brothers, Joseph and Michael Hofer, were abused so badly they both died in Leavenworth. After this came a lengthy chapter on various traditional Hutterite animal husbandry practices. It was dry reading, and before long August dropped the book on the porch and finished picking at the chicken.

He had his feet propped up on the railing and was finishing the last beer when there was a loud huffing noise, like a stubborn engine refusing to turn over, followed by the sound of hooves churning, a crack of wood splintering. August got to his feet just as Chief came around the corner of the shop. Broken free of the corral, he was walleyed, with a long string of viscous snot running from his muzzle. He made one final stride and then went down, legs tangled, skidding in the long grass at the edge of the yard. His raised his head one more time, the cords of his neck clear as ropes under his skin as he struggled and failed to get up. August could feel the thump of his head hitting the ground through the soles of his boots. The horse's sides heaved, and then he was still. There was the long, slow sound of flatulence, and then Chief was just a brown mound in the weeds, unmistakably dead.

The next day Ancient rented a small excavator and dragged Chief out to the pasture. Before starting on the hole he walked to Chief's dead form, stood there looking down for a moment, and sat down on the horse's large haunch. August was there with a shovel, and he tapped the blade on his boot a few times. Waiting.

Ancient took his hat off and held it between his hands, his head bowed slightly. "Chief was a good horse," he said. "I've never much cared for horses, but Chief was all right. My old man's last horse. I buried my father and now I bury his horse, and it's like somehow this is actually it. Like, now my old man is truly dead, because as long as something he'd trained was still around, then part of him was still alive, too. But now we put Chief in the ground, and it's just poor orphan boy Ancient. But I guess the show goes on. No sense being all shmoopy about it."

Ancient stood and jammed his hat back on his head and slapped his hands on his thighs. He laughed and toed Chief's shank with his boot. "Maybe this is the universe's way of keeping us hopping along. Every time someone or something close to you dies, there's a carcass you have to attend to before it starts to stink. If bodies didn't decay, the dead would be stacking up everywhere, and soon enough the living would become enslaved by them. Memories are bad enough as it is. Let's get this thing dealt with."

August stood by with the shovel to help him but there wasn't much for him to do. The excavator bucket scraped and sparked, and August could smell the ozone odor rising from the bruised stones in the pit. He leaned on his shovel, and when a magpie landed on Chief's flank, August scuffed his feet to make the bird fly away. When the hole was dug Ancient hooked the bucket around Chief's long back and dragged him over the edge into the hole. August felt Chief's final thud broadcast through the dirt, and then Ancient began shoving the loose, rocky soil back into the grave.

Hole filled, Ancient ran the excavator back and forth over the grave a few times to tamp everything down, and soon there was just a disturbed patch of dirt that would be indistinguishable from the rest of the pasture in a matter of days. Ancient drove the excavator back to the yard, up the ramp, and onto the trailer, where August helped him hitch the safety chains around the tracks.

"I rented the thing by the hour," Ancient said. "Probably some other little jobs I could do around the place while I have it but I don't really feel like messing with it right now. I'm just going to take it back. You eat yet?"

August shook his head no, and then they were heading into town.

They dropped the excavator at Northern Rental and went to the Mint for dinner.

Ancient was drinking whiskey, barely picking at his hamburger. August stuck to beer; he was suddenly ravenous and ended up eating half of Ancient's burger on top of his.

"How's it going with Kim?" August said. "None of my business. I just hope it's going okay."

Ancient swirled a fry around in ketchup. Chewed and sipped his drink. "It's all right, you asking. I've been leaving you in the lurch a fair amount lately, and I'm sorry. You've been doing a good job. And, when I'm gone, I don't worry that things aren't being taken care of. I lucked out hiring you, and I hope you know that I feel that way. I've never met your old man, but I have to think that it was him that taught you how to work. Hopefully you thank him for that on occasion. If I ever met him, *I'd* thank him. Anyway. She's got a job down there now. She's working as a receptionist at an orthodontics office. I go down there and we go to counseling. She's still staying with her sister, and so we go to counseling, and after, we go have dinner or something and then we go sleep in her sister's basement on the pullout couch. I've seen enough of Billings to last me a lifetime. Smells like burning oil all the time, and the streets are littered with bums and drunks and other defects."

"You're doing counseling?"

"Yeah. We talk in circles and pay someone to listen. She's got the job now, though, and it's hard to see that as anything but one foot following the other out the door. Your parents are split, aren't they?"

"For a while now."

"What happened? If you don't mind me asking."

"My dad started messing with a girl he had helping out in the barn. At the time, she was younger than I am now. She'd just graduated high school. Was actually working for my dad when she was still in high school, so who knows."

"That must have been a hard one for your mom to swallow."

"Well, she can be difficult in her own way. Her family had some money. My dad's people never had much. Whenever he couldn't afford something she wanted, she could come up with the funds easy enough with a phone call or two. That had to get old. They fought about this couch she bought—it was fancy upholstery, real expensive. He'd put his boots up on it whenever he got a chance and it got stained, and then one day she had me help her drag it out into the front yard and she lit it on fire and it sat there burned out and smoking for a few days before he took an ax to it and hauled it off. He laid on the floor to watch TV for a long time. My mom never watches TV. That's a small thing, but I guess it's the buildup that happens over the years that does it. Never any one major problem. Who knows? At least you and Kim never had any kids."

Ancient shook his head, his eyes widened in fake surprise. "I think that's the most words I ever heard you string together." He laughed. "But the problem is, when you get to my and Kim's age, the kid aspect is the biggest issue, believe it or not. I want kids, I think. A child keeps people together and gives them a reason to behave better than they might on their own. Without a kid, it's way too easy to just pull up stakes and go down to Billings and take yoga classes and get a job as a receptionist." Ancient downed his whiskey and ordered another.

It was well past dark by the time Ancient slid, none too steadily, from his stool and fumbled his keys from his jeans pocket. "Want me to drive?" August said as they headed toward the truck.

"Shiiit," Ancient said and swung into the driver's seat. It took him two tries to get the key into the ignition, and when the truck rumbled to life he paused before putting it in gear. "Guess maybe I'll take the back way," he said.

As they drove out of town, August said, "We've had that hay down for a while now. How's that baler coming along?"

"The main problem with that baler is that it is a giant hunk of crap. Was a problem almost from the time my old man bought it. I put a new idler and V-belt in it, though. I'm cautiously optimistic."

"Should I give it a shot tomorrow?"

"Yeah, we'll give it a shot. You know how much a new baler costs?"

"I'm guessing it's not cheap."

Ancient was about to say something but stopped. He'd taken the Dry Creek turnoff. They were rattling along the dirt road, and then Duncan's signs bloomed white in the headlights. Ancient slowed. "You've got to be kidding me. Looks like he even added a couple new ones. GOOD FENCES MAKE GOOD NEIGHBORS. SMILE, YOU ARE UNDER SURVEILLANCE. *Good fences make good neighbors?* Seriously? Isn't that from a poem?"

"I believe so."

Ancient let the truck idle. "I told Kim about Big Tim coming and tearing up the fence, and she said that now it was even and I should let it alone. You said he just came in and tore it out and left, right? You didn't see him messing around with Chief at all or anything like that?"

"No. Nothing like that."

"I suppose not. Fences are one thing; killing a horse is another. And Chief was older than dirt. Still, I have a suspicious mind. Wish I had my chainsaw. The ignorance of these things just irritates the hell out of me."

"Saw probably wouldn't do it anyway."

"What?"

"I came by the other day, in the daylight, and he's got T-posts behind the two-by-fours. Probably hoping you try to cut one and mess your chain up."

"Seriously?"

"There's definitely metal fence posts behind the wood. Yeah."

Ancient shook his head. "Where does this asshole find the time? How many days' work are we looking at right here? For what? To make some people driving by feel shitty? Kim's always telling me that part of her problem is the small-mindedness of the people around here, and I try to tell her that people are people wherever they're at, not much difference, but when you come across things like this, you have to admit that she might have a point. It's hard to make a go around these parts and everyone hunkers to their own to survive, and sometimes that itself starts to feel like an injustice, and then pretty soon we're all just rats eating at each other for no reason other than to get out our internal meanness. And she's wrong about me and him being even. There's the note that started it all, then I cut his signs, then he tore down the fence, and if my math is correct that puts him up one." Ancient looked off the road and tapped his thumbs on the steering wheel. "There's people I'd be willing to concede a point to. Big Tim is not one of those people."

He drove down the shallow ditch and backed the truck up next to a corner post on the fence line. He put the truck in park and hopped out. August turned to watch Ancient moving around in the red taillight glow. He had removed a tow strap from the toolbox and was looping it around the post, ducking low to hook the other end around the ball hitch.

"Fences make good neighbors, my ass," he said, returning to the cab, shifting into drive, and accelerating out of the ditch.

In the rearview mirror August watched the corner post jolt and then pop. There was a high-pitched wail of barbed wire stretched to the max and the deadly whang of strands snapping. Several of the signs tipped and came thrashing along for the ride. Ancient drove up onto the Duncans' driveway, and August thought he'd stop and undo the tow strap but he kept going, heading toward the lights of the house in the distance.

"Looks like someone is home," August said.

Ancient was looking straight ahead, a knot in his jaw. "I hope so," he said. "Should have come down here first thing, and now it's gotten out of hand. It's all going to be done, one way or another, after this."

Ancient sped up, and the trailing signs splintered and bucked. He pulled halfway around the circular drive in front of the Duncan house and put the truck in park. The dust that had been billowing behind them caught up and swirled, motes floating through the headlights like a brown fog. Ancient laid his fist on the horn and then opened the door. Before getting out of the truck he looked at August. "Sorry to involve you in this. It's not your deal, but I'd appreciate it if you'd make sure no one shoots me from behind." And then he was out of the truck, heading toward the porch, the front door already opening to greet him.

Big Tim stood backlit in the doorway. He was barefoot, in jeans and a white undershirt. His beard trailed down his chest, and his hairline receded halfway back his skull; what was left of his hair a thin, wispy mess above his head. He had his arms at his sides, and he held something in each hand, down low next to his legs. Ancient was approaching the porch, and August got out of the truck. There was a tire iron under the seat and he gripped it, leaning against the truck in the shadow.

Ancient stopped at the foot of the porch stairs and hooked his fingers in his belt loops. "Let's talk about fences, neighbor," he said.

Big Tim stepped out of the doorway, and August still couldn't make sense of what he was holding. His voice came low and calm. "I saw you coming, and I know that you've got a deep-seated problem, Ancient. I talked to your father about you once before he died, and he asked me to keep an eye on you. He was worried, I think."

Ancient shook his head and spit. "Don't even talk about my father. No more of your bullshit now, Tim. You never got over the fact that you had to sell that piece of pasture to me, and then you tried to run my fiancée out of town because you're a small-minded, conspiracy-theory-spouting backwards ingrate."

"The only question," Big Tim said, "is just how deep your problem lies. It's come to the surface now, but how far back are the wellsprings?" Big Tim came across the porch, his bare feet whispering on the boards. He was raising his arms, and in each hand he had a long, thin piece of black wood or metal. They were rods, no thicker than car aerials, cylindrical and L-shaped, each with a ninety-degree bend. He had his index fingers pointing, each hand in a gun shape, the rods balanced and swaying on the protruding digits. In the headlight glare, the angled rods cast long shadows, and Tim was an arm's length away from Ancient, moving in slowly.

"I've been practicing rhabdomancy since I was young," Big Tim said. "You know that before you were born your old man came to me because his well was drying up, and in an afternoon I dowsed up the spring for the new well that you drink from to this day? Did you know that it was me that delivers your everyday water, boy?"

"Get that goofy shit away from me and talk to me normal," Ancient said, taking a small step back.

"I can find the problem you're having, Ancient. Springs below the earth's surface are not so different from the springs beneath a man's skin. If you let them, my tools will find the source of your pain, and from there we can start the work of healing."

"I'm sorry your kid died, Tim. I truly am. But that's no excuse to unhinge. Look at yourself, man. Do not touch me with those things. Tim, I'm telling you."

"It's the drink, in part. I don't even need my tools to tell me that. I can smell your breath from here. But drinking is just a fool's attempt to bandage the wound. Let me do my work, son."

"I'm not your son, you loon. If you touch me, I swear to God, Tim. Get away from me with that."

Tim appeared on the porch. He was in plaid boxer shorts and a white T-shirt. He held his Marlin .22 low, pointed toward the ground. "Dad?" he said.

August stepped away from the truck, and from the corner of his eye he saw Big Tim stretch his arms toward Ancient, balancing rods trembling between them.

"Dad?" Tim was coming off the porch.

"Just relax," Big Tim said, and then his rods made contact with Ancient's chest, both of them touching at the same time just beneath his breastbone. August saw Ancient's fist flash and connect with Big Tim's jaw and they were down in a tangle, the dowsing rods landing on the rocky driveway with a tinny sound.

"Dad!" Tim shouted and came toward the downed men, rifle coming up. Big Tim and Ancient were grappling, dust raising, their limbs nearly indistinguishable. Tim saw August and stopped.

"Put it down," August said, still holding the tire iron.

"Or what?" Tim said. "You'll hit me with that? Why are you even here? Dad!" he shouted. "What the fuck?" He had the gun pointed in a vague place between August and the men on the ground.

"Come on," August said. "I'm not trying to hit anyone."

August was watching Tim, but on his periphery he could see Ancient roll atop Big Tim. He straddled him on the ground and was punching slowly and deliberately into Big Tim's face, Big Tim's arms trying to block but faltering. Tim took several strides closer, .22 to his shoulder. "Ancient!" he shouted. "Ancient, lay off, you fuck." And August was coming, tire iron gathering. Tim, feeling his approach, turned, and the small black eye of the .22 focused on August, and he stopped. There was one more wet thump of fist hitting meat and then, a bass line.

Taxi!
. . . driver . . . take me . . . ride?

A slim figure was coming down the porch stairs, shirtless—a pale torso with hip bones jutting above the waistband of sleek leather pants, a large boom box propped on the shoulder, trailing an orange electrical cord, a strange, halting, skipping, strutting walk, a dance. The music was extremely loud, Prince's "Lady Cab Driver," but there was a bad connection somewhere and the song kept crackling. August could see the figure's long black hair flowing from one side, shaved to stubble on the other. Avery. His eyes closed, nodding, he made his way toward the men on the ground, a jaunty step back, two shuffling steps forward. Everyone stopped, watching in disbelief.

He grabbed the electrical cord and resumed stepping, twirling the cord in time. He was singing along, pelvic-thrusting, moonwalking. Ancient rolled off Big Tim and got to his knees, breathing heavily, his eyes wide in the gloom. Big Tim sat up, blood on his face. Tim had the gun barrel down in the dirt, rubbing his jaw. Avery spun a complete circle as the song continued to cut in and out.

> . . . *brother, handsome . . . tall*
> . . . *bored . . . believe . . . war*
> . . . *for me, that's who . . .*

He wasn't looking at anyone, eyes closed, overpowering Prince's falsetto with his own more desperate voice, sending it out over to the black behind the headlight beams. And then he reached up, pressed a button on the boom box, and the music came to a sudden stop. He opened his eyes, and his gaze passed over all of them.

"You people are ridiculous," he said quietly. He tucked the boom box under his arm, retraced his steps up the porch, and went inside the house, slamming the door behind.

III

A t the Two Dot Bar, August sweated, waiting for his hamburger. He'd been haying all day, and when he sat on the barstool he could still feel the tractor rumbling underneath him. *Painin' from tractor back.* He was exhausted, and he hadn't even stopped to mend the broken legs of any meadowlarks. Where was Paul Harvey with a pep talk when you needed him? He had a beer on a napkin in front of him, and it was a warm evening, so Theresa had the door propped open. In the mirror of the backbar, he saw Tim coming. Saw him pause for a moment on the threshold before entering and sitting at the far end of the bar. He ordered a shot of Jim Beam and a PBR back, and while Theresa poured his drink he sat, spine rigid on his stool, staring straight ahead. He did his shot, put the glass down on the bar softly. The bar was quiet, the jukebox silent, TVs muted, the clank of pan against stove from the kitchen.

"That one time, in the snow, when you called me a figment," August said. "What did you mean by that?"

Tim met August's eyes in the mirror, and he spoke to August's reflection. "It meant something at the time," he said. "Now I don't know."

Tim drained his beer in three long gulps. He laid his money down and then set the empty shot glass on top of the bills. "The change is for you, Theresa," he said. Then he stood and settled his hat back on his head and walked out into the evening.

August was awake in the early dark, lying there in his bunk waiting for the burble of the coffee maker to begin. When it started, he heaved out of bed and ate a bowl of Frosted Shredded Wheat standing at the kitchen sink, watching the light creep up from the rise on the other side of the pasture. He made toast spread with a thick layer of apple butter. He had the radio on for the weather. It was going to be a calm morning with winds building in the afternoon. Twenty percent chance of thunderstorms. While he was finishing his toast, Ancient called.

"I'm still in Billings," he said. "I was planning on being back bright and early, but I got hung up." He was silent for a moment and then he laughed. "To be honest, I'm going to a damn AA meeting later. That talk we had the other day. You wouldn't tell me that I hadn't been acting erratic. That kind of made a light go on for me. I'm taking a month off the sauce. No beer, even. And I don't think AA is necessary, but I'm going because I said I would. Anyway, looks like I won't be back till this evening. I was listening to the weather. There's a chance of some rain this afternoon."

"I just heard that."

"You think you can roll up that last little bit today by yourself?"

"I don't see why not."

"You pretty much did all that piece by the river yourself anyway. I think you'll be fine. If it binds, just toggle reverse and forward until it comes free, and if that doesn't work, lower the speed and use that broom handle to get the stuff unstuck like I showed you."

"I know."

"Grease the fittings, too."

"I will."

"That soil moisture tester is in the cab. Test the first bale and then every few after that. Thirty percent is what we're looking for, right?"

"Don't you mean twenty?"

"Exactly right. Just testing you there. Good catch. I think you should be set. If anything comes up give me a jingle. And you know what?"

"What?"

"Get that finished up and take the afternoon off. Probably going to be a hot one out there. Go down to the lake or something. I talked to old Brody at Feed-n-Need the other day, and he said he caught a bucketful out at the reservoir. Or whatever, take a nap and jack off for all I care. Just relax. Sound good?"

"Sounds fine."

"All right. I appreciate you. See you tonight."

August filled his thermos and headed out to the shop. The baler was already hooked up, and he spent a few minutes greasing the fittings and spooling up a new twine roll. They'd finished the second cutting and there was only one of the small side fields adjacent to the house left unbaled. August fired up the Deere and headed out to the road. He drove straddling the white line on the shoulder for the short distance to the field entrance and then turned up and into the section of mowed grass.

The first bale came out tight and symmetrical. It tested at 17 percent and August gave it a fond slap before swinging back into the cab. He watched the intake, and when the baler jammed he stopped and reversed the feed, and it started rolling again. Three more bales came out clean and tight. August was keeping an eye on a line of dark clouds forming over the low hills toward the river. He was over halfway done and it looked like he was going to get it all stitched up, just in time.

The wind was intensifying and bits of hay chaff blew in from the opened windows, the good clean herbal smell of it filling the tractor cab. August was nearly ready to spit out another bale when there was a bang, barely audible over the tractor noise, and the baler dipped and lurched, wobbling on the hitch. August slowed the tractor to a halt. He left it in idle while he hopped out. The situation was immediately apparent. The baler sagged heavily to one side, a tire completely blown out, the sidewall shredded, so the machine rested on the metal wheel rim. August considered the pregnant clouds, still a ways off. Considered the blown tire. Considered the windrows of hay still down in the field. The wind caught the brim of his hat and flipped it to the ground, and he scooped it up and tightened the band, jamming it back down on his head. He shut off the tractor and jogged the short distance back to the yard to get his truck, driving it around and out into the field next to the hobbled baler. He took the jack from behind the truck seat and spent a few moments puzzling out a spot to get it set, finally deciding on a flat area near the baler's axle.

He loosened the lug nuts with some difficulty; they were rusted tight, and each one took several jolting stomps on the tire iron to get unstuck. When they were finger-loose he started cranking the jack. The ground was soft and as he rotated the handle, the weight of the full baler sunk the jack stand down into the dirt. August shifted position and kept turning the handle. Finally the baler started to rise, almost imperceptibly, with each turning of the screw. When there was an inch of daylight between the flat rubber tire and the ground, August backed the lug nuts the rest of the way off. He took off his hat and placed the nuts in it so they wouldn't roll off into the grass.

When he tried to pull the wheel off the hub, it didn't want to come, everything rusted and coated with layers of hardened axle grease. In an awkward half crouch, August gave another hard tug, and with it he fell back slightly. The baler rocked under the wind and the force of his pull, the jack stand rolled, and the baler was down. August knew he must be in shock, because he didn't feel much of anything. He was still on his knees and half of his left hand was under the flat tire, and when he tried, stupidly, to pull it out, it wouldn't come. The full weight of the baler rested on his hand with nothing but a layer of demolished rubber between fingers and metal rim, and already the light gray of his glove was turning a muddy red with the pooling blood.

Seeing the blood immediately brought his stomach to his throat, but there still wasn't any pain, just an immense pressure and a thumping in his ears. He dug at the ground with his right hand, trying to make some space, tearing at grass roots and stones, but it seemed that the baler had some sort of evil intelligence, settling itself more firmly into the ground with his every frantic scrabble, his hand coming no closer to being freed.

From where he sat he was able to reach the tipped jack. He tried to get it back into place with one hand, but since the baler had slumped, it was set at too high a level and he couldn't put it back into position until he lowered the head. His right hand was shaking badly as he turned the handle, an impossibly big patch of blood on the grass under the tire, and then August did heave his stomach. He could smell apple butter gone sour and the blood and the cut grass, too, and he finally got the jack in place.

When he made the crank that freed his fingers, that's when the pain came like a dam had burst. Black pinpricks swirling across his eyes, he held his injured hand to his chest without looking at it. He stumbled through the windrows of unbaled hay to his truck, leaned on the bumper, and pulled his shirt over his head. He put the injured hand through an arm hole with his eyes averted and then wrapped the fabric around as best he could. The shirt was white cotton, and with the red bloom upon it growing, he headed for town, trying to take deep breaths of air.

At the clinic he stumbled from his truck and crossed the flat parking lot like he was wading over the snot-slick rocks of the Musselshell. He hit the double doors with his shoulder, and bright splatters of blood marked his path across the tiles of the waiting-room floor. He slumped into the first chair he came to. Seeing him, the receptionist dropped her clipboard and reached for her intercom.

―――――

August was laid up in bed at his mother's house when Tim stopped by. August had just had a second surgery on his ring finger. The specialist in Billings had thought that maybe it would heal up, but after a few weeks came to the conclusion that the damage was too great and that it, like the pinkie, would have to be amputated at the second joint. His hand was swaddled in white gauze, and he wore a sling to keep it immobile.

His mother had been hovering but finally, at his insistence, she'd gone back to staying with Art. The two of them had decided to push the wedding back to early November, and they were all going to have a little dinner just as soon as August started feeling better. Art had a son, and he was coming out from California for the wedding. He was about August's age, and maybe the two of them could go fishing or something. At the very least there was going to be a little dinner. All of them together. These events were on the horizon, but hazy. August watched TV and slept, getting up only to take a piss or drink a glass of water. The painkillers made everything seem far away, events unconnected. For instance, Tim was just there, straddling the high-backed chair across the room from August's bed, and they were talking. August had no recollection of the doorbell ringing or letting him in. Tim had a small Igloo cooler and there was a twelve-pack of cans on ice and he acted like he was going to toss one to August but then laughed, popped the tab, reached over, and handed it to him.

"They probably got you pretty doped up," he said. "Beer usually helps a little to clear your mind in these situations."

Tim opened himself a beer and raised it in August's direction. "When are you going to stop feeling sorry for yourself and come on back up to work?" he said.

August sipped his beer. His tongue felt thick, but the beer was cold and it tasted good. "Just got out of surgery yesterday," he said. "They had to go back and take off another part of my ring finger because it was too fucked up."

Tim regarded August with his eyebrows raised. He shook his head. "At least you're not a lefty. Is that cheap asshole Ancient paying your bills?"

August shrugged. "I'm still on my mom's insurance. She gets good insurance. I guess that part's not a problem."

"How about for your missed work? Is he giving you wages?"

"I don't know. He stopped by the other day, but I was passed out. He left me some of my stuff from the bunkhouse."

"Well, if you want me to go over there and shake him down, you just say it. He's the kind of snake that will try to weasel out on giving a man his wages. He had you up there all spring and summer doing the work of two men and then you get hurt because of his janky equipment and he tries to gyp you."

"It was just an accident. Anyway, I don't think I'm going to go back up and work for him."

"No? What are you going to do?"

"You know, I don't know. You know?"

"I'd say the drugs are making you funnier, that's for sure. I guess your hand-modeling days are over. But really, if you have to lose a couple fingers, those are probably the best ones to have gone. Could have been your right thumb or something. That'd be way worse. Can you still feel where your fingers should be? Like, what do they call it, phantom pain?"

"Nah. I've got enough real pain at this point I don't think the phantom kind would even register yet. Maybe it's something I can look forward to."

"You got more to look forward to than that. Hold on, I have something for you. I didn't bring it in right away because I didn't know what kind of shape you were going to be in, but it's clear to me now that you're mostly fine and just milking it for sympathy. Hang on. Be right back."

When Tim returned from his truck, he had a squirming ball of mottled fur under each arm. He set them down on the bed, where they immediately beset August, licking his face, one wagging its tail so hard it fell off the side of the mattress.

"They're miniature Aussie/border collie mixes," he said. "Got them from the shelter down in Billings. The lady there told me they came in from Fort Smith, on the Crow rez. A rez dog is always the best kind of dog, in my opinion, because they can sense the sort of life you've saved them from and they'll do anything for you—they're grateful. Some of those old boys down there on the rez still eat dogs. No shit. They're both females, of course, because you don't want to deal with any animal that's got balls if you've got balls yourself. I'm sort of partial to that one there with the mismatched eyes, but I'm giving you first pick, pal."

"Jesus, Tim. You can't just get people dogs without asking first."

"I figured you'd say that, and that's why I didn't ask. I've come to realize you're a person that needs to be talked into everything at first. How about dancing? Remember that? Turned out to not be so bad, eh? Bottom line—you need a dog, I need a dog, and these are going to be great ones. See how that one is looking at you? When they tilt their head like that it's a sign of intelligence. She's trying to figure out what kind of person you are."

"Oh yeah?" August pinned the wriggling puppy to his side and rubbed her ears. She gave a small squeaky growl and nipped at his thumb. "Her and me both," he said.

Tim scooped up the puppy with the mismatched eyes and held it up to his face. She stuck her tongue out and licked his nose. "I think I'm going to have to call dibs on this one. I'm sorry, but we've already bonded." He had the puppy on its back on his lap, rubbing its stomach. "I'm thinking Chica, for a name. What do you think?"

"Chica," August said. "Yeah, that's pretty good."

Tim put his pup back on the bed, and the dogs immediately began wrestling, mouths agape, chewing on each other's feet and ears and tails. "Look at those little shits get after it," he said. He opened another beer and sucked the foam off the top of the can. "That was some scene at the house the other night," he said. "Ol' Avery—quite the show stealer, eh?"

"He's something, all right."

"He's probably going to be a millionaire someday and live in California, or France, or someplace like that. Wouldn't surprise me in the slightest. And I'll just be here, and that's okay, because I'm suited to it fine. Being suited to where you're born is a lucky thing because, as far as I can tell, it saves you a lot of heartache. Anyway, you know that letter Ancient was whining about to my dad? The one about Kim being a pervert and all that?"

August nodded.

"About five years ago, a while before the thing with Wes, my old man set us down and said that he knew that after he passed, chances are we wouldn't want to just keep on ranching forever, because he could see the writing on the wall as well as anyone. He said he didn't like the thought of us fighting over things when he was gone, so he wanted to get it straightened away while he was still of sound mind and body. He let us pick that day, divided the place up by even sections, and gave Weston first choice because he was oldest, then me, then Avery.

"Wes took the piece that the house is on. Good well and outbuildings and all that, so it was probably the smart move, but I was happy because I didn't want that anyway. I wanted the section down by the Musselshell. There is a little rise there where eventually I was going to build a house. The grass is good on the river bottom and it has the best view on the ranch, in my opinion. That was mine. And knowing it was mine made my day's work different somehow, because that piece was there, waiting for me to do with it what I pleased. It's one thing to own something within a family, but it's another to own something as an individual. It was going to be mine free and clear. I already had my house site all picked out, and then, after Weston, my dad had to sell it. It's been a couple years now, driving by it every day, knowing it once belonged to me but not anymore. That put a bad taste in my mouth. No two ways about it."

"So you wrote that note to Kim."

"I suppose. Although it wasn't really *to* Kim. It was to Ancient *through* Kim."

"I don't think they're going to end up getting married. Doesn't seem like things are going too well."

"He'll probably want to blame me, but any marriage that can be broke up by a little thing like that wasn't meant to be in the first place. Probably at some point he'll thank me for helping him dodge a bullet."

"Maybe he could say the same thing about you."

"How do you mean?"

"He bought that section of your family place, and now you won't have it hanging over your head. Your old man passes, and you and Avery can just sell the rest off and all of a sudden you're free. Go down to Austin. Go wherever. Maybe Ancient lifted a burden from you."

Tim laughed. Scratched a puppy behind the tail. "I don't know about all that. That's a theory I'll need some time to get caught up to. Austin." He shook his head. "Goddamn. They got this whole part of town that's full of taco trucks. Food of all kinds, really, but all of it served out of trucks. In one afternoon I think I had six different kind of tacos and saw three girls holding hands wearing cutoff jean shorts and shirts made out of bandanas."

"Bandanas?"

"Yeah, like handkerchiefs. They had them tied up in some way.

Barely covered the items. There was a blonde, a brunette, and a red-head. Like *Charlie's Angels* or something. Real good tacos, too. Way better than anything you get around here."

"Well, there you go."

"Yeah. There I go," Tim said. "Me and Chica roaming free in the Lone Star State." He lifted the puppy and rubbed his nose against hers. "Just hitting the open road." He put the dog down and finished his beer, stretching and belching. "Well, I guess I ought to be getting on. You look about half-asleep as it is."

"Nah, I'm fine. Hand me another beer. And I was meaning to give you something I found a while back. Open up that book on the desk there. I was using it as a page marker."

Tim hefted *The Hutterites: A People's History* and raised his eyebrows. He flipped the book open and held the Polaroid out at arm's length. He brought it in close and then reached it back out to arm's length again. He swallowed and rested his chin on his fist. "I'll be damned," he said.

"I found it down on the Musselshell, in a little bundle of stuff. Some cigarettes and things, nothing too interesting except for that. A graven image. Her name was, *is*, Sarah Jane," August said.

"She goes by SJ mostly," Tim said.

"You knew her?"

Tim nodded, sipped his beer. "Weston had her over to the house once for dinner. I have no idea how she worked that out with the elders. She came to the funeral, too. Walked right up and hugged my dad in front of a whole church-load of people. Crying her eyes out. She came up to me after the service. Telling me stuff about how Weston had asked her to leave the colony, for him. He'd come back for spring break and told her that if she left the colony he wouldn't go back to school; they'd figure it out some way. He didn't want to be there without her. He was half flunked out anyway. But she just couldn't. That life is all she ever knew. She'd be trading everything she had for him, and in the end she just couldn't.

"So he goes back to school and we know how that ends. She's crying out all this on my shoulder in the fellowship hall of the church. Saying maybe it's her fault. Saying he told her he'd rather die than be without her. That didn't sound like Wes to me, but when it comes down to it, it's impossible to understand how another man is with his woman, even if he's your brother. It has no bearing on how he is in real life. But don't they look happy right here, though?" Tim held the picture up one more time, blinking.

"There's some interesting stuff in that book," August said. "Did you know that the Hutterites don't have a problem with people taking pictures, as long as it's candid? It's the posing that they don't like. Graven images. Up in Canada they're in a lawsuit to make it so they don't have to get their pictures taken for driver's licenses."

"And then you see them in the Feed-n-Need talking on cellphones and eating Doritos. I don't really get it. They've got all the fanciest shit, too. GPS in their tractors. My dad says they don't have to pay taxes. That's how they do it. Got it set up so they're a religious group, like a church. Big scam, if you ask me."

"In that book it talks about something called *Eigennutz*."

"Say what?"

"*Eigennutz*. I'm not sure I'm pronouncing it right. I guess it's German, but it's a word with no direct translation into English. It basically means acting in your own best interests, like, being selfish and not putting the community first."

"How does that work? If a community always wants you to put it first, then isn't the community itself being *eggnuts,* or whatever?"

"But it's a community. So how can a community be selfish if it's made up of a bunch of people?"

"Every community has a guy in charge. The Hoots have elders, and amongst the elders there's got to be one that's the *boss* boss. Even if it's unofficial. I don't think there's any such thing as a real communal sort of community. Hippies tried that and failed." He tapped the Polaroid's edge on the desk and shook his head. "My bro and his uncommon Hoot girlfriend. They could be anyone, looking at them like this. Just two good-looking people. Weston, you stupid bastard. The whole world under your thumb. Most *eggnuts* person that ever lived. If you weren't my brother I'd probably hate you."

There was no scaffold of poles this year. Just a regular-sized bonfire, a small pile of pine logs burning by the river. August was standing there talking to a few of the guys when someone came up behind him, got him in a headlock, and jabbed him in the ribs before letting him go, laughing. It was Veldtkamp. He had a Jack Daniel's bottle by the neck, and his teeth and eyes were wet white in the firelight.

"Goddamn," he said. "Look who it is. I thought you'd dropped off the face of the earth. Someone told me you got your hand cut off in some kind of accident. You got a hook on the end of that thing or what?"

August eyed Veldtkamp warily. He had already developed the habit of keeping his left hand jammed in the pocket of his jeans. The stitches had only recently come out, and the stumps of his pinkie and ring finger were still red and raw looking. Dry and scaly on the very ends. If he accidently bumped them against something, a shooting, tingling pain ran all the way to his elbow. The doctor told him this would lessen as time went on—the nerves deadening, getting used to the new terminus point. He pulled his hand out and held it up. "Just part of a couple fingers," he said. "Not that big of a deal, really."

"Well, look at you. Ol' Stub-Fingers McGee. How'd that happen?"

"Just a stupid thing with some machinery. A baler fell off a jack. It was my fault."

"Could have been worse, I suppose. Could have been your whole hand, or leg, or something."

"Exactly."

"Could have ended up like Ramsay. Burns over seventy percent of your body."

"Everything could pretty much always be worse."

"Even with Ramsay. A person might think that dying with burns over seventy percent of your body is about as bad as it gets, but then I'm sure there's people out there that get burns over eighty percent of their body. You know?"

"Without a doubt."

Veldtkamp passed August the bottle and watched as August took a long swig and handed it back with a cough. "Decent turnout tonight," Veldtkamp said. "But nothing like last year. Last year was crazy. I guess that's how it goes when somebody dies. The party gets a little smaller every year, and then at some point there's not even enough people around that remember to make it worthwhile."

"Last year *was* crazy," August said.

Veldtkamp screwed the cap back on the bottle and put it at his feet. He stepped close enough that August could smell the whiskey on his breath. "What does that mean?" he said.

"What we did."

"And what did we do?" He stepped closer so his chest bumped August's. "What did we do?"

"Uh-oh," someone said from the other side of the party. The smattering of conversations silenced.

"I said, What did we do?" Veldtkamp bumped August's chest again, and August took a step back.

"I don't have to tell you," August said.

"I remember getting drunk and celebrating the life of a great friend. That's what I remember."

"June," August said. "That's what I remember."

"You don't know a thing about her. About what she wanted. Nothing. You're making it out to be something it wasn't. And that says more about you than it does about her."

"I know what it was."

"You don't know shit. No one forced anyone into anything. You were right there. Now you're trying to act like you're a saint."

"I'm not trying to act. I'm just saying it was fucked up."

Veldtkamp had August's shirt bunched up in his fists and was walking him back, August shuffling, trying not to stumble. He slammed August back-first into a cottonwood. They stood this way eye to eye for a long moment. And then Veldtkamp released August's shirt, shook his head, and turned away, picking up the whiskey bottle as he walked off into the dark at the edge of fire.

Someone laughed, and someone shouted, "Can't we all just get along?"

August followed Veldtkamp and found him sitting on his lowered truck tailgate, bottle between his legs.

"Can I sit?" August said.

Veldtkamp shrugged, and August heaved himself up next to him. From where they sat they could hear the music of the party, a blur of indecipherable voices, see bodies passing in front of the fire.

"I didn't watch much football this fall," August said. "But I caught a couple games on TV. I looked for you."

Veldtkamp laughed. "Well, you wouldn't have seen me," he said. "Unless the broadcast showed the inside of the Rhino Bar. I didn't really pan out too well up there."

"Was it because of that day with the truck? Your leg?"

Veldtkamp shook his head. "Nah. Not really. I had a deep bone bruise and an MCL strain from that. But I was fine in a few weeks. I mean, I definitely told a few people around here that was the problem. Made it out to be that if I wouldn't have gotten my leg run over I'd have been an all-American. That was pretty much bullshit. College ball is different. It has a different feel. Everyone's faster. Everyone's stronger. I think I was fast enough and strong enough to hang, but it got to be mental. In high school I *knew* I was faster and stronger, and so I played a certain way. Up at the U, I just couldn't get that confidence, because I wasn't much different from anyone else. Does that make sense? I didn't have the knowledge that I was bigger, so I couldn't play bigger. Some people can play their size, but I could only be good if I was bigger. Anyway. I figured all that out in practice, real quick. Never even suited up for a game or made the travel team. I could have stuck it out, probably, and seen some playing time in a year or two, but I said fuck it. My old man has the contracting business, and he needs help. Not the end of the world. Could be worse."

"Remember in practice, that one time, when Coach had us doing that stupid drill—bull in the ring?" said August. "You cleaned my clock. I was in the middle, chopping my feet, head on a swivel, and Coach called your name, and I remember thinking, *Oh fuck, Veldtkamp, here it comes,* and when I turned you were already there and I was flat-out on my back seeing stars. Coach about lost it. I think he got off on watching us cream each other like that."

"I have dreams about it. A couple times a week while I'm sleeping I still see things through the face mask. I'm always in the middle of a game, and I just can't get traction. The field is slippery and I'm spinning out. I give out these spastic kicks and then I wake up. When June would stay over she'd always laugh about it."

"I thought maybe she'd be here, actually," August said.

Veldtkamp reclined until he thumped back on the truck bed. "I doubt we'll be seeing Miss June around here for quite a while," he said. "She's on the East Coast for school. She has an internship or something. Didn't come back this summer."

"Brown?"

"Yeah, Brown. She deferred her enrollment last year when all that stuff happened. With her dad and everything. We hung out almost every day right up until she left, and we said that we'd stay in touch and I'd maybe go out there to see her and we'd make it work somehow." Veldtkamp laughed. "Shit. She called me after she'd been out there for about a week. Told me straight up that it wasn't going to work long-distance. I told her I'd come out there. I'd find a job, whatever. She told me it wasn't a good idea.

"I just—I go to work and I come home. I get shitty on the weekends. I go to work and I come home. My dad's done this for thirty years and she's out there at Brown and I'm just getting up and going to work and coming home. One time she told me that I possessed the highest level of kinetic intelligence she'd ever come across in a person. *Kinetic intelligence.* Can you believe that? She was calling me a dumb jock, basically, putting it nice. And now some other fuck probably has her. Out there at *Brown.* I could hear it in her voice when I talked to her last. She was a million miles away. Like she was so happy she was on a balloon up above me shouting down with a megaphone. There's nothing harder than a girl telling you it's over and her voice sounding so happy."

"Maybe you deserve that."

Veldtkamp sat up quickly and leaned in so his face was inches from August's. "You think you've got some magic ability to tell right from wrong that I don't have? If you felt so bad about the whole thing, you should have let me beat your ass instead of running me over with your truck like a pussy. The other guys felt bad and they faced it."

"Maybe. Who beats your ass, then?"

"I'm doing that myself just fine."

"Did you ever apologize? I always wondered about that."

Veldtkamp shook his head. "You can only solve problems by talking if they were caused by talking in the first place."

August hit him then. It was an awkward angle, sitting as he was, but it landed well, and he felt the mash of lips under his knuckles. Veldtkamp went down off the tailgate but came back immediately, a slick of blood on his chin, grabbing August's boot and dragging him to the ground. His teeth were grinning red and his fists were finding August's face like falling rocks. August tried to jam his knee up into Veldtkamp's groin, but he just twisted and kept punching. August covered his face with his forearms and absorbed a few more blows before someone hauled Veldtkamp off. There were people standing around, faces appearing and disappearing in the dust they'd raised. August's eyes were already swollen to slits. There was a hot slug of blood moving down his throat, and he swallowed. Veldtkamp struggled to his feet and August thought he might come for him again, but he stepped over August's legs on his way to the truck. August heard him gargle and spit. He dropped to the ground next to August and put the Jack Daniel's bottle close to August's good hand.

No one said anything, and seeing the excitement was over, people started filtering back to the fire. There was a loud laugh, and someone turned the music up. Veldtkamp sat back with a groan. "You tagged me good," he said, probing his mouth with a finger and spitting. "I think you put my teeth damn near all the way through, you fucker. Might need to get it stitched."

August tried to stand, but it was too much and he thumped back down. Eventually Veldtkamp got to his feet and extended his hand to pull August up. They sat on the tailgate again, blood on their shirts, dirt on their jeans, watching the party die in front of them. "I know it's pathetic," Veldtkamp said. "But I'd give a whole lot for one more practice. High school practice, not college. Just all of us guys out on the field after school. Coach screaming his stupid head off, making us do laps around the baseball field. Bull in the ring. All of it." He uncapped the whiskey, took a wincing drink, and reached it toward August. When August shook his head, Veldtkamp shrugged and had another drink himself. "Our boy Ramsay," he said. "Way to do it. Die young and you're a fossilized hero. Leave the rest of us to muck it out down here."

August's mother came home and made him pork chops—seared in a cast-iron pan on the stove top, swimming in herbs and butter. She served them with thin-sliced red potatoes fried in bacon grease and a wilted spinach salad that August only picked at. She sat across from him at the table, drinking a glass of iced tea, clearing her throat loudly several times but not actually saying anything about his fading black eyes. When she picked up her glass, her new engagement ring clinked on the rim. Several times he'd caught her looking at it when she didn't realize he was watching. Her lips would be slightly pursed. The beginnings of a frown, or her own peculiar grin, it was hard to say.

August finished his pork chop and polished off the potatoes. He wiped his mouth and drained his glass of water and handed the pork chop bone to the pup, who'd been staring at him imploringly from the floor near his chair. She retreated under the table, and soon the sound of her sharp little teeth working on the bone filled the room. He'd named her Sally.

August did the dishes and then went upstairs to his room to get the papers he'd been puzzling over all afternoon. His mother was at the table listening to the radio, and he put the stack of computer printouts on the table between them. "I can't make heads or tails of it," he said. "I think I need your Social Security number. Dad's, too. It's a FAFSA."

She sat up a little straighter. "Oh? Well," she said, "let me get my glasses. And I'll put some coffee on." This last bit from the kitchen—

she was already at the sink, running water into the carafe—she nearly sang it out.

* * *

When his father called, August was pondering the bewilderingly abundant contents of the refrigerator. His mother kept bringing home groceries, even though he'd told her repeatedly it was unnecessary.

"How you feeling?" his father said.

"I'm doing all right. Hot day here. Might go jump in the river later."

"That sounds good. Indian summer is always nice. We had a bit of a cold snap here this week. Hard to believe, but it already feels like fall is in the air."

"Last week they forecasted snow above six thousand feet. Never happened, but still. Got cold for a day."

"You able to feel that in your fingers? The change of weather? My old man's brother lost the tip of his thumb in a log splitter, and he could always feel it there when the barometer changed. I've heard that's pretty common."

"No. It just feels weird all the time. It hurts but also something different. I don't know. It's hard to explain."

"Well, hopefully your little lady, June, is around treating you nice and helping you with things you need helping with."

"I guess that's over."

"Oh? What happened? Seemed like you two were getting kind of serious."

"It's basically like you said. She was out there at school, doing all the extracurriculars. She called me and told me it wasn't going to work out, the long-distance thing. Probably she met someone else. It seems like she's real happy out there, and even though she grew up here she doesn't like it the way I do. I'm glad she's happy, though."

"Well, that's tough. But look at it this way; now you're free to play the field and mingle, which is what you should be doing anyway. There'll be plenty of time for the shackles later. My advice is to stay busy. And put yourself out there, too. Introduce yourself to one woman a day, old, young, pretty, ugly, it doesn't matter. Just get used to talking

to them. You start doing that, and it won't seem like much but eventually it will start to snowball and you'll have your hands completely full.
When it rains, it pours, that's how these situations go. So keep your
chin up."

"Okay. I will."

"How's the dog coming along?"

"Good. She seems smart. Doesn't give me any trouble."

"What are you going to do with her when you're in class?"

"I figured she'll just sleep in my truck. That's pretty much what she
wants to do anyway. I think she knows that if she's in the truck, then I
can't get too far away from her."

"She a chewer?"

"Nah."

"Barker?"

"Nah. Hardly had any accidents in the house or anything like that,
either. She just kind of follows me around and looks at me. Who
knows, maybe she'll all of a sudden turn difficult as she gets older, but
I think I lucked out."

"Sounds like it. But it's probably not luck, actually. I always had a
theory about dogs. Seems like dogs kind of take on the personality of
their owners, you know? I just have a really hard time picturing you
having a dog that's high-strung, or neurotic, or a pain in the ass. You're
too levelheaded to rub off on a dog that way."

"We'll see."

"I'm just saying that I think you're on track is all. Seems like you got
things figured out, more than I did at your age. You work hard and
your head is on straight. I'm proud of you, kid."

"Thanks. So how are things going back there? Is Lisa good, and everything?"

"She's fine. We're doing fine, mostly. We're going to the lakeshore
next weekend. She rented us a little house on the water, and we're just
going to go up there and hang around. Although I don't doubt she has
things planned for us to do. That girl has all sorts of plans. More and
more I'm figuring that out."

"You check the forecast? Weather supposed to be decent for you?"

"Looks pretty good. Partly cloudy on Sunday, but Friday and Saturday are all sun and hardly any wind. There are a million things I should be doing around here, but Lisa wore me down. She's got her brother and cousin coming over to take care of chores while we're gone. Twenty percent chance of storms on Sunday, but then a storm at the lake isn't the worst thing. I remember going with you and your mother that one time, and it was stormy every single day. The waves came up big and the water was actually warmer than the air."

"I remember that. We had those inflatable rafts and we swam out a ways and kind of rode them in on the waves. We had a fire on the beach, too."

"We did, that's right. I think you ate about a dozen s'mores and fell asleep on a blanket in the sand."

"I haven't thought about that in a long time."

"It was quite a while ago now. Lisa would probably like it to be hot and sunny so she can work on her tan or whatever. But either way, I don't really care. If it storms, I'll get one of those rafts and do a little body surfing with it for old times' sake. I'll let you know how it goes. And, while I've got you, I'm sorry about what happened to your hand. Seems like you're doing okay, but I just wanted to say that."

"Could have been worse."

"Sure. Of course. Still, for some reason I feel slightly responsible. You're a grown-ass man now, and I'm a thousand miles away, but I feel a little to blame. I sometimes think about you out there in Montana, alone in that field, under that baler, and I don't like it at all. I can't help but feel that, in a roundabout way, something about the way I was with you as a kid led to you being under that machine. It's ridiculous. But there it is."

"Wasn't your fault. You did fine."

"If you'd have been working here it wouldn't have happened. Even though you might not want to hear it, I feel like I need to mention it."

August didn't say anything for a moment. He'd taken the phone out to the porch and was sitting on the steps. Sally had come to lie down next to his leg, and he rubbed her behind the ears, her tongue lolling in the heat. From where he sat he could see the gray haze of smoke from a fire that had been burning for weeks in the Bridgers. The news said it wasn't threatening any homes and so the fire crews were just keeping an eye on it—letting it go until it burned itself out or the snow blanketed it.

"I got my old job back at the Heart K," he said. "I've set up my schedule so I have school three days a week. I'll be able to work at least two days; weekends, too, if I want. I was out there the other day and we were moving some of the herd down to a lower pasture. I had Sally with me and she was running around like crazy trying to follow the older dogs they've got out there. You could just see her watching, figuring out what she was supposed to do. She already rides on the back of the four-wheeler just fine. Gets her nose up in the wind and her ears start flapping. Pretty funny."

"Don't get me wrong. I understand that you need to get out and see a bit of the world. I'm not stupid enough to think that you'd want to just spend your whole life here doing this. But it's going to be yours. You know that? It's not a ranch, it's not a *spread*. But it'll be yours, and you can do with it what you want."

There's was a two-hour time difference, and August figured his father was done with the chores for the day. Sitting on his porch with his boots off, dirty white socks, lighting the citronella candle to fend off the last of the summer's mosquitos. "You look at the almanac to see what they're forecasting for this winter?" August said.

There was a momentary silence, then a long exhale. "No, I haven't looked yet. Never seems to be all that accurate anyway."

"I guess not. Something to talk about, though."

"When we first started dating and I would start in on the weather, your mother would just raise her middle finger at me until I stopped. Amazing how hard it can be to keep coming up with other stuff to say. I guess I stopped trying after a while. Probably that was a good chunk of the problem, to tell the truth."

"That sounds like her. I heard a good one the other day. *Wherever you go, you always take the weather with you.* Made me think of you."

"That is a good one. I like that. I know you understand, even though your mom never did. Most of the time I feel like the weather is the only subject that's worth wasting talk on. Who said that, about taking the weather with you?"

"It was in a song I heard. Jimmy Buffett."

"Jimmy Buffett? Seriously?"

"Yeah."

August's father was laughing now, and August joined him. He laughed so loud that Sally jumped to her feet, looking at him with her ears cocked back. His strange behavior continued on long enough that eventually she thought something was wrong and started barking out her concern.

On his way out to the Heart K, August swung into the diner to fill his coffee thermos. The fire was still burning out in the Bridgers, and this morning the sun had risen a murderous red through the smoke. Back when he was at the Virostok place they'd gotten their eggs from the Hutterites. On several occasions he'd cracked one in the pan for breakfast only to discover the yolk was a watery, bloody mass. He thought the sun coming up through the wildfire haze looked just like that. This time of year, everyone held their breath. Summer was still hanging on, but it was stretched and faded. A certain metallic smell on the clouds. Every day he heard the snarl of chainsaws, people out in the Forest Service land cutting deadfall for firewood.

The diner was busy with the usual mix of early risers. August left his truck running, and Sally stuck her head out the lowered window and watched him intently through the diner doors. August had capped his thermos and paid his two dollars and was turning to leave when he saw her. June was in a corner booth, facing him but with her head lowered, a half-eaten pancake next to the book she was reading. She had her blond hair pulled back into a ponytail. She wore oversized tortoiseshell glasses and a loose blue tank top with one of the shoulder straps fallen down her arm.

Before thinking it through, he walked to her table. He realized he was repeatedly tightening and loosening his thermos cap, fidgeting, and he forced himself to stop. He stood before her, and she raised her eyes from the book. She regarded him without saying anything, then picked up her fork, cut a piece of the pancake, swirled it in the syrup, chewed. Watching him the whole time. August wondered why she was up so early. He wondered if she had a hard time sleeping. Had she dropped out of school? Was she just visiting? He stood, face growing hot, mutilated hand jammed awkwardly in his jeans pocket.

"Can I buy your breakfast?" he said. He immediately knew it was the wrong thing. He should have just said hello. He should have asked her what she was reading. Said something stupid about the weather, the fire smoke, anything. But now the words were out and he couldn't stuff them back down his throat.

Her face registered no change. She took a sip of her coffee. "No," she said.

August knew he should leave. He ground his heel into the floor and lowered his head.

"Are you having a good summer?" He'd said it too loud. He was standing over her at the table, and he felt that other people in the diner were watching. He would have liked to sit down but there was no way to ask.

"My summer was fine," she said.

"Mine is going okay, too," he said. "I had an accident. Lost some fingers." He had his hand out of his pocket now. He looked down at it, as if seeing it for the first time.

She raised her eyebrows.

"It doesn't bother me too much anymore."

"Oh. Good." She had a small smile fixed on her face, looking past him, out the window over his shoulder.

"That's my dog, Sally," he said.

"Cute."

"I guess." There was silence, and someone dropped a plate back in the kitchen. A muffled curse. June was looking at him, and he knew he had to say something now. Something real. But there wasn't a single thing to say. All the words in the world and no combination of them made any sense. He tensed to leave. Then blurted it out: "Did you ever jump off the railroad trestle bridge?"

Her eyes came back to him. The smile she'd had was gone. "Is there something you want? Because I'm just kind of enjoying reading my book here."

"I'm sorry," he said. "I'm leaving." And then he bolted through the doors to his truck. He drove the back roads blind. Taking the corners too fast, sliding on the washboards. He thought that if everyone in the world felt this way it wouldn't be so bad, he could chalk it up as a reality of the human condition, but as far as he could tell, everyone else was fine and it was just him that couldn't find a way to properly live. Most of the time he didn't want to be in his own company, but he couldn't think of any good way out of it.

It was early October when his father called to tell him.

"Your mom already knows, of course. We're doing this in a friendly way; everyone is getting the percentage they deserve. I was rather surprised—we're making more than I thought we would. The Amish are going to buy it, believe it or not. Cash. They like the fact that there's two houses up already. I think they're going to make the old house into their regional school building. Good thing I didn't burn it down, I guess."

"Selling?" August said, trying to keep the surprise out of his voice. "The whole place? Why? I mean, what are you going to do?"

His father laughed. "Well, believe it or not, a guy like me might have some ideas occasionally other than getting milk from the teat. Remember last month, me telling you that Lisa and I were going to the lake? We went up there, to Traverse City, rented a little place right on the water. I'm not going to lie, she and I have had a bit of a rocky patch, but something about it up there, the water, the sand, I don't know, it felt like a breath of fresh air. It's easy to put your head down in a rut. You do it as a man because that's how they raise you up, but life is short, you know? You actually inspired me a little."

"Me? How?"

"Just the way you took off in your own direction and didn't look back. I said to myself, *Look at that, my son is not afraid to adapt to new circumstances, he's not tethered to some rigid idea about how he needs to operate. He lives in the goddamn Rocky Mountains, you know?"*

"But I thought farming was what you liked to do."

"It was. It is. I'm sure I'll have some minor regrets here and there, but I shipped all the cows yesterday and I was actually surprised, those trucks heading away, kind of a weight off my shoulders. I slept in till seven-thirty this morning. It was a revelation."

What about Skyler's grave? August wanted to say. *What about fresh milk from a mason jar in the pump room? What about wrestling matches in the haymow and Tigers games on the radio and fireflies and sun tea?*
"The houses have electricity, and plumbing, and stuff," he said. "What are the Amish going to do with that?"

"I really have no idea. They're buying up a lot of old farms around here, though. I'm sure they have some way to render everything to their liking. I know for a fact they've had their eye on the hardwood stand. They'll probably cut some of the oaks, tap all the maples for syrup. They've been on me to tap the trees for years, and I never let them. Now they'll be up to their beards in sap. Industrious folks. I'm actually happy it's going to them and it will still be run as a farm. Better than some asshole trying to turn it into a trailer park. Enough of those around here as it is."

"It seems kind of sudden. You went on vacation and then you decide to sell the farm? I mean, what are you going to *do* now?"

August could hear a voice in the background, Lisa saying something. "Lisa says hi," his father said. "And, yes, it may seem sudden, but it's a decision that's been building for a while, and then a few events occurred and here we are."

"What events?"

"For starters, it became clear to me that you had no real interest in stepping in and taking over, and I don't blame you for that, I really don't. This day and age, a dairy farm is a bit of a losing proposition. Actually, I'm not sure if it was ever a winning proposition, but these days you have to get big or get squeezed out. I could read the writing on the wall. So there's that."

"What other events?" There was something in his father's voice, an undercurrent that he'd rarely ever heard, as if each word was saturated, a happiness threatening to leak around every syllable. His father was barely containing his excitement. August could hear something on the line, a jostling, Lisa's laugh. His father saying something off the phone that sounded like, "Damn woman, you're getting heavy." August wanted to hang up. He didn't want to have this conversation with his father with Lisa hearing everything.

"What other events?" he said.

"We went up there to Traverse City, like I said. We had such a good time."

"It's beautiful up there," Lisa said, in the background. "So amazing. When we get settled you have to come visit, Augie."

"What does that have to do with selling the farm?" August said. "You went on vacation and decide to move, just like that?"

"Well, let me finish," his father said. "We went up there, and Lisa— you know she just wrapped up her vet tech training—she went off one afternoon and sniffed around a little and got a job offer at a fancy new shelter they just built up there. There's a lot of money in Traverse City these days. Second-home people don't want to see stray dogs uncared for or sad little kitties sleeping outside. So Lisa comes back and kind of lays it out straight for me. She's going to take this job, and she doesn't really see how a long-distance sort of deal is going to work. She gave me an ultimatum, basically."

"No I didn't!" Lisa was giggling. August wanted this whole thing to be over.

"No, you're right, it wasn't really an ultimatum. But I felt like I was coming to a crossroads where some decisions were going to have to be made. I told her to give me a couple weeks to think about it, and she was fair enough to agree to that."

"Are you going to tell him or not?" Lisa said.

"Tell me what?" August said. "What in the hell are you guys talking about? You're selling the farm because you went on vacation? I just don't see it."

His father stopped laughing, and Lisa fell silent. His father cleared his throat. "I was already considering selling, and then Lisa came home one day and told me that she was pregnant, and in that instant I pretty much made up my mind. There it is. This was not in the script, I admit, but in about six months you'll have a sibling, and we couldn't be happier. What do you think about that?"

"What?" August said. "Wait, what? Really?"

"Yes!" Lisa shouted. "Really! So exciting!"

"So exciting," his father said. "We're on cloud nine over here."

August took a week off work. His mother rented a U-Haul truck and they set out before dawn, August behind the wheel, bleary-eyed, sipping coffee, his mother fiddling with the truck's radio. Sally slept, curled on the seat between them. They were quiet for most of the morning until, somewhere in the sun-blasted, flat expanse of eastern Montana, his mother yawned and stretched and reached over to pat his leg. "This is kind of nice," she said. "A little bittersweet, maybe, but there's a certain symmetry."

August glanced at her. She was leaning her head against the glass, looking out over the scrolling sagebrush hills. "What kind of symmetry?" he said.

"It's like when we originally came out here, the U-Haul, the same sense of things ending. Just this time you're driving. I'm older, relinquishing the role of caretaker, adopting, slowly, the role of care receiver."

"I don't think we're quite to that point yet," August said. "I'm sure I'll get tired eventually and you'll drive."

"Maybe, but I'm just thinking of the greater symbolism. The young son drives the aging mother across the country to retrieve the few valuable artifacts that remain of a broken home before the home is sold and the chapter comes to a definitive end."

"You're the librarian, but I'm pretty sure metaphors don't actually happen in real life. I'm driving you, but it's not symbolic of anything. It's just what I'm doing. It's happening."

She turned her eyes from the fields to look at him. She smiled. "I'm your mother," she said. "Whether you like it or not, I created you to be a character in the novel of my life. Every child exists in part to further the narrative of the parent."

"How am I a character? We're all just living our lives."

His mother pursed her lips in thought. A few miles later, she said, "You didn't get to choose when and where and to what circumstances you were born, did you?"

"No."

"Then why would you expect choices to appear magically once you've arrived? That's like creating something from nothing—it goes against the laws of physics. Trust me on this one, until a human being can choose his or her parents, they'll be no such thing as true freedom on earth."

"Are you thinking of Dad and Lisa's kid? Is that what this is all about?"

She laughed and dug in her purse for her Swishers. She lowered the window and lit her cigar, blowing a stream of smoke into the rush of air. "How do you feel about having a sibling?" she said.

"Half sibling."

"If you want to think of it that way, I guess that's your prerogative. I'm actually happy for him. He always wanted more, but having you just exhausted me in some way. I didn't have it in me to go through it again. The world conditioned me to feel guilty about that and I did for a long time, but at this point I've mostly moved past it. When that kid is eighteen your father will be damn near seventy." She shook her head and coughed. "No thanks, buddy."

They arrived in the late afternoon, and right away August realized there was something naked about the place. The pastures along the driveway were still cow pocked and trampled, but empty now. For the first time he could remember, there was not a single Holstein to be seen. His mother took a deep breath and then let it out slow. "Here we are," she said.

August, stiff from the driving, did some stretches and watched Sally prowl the pasture's edge, looking around warily for the missing cattle. "Nothing for you to do here, Sal," August said. "Relax."

The maples and oaks had already turned colors, but it was an unseasonably warm day. His father came down the steps, wearing jeans and a T-shirt, and walked barefoot across the grass. When he reached to shake August's hand, he did so with his left so August had no choice but to follow suit. His father grabbed his wrist and held it up for inspection then released it and raised his own, waggling the pinkie finger that stuck off at a strange angle after some long-ago accident. He gave August a punch on the shoulder. "I say never trust a man that doesn't have at least one bum digit," he said. "Trademark of an honest living. Good to see you, son."

August could sense his mother behind him, and he stepped to the side.

"Dar," she said.

"Bonnie," he said. They hugged quickly, and then his father stepped back and bent down to rub Sally behind the ears. She was groveling at his feet, thumping her tail. "And you must be Sally," he said. "Did she do good in the car that whole way?"

"She mostly just slept," August said. "Got out and ran around with me at gas stations."

His father gave Sally one more rough scrub behind the ears and then stood up, knees popping. He nodded at the U-Haul. "That thing probably guzzled the gas, eh? Fifteen or sixteen miles to the gallon, something like that?"

"I'm not totally sure, but that sounds about right."

"Under twenty for sure. My truck gets about twenty on the highway. You guys hungry? I've got some potato salad and sandwich stuff. Made some tea."

As he followed his father up to the house, August tried to remember if he'd ever seen him like this, going barefoot over the lawn, or wearing a T-shirt in the middle of the day. Stubble on his face. He had some new glasses as well. Thick black frames that Lisa had probably picked for him. He looked like a middle-aged professor bumming around the house on the weekend. It was as if, along with shipping the cows, he'd shipped the farmer.

They made sandwiches in the kitchen, talking about which pieces of furniture his mother wanted to take and which she could live without. Then they settled on the porch, paper plates balanced on their legs, Sally there giving imploring looks.

"So," his mother said, raising her glass of iced tea, "I think some congratulations are in order. Will we get to see the lucky young mother-to-be?"

"Thanks. We're very excited. But no, Lisa won't be around. She's already up in Traverse. She wanted to get on her feet at her new job before she goes on maternity leave. We rented a little place up there, and she's getting settled in. I'll be headed that way when I get things wrapped up around here."

"Are you going to get a job?" August said.

His father laughed and threw a chip to Sally. "I've been kicking a few things around. I actually think I'm going to buy a little snow removal business."

His mother snorted. "You're going to shovel sidewalks?"

"Something like that. Maybe on a slightly larger scale. You know how they get pounded by those lake-effect storms up there? It just piles up all winter, and there's really only a couple guys doing residential plowing. One of them is getting older and wants to bow out. He's got a big client list, a half a dozen plow trucks, a bunch of drivers. We're in negotiations. I think we'll hit on an agreement." He tossed Sally another chip, and August waved a hand at him.

"Stop with that," he said. "She doesn't need those."

His father acted like he was going to throw one more, but then he ate it himself. "Anyway," he said. "I'll work hard in the winter and then take it easy in the summer. Spend time with the new little monkey, of course, maybe come out and visit you, August. Finally see those damn Rocky Mountains."

"Sure," August said. "That sounds good."

The shadow of the old white oak in the front yard was beginning to stretch into evening. A few hardy mosquitos showed, and his father lit a citronella candle. August was struggling to keep his eyes open. "So," his mother said, firing up her cigarillo with the candle's flame, "Traverse City, eh? I wonder if they have the cherry festival still."

"I'm sure they do. They've been having that forever."

"Remember that street dance?"

"Long time ago now."

"Still a good memory, though, right?"

"Of course. Lots of those floating around out there."

His mother and father were talking, and August started to drift. He caught himself tilting out of his chair and jolted awake. He stood and stretched. "I'm beat," he said. "Good night, guys." He started down the steps, whistling Sally up. "I've got your bed made up in your room," his father said.

"And I'll be down in the old house," his mother said. "The spare bedroom is open, of course."

August, standing in the yard, watched the vapor light over the barn door flick on. "When's the last time you started my old truck, Dad?" he said.

"It's been a while. Should fire up, though. I know it has gas."

"Okay. See you guys in the morning, then."

August grabbed some bedding from the old house and went to the shed. The Ranger coughed to life on the second try, and he honked at his parents, still sitting on the porch, as he drove by. He took the back roads slowly out to Brockway Lake. The surface of the water was like glass, a few nightjars out swooping low. He arranged the blankets and pillows in the back of the truck while clouds formed and obscured the stars. A gray mist rising from the lake enveloped the truck in its damp fold. August lay on in his back, covers to his chin. Sally burrowed her way under the blankets near his hip, and he dug his fingers in the thick ruff of fur under her collar. The possibility that his father's new child would never come to this lake—would never jump from the stacked bales in the haymow, would never climb the beeches that lined the back fence—had some vague but important implications for the relationship August was likely to have with him or her. As far as he could tell, a siblingship was made as much by the setting of one's childhood as it was by the sharing of parents. He'd give the kid a chance, of course, but he had to guess that growing up in a town full of sailboats and vacation homes was bound to render some lasting negative effects on one's development.

He was starting to think that every childhood existed as a unique set of problems, and most of what people called living was just the act of trying to decipher, after the fact, what in the hell had happened to them. When it came down to it, he figured that his parents had done what they could. Back at the house, when he'd gotten up to leave, he'd thought that his mother and father would soon follow suit. But, as he was driving away, he could see them there in the rearview mirror. It almost looked like they had moved their chairs closer together so that they could sit side by side. He wondered if they were out there still, and what in the world they were talking about with him gone.

ABOUT THE AUTHOR

CALLAN WINK has been awarded fellowships by the National Endowment for the Arts and Stanford University, where he was a Wallace Stegner Fellow. His stories and essays appear widely, including in *The New Yorker, Granta, Zoetrope: All-Story, Playboy, Men's Journal,* and *The Best American Short Stories* anthology. His first book, *Dog Run Moon,* was short-listed for the Dylan Thomas Prize and received a PEN/Hemingway Award Honorable Mention. He lives in Livingston, Montana, where he is a fly-fishing guide on the Yellowstone River.

ABOUT THE TYPE

This book was set in Minion, a 1990 Adobe Originals typeface by Robert Slimbach. Minion is inspired by classical, old-style typefaces of the late Renaissance, a period of elegant and beautiful type designs. Created primarily for text setting, Minion combines the aesthetic and functional qualities that make text type highly readable with the versatility of digital technology.